WILDEST LOVE

LOVELOCK BAY
BOOK ONE

ASHLEE ROSE

Cover: Irish Ink Publishing
Editing: Lea Joan
Cover Photographer: Sydnee Rayl Photography

OTHER BOOKS BY ASHLEE ROSE

STANDALONES

Unwanted

Promise Me

Savage Love

Tortured Hero

Something Worth Stealing

Dear Heart, You Screwed Me

Signed, Sealed, Baby

DUET

Way Back When Duet

NOVELLAS

Rekindle Us

Your Dirty Little Secret

A Savage Reunion

RISQUÉ READS

Seeking Hallow

Craving Hex

Seducing Willow

Wanting Knox

Pursuing Hartley

Tempting Klaus

ILLICIT LOVE SERIES

The Resentment

The Loathing

All available on Amazon Kindle Unlimited

Only suitable for 18+ due to nature of the books.

*For those who have ever felt incomplete and lost; be patient, your
other half will make its way back to you.
Soulmates come in many forms.
Don't give up.*

PLAYLIST

Tolerate It - Taylor Swift
Die From A Broken Heart - Maddie & Taw
White Horse (Taylors Version) - Taylor Swift
this is me trying - Taylor Swift
Heartbroken (feat. Jessie Murph) - Diplo, Jessie Murph,
Polo G
Mountain With A View - Kelsea Ballerini
7 Summers - Morgan Wallen
Religiously - Bailey Zimmerman
Going, Going, Gone - Luke Combs
Heartless (feat. Morgan Wallen) - Diplo, Morgan Wallen
exile (feat. Bon Iver) - Taylor Swift, Bon Iver
More Than My Hometown - Morgan Wallen
cardigan - Taylor Swift
Wild Love - Acoustic - James Bay
Forever After All - Luke Combs
Love You Anyway - Luke Combs
invisible string - Taylor Swift

DECEMBER 2023:

GOALS FOR 2024:

- Get married to my love.
- Buy our forever home.
- Live our happily ever after.

JANUARY 2024:

GOALS FOR 2024:

- ~~Get married to my love..~~
- ~~Buy our forever home.~~
- ~~Live our happily ever after.~~
- Move back home to Lovelock Bay.

PROLOGUE

This is not how my life was supposed to go.

Everything was planned.

Mapped out even.

This was not the happily ever after I was promised.

Luke was that promise. College was that promise.

But these broken promises are just a reminder that everything can change in a split second.

In a blink of an eye.

In an instant.

There have been three men in my life.

Riggs.

Pacey.

Luke.

One was my epic love.

The second was unrequited love on my part.

And the third was my promise of a happy ever after.

. . .

BUT THE TRUTH WAS, I had only *really* loved one of them; love felt too weak of a word to explain just how much my first love meant to me. I adored him.

What I had with Luke was what I thought I needed.

What I thought would help me heal.

But it turns out, I didn't need him as much as I thought I did.

With Luke my world was merely gray with the odd speck of white. I existed, but I needed the kaleidoscope of colour. I needed to live.

And as much as he hurt me, he pushed me to my forever.

MY FIRST LOVE BROKE ME, my second destroyed everything, and my third... well.

With him I had everything, and without him, I had nothing.

Or so I thought.

CHAPTER ONE

A heavy sigh vibrates through me at my mom's voice that floats through the speaker of my phone.

"I know mom, but Luke has so much going on with work, plus he has just begun filming his new movie," I nibble on my bottom lip as I rest the phone to my shoulder and slip my oven mitts on. I hate disappointing her, I can hear it in her voice and it surges a pain deep inside of my chest, winding me.

"I understand that sweetheart, but this is the third Christmas that you haven't come home," I can hear the crack in her voice, I know me not returning home to Lovelock Bay has been hard on them, but my life is here now. "Me and your daddy really miss you," she slips in and my heart stutters in my chest, a heavy ache prominent behind my rib cage.

"And I really miss you both too, but I can't just up and leave mom, Luke needs me here." It wasn't a lie. I did really miss them.

"So you always tell me," her tone has bite to it but I

brush it off. I love my parents dearly, but everything I want is here in LA. Not back home in Lovelock Bay, not anymore.

Placing the cooked chicken on the stove top, I close the oven and pull my mitts off. My mom is still talking in my ear but I'm not paying attention. I am too busy making sure everything is perfect for when Luke comes home.

"Mom, look I've got to go. I'll call tomorrow, okay? Send love to pops and Austin for me. Love you."

"Okay sweetheart, speak soon. Love you," and I hear the defeat in her voice, setting a coolness off deep inside of me, making me shiver as the ice dances up and down my spine. The phone cuts off and I pull it from my ear, pinching my brows so it causes a deep V to set in as I stare at the screen but whatever I was feeling leaves me as I see the background on my phone.

Me and Luke on our engagement shoot. Standing in the middle of Central Park, the blossom cascading down over us, my left hand is held out and towards the camera as I showcase my huge oval diamond. Luke is kissing me on my rosy cheeks and I'm bearing a wide, full tooth grin. I really was living my fairytale. My heart thrums in my chest.

I met Luke one evening in downtown Manhattan at a cocktail bar with my college friends, he was cocky and so sure of himself. I liked that about him. He wouldn't take no for an answer and when I agreed to date him, everything fell into place. I had no idea who he was until he sat me down and showed me an old sitcom that he starred in, but now, his name was in shining lights.

Luke Montgomery.

Hollywood actor and most women's fantasy. But I didn't have to fantasize, because he was mine.

We lived on Plymouth Boulevard, Windsor Square, Los Angeles in a stunning house that was fit for a King and

Queen. Large windows, spacey rooms and everything you would expect from a mansion in Los Angeles. I was a thousand miles from home. But this was my home now. Luke was the new home I had tied myself to after leaving a piece of myself back in the country.

My parents and brother live in Lovelock Bay. It's all rolling green hills, beautiful mountains that were tipped in glistening whites and pretty little rivers and streams that flowed through the valleys. It's idyllic.

Picture perfect.

But that's not me anymore.

I grew up on a farm; my pops has worked all of his life growing crops and breeding, raising and selling horses, and when I was younger, I never wanted to leave. But when I got into Cornell, I never looked back. I loved the city life, the hustle and bustle. I never wanted to stay on the farm. The dreams I once had as a young girl were not the dreams I followed as a young adult. Life changes quickly, and I soon adapted to a new dream.

Happiness radiates from me as I look out the window to the front yard, our house was beautiful, but it wasn't our forever home. Luke was given this when he was picked up for his movie, but once it wraps up late next year and we're married, that's when we will move into our *own* home.

Pulling myself from my wandering thoughts, I spin and turn the stove top off, the potatoes soft boiled and ready to be mashed, the vegetables cooked and resting. One thing I missed about living back home that wasn't my parents, was the fresh produce. I'm sorry, but you can tell the difference between fresh, home grown and store bought. But it's a small change I can live with.

Turning my wrist to face me, I check the time on my diamond encrusted Rolex, and it's just gone seven p.m. He should be home soon. Placing a lid over the potato saucepan and covering the vegetables, I untie my apron and hang it up just inside the pantry as I walk past. Turning out into the long hallway, I climb the stairs and turn the light on in the main bedroom and I smile. Floor to ceiling white panelled walls, coving wrapped round the high ceilings and a beautiful ornate gold light hung from the middle of the ceiling. Our bed sat perfectly in the middle of the room, large sash windows that line one side, white, linen drapes tied back with gold tiebacks. I move forward, walking into the walk-in wardrobe and slip out of my jeans and tee. Grabbing a cream knee length fitted dress, I slide it over my head and am careful not to mess my blowout. I reach for nude *Jimmy Choo's* and slip my feet into them. I take a moment to look at everything I have and think about just how grateful I am.

When I met Luke I was drowning in student debt and I was too proud to ask for help from my parents. I knew they just about made ends meet when I left, so I worked two jobs. An office job in the day and a cleaning job of an evening.

But then Luke happened. He paid off my debt and asked me to be a stay-at-home fiancée. At first, I was a little hesitant as I never wanted to not work, but I have fallen into my new life easily, though I do feel guilty sometimes. I miss having my own life and independence, but I know this makes him happy. He likes having me at home, dinner on the table waiting for him, the house clean and tidy. I spend my days reading, lunching, shopping and when inspiration hits me, I sit at my laptop and work on one of my hundreds of unfinished manuscripts. My old dream was to become a world champion show jumper; my new dream is to become an author, but I have never typed *the end* on any one of them.

Maybe one day.

Maybe this was my new dream.

But I knew Luke was in this new dream and to me, that's all that mattered.

I brush the ends of my loose curled dirty blonde hair and smile at my reflection. My hazel eyes are glistening, freckles scattered over my button nose and across my high cheek bones. Running a lipstick over my full lips, I paint them in red and I spray myself with a perfume and let it settle into my skin.

The reflection of the light on my *Harry Winston* engagement ring catches my attention and my heart stutters in my chest, and suddenly I feel an unbearable weight. My chest aching, my pulse throbbing beneath my skin and my stomach knotting with an unknown anxiety.

I was twenty-three when I met Luke; I'll be thirty next year in May. Luke is in his late thirties. I know people speak about our age gap. But I love him with every fibre of my being. The love I felt for him was different than I've felt before... I just didn't know if it was the *good* different.

I hear Butch, our Pomeranian, bark and my heart thrums in my chest.

He's home.

I rush down the stairs, careful not to break my neck as I do and my smile widens as soon as I see him. Copper brown hair, beautiful blue eyes, but when they meet mine, they're not glistening like they normally do. There is no wide, toothy grin and there certainly isn't the look of adoring love when he looks at me.

"Baby?" I test his nickname out on my tongue, and I don't miss the way it tastes bitter somehow.

"We need to talk," he just about manages, his jaw is wound tight and his fists are balled. He is on edge, tense, anxious. His eyes fall from mine as quickly as they found them and he walks with his head down towards the kitchen.

"Okay," my voice cracks as I try and hide the panic that is clawing at my throat, thickness growing and it doesn't matter how much I swallow, I can't seem to stop it. I follow him, Butch on my heels as they click on the tiled floor. The knot in my stomach grows, the small beads of sweat that prick under my skin grow more with each step I take, a prominent throb starts behind my eyes.

"Let me get the dinner dished up," I rush out and try to hide the panic that laces my soft voice. I reach for two plates then mash the potatoes before dishing them up along with chicken and vegetables. My nerves vibrate through me, my fingers ache as I try and stop them trembling. Something is wrong.

I ignore the feeling of impending doom that simmers at the bottom of my stomach and turn, smiling wide, trying my hardest to mask the worry that is likely etched onto my face. I walk over to the table before I gently place his plate in front of him and his eyes still don't meet mine. I tuck my now trembling hand behind my back as I take my own seat before burying both of my hands into my lap to hide the shaking from view.

He normally kisses me on the cheek when he comes home.

He struggled to even look at me today.

I ignore the sting behind my eyes that is intensifying with every passing minute and desperately try to swallow the large lump that has formed in my throat. Grabbing the bottle of red wine from the middle of the table, I pull the cork out and pour us both a glass before placing it back in its exact spot. Luke hasn't picked his knife and fork up. He just sits, his elbows resting on the table, his fingers locked together as his chin rests on his knuckles, his gaze is misty but focused ahead.

"Luke, what's wrong... you're worrying me," I just about manage, and I try to laugh it off, but it somehow changes from a laugh to a choked sob. I blink softly and feel a lone tear escape and roll down my cheek, my trembling left hand lifts and swipes it away before he can see it. I hear his sharp intake of breath and only then do his icy blues meet mine and I brace myself for what he is about to throw at me; my shoulders sit a little higher, my back a little straighter and my chin lifts as I turn to face him. A copper taste fills my mouth from where I have bit a little too hard on the inside of my cheek to stop my bottom lip from trembling.

"It's over Aspen. I don't love you anymore..." he begins, his voice like steel. Hardened, cold, thick.

My lungs crush, the breath catching at the back of my throat as I try to fill them with air after he winded me with his words. My whole world is collapsing, everything slowly crumbling around me and there is nothing I can do to stop it from happening. I am merely a witness in this colossal event that is unfolding in front of me.

"Luke," I whisper, because saying his name out loud is too painful, "please, you don't mean this. I have given you everything. Every piece of me is yours." And it's true. I built myself up for him, changed who I once was to be his perfect bride. I reach over to try and grab his hand, but he snatches it away, shaking his head from side to side as he pushes away from the table.

"I love you," I tremble, and I sound pathetic. I blink for a moment, letting my eyes fall and I don't even recognise myself. I am catapulted back to a time when I stood in the pouring rain, begging a man I loved to love me back.

"I've met someone else." His words pierce through me, and I am back in the room. A hot pole scalds my throat as I try and push away the tears, but I feel the pressure building, the feel of a thousand needles behind my eyes. Standing from the table, he pushes his hands through his hair before he turns and faces me. "Tammy," he rushes her name out as if it's burned his tongue.

"Tammy." I repeat, eyes wide and suddenly the pain that penetrated me and the tears that threatened dissolve into nothing. "As in your co-star, Tammy."

He nods, unable to bring himself to even mutter the word *yes*.

"The one that you assured me I had *nothing* to worry about after her notorious streak of being a fucking home wrecker," my voice gets louder as blind rage consumes me.

"It's different with us," he tries to defend his actions and I scoff on a laugh, hot air filling my nostrils.

I stare at the man I love, silently searching for anything that shows me he is still in there, still tucked away and hiding somewhere safe as he shatters my world.

"Don't do this... please, Luke." I'm back to begging, the rage simmering once more, and I hate myself for being *this* girl. "Don't throw away what we have for some stupid *fling*." The words are poison on my tongue as I spit them out, standing from my seat and hovering in front of him, my eyes bouncing back and forth between his.

"It's. Over. Aspen." He drawls out in a slow and vicious manner and my heart combusts in my chest. *It's over.*

I say nothing and I am ashamed of the tears that I am crying over this man. This man that humiliated me in ways he should have never done. Wasting tears over unrequited love. Or was it even *love*. Everything I knew or thought I knew has been pulled away like a rug under my feet and now I am left on the cold floor wondering what the hell I am going to do.

I am disappointed in everything I have given up for him. I am disappointed in *myself*.

He walks over to me, cupping my face in his hand as he lowers his face, his eyes searching for mine.

"Can I ask one thing of you—and I know I have no right —but..." his tone is soft, caring almost, but it's all an act. He is paid to switch his personalities. It's basically his job.

I stay silent, completely numb as I replay everything that has unfolded in my mind.

"Can we keep our separation quiet until this movie is wrapped up. I don't want to bring any unnecessary attention to myself whilst I have this going on." His blue eyes bounce back and forth between mine as he waits for a response.

Of course not you selfish, self-entitled piece of shit.

No, you selfish pig.

No.

NO!

But, for some fucking reason, I am nodding my head like a good, dutiful fiancée as I agree to this and shame flames across my cheeks.

In my head, I am trying to make sense of what the fuck I am doing and maybe, just maybe it's because he will realise that this is a fling and he will come back begging on his knees with tears in his eyes.

I swipe a stray tear away from my cheek angrily.

"You need to leave," his icy tone is back and it makes me shiver. How can he be so cruel and callous.

"Sorry?" I mumble, blinking as I allow myself to look at him, my heart pounding so hard in my chest that my breaths stutter.

"I want you to leave." He drops his hand from my cheek and turns on his heel. My fingers dance where his hand once was and somehow, I can feel a sting. Maybe it's the sting of betrayal that he marked my skin with, seeping deep beyond my layers and laying heavy on my heart for the rest of my life.

"Where am I going to go?" my bottom lip trembles as I look up at him standing tall over me, his hands tucked deep in his suit pants and there is nothing behind those beautiful blue eyes for me anymore.

"That's not my problem. You can take your car, but you need to leave..." his tone was flat and monotone.

I choke on my intake of breath, and I cannot believe the words that have left his lips.

Turning my wrist to face me, I look at my watch, it's seven thirty.

"Don't kick me out Luke, just give me a couple of days to sort myself out," my voice comes out on a whimper.

He shakes his head from side to side and he can't even look at me.

"It's because of her, isn't it?!" I snap, bile rising in my throat as I stand from the table. "Are you moving her into *our* home?"

"My home," he corrects me.

"What the fuck," I whisper as hysteria consumes me. "What the fuck is happening?" I drop my head and let out a deep breath as I count to five.

One.

Two.

Three.

Rage consumes me on my third deep intake of breath and the fire that was softly simmering in my stomach is back to raging with full force. Luke was the gasoline it needed to spark back into a raging, burning, ember.

"I've just agreed to *help* you, yet you can't help me. After six years together you can't even let me stay here until I am back on my feet." My eyes are wide and I am furious.

He says nothing, just rolls his lips and looks at his watch as if I am an inconvenience.

"You're an asshole," I scream, stepping towards him and slap his face, hard. I hear him suck in an intake of breath but I am already walking out the room.

My heels click quickly over to the kitchen and I grab a sharp knife from the drawer before reaching for my car keys to my McLaren P1. Stopping at the side unit in my office, I grab my laptop and move for the door.

"Aspen," Luke's panicked voice follows me but I ignore him. I rush for the front door and welcome the cool night air that fills my lungs as I swallow in a deep breath. Walking out onto the large driveway, I see Luke's *Porsche 911* sitting at the foot of the drive. I smirk, a wicked glint in my eye as my eyes focus on *her*.

Storming forward, the winter air nips at my skin. Tears stream down my face and I see Tammy's eyes widen at what I must look like hurling towards her with hysteria covering my face and my hand wielding a knife. I stop at the front of the car, the panic evident in her eyes but I don't care. I want her to feel like shit. I want her to panic and feel fear as it slowly seeps into her. I hold her gaze for a moment before I lift my hand high which is gripping the knife, my knuckles already turning white. A small smirk pulls at the corner of my mouth before I kneel down and stab Luke's front tire. Satisfaction blooms in my chest as I stand tall and move towards the back of the car and slice the rear.

Fuck, that felt good.

Turning, I throw the knife to the side and it lands on the front lawn. I turn back and see Butch running up behind me. I sweep him up into my arms and I ignore the way Luke is shouting at me.

He is more upset about his car than he is about breaking my heart.

Unlocking my graphite gray car, I open the butterfly winged doors and drop Butch into the passenger seat as I slide in and place my laptop next to him. I am fully aware what this must look like to the neighbors but I give no fucks.

He will deny all and want me to keep his dirty little secret.

Pulling the door down, I start my car and the engine roars, my small frame vibrating in the seat as the engine purrs.

"This is fine," I say to myself, over and over.

Lowering my rear-view mirror, I slip the car into reverse and see Tammy rush from the car that is nestled behind me and into Luke's arms.

My stomach rolls.

Nausea rips through me.

How could I have been so stupid. My body hardens like steel at the sight in front of me and I narrow my gaze on the two of them. I swallow down the thickness, but it stays firm at the back of my throat.

My heart thrums, my blood pounding in my ears.

"You know what," I mutter to myself, "fuck it."

Pushing the car into park, I open the door and slide out. Walking over to where Luke's Porsche is, I lean in and release the parking brake. I stand, watching it roll down the hill of our driveway and dust my hands off as I stand proud.

"You're fucking crazy!" Luke shouts out, his arms in the air before he tugs at the root of his hair.

"Yeah well, you only have yourself to blame for that," I counter back, flipping him off. Walking back towards my car, I slide in and push the pedal down as I reverse off the drive too fast and as I do, I catch the back of my car on the front of his.

Shit.

It's fine.

I'll get it fixed.

I slip the car into drive, ignoring everything in me telling me to look at him one last time. I drive away from the heartbreak and devastation and swallow down the tears.

Turning my radio on, *tolerate it* by Taylor Swift plays as I head for the only place I know.

Lovelock Bay.

CHAPTER TWO

Too many hours in the car.

Numerous toilet breaks—mainly for Butch.

And a shitty few hours sleep in the car, by the time I roll into the small town, the winter sun is nestled between the mountains, and suddenly I feel exhausted.

But now I was here.

And I never thought it would feel as good as it did when I saw the sign, 'Welcome to Lovelock Bay'.

Slowing the car as I hit the low-speed limit, my heart bangs in my chest. Three years since I have been back. Three years is a long time.

I grew up here; me, my brother Austin, Riggs, Tripp and Pacey Rivera and my best friend, Harlow. Not that I can really call her a best friend anymore. We never speak. She knows nothing about me and vice versa.

It's sad really, how someone who once meant so much to you is now a stranger.

I have friends back home in LA; back *home*. The bitterness coats my throat as I swallow. Well, they were Luke's friends really. They just most likely tolerated me and what makes me sick to my stomach is they've probably known about him and Tammy the whole time whilst I sat like the good wife-to-be completely unaware of what was happening right before my eyes.

Shaking my head free of thoughts of Luke. My mind drifts to our childhood here.

Running through my pops' fields, racing along the fence line and climbing into Rivera Ranch with Austin just so we could hang out with the Rivera brothers. Tire swings, swimming in the streams, fishing, rolling down the hills and horseback riding whenever we wanted.

I loved growing up here and I am so glad my parents lived here. It wasn't a bad place to grow up. Blissfully unaware of the rest of the world. I felt like we were hidden here, protected somehow from the realness that sat just over the town line. We were in our own little bubble here. Most people never leave Lovelock Bay, but I wasn't most people. I wanted so much more than to be cooped up in this small town.

My pops and Jorge Rivera had a love-hate relationship but as they've grown older, they have both mellowed out. Or so I am told.

My pops supplied him with his reared horses for his cowboys and in return, Jorge gave my pops meat and use of his land whenever he wanted.

They had a silent agreement.

The big suits have been trying to snatch a lot of this old land up but they've not been successful; not yet, anyway.

People seem to love the idea of building up the countryside and making it a tourist hot spot, but what they don't see is the family lineage of everyone who has grown up here and made this their home.

I swallow hard when I pull into the winding drive of

Maple Farm. The trees that line the dusty old driveway blowing softly in the winter breeze, the dark clouds rolling in and ready to eclipse the winter sunlight.

My mind wanders to the Rivera brothers.

One more than the others.

Riggs.

Riggs was the oldest Rivera brother followed by Tripp, then Pacey. Austin was the same age as Tripp, thirty-three. Riggs was thirty-five and Pacey was the same age as me, twenty-nine.

My favorite Rivera boy had dark brown curly hair, a little longer than average which travelled to the nape of his neck just enough for you to curl your fingers in. Light, beautiful, sage green eyes that consumed you completely and full, rosy lips that you silently begged to cover yours at every given moment and a smile that made you weak at the knees. His jaw was sharp, his cheek bones high.

He was beautiful.

He was rugged.

Dirty, rough, calloused hands, toned body and broad, heavy shoulders.

Everything about him screamed *big boy.*

I crushed on him so hard growing up, I would like to think I kept my cool around him but thinking back, I doubt I did. He was always tall and a little heavier set than his brothers, his hair was always wild but he was baby-faced, we all were. Where now, he was a man.

Puffing my cheeks out, the noise of this car is not ideal on making a silent entrance.

My parents' farmhouse comes into view, the front yard rolling into the fenced off fields as I approach. Their house is beautiful. Timber built in a teak stained wood; it's impressive. Large windows that stream in the sun perfectly, a wrap-around porch with the perfect veranda. The views overlooking the snow tipped mountains makes my heart gallop like a wild horse.

My heart stutters in my chest when I see Austin leaning against the fence to the left of the house where the horses are turned out and Riggs is leaning next to him, his elbows resting on the wooden post.

Bang.

My heart thuds and my anxiety swirls in my chest.

I see Austin's head turn in my direction when he hears the commotion of my car. The windows are tinted so I have no idea if he even knows it's me. The blood pounds through my ears, my palms sweaty as I approach.

I crack the windows slightly for Butch and I hear Riggs growl, his voice low as he grumbles to my brother.

"What's the betting it's an outsider who took the wrong turn on their sat nav? We don't get them sort of cars here," he scoffs, shaking his head from side to side, tipping his face down slightly and running his gloved fingers over the rim of his black cowboy hat. I roll my eyes at his stupid statement. *Ass.*

Austin whistles through his teeth as he steps a little closer to no doubt admire the car and offer some friendly help but he doesn't get a chance to even reach me. Opening my door, it swings up and I try with all my might to get out with some sort of dignity, pressing my knees together as I twist. My hair is a mess and tangled, my dress creased, and my feet are killing me. My heel slips on the pebbled drive as I try and balance myself. I feel the humiliation mark my cheeks as I feel Riggs' eyes on me. This is not how I wanted to return.

"Penny?" Austin squints and I am doing everything to stop the tears from falling at the use of my nickname.

"Aussie," I choke as he runs towards me and envelopes me in his arms and only then do I collapse into a heap. Eyes blurring as I finally give into the tears, the burn in my throat feels like I have swallowed lava but I let it erupt and flow, burning me as it does.

I hear a commotion of loud whispers and surprised gasps behind him and reluctantly lift my red rimmed eyes from his plaid shirt which is soaked in my tears, to see my pops standing on the veranda and my mom next to him, wide eyed and mouth a gape.

"Aspen!" she calls out as she begins running over to me, my pops standing guard on the front porch and Aussie doesn't let me go, his arms still firmly wrapped around my small frame.

"Are you okay my sweet girl?" my mom says as she pulls me out of Austin's grasp and clasps her cool, soft hands around my face, her eyes searching for something, anything to give reason as to why I am here. As to why I am in the state that I am, broken and wounded. Tears seep from my eyes once more and all I want to do is hide in a corner and lick my wounds.

"I'm fine," I managed to muster the two words that I have felt myself repeating either out loud or in my head. My throat bobs, thickness catching at the back of my throat and I ignore the burn, my stomach knotted and twisted with anxiety. Nerves coat my skin in the form of goosebumps and the pressure builds behind my hazel eyes once more. "I just needed to see you guys," I lie and I hate that it slipped off my tongue so easily. I didn't want to tell them the truth. I didn't want them to know that he kicked me out on the sidewalk and left me in the cold. I didn't want them to know that he in fact had broken my already broken and battered heart. I didn't want them to know that I needed them.

"Oh," she drags me in for a hug, holding me tightly and I feel my body quiver in her motherly embrace. "Where is Luke?"

The burning question hits me like a freight train and my heart obliterates once more.

"Tied up with work," I try and give my best upbeat tone as the lies fall from my lips but I am failing.

Miserably.

I was never a good liar, and I haven't got any better with age.

"Come, let's get you inside. You must be freezing," her blue eyes scope over my outfit and I see her brow lift. This wasn't who they were used to. They were used to me in my *Levi's*, plaid shirts and hair in a braid. Yet here I am standing in *Jimmy Choo* heels and a fitted knee length dress. I was too scared to look at myself, my eyes black and puffy from the constant flow of tears, my painted red lips no doubt smudged and messy. I was broken. Falling apart, piece by piece as the seconds past.

I follow my mom, her arm tucked round my shoulders as she leads me to the house, Butch following and I can't stop my gaze from drifting over to where Riggs was once standing, but he is no longer there.

"Austin, grab her bits from the car," my mom calls out.

"It's only my laptop," I stammer out and nausea swells in my throat. My eyes are cast down to the floor as I try to watch where I walk so I don't break my flipping neck in these ridiculous heels.

Mom's grip tightens on me. *Don't let me fall.*

Stepping onto the porch, my pops icy gaze skims across to me but I don't meet his eyes. I am too ashamed.

Buck, my dad, my pops, my daddy, and my mom, Blue, are both in their sixties. Mom is a couple of years younger. Her once dirty blonde hair has streaks of gray running through and it's as if she has given up trying to cover it. And my dad's once full head of dark brown hair is now completely gray. Only tufts remain around the sides and a thin layer on the top of his head, apart from his crown which is completely bald. Sucking in a breath, I can't believe how much they've changed in just three years. I love my mom and pops with every fibre. They were honestly the best kind of parents a kid could wish for. Of course, my childhood wasn't perfect, but it was pretty damn close to perfection.

The warmth of my childhood home smothers me as my mom ushers me through the door, and the smell of apple and cinnamon fills my nostrils. My mom's apple pie. My stomach groans and I realise how hungry I am. I haven't eaten since lunchtime yesterday.

"Go get showered, I'll get some of your old clothes out... I'm sure I have some somewhere from when you were last here." My mom gives me a small smile and I know that was a little dig. They were allowed to be hurt, but they weren't allowed to throw it in my face because of my lack of visiting. It was wrong and I already feel awful, I just don't need my nose rubbed in it at every given moment.

"Okay," I just about manage and my gaze skates over towards my dad who is sitting at the table reading a newspaper. I will for him to look at me, but he doesn't.

I kick my heels off and instant relief fills me, the balls of my feet ache, my arch throbbing and all I want is a hot bubble bath.

I hear the front door close, a gust of icy wind blowing through as it does, and I hear the tap of Butch's claws on the cherry mahogany floor. Looking over my shoulder I smile when I see him.

"Hey buddy," I crouch and give him a stroke behind the ear, his head tilts and his back leg thumps on the floor as I hit the spot.

Austin glares at me with a million unanswered questions and I know I owe all of them a massive explanation but right now, I haven't got it in me. I am exhausted. I am broken and I have no idea what to say.

I got dumped.

You were right.

He broke my heart but wants me to pretend we're okay for his career.

I roll my lips and run my toe across the floor beneath me.

Austin lifts his cap off his head and places it on the coat hook in the hallway before walking towards my dad. My mom is off looking for clothes and Butch goes exploring so I take this moment to slip away and trudge towards my childhood bedroom.

STEPPING FROM THE SHOWER, the steam fills the room. I stand for a moment, towel pulled tight around my chest, my head tipping back as I inhale the warm, wet air that surrounds me. My mind is racing, and I have no idea how to calm it down. How did everything go from being so perfect to so... *fucked.*

I pad across the large, airy hallway, my wet footsteps marking the carpet as I walk and open the door to my old bedroom. My mom has laid out a pink and beige plaid shirt, a white tee and bootleg jeans. I scrunch my nose up at the outfit and internally cringe. I don't remember ever wearing this. Fuck, I sound like a spoiled brat. I haven't always worn designer, and I know deep down that I was a jeans and plaid shirt girl. It just feels like it was a million years ago.

Nostalgia burns through me like wildfire as I look around my childhood bedroom. Everything was exactly how I left it. Light, blossom pink walls wrap round the large, square room. I had the biggest room between me and Austin and he always hated it. I'm surprised he didn't convince mom and dad to let him move in here and put my stuff in the attic as storage above the old stables. Large sash windows overlook the paddocks with a pretty cream, cushioned window seat which is scattered in pink daisies. The white sheer curtains are tied back with light pink rope and I let out a soft sigh.

Stepping a little further in, I turn to see all of my old medals and rosettes that I won once upon a time hung like the showpieces that they were. I was so proud of myself and so were my parents. I was an avid show jumper until I had a nasty accident and broke my shoulder, collar bone and femur as well as bruising my face pretty badly. The trip down memory lane stirred old feelings deep inside of me, my chest ached, my stomach was tied in a thousand tiny knots and suddenly it all felt painfully raw.

After my accident, I couldn't get back on a horse, the fear crippled me. I tried, I really did but I just couldn't do it. Reluctantly, I gave in and retired my beautiful Palomino, Blossom and she spent the rest of her days being a companion horse. I sobbed all day, watching her live her days out in the paddocks. It broke my heart but I had to do what was right for me at the time. The familiar burn rises up my throat and I feel the pressure heavy in my chest and suddenly I am thrown back to that day. A sniffle escapes on my shudder of breath and I honestly don't even think I have any tears left to cry.

My eyes skim across to the photos and I pick one up from the side unit, a small smile lifting the corner of my lips, my eyes glassy and glistening as I gaze with intent at her. She was a beauty. A perfect white stripe down to her nose, her blonde mane and tail glossy and long. In certain lights you could see the dapple spots under her cream coat. I missed her. Truly. And part of me wishes I could go back in time and overcome my fear. But everything happens for a reason. Maybe I was never meant to get on the back of a horse. Maybe I was meant to run out of town and leave a crumpled mess behind me and just maybe, I was meant to return all these years later.

Placing the photo back down, I skim my fingertip over the edge of the photo frame before sitting on the white metal framed single bed, the spring mattress creaking as I did.

I was so tired. Mentally and physically tired. It had been a long few hours. I thought the drive would clear my mind but all it did was burden me even heavier with all the *what ifs'*.

Flopping back, I gripped the top of my towel with my fingers holding it close to my body as I stared at the ceiling. My heart galloped in my chest, my pulse throbbed, and my eyes welled.

"What the hell am I going to do?" I whisper to the empty room, and the next thing I know, my eyes fall heavy and darkness takes over.

RIGGS

Leaning over the fence, I am lost in easy conversation with Austin. I see his eyes cast behind me and my ears are met with a loud rumble of an engine. I turn to look over my shoulder, the low winter sun peeping over the mountains as I watch the low, plastic sports car clattering down the dusty driveway of Maple Farm. I wince when the front of the car hits a few dug outs.

"What's the betting it's an outsider who took the wrong turn on their sat nav? We don't get them sort of cars here," I scoff, shaking my head from side to side and letting my head roll forward, my fingers running across the edge of my cowboy hat.

Turning my body round, my back rests against the fence, my arms crossing against my chest. My eyes eclipsed behind my tinted sunglasses as I watch the car roll to a halt. I turn my face to look at Austin, but he isn't there anymore. He is moving towards the car, his baseball cap sitting on top of his head, his hands tucked into the front pockets as he walks with swag and a boyish grin on his face.

I stand tall, lifting my leg to rest the flat of my boot on the bottom fence.

Who the fuck would drive a car like that in a town like this.

Curiosity piques my interest when I see Austin's facial expression change, his shoulders sagging as the butterfly door to the McLaren lifts. A set of long, tanned legs swing from the car, a high, stiletto heel slipping on the dusty gravel beneath it.

Stepping forward, my arms slowly unfold from my chest, my heart slamming forward when my eyes cast on her. My body stiffened like heavy, cold metal.

The one that broke my heart.

I've avoided her for years, but now, everything I once felt comes flooding back. The feelings I pushed so deep down into the depths of my soul, switching everything off when it came to *her*.

But now here she was. Wrapped in a designer dress and heels, her hair curly and wild. Make-up smudged down her face and when she looks up, her eyes cut to mine and everything in me freezes. My heart stops beating for a minute, my blood stops thrashing through my veins and the once loud thumping in my ears turns into deathly silence.

For just a minute.

Gazes locked; her pretty face is flushed with humiliation. I swallow down the apple sized lump that is lodged in my throat, thickness growing. I watch as Austin wraps his arms around her and only then, when her hazel eyes are off mine, can I breathe. My heart pumps a little harder, a little faster like a steam train in my chest. My blood floods through my veins, riptides forming deep within my bloodstream and the silence that once consumed me is replaced by a hundred drums, banging inside of my ears.

Blue comes rushing out, running towards her daughter and whilst they're consumed in each other I turn to look at Buck who gives me a knowing look before his hard exterior moves to his daughter.

I can't do this.

I won't do this.

I allow myself one last look, scoffing then kicking my boots across the dust as I take my wounded self back home.

Aspen Warren was back in Lovelock Bay.

Home.

CHAPTER THREE
ASPEN

I startle myself awake and sit up too quickly. It takes me a moment to realize that I am back in my childhood bedroom as I turn to look over my shoulder and out the window to see dusk starting to set in.

Damn.

My neck felt stiff, my hair is still damp and wrapped in my towel on the top of my head and I feel as if I have been hit by a bus. I scrub my face feeling irritated with myself suddenly. My arm falls and hits the bed and I puff my cheeks out, then slowly release the breath I had been holding.

Reluctantly, I pull myself up and let the towel around my body fall to my waist. Leaning across, I grab the white tee my mum had left out for me and pull it over my head. Standing, I hold the towel around my waist and move towards my drawers to find some panties. Letting the towel fall at my feet, I slip my panties up and then move towards the bed and tug on my light wash denim Levi's. They swing round my waist, and I drop my head down to look at them. These used to fit snug, but I suppose eating clean with Luke helped me shift some unwanted weight without me even realising.

Reaching for my plaid shirt, I pull it on and let the towel unravel from my long, damp hair. Running my fingers through the ends as I walk towards the door, a small smile creeping onto my face when the familiar creek of the floorboard sounds. I would dodge that board when me and Austin used to sneak out and meet Riggs, Tripp and Pacey. A pang shoots through me, but I ignore it.

Tugging the stiff drawer on my dresser open, I fish for my brush and run it through my hair. I bend slightly and look in the oak rimmed mirror at my reflection. My eye bags are heavy and have a purple shade to them, standing out against the paleness blanketing my usually tanned skin. Washed out and exhausted.

I have no idea how I am even feeling. The tears are there, and the pain is prominent, but covering it with a mental band-aid is not helping, my wound still bleeds and seeps through the thin material. All I know for certain is my heart feels like it's been through a stampede of galloping wild horses and pushed back into my chest. Battered and bruised. It ached. Heavily. I was wounded. I just needed time to get over whatever the hell was going on and I know I will heal from this. Like I always do. It was just going to take time.

Closing my eyes for a moment, I stand and press my hand to my forehead, instantly feeling the cool metal of my thick engagement band on my warm skin and my heart sinks. Slowly, I lower my left hand and hold it out in front of me, my beautiful engagement ring didn't feel as beautiful anymore. It was tarnished with infidelity and heartbreak. I gently touch the band with my index finger and thumb and give it a soft pull before I am met with mental resistance telling me that I'm not quite ready to take it off yet.

Not yet.

I ignore the roll of nausea in my stomach. I still couldn't quite get my head round it. I was in such a rush to get out, I packed nothing. I didn't even grab my phone. Just grabbed my keys, Butch and my laptop.

Puffing out my cheeks, I place my hands on my hips and just give myself a moment, willing for this sickness that I feel in my stomach and the crushing pain that's radiating in my chest to leave.

I hear the stairs creak and I see my mom walking up them as I open my bedroom door.

"Hey, mom," my voice is rushed. Stepping out into the hallway, I stop in front of her.

"Hey sweetheart, I was just coming up to wake you. You feeling a little better?" she asks, her head tilting to the side, her eyes bouncing back and forth between mine. I know she knows the story I spun her was bullshit. The fact I turned up in a designer dress, *Jimmy Choo* heels and nothing but my dog and laptop, well, it was pretty obvious.

"I'm fine," my tone is curt.

Those two words again.

I wasn't fine.

At all.

"Okay sweetie. Come, I am just about to serve dinner up. Austin and your pops are bringing the horses in, then we can eat."

Giving her a gentle nod, she wraps her arms round me and holds me tightly for a moment before unravelling me from her grasp.

"Let's go," she smiles, her eyes a little glassy and I force a tight-lipped smile across my lips. "For what it's worth..."

she stalls at the top of the stairs, "I'm glad you're here," the honesty of her words spreads across her expression like the sun beating down on the rolling green fields.

"Me too," I whisper. "Me too."

WALKING INTO THE LARGE, rustic kitchen my stomach grumbles with hunger. It smells amazing. Sage green kitchen units, solid oak countertops with matching ceiling beams. This whole house screams *farmhouse* and I adore it all. It was so different to our—I mean *his*—mansion back in Windsor Square with its high ceilings and modern finishes; it screamed pretentious.

The downstairs of my childhood home was mostly open planned, there aren't many walls separating the rooms. A large archway leads to the dining room, a wide hallway breaks the kitchen from the living area. At the back of the living area is my dad's bar and to the left of the bar is a study area where he works. It's a cosy little room overlooking the rolling greens of Rivera Ranch and the mountains on the horizon. It's the perfect place to sit and work. *Maybe I'll slip in there if I get the urge to write.* I scoff at my own thoughts knowing I wouldn't finish anything regardless.

"Do you need any help?" I ask, feeling like a spare part suddenly.

"You can lay the table?" My mom offers, looking over her shoulder as she drains the potatoes from the pot.

Walking through the rooms of my childhood home, I feel myself warm with the memories that we had here. We had a hard childhood, but a happy one. My mom and dad weren't perfect, but they were happy. We were happy. My dad worked hard, harder than most I knew and we'd never had a lot of money until my dad sold an amazing horse to a well-known dressage and show jumper named Lillian Savoy. She was who I always wanted to be like, but that dream soon diminished into nothing. It became splintered and fractured into tiny pieces and it didn't matter how much my heart wanted it, I couldn't put the pieces back together again no matter how much I tried.

Heaviness crushes my chest and I pull myself from my thoughts.

Placing the plates on top of the placemats, I lay the cutlery out and finally the wine glasses.

"All done," I chime as I walk back into the room to see my mom loading the serving dishes with mash, vegetables and beef short rib. I licked my lips. I was *so* hungry and my mom was the best cook.

"Can you get the red from the wine cellar? The pinot noir."

Anxiety cripples through me, but I moved to do as I was asked.

I twist, turning my back to my mom and walk slowly towards the back of the house. I kick the small, rectangle rug away with the ball of my foot, sliding it along the hardwood floors before I bend, pulling up the cellar door and stepping down into the basement.

The cellar runs the complete underside of the house. It's always fully stocked.

Champagne, white, red, rosé.

You want it? We have it.

Dragging my fingertips over the dusty bottles, I grab the 2018 pinot noir. I pause for a moment, looking at the boiler that sits in the corner and I remember I used to be so scared to come down here as a kid. I know I am lying to myself. I am still terrified to come down here. I used to cry, and

Austin would trap me down here thinking it was funny. I have been scared of the dark ever since.

Everyone has fears. And mine happens to be the dark. A silly childish prank turned into a crippling fear that grips me by the throat every time, along with riding horses.

Ice coldness trickles down my back, but I ignore it.

After that, my mom and dad made sure that the farmhouse was scattered with nightlights so I could always find my way and never have to walk through pitch-black darkness again. Austin eventually apologised, but it took me a while to forgive him fully and he has never forgiven himself for causing my lasting fear.

I wasn't going to be labelled a scaredy cat so I used to scream till I was blue in the face trying to prove to him and the Rivera brothers that I was brave like them.

But they never believed me because of Austin.

A shiver dances over my spine and I rush up the stairs, cutting the light and closing the cellar door quickly.

Just as I walk down the hallway, I see my dad and Austin walking through the back door, all rosy cheeked from the cold and laughing about something. No doubt a private joke that I'm no longer privileged to.

"Penny," Austin beams at me and his hazel eyes dance with mine, "you're awake," his tone is laced with kindness and my heart swells. Austin was a good man; hardworking, loyal and loved his family fiercely.

I nod, rolling the bottle of wine in my hands to keep them busy.

He squeezes my shoulder as he walks past me and straight into the kitchen, pinching a string green bean off one of the plates and I watch as my mom swats him away.

"Hands!" she bellows and he laughs as he leans over the

sink, turning on the faucet. I turn my attention back to my dad and my heart races.

"Pops," I smile, my nose scrunching softly.

"Darling," he smiles wide, and I see how the coldness has marked his skin, his cheeks are scarlet, his nose cherry red and his lips are cracked and dry.

He steps towards me and pulls me into his embrace, holding me tightly.

It felt good to have his arms wrapped around me. One thing I hated most in the world was upsetting or disappointing my parents, especially my dad. They would never admit it, but I know I disappointed them when I left town. Sure, they understood, but it didn't mean they had to like it or approved for that matter. The longer I was in his embrace, the more I could feel the tension crackling between us. I hated that I had just turned up, but I hated myself more for lying to them.

But they weren't stupid.

They knew what the hell was going on.

I just didn't want to admit it and they didn't want to ask.

"I'm so glad you're home and out of la-la land," he whispered, and I feel his shoulders rise and fall as he chuckles.

"Me too, pops."

It wasn't a lie.

But it also wasn't one hundred percent the truth.

He gives me a soft pat on the back as he lets me go and walks over to my mom, kissing her on the cheek and then washing his hands without even having to be asked.

I move forward, reach for the corkscrew and walk into the dining room to place the bottle in the center of the table, laying the corkscrew next to it.

Mom and dad walk into the dining room carrying the *Le Creuset* orange dishes.

"Mom, this all looks..." I pause for a moment.

"Delicious," Austin nods and dives straight in, scooping a large spoon of mash and dropping it onto his plate.

"You're an animal," my dad scoffs, shaking his head from side to side as he unscrews the cork.

"I know," Austin winks, his cap backwards on his head and as my father places the bottle on the table uncorked, he leans across to his left and swats Austin's hat off his head.

"Manners, boy." He groans, wrapping his fingers back round the bottle and topping all of our glasses up.

I smile, my eyes roaming the table. I hadn't even realized I sat in my exact seat I used too as a kid. We all have.

Dad at the head of table, naturally.

Austin to his left.

Mom to his right.

And me? I was nestled next to Austin.

"I just want to say," my dad clears his throat as he holds his glass of wine in the air, "we're glad you're back and home, Penny," he uses Austin's nickname and my cheeks pinch scarlet, my eyes glassy. "And I will pray every night and every morning that this is for good, because God, we have missed you," he chokes slightly and my mom gives him a sad smile, her hand resting on his and I feel a snap on one of my heart strings.

"I'm here for a while, so..." I smile but keep my eyes down on my empty plate. I couldn't look at them. I couldn't let them see the truth that dances in my eyes.

"Well, my prayers are already being answered," my dad beams as my mom begins to dish his food up which causes a tut and roll of the eyes. "I don't know how many times I have to tell you woman, I can dish my own damn food up," he growls but not in an aggressive way. My parents are the definition of soulmates. They adore each other. Sure, they piss each other off; but at the end of the day, they always say good night, I love you and seal it with a kiss no matter how mad they may have been earlier in the day.

We were always bought up to never go to bed on an argument with someone you love.

"I know darling, and like I have told you for the past forty-eight years, I like doing it for you," she leans across and kisses him on the cheek and my heart thumps in my chest.

I dreamed for a love like my mom and dad's, and I thought I had finally found it, but me being here alone just proves that it wasn't meant to be.

I swallow down the bile, my chest tightening as I try and will my mind to not go back to Luke and eventually, I dish my own food up.

"I heard Tripp has had a few issues with the ranch a few miles down; Bluebeak." Austin breaks the comfortable silence and my eyes volley between him and my father.

I watch as my dad's brow forms a deep V, wrinkling his forehead more prominently.

"Why?" he asks, but not lifting his eyes to meet Austin.

"Clay has been trying to sell livestock along to a farmer out of town, and without papers nonetheless, so he can avoid Marty because he is the livestock commissioner. I'll be honest, from what Tripp and Riggs were saying, Clay down at Bluebeak is just pissed because his old buddy Trevor has left. We both know he was lining his pretty pockets now," Austin shakes his head from side to side and his lip curls with disgust, his eyes blackening as he stabs his vegetables with his fork.

"I don't get these young fools. Rules are rules." My dad hums, speaking with his mouthful and my mom tuts at his manners.

"Well, rules are garbage according to Clay."

My dad grumbles something under his breath that none of us can decipher.

"What does Pacey think of it all?" My mom pipes up as my dad continues to ramble to himself, the odd head shake from side to side occasionally as he listens.

"Ugh," Austin sighs and I can see the weight bearing on his slim shoulders, "you know Pacey. He is a big kid. Tripp thought by making him a livestock agent that he would knuckle down a little... but he just sees this as a joke I think."

"Silly boy."

"Yeah," Austin roughs his hair up with his hand as he shovels a spoonful of mash into his mouth.

I sit quietly, nibbling on my food because my anxiety is suffocating me. I feel so welcome but so out of place at the same time. Like a misplaced object that doesn't quite know where it should be sat.

"Aspen, sweetie, are you okay?" my mom asks me and forces my eyes up to meet hers. My eyes pin to hers and my mouth drops open softly as I swallow the dryness down.

"Yeah, well, I think so," I laugh softly, my eyes moving from her to my dad then Austin. "I am very out the loop," I nod quickly, pushing my food round my plate, "and I know that's my fault," I rush out before any of them can swipe me down with a comment.

"Well, I can give you a quick rundown if you want?" Austin's brows lift, his hazel eyes glued to mine.

I nod, because this way it takes my mom's attention off me. "That would be a big help."

"Okay, so, Riggs runs the ranch. He is the top dog now; he has eight cowboys underneath him and in the bunkhouse. All new faces from when you last visited. Young blood with a couple of older guys to keep them rowdy asses in line," Austin scoffs.

"Bet Jorge is happy that Riggs stayed home," I mutter quietly and I feel my heart constrict. I always knew Jorge wanted his boys home, here in Lovelock Bay and to continue their legacy.

"Yeah, he is." Austin's tone is clipped and I notice how he sits a little taller, but I don't push for any more out of him even though I want to know everything there is to know about Riggs Rivera.

"Obviously as you heard, Marty is now commissioner, we're pleased for him. He is so much more than a cowboy. Tripp is now Sheriff, Chip went out with a bang though."

"Oh really?" my brows raise, I remember Chip. He was the livestock commissioner when I lived back here, he had always been the Sheriff and I am surprised it didn't go down to one of his three sons.

"Yeah, bullet straight through the chest." I don't miss the glint of a smile that crosses Austin's lips.

"Oh, you meant literally out with a bang," I choke on my intake of breath and reach for my wine, swallowing a large mouthful down and it instantly warms my throat. It's earthy and has hints of dark cherries and liquorice. It's delicious. Licking my lips I take another mouthful and get ready for the next lot of information that Austin is about to drop on me.

"Yeah, the sheriff got a tip off that it was something to do with the Rivera's because Jorge is one of the biggest livestock movers on this side of the state, but they couldn't find anything. Jorge is a lot of things, but a murderer or fraudster is definitely not something you could pin on that grumpy fucker."

I snort a silent laugh as I take another mouthful of my wine. It was the truth. Jorge was a lot of things, maybe a little twisted in the name of the law and I wouldn't be surprised if he didn't have a few people buried deep in his pocket, but he wouldn't harm anyone intentionally.

"And here, all is well?" I ask as I place my wine on the table, my fingers tapping the base of the wine glass in a steady rhythm.

"As well as it can be, we're still selling and raising beautiful, strong horses. We're all ready for spring, you'll have to come down to the stables tomorrow. Meet some of our girls. We only have two stallions now, one Mustang and an American Quarter Horse. We have a couple down at Bob's in the next town along, Norwood Bay. He has a couple of Arabians, some Morgan horses and an American Paint Horse. So, we have a nice variety." Austin beams. "I hope you can witness it; I really do hope you're here for good, Penny." His hand reaches for mine as he gives it a squeeze and I have to swallow the lump down in my throat at his small show of affection.

I just about manage a hum in agreement as my tears build behind my eyes.

"I've started going to a couple of the shows to see some of our bred horses compete. There's something enchanting about watching the horse you reared, broke in and sold on. You'll have to come with me next time, I'm trying to rope Riggs and the boys in, give us a little weekend away."

He elbows me.

"You sure you want me to gate crash your *boys'* weekend?"

"Ah come on Penny, don't be like that," he nudges me a

little harder now and I smile like crazy. In that moment it makes me realise just how much I have missed our simple family dinners.

"The next one is March, so, hopefully if you're still here you can ride up with us. It's in North Dakota, you up for it?"

"Let's see, yeah?" I say softly not wanting to get his hopes up because honestly, I have no idea where I'll be in March.

Silence fills the room for just a moment as I pop a carrot into my mouth and bite down.

"We're heading down to the Old Dusty Boot tomorrow night; me, the Rivera boys, Harlow and Marty."

Harlow.

"Sounds good," I lie. Nerves cascade through me, my skin prickling with anxiousness, but I mask it well.

"Great," Austin chimes and we fall into light conversation whilst we finish our dinner, I felt stuffed but then mom served up her apple and cinnamon pie and my god, it was delicious.

***

WRAPPED UP IN A SCARF, large, padded coat and fluffy socks, I sat on the decked porch and looked into the night sky. The sky was so clear here. We didn't get nights like this in LA. It was too bright. There was something so calming and almost healing looking up at a clear night sky; at small, burned out stars thousands of lightyears away, still burning bright in our atmosphere. Sipping my fourth glass of wine, my head was beginning to get a little hazy, but it was warming me from the inside out. My cheeks were no doubt flushed and the sadness that was suffocating me was also slowly seeping away.

It was just me and the night.

The stars twinkling above me.

Crickets dancing.

The odd fireflies lighting up and my eyes fixate on them.

I felt at peace here. I had forgotten how good the country air felt. How much I missed it. Why the hell did I run to the city?

Because I was an idiot wanting to leave behind a past.

To leave behind a broken-hearted boy, because the broken-hearted girl wanted someone else.

It was messy and complicated, so it was easier to run. And that's what I did.

I studied English literature and took a creative writing class which really, in hindsight, was a waste of time.

And now I was back. And I was petrified of seeing Riggs, Tripp and Pacey.

They hold grudges and I'm sure they weren't as happy to see me as my family was.

Thirteen Years Old

THIS WAS the first time I really noticed Riggs Rivera.

It was spring, the air smelt sweet, the sun was shining and life was good.

Me and Austin made plans to meet the Rivera brothers on their fence line at one p.m. I was excited and nervous. It was the first time I was 'invited' out with the boys. I didn't want to be the annoying little sister, even though Austin was only three years older than me, I was still considered the 'baby'.

"Bye mom!" Austin called out as he pushed through the front door, me following, eyes wide and all starry.

"Be back at dusk and not a minute later Austin Warren and don't go past the river bend!"

"I won't!" he calls back as he jumps the three steps off the wrap around porch and I follow, but I don't jump. Just in case I tumble and fall. We climb the first fence of our front paddock and we run and run into the distance until we make it to our neighboring fence.

They were already there, standing tall and proud.

Riggs was the oldest, he was five years older than me and I felt embarrassed for having a crush on someone that much older than me but there was something about him. His chocolate brown hair sat in curls on the top of his head, you would think he had it permed. But it was all natural. The only one out of the boys with their mom's curly brown hair. Tripp was more a dirty blond and Pacey had light brown hair. Riggs' eyes were a light sage, like the clear summer ocean that you see in the movies, where his brothers had dark brown eyes.

"So, you brought her with you then," Riggs smirks and I place my hand on my hips.

"'Her,'" I quote, "has a name, thank you," I tap my foot on the dirt at the edge of the grass.

"I know that Dinks," he gives me a smile and my heart flutters. He has a perfect smile. He is so beautiful.

"Okay, so, shall we head down to the river creek?" Austin leans over the fence, we're still on our land, the boys on theirs.

"Shall we race?" Tripp says playfully.

"Foot or horse?" Pacey asks.

"Horse," Riggs scoffs.

"Lazy boy," I hum as I put my foot on the bottom of the fence.

"Hardly lazy; come, let's get saddled up."

Me and Austin climb over the fence and jump onto the

ground, the dust flying up round our ankles from the dirt path that runs alongside the grass.

We pass Jorge and Orla as we head into the stables. The cowboys are out so the ranch is deadly quiet. We always go for the same horses.

Riggs goes for the American Paint horse, Rhodes.

Tripp goes for the Arabian, Casper.

Pacey goes for the second Arabian, Zayn.

Austin goes for the American Quarter horse, Monty.

And I go for the Appaloosa, Dotty.

She was my favorite anyway.

Plus, the only mare.

We tack up and mount the horses, Tripp's horse, Casper, is probably the rowdiest one of the group; its tail held high, ears pricked forward and nostrils flare as he gazes out onto the open fields.

"Last one there has to swim in the creek!" Riggs shouts as he kicks off his horse, moving straight into a canter.

"Cheater!" I call as I spur Dotty on and let my hands reach up her neck as I lower myself over her and kick her into a gallop. "Come on girl, don't let me lose."

I blaze past Tripp and Austin, lifting myself from the saddle and looking over my shoulder, giving them both a small smile as I chase the pretty Arabian in front of me. Zayn was completely black, he was stunning. Dotty was a Grulla blanket with a thick white blaze down her pretty face.

"I'm coming for you, Pacey!" I call out and I hear his boyish giggle as he shrieks, kicking Zayn on.

"Dream on, Penny!" he calls back, looking over his shoulder and throwing me a wink. Pacey isn't hard on the eyes; in fact he is beautiful. Freckles scattered over his cheeks and the bridge of his nose. He is cheeky, playful... but he isn't Riggs.

Something about Riggs pulls me to him, like a moth to a flame.

But he doesn't see me like that. I'm just the girl next door. His best friend's kid sister.

And I'm okay with that.

I can admire him in secret.

I give Dotty another kick forward, loosening the reins slightly so she feels it on her bit, and she surges as we pass Pacey and Zayn, the sound of her hooves beating down on the grass is all I hear, my heart beating along with the music that she is making.

This is where I belong.

Lovelock Bay, on the back of a horse and riding free.

This is what life is about.

This moment right here.

I was never going to give this up.

My life revolved around horses, I was good at riding, I knew I was, and I wasn't going to let anyone stop me from reaching the goals of becoming a world renowned show jumper.

"Riggs," I call out, he's out of the saddle, cowboy hat sitting on his curly hair, and he looks amazing. He was made for this life as well.

"I can't hear you!" he mocks and I laugh.

"You're a liar, I'm so close to you," I shout, but I don't have a chance to catch him. I can see the creek and I can't push Dotty any more.

I watch as he slows, Rhodes moving from a gallop to a canter, to a slow and steady trot before Riggs lets go of the reins and Rhodes walks towards the creek, taking a well-earned drink. I slow myself and Dotty, my heart is racing, my breaths ragged, and I pat Dotty on the neck.

"We would have beaten your ass if you didn't cheat," I shake my head from side to side as I swing my leg over the back of

Dotty and dismount her before I close the gap between me and Riggs and I shove him in the arm.

"Of course, you would," he rolls his eyes and I don't miss the sarcasm that drips from his tone. Riggs swings his arm round my shoulder and pulls me close and I swear my heart stills.

He smells like fresh mountain air.

Crisp, clean but earthy at the same time and I don't miss the hint of tack cleaning soap and leather that surrounds him.

Delicious.

A blush creeps onto my cheeks and I dip my head because I don't want anyone to see. Especially him.

We hear the sound of whistling and hooves beating the ground behind us and I pull away from Riggs quickly as if suddenly, he has burnt me. Twisting fast, I smile when I see the boys approaching.

"You took your time," I put my hands on my hips, a lopsided smirk pulling at my lips.

"We know when to accept defeat," Pacey scoffs as he jumps from his horse, followed by Austin and Tripp.

I lean against a large tree, sliding down the trunk and watch as the guys flop down beside me.

This is perfection.

Me.

Them.

Us.

Sure, I was the kid sister but they were everything to me. Every single one of them.

I adored them, and I knew deep down, all three Rivera brothers adored me too.

"So, seems Tripp is going for a swim?" I tease, a soft laugh bubbling out of me.

"Doesn't bother me," he shrugs nonchalant as he begins to undress, and I cover my eyes and shriek.

I hear a large splash and when I finally lift my hands, my smile widens. Tripp is sitting in the middle of the creek, completely and blissfully at ease.

It really was the best day.

We all rode home, and Orla made hotdogs and corn bread with ice cream and pie for dessert. And of course, she made sure we were home by dusk, but the Rivera brothers came with us. We spent our evening melting s'mores over a little campfire and sleeping under the stars.

This was just the start of our adventures.

CHAPTER FOUR
ASPEN

It had been a week. A week since I returned home. It felt weird calling it *home* when I hadn't been here for so long. I was a little bit lost. I didn't quite know where I belonged. I hadn't seen Riggs. I hadn't seen any of them. I've stopped myself from walking down to the paddocks and to the fence line but curiosity still burns deep inside of me, wanting to see if everything is the same as it was all those years ago.

A heavy, burdening sigh passes my lips as I watch my dad and Austin round the mares up for their new hooves. I'm standing at the large kitchen window, my arms wrapped around my body and my visible breath dancing in front of me from the coolness of the open windows; the winter air filling the once warm and cozy kitchen. My eyes flick over to the farrier getting ready to shoe the horses; tall, burly, clean-faced. Opposite to Luke. Very good looking. I let my eyes roam over him, he is only wearing a muscle tee and dirty chaps over light wash jeans. He must be *freezing*. Dad and Austin are all wrapped up in layers and the hot farrier is dressed for summer.

"Why don't you go and see the horses... see if your dad wants any help," I hear my Mom's voice vibrate through me.

I turn my face and look over my shoulder, my cheeks blushing crimson at being caught staring at said hot farrier.

"He doesn't want my help, I'm about as helpful as a cowboy without a horse," I snort.

"Just go, I'm sure he would appreciate it," she urges and my stomach knots.

My nerves prick. Anxiety creeping up and slowly drowning me in my own body, my breaths labored and harsh as I gasp for the air I so desperately crave.

"You need to try and beat this fear, Aspen."

Easier said than done.

"It's not that easy," my throat constricts and tightens which causes my voice to come out more like a squeak. "When something happens and completely destroys you mentally and physically..." I pause, squeezing my eyes shut as I try and stop myself from crying into a crumbling mess. My words sound harsh, whipping across my mother's skin and I instantly regret it. Sniffling, I turn my face forward and focus on the three men in front of me, my chest rising and falling a little slower now.

My mom walks towards me, standing next to me and twisting her body so she is facing me. She is wearing old, worn denim overalls with a cream crew neck tee. She places her soft hand on my cheek while her eyes probe mine as if she is searching for something, anything, to give her a glimmer of what may or may not be going on.

"Darling, it's not meant to be easy. You can get through this; everyone goes through something at least once in their life that destroys them in one way or another." She pauses for a moment as if remembering something that may have happened to her once upon a time. "It's when you *choose* to overcome it, that's when you'll start healing. Be brave my love, don't let what happened in the past cripple your future."

I choke on my inhale, my throat burning as if hot coal was being pushed into my mouth and being forced to swallow, but I won't let the tears fall. Because if I start, they won't stop. I don't want to admit just how broken I am, how fragile my heart is. One small movement and it will shatter into a million pieces. I don't want to explain *just* how much of a spare part I now feel because I have no place, I have no reason or motive. I gave up *everything* for Luke.

Everything.

And for what?

To come back home with my tail between my legs with just my dog, my laptop and my McLaren.

I suck in a breath just as my mom's hand drops and I instantly miss her motherly embrace.

"Are you going out with them tonight seeing as you blew them off last week?" I watch as she steps back and lifts the cast iron teapot from the stove, giving it a gentle shake from side to side to see if there is any water inside.

"I don't know mom, I'm not sure if I am feeling up to it." It wasn't a lie. I had no idea if I wanted to go out with them or not. Old feelings will resurface, blurring into new ones and I'm honestly not sure if I am quite ready for that just yet.

"Well, me and your dad are going out with Jorge and Orla so you'll have the house to yourself. Whatever you want to do," she waves her hand at me. Rolling my lips, I push my hands into the back pockets of my jeans and turn to look out the window again, watching the farrier just a little bit harder now.

"I'm going into town and to the mall tomorrow, need to get some last bits for Christmas. Why don't you come with, get some new clothes and whatever else you need."

"I have no money," my voice is tight, and I refuse to turn to look at her because my eyes are misting, the intense pressure building and my chest heaves, ready to cave in at any given moment.

"Our treat," she quickly replies.

"Mom..." I swallow down the tears, swallow down the remorse and guilt I am feeling for ever leaving and pushing them aside as soon as Luke came along.

"It's okay Aspen," her tone is soft and she continues waiting for her teapot to boil, my eyes find her over my shoulder and as I blink, a tear rolls down my cheek.

"I just..." I stammer but struggle to form the words, tightness coats the narrow column of my throat, swallowing hard.

"I'm here when you're ready," her voice stays soft, but I appreciate her kind words. She pours the hot water into a mug of chamomile tea. I didn't ask for one, but she's made one anyway and my heart warms.

I take it from her and lean against the kitchen counter as I blow on steam before taking a tentative sip. We stand in companionable silence for a few minutes, my mom somehow knowing I need to process all of our conversation. Decision made, I place my still half full mug by the sink and head for the front door, my heart thrashing in my chest as my fingers curl around the doorknob.

"I'm going to be brave, mom," my voice is a little louder as she follows me out into the hallway.

"I have no doubt, sweetheart."

Walking onto the porch, the cold air hits me and causes me to cough as the chill hits my lungs. My dad, Austin and the hot farrier have disappeared, and something surges deep in my chest but I am unsure of what emotion has caused it. Pinching my brows, my eyes search the front of the house as I step down the steps and onto the dusty gravel path. My boots crunch and my head tilts down as I move my feet from side to side, digging the toes of my boots into the gravel a little further. After a quiet moment with myself and my ever-noisy thoughts, I will for my legs to move me forward, to carry me towards the large stables. With each step that brings me closer, the quicker my heart gallops inside my chest at a steady, even beat. But with each step comes anxiety. Soul crushing, chest caving anxiety.

I can do this. I remind myself on loop.

My boots crunch across the stones and the smell I once found so comforting fills my senses and fear surges inside of me; so much that I almost feel paralyzed.

I hear my dad's voice and Austin letting out a small laugh that fills the large space ahead of me.

"Pops?" I call from the wide entrance of the stables, the sliding door hooked back.

"In here Penny," his voice echoes through the stalls. I inhale deeply, holding my breath for a second as I take a small step forward, but not a big enough one to be able to step across the threshold. The familiar smell teasing at my senses, my fingers knotting as I take another step forward and this time, I step over the metal grate. The warm smell intoxicates me, musty like hay in the spring, sweet and addictive. This used to be one of my favorite smells. I would have rather buried my nose in a horse's neck and inhale than smell a bouquet of flowers.

There was something poignant about the smell and comforting at the same time. A warmness burned in the depths of my stomach and my heart thumped in one large, heavy beat.

Gliding cautiously through, I ignore the burning ball of anxiety that presents itself deep in my stomach. I walk to the end of the stables, turn the corner and that's when I see my dad, Austin and the hot farrier all standing in one of the corner stalls.

All eyes on me.

Blinking, smiling, waiting with bated breath for something to fall from my lips.

I shrink back and stand just the other side of the stable door, not quite ready to push myself any further.

Dark brown eyes crash over me and a small sense of calmness washes over me like gentle waves lapping against the shore.

"New shoes?" I ask the most ridiculous question, blurting it out and embarrassment flames my cheeks.

"Just a repair for Sapphire today," the farrier lifts his eyes back to mine before he focuses on the hoof that is tucked between his thick thighs, covered in dirty denim and leather chaps.

"Cool," I roll my lips, crossing my arms across my chest when I hear the sound of heavy boots kicking down the stable halls.

"Austin!" Riggs' deep, husky voice calls out and my skin prickles in goosebumps, swallowing hard.

"In the end stall," Austin shouts as my dad strokes the mare's neck.

"Right, Conrad, I'll let you get on with it." My dad grunts, turns and walks out but not before giving me a lingering kiss on the cheek.

"Need help?" I rush out, silently praying that there is something, anything, that I could do so I am out of the hell that I am about to endure. Me and Riggs haven't been in the same room together in years. When I returned home three years ago he kept his distance, before then was when I ran. My eyes widen, waiting for my dad to respond but all he does is shake his head from side to side.

Damn it.

The air leaves my lungs, screaming and burning as they beg for oxygen when Riggs turns the corner and stops in front of me. Pulling his tinted glasses down the bridge of his nose, his sage green eyes lock on mine; they sweep over me in a look of disgust and rage. Pure fucking rage.

The tension grows.

My cheeks burn a flaming red, my chest aching along with my thrashing heart.

The atmosphere crackles, tension building as the seconds tick past.

I can feel it.

Austin must feel it.

Riggs definitely feels it and I am sure as shit that Conrad the farrier could likely feel it too.

"Well, our spoiled princess returns, it's been a while, hasn't it? What brings you back here? Trouble in la la land?" his glare ice cold, his voice like steel and his whole body stiffens as his shoulders roll back. Riggs' deep, low laugh rumbles through the stalls and I feel my temper begin to simmer deep in the depths of me.

Our spoiled princess? There is no 'our' about it. My rage continues to bubble away.

"Where is the McLaren?" the sound of his voice blankets me in a hot sweat.

"Our?" I scoff, trying to ignore everything else that he

said, my small fists balling at my side, my nails digging into my clammy palms.

"Yeah, *our,* darlin'"

"You're insufferable," is all I can manage, my tongue swollen in my mouth and my throat is dry like I have swallowed a mouthful of sand.

I can't stop the roll of my eyes, annoyance swimming in my veins.

"Ugh, I forgot how annoying you both are," Austin snaps as he stands tall, hands on his hips, his hazel eyes volleying back and forth between us.

"He started it!" Pointing my index finger at Riggs, my brows dig into a frown, my lips turned down and my teeth grind together as I bite down, hard.

I know I sound and look childish and immaturity doesn't look good on me but he makes me seethe.

Riggs chuckles before tucking his gloved hands into his jean pockets and I suddenly want to punch his handsome, stupid face.

"And the McLaren is in the garage, I need to get it fixed up. May or may not have fucked the back of it," annoyance bites at me as I answer his question.

"Lemme take a look at it," a softness masks Riggs' usual hard exterior, his kind offer wavering between us but I shake my head, turning it down in an instant.

"No thanks, I'll sort it. Don't want you to think I am *too* spoiled to get my car fixed."

The softness that was once there was now gone, darkness filled his eyes momentarily before a glint of softness returned. "Pen," he breathes out and I can hear the exasperation in his voice.

"Whatever," I drop my eyes to the floor and I can feel Austin and Conrad's eyes burning into me.

Inhaling deeply, I ignore the silence that is screaming around us and walk towards the main doors of the stables. My cheeks burn as humiliation slaps herself across them and my throat burns from trying to push down the lump that's lodged itself there, growing thicker and larger as the seconds pass.

I have no idea what I ever saw in Riggs Rivera, but whatever it was, it's long gone. He is an entitled ass who holds grudges over childish, stupid shit that happened *years* ago.

"Hey, Pen is it?" I hear Conrad's voice echo through the stalls, footsteps falling behind me and I spin quickly, angrily swiping away the stray tear that escapes.

"Aspen, actually," my voice quivers and I ignore the way my heart weeps in my chest. Ignoring the urge to knot my fingers, I slip them into the back of my jeans.

"Aspen," he smiles back at me, his lips widening, and I focus on just how beautiful he is. Conrad is clean beautiful. Tidy, clean shaved and most likely a well-dressed man, hard to tell with his dirty jeans and old leather chaps. Not like Riggs who is dirty, burly and scruffy... but not even in a bad way. In an absolute delicious way.

In a way that makes me want to spend hours undressing him, to have him ruin me in a way no other man has then piece me back together between the bedsheets. Tangled deep within them, losing ourselves in each other.

"Sorry," I blink, knowing full well I have missed everything Conrad has just said to me.

"Drinks? Tonight? Are you free?" he smiles, a glint in his eye. "The Old Dusty Boot and maybe a little stargazing?" he chimes, stepping closer to me.

I smile. A real, genuine smile. My eyes crease and my stomach flips with anticipation.

"Sounds perfect, I would really like that." I break eye contact for just a moment because it feels a little *too* intimate. Inhaling a breath and calming my erratic heart, I lift my face, my eyes on his. A piece of loose hair falls in front of my eyes and my hand reaches up, my nails pushing it back into place and I see his eyes widen at my engagement ring.

Shit.

My stomach drops.

"I didn't realize you were spoken for, I'm sorry, please..." he stammers, slowly stepping back but I hold my hand up to stop him. My eyes frantic. I am so used to wearing the ring I forget I have it on.

"I'm not, I mean, I am... maybe? I was. I don't really know," I whisper, confusion and guilt consume me and I feel the shameless tears pricking at my eyes. I refuse to blink because I don't want a single tear to fall over what Luke did to me.

"Right..." he cocks his head as he stares at me, he thinks I am lying. He doesn't believe me.

"It's complicated," I admit, because it is complicated. My tongue feels too big for my mouth suddenly, my throat dry.

After a beat of silence, a slow, crooked smile creeps onto his lips, his eyes narrowing and I watch his throat bob up and down. "Isn't everything?"

"I've not handled this very well," a nervous laugh escapes and I drop my head for a moment as my brain whizzes a hundred words at me. Tilting my face up, I catch him staring at me. "I'm not with him, but I'm not quite ready to..." I pause and suck in a deep breath.

"It's okay," he moves closer to me, one large step and he

is in front of me, his neck craned and his wide-eyed gaze on mine. "I'll pick you up at seven?"

"That sounds perfect," I purse my lips.

"Cool," he gives a slow, sexy wink and turns from me to head back to where Sapphire is stalled, my eyes roaming over his back and it's not till he steps back inside the stables that I see Riggs.

Eyes ablaze with rage, jaw locked and ticking, fists balled by his side. He takes a slow step towards me and I back away by two.

"Aspen." And I don't miss the warning tone to his deep voice.

"I don't owe you anything," my voice vibrates as I raise it a little louder and the smile that once sat on my face at accepting a date with Conrad soon slips and fades. My hands tremble and my heart thrums in my chest. "I owe you nothing," an evident crack taints my voice before I turn and walk away.

"Maybe I should cancel," I twist my wrist to face me, my watch ticking. Six-thirty.

"Absolutely not!" my mom tuts, shaking her head. "I have no idea what has happened between you and Luke but I think you need this. Just go, have fun, let your hair down, but don't let that man in them pretty panties of yours," her brows wiggle and I stand, lips parted and eyes wide at her words.

"Mom!"

"I'm just reminding you." She rolls her eyes as she runs a brush through my hair like I am a child again.

"I don't need reminding, I'm not easy. I'm not going to

jump into bed with him." She runs her fingers under my hair and lifts it from my nape before letting it fan out down my back. I smile at her as I stand. She moves to the side so I can see my full body reflection in the mirror opposite me.

I'm wearing an old emerald jumper dress, black thick tights and black knee-high boots. This wasn't a look I would wear in my life in LA, but I don't have a choice until I go shopping with mom tomorrow.

"You look lovely," her voice floats over me as if she can hear my thoughts, and I give her a small shrug. I wasn't so sure. My dirty blonde hair sits in waves, the once tight curls are now brushed out and loose, tumbling down past my ribs.

Pushing medium gold hoops through my ear, I spray my perfume and step into the mist, coating my skin.

My head falls forward, my fingers locked round the band of my engagement ring, and I softly tug at it when I hear my mom's question slice through me, causing me to push my ring back onto my finger.

"What happened, Aspen?" Rolling my head up to look at her, her soft eyes focus on me and the question lays heavy on my shoulders.

"Mom," I whisper because I am too scared to say it out loud, the flood of emotions drowning me and it doesn't matter how much I tread, I can't keep my head above the choppy waters.

"You can tell me, there will be no judgement or anger towards the situation..." she steps closer to me and my heart hammers, slamming against my chest and my breaths slow.

"I can't," my voice cracks and it's the truth, I can't tell her because I am weak and still care what Luke thinks, still think that he will turn up and beg on his knees for me to return home. Still agreeing to keep my mouth shut for *his* career.

Her gaze doesn't harden, there is no anger brewing in her frown but there is concern laced through her expression. I refuse the blink when my eyes beg for it, the tears forming in my bottom lid, my tear ducts overflowing and I know as soon as I give in, the tears will cascade down my cheeks.

"Okay, sweetheart," she scoops me up into her motherly embrace and just holds me close, her heart softly beating through her cashmere sweater, and I have never felt more at home and content than I do now with her. "Don't waste your tears on whatever has happened my darling. I know how much you love Luke, but don't let whatever has happened consume you, you deserve so much more than this. He doesn't deserve your tears or your beautiful soul."

And I sob into her sweater, my tears soaking through the small gaps in the material.

"I'm assuming it was him and not you…" she trails off and I nuzzle deeper into her hold. "Thought so," she whispers to the top of my head and places a kiss there, her arms wrapping around me a little tighter.

Minutes pass and I begin to compose myself; the odd shudder of my breath still vibrates in the back of my throat but the tears have dried up.

"Come on, McHottie will be here soon. You don't want to go out puffy eyed and a quivering mess, do you?" she lets me go, her head tilting to the side as adoration fills her eyes as they hold my glassy eyed gaze.

"No," I whimper, frustration boiling deep inside of me at how upset I am over that worthless, cheating piece of shit and I am even more frustrated that I am allowing myself to still lie and hide what he did.

Her hands drop from me and my arms cross over my body, hugging myself.

"Well then, fix your make up, give yourself a minute and I'll see you downstairs."

I sniff, heading towards the small dressing table, sitting back down and looking back at myself.

"Oh, and Aspen," my mom says as she reaches the door.

"Yeah," my voice cracks.

"You don't owe him, or anyone, anything. Don't feel like you *have* to stay committed to him. He doesn't own you. You're not imprisoned by him. You do you," she smiles before disappearing and I let out a shaky breath.

My eyes fall to my left hand, the large, opal ring sitting on a thin gold band, and as much as I want to take it off, I don't.

This is all I have.

This is all I know.

Everything I was before Luke I masked with the woman I am today and I'm not sure if I am ready to take the mask off.

Not yet.

CHAPTER FIVE
ASPEN

Pulling up outside the Old Dusty Boot, my nerves are shot. I spent the duration of the journey chewing my bottom lip and playing with a loose strand of wool on my sweater dress which I am now internally cursing myself for as I've made a pull.

Sitting up front in Conrad's truck I scan the area. The town is quiet and I am grateful. No one knows who I was with here, or who I was back in LA, apart from the Rivera's and my family.

At home, I couldn't go anywhere without someone following. But here? I was just little old Aspen Warren from Maple Farm, the daughter of horse breeder extraordinaire. The down and out show jumper who ran away from it all to go to college in the city.

The girl who broke two of the Rivera brothers' hearts.

That's who I am here.

I'm not Aspen Warren, fiancé of Hollywood's new up and coming actor Luke Montgomery.

I was safe here.

Well, from the paparazzi at least.

Not from the local town folks gossip. There's one thing Lovelock Bay loved more than their land and livestock. Gossip.

I twist my engagement ring on my finger when I feel Conrad's hand on my thigh. Unfamiliar feelings stir inside of me.

"Hey, you okay?" his kind voice pulls my eyes from the window and back to him and I give him a solemn nod.

I watch as he cuts the engine of his gray pick-up and jumps out. I wait, knowing full well he will want to open my door and like the perfect gentleman, he does, swinging it wide and taking my hand as I slowly lower myself out the truck.

"Thank you," I give him a sweet smile as he closes the door behind me and places his hand on my lower back, ushering me towards the pub.

Nerves prickle through me at the familiar stomping ground and I stall at the entrance. Overwhelming memories suffocate me. Squeezing my eyes shut, I will for them to stop flashing in front of my eyes.

"We can go somewhere else?" Conrad offers and my heart tugs at his kind offer, his hand slowly slipping from the small of my back and I inhale sharply. Forcing my eyes open, I turn my face up to look at him as I try to read his expression. His brows are furrowed but smooth as soon as my eyes meet his, his lips parted ever so slightly as he waits for my answer.

"No, it's fine. Just a lot of old memories here," the corner of my lips tug into a small smile and I ignore the feelings that are igniting deep inside of me.

"Good ones I hope?"

My mind flashes back to the memories that have plagued me during the drive down here.

Me having a screaming match with Riggs.

Pacey declaring his love for me in front of everyone.

Tripp and Austin dumbfounded.

Harlow betrayed because I was leaving, but little did I know she done some betraying herself.

"Yeah," I nod, ignoring the familiar sting and I lick my lips. "Shall we?" I turn and look up at him.

"Let's," his hand is back where it was and we walk side by side and straight into the hellish hole that is my past.

The soft country music plays through the speakers that sit in the corners of the room, a wooden bar made out of pallets and a thick oak countertop stained in a dark mahogany. Bottles of alcohol lined up behind the bar, some a little dustier than others, deep cherry red bar stools lined and all filled with the usual locals of our small town, Lovelock Bay. Most of which are the local cowboys, ranch owners and the small business shop owners.

There are six cherry red leather booths situated around the large bar, the floors untreated wood giving it a rustic feel, the ceilings covered in beams. The walls are a light cream with *Levi's* jean posters and *Wrangler* jean posters; of course, all with cowboys modelling them. A few animal's skull artwork pieces are hung on the walls and the odd cowboy hat pinned to the wall, with little gold plaques underneath of those that we have lost.

Conrad leads me over to one of the booths and I am grateful that we're tucked away in the corner. My eyes scan the room as I look for my brother, Riggs and the gang but they don't seem to be here yet and relief circles me. The wildfire that is anxiety is blanketed out as the flames flicker into nothing.

"What would you like to drink?" Conrad asks, not

sitting down and resting his large hand on the wooden table.

"Um," I lick my lips as I try and think of something. I've only drunk good wine and expensive champagne for the last six years so choosing something other than that is proving difficult.

"You choose?" I suggest, a sweet smile painted on my lips and he gives a curt nod and tips his invisible cowboy hat. I giggle as he turns and walks away, my eyes roaming over the back of him for a moment and a soft outbreath passes my lips. He is very good looking.

Whilst I am alone, I people watch. My eyes scanning the room as they land on familiar faces. It's as if no time has passed at all.

Everyone looks the same, everything seems the same, everything feels the same. As if the seasons had paused, the years frozen in time.

"Oh my god," I hear her terse tone before I see her. "Do my eyes deceive me or is it little miss 'too good for the country so I leave for the city' sitting here in *our* stomping ground?" I am glued to my seat. Frozen.

Fuck.

"Nope," the word passes my gritted teeth, "your eyes are not deceiving you," I push a fake ass smile on my face, my head tilting as my eyes land on her, narrowing my gaze.

Harlow.

My old best friend.

My old best friend that was going to miss me so much she didn't make one phone call.

My old best friend that fucked my crush and my brother. Not at the same time, just wanted to throw that in there.

"Well..." she scoffs, disbelief coats her tone and I don't

miss it. Her hips sway from side to side as she struts towards me. Her dark hair bouncing in its loose curls as she leans across the table.

"What brings you back home?" Her tone is vicious, sarcastic and downright fucking rude. "Because it sure as shit isn't me." She rolls her eyes in an exaggerated manner. "Is it Riggs?" she continues, her lips pursing and pushing over her teeth, baring her perfect white smile. "Ohhh, Pacey?" she jibes me, waiting for me to bite back.

"Give it a rest," I hear Austin say, his words sniping at her, lashing against her skin and I see her cheeks turn a pretty pink shade. He walks up behind Harlow, but his eyes are on me. I have never felt as small as I do now.

"She came back home because she wanted to, it's not a crime, she doesn't have to ask your permission… jeez Harlow give it a fucking rest. You're like a dog with a bone." Austin pushes past her, disregarding her in an instant and I hear the sharp inhale of breath she sucks in before letting out a huff.

Austin slips into the booth and cocoons me in his arms.

"Ignore her, she is just showing off because she has an audience," he whispers in my ear, then gives me a kiss on my cheek and I am grateful that he is here.

He breaks away and when I look up, my eyes fixate on them.

The Rivera brothers.

Riggs, Pacey and Tripp and my heart flatlines in my chest.

Where the fuck is Conrad with my drink?!

"Anyway, we will leave you to it, feel free to join us if you want to," Austin half shrugs, his smile lopsided. He throws me a wink as he turns. I watch as he grabs Harlow by the wrist and drags her away.

The three Rivera brothers don't move.

They just stand as if anchored to the floor, all sets of eyes on me and suddenly, I am finding it hard to breathe.

There is so much I want to say.

But words don't come.

I just stare back, lips parted as if I am ready to say something, but I stay mute.

My eyes shift between the three of them, willing for one of them to speak, but just as I see Pacey's mouth open, Conrad walks between the three of them, completely ignoring them and placing a whiskey sour in front of me, my eyes pull from the three men who have consumed me whole and I let them fall to the table.

"Hey," Conrad says softly, and I watch his brows furrow when my eyes are glued behind him. He follows my gaze, twisting to look behind him to face Riggs, Tripp and Pacey.

"Can I help you Riggs?" Conrad asks.

"Nope," his tone is clipped, and it slices through me. I miss the old me and Riggs. The old friendship between us. I cared about them all, they were my best friends—along with Harlow—but those bridges are well and truly burned into nothing but ash. Even if we spent time rebuilding, they would never be the same.

"Okay then, can you give us a bit of privacy so I can spend the evening getting to know this beautiful lady?" Conrad gives him a wink and I can't help but hear how condescending his question sounds.

Riggs rolls his eyes, but lifts his hat off his head in some sort of peace offering.

"You okay?" Conrad tips his head down, looking up through his lashes at me.

"I will be," I swallow as I slowly sit a little taller and wrap my fingers around the glass, picking the glacier cherry from the top and pursing it between my lips, before locking my tongue round it and sliding it off its stick. I watch as Conrad rubs his lips together, his eyes blaze and my cheeks pinch the same color as the cherry.

I was flirting; it was shameless.

I'm still wearing my fucking engagement ring and the two guys I destroyed won't stop staring at me, consuming me completely and all I want to do is back away into the depths of the darkness to never be found again.

This was a mistake.

I should have never agreed to come here.

It was like pouring gasoline on an already burning, angry fire.

The Rivera boys the fire.

Me, the gasoline.

It was reckless and stupid, but I still agreed knowing the damage was going to be catastrophic and we would never be able to recover from it.

I lift the glass to my lips and down the drink in one, slamming it down on the table and instantly feeling the warmth smothering me.

"Tequila?" I rush out as I stand motioning to the bar, the alcohol burning through my veins, and I watch as Conrad sits back in his seat, leg crossed over the other and a wide smile across his lips.

"Absolutely," he beams, "you, Aspen Warren, are going to be a lot of fun."

Smirking, I give him a one shoulder shrug then walk towards the bar, keeping my head high as I walk past their table and not giving in to look at any of them. I feel their eyes on me and I feel like shit, but it's not about me and them tonight. It's about me and Conrad. Beautiful, caring and kind Conrad.

"Well, well, well..." I hear Tabitha sing as she struts towards the bar, a huge smile on her face. "If it isn't my little beauty Aspen!" she squeals and leans across the bar, pulling me into her.

"Hey," I embrace her and take in her vanilla scent, finding comfort in it.

"How long you been back for?" her southern accent prominent.

"Just a week," I beam, pushing my feet flat to the floor once she lets me go.

"And how long y'all staying for?"

"It's just me, and I'm not sure yet. I haven't quite decided" I shrug, turning to look over my shoulder and see my brother having what looks like a heated conversation but I'm not sure if it's between him and Harlow or him and the brothers.

"Well, I for one am super glad you're home."

"Me too," I exhale a shaky, whiskey coated breath, ignoring the burn that is radiating deep inside of me, my ears pricking a little hoping to hear just anything of their conversation but it's no use. I'm too far, and they're too quiet under the country music that floats over the room.

"What can I get ya sweetness?"

"Four tequila shots."

"Coming right up," she winks and turns to grab the tequila bottle and I watch as she pours four shots out. I pull a couple of notes out my purse, but Tabitha shakes her head, shooing me away.

"On the house, darlin', little welcome home drink from me to you," she bunches her shoulders up and smiles, scrunching her nose as she does.

"Thank you," I mouth, "that's so kind."

"Anything for our little Aspen," she coos before turning

and serving the next customer. I collect the four glasses between my fingertips and walk back over to Conrad who is smiling from ear to ear when he sees me approach.

"Here," I chime, placing the shots down gently, careful not to spill any of the poignant liquid.

"Cheers," he holds one up as I slide back into the booth and pick my own glass up.

"Cheers," I sing, letting our glasses clink before we knock them back.

Shit.

I wince, the burn coating my throat, but I don't dislike it. It makes a change from the burning coal that lodges in my throat, making me feel sick constantly.

"So, little miss Aspen, tell me… what brings you back to Lovelock Bay?" Conrad asks the burning question that is no doubt on the tip of everyone's tongue at my return while reaching for the other two shots and sliding one across the table for me.

I puff out my cheeks, holding my breath for a moment before letting it out.

"Does it matter?" I ask him back, my tone a little blunt, my eyes striking back and forth between his and I hear him click his tongue to the roof of his mouth.

"Of course not, I am just trying to get to know *Aspen Warren.* I kind of got the impression that something has happened between you and them… just color me curious." His tone is nonchalant.

"It was all a long time ago, things happened, people got hurt, I left… That's about all there is to it," I knock the shot back, wincing again and I catch Tabitha's attention, holding my hand up, spinning my finger and I get a wink back confirming my order.

"And that's all," he sits back with his arms crossed

across his chest smiling, not quite sure if he is buying my story.

"That's all ya getting buddy," I nibble on my bottom lip to stop my smile spreading.

"Fair," he smirks just as Tabitha returns with the tequila shots.

"Just keep them coming," I say as she slides them across the table.

"You sure about that sweetness?"

"Never been surer."

THE ALCOHOL SWIMS in my veins, I feel warm, tingly and happy.

"I'm just popping to the ladies room," I try to whisper, but we both know that I am far from quiet; I am happy drunk. Quiet is no longer an option for me.

"Okay princess," he gives a slow wink and he sits back, calling Tabitha over. Scooting out of the booth, I stand on shaky legs and give myself a moment for my feet to anchor to the ground, to find the steadiness I need to actually move forward. My head is spinning one way, my eyes the other. I have a stupid grin on my face and it feels good to be actually smiling. Flicking my hair over my shoulder as I saunter towards the restrooms, passing the table of *them* as I do and confidence bubbles away with each step I take.

I look over my shoulder and see Conrad's eyes on my behind and my cheeks flush. Pushing through the door, I inhale deeply before locking myself in the stall.

Washing my hands and drying them on a paper towel I look at myself in the reflection. My cheeks are rosy apple red, my lips plump and swollen because I keep sinking my teeth into my bottom one no doubt.

I like this look. I like looking happy. It's only momentary, it won't last. My heart aches when I think back to Luke, not that I should even let him have any of my heartache or thoughts, but, I did love him. I still do. I think? He hurt me. But at least we weren't married, right? Imagine having to tell everyone that my marriage broke down because he fell for the LA homewrecking tramp.

"Ugh," I groan, "they deserve each other. They can be tramps together." I say to the empty room.

Throwing the paper towel in the bin with a little more anger than intended, I tug the restroom door open and wince as it hits into the wall.

"Damn it," I sigh as I walk forward but look over my shoulder at the door to make sure it swings back to close when I hit into someone. "Oh my God," I whisper ready to apologize when I hear a burly growl and my skin prickles. Snapping my head forward, my eyes trail up to see Riggs.

Fucking beautiful Riggs.

I'm flush with his body and I quickly push away from him, my chest heaving up and down.

I expect Riggs to step away, but he doesn't. He steps forward, backing me towards the wall. His head dipped, and I smell the bourbon on his breath, his musky scent filled with leather and a lot of everything I shouldn't still want.

"Riggs, I..." I stammer as my eyes search his face and I'm not sure what he is feeling. His eyes are soft, his breaths calm and not ragged like mine. His green eyes glisten with a streak of the old Riggs; kind and caring.

He goes to say something but stops and just as I go to question him, someone knocks into him, pushing him into my body and I feel him stiffen against me.

A low growl vibrates through him and he spins, shoving the poor guy into the wall opposite.

"Fucking watch it," he bites, shaking his head from side to side and storming out of the cozy hallway, not looking back at me or the crumpled man on the floor.

"Well shit," I breathe, my chest rising and falling as my eyes follow him until he disappears.

I take a moment to compose myself, clearing my throat, then I make sure the guy is okay but he just keeps his head down and scarpers away. Everyone knows the Rivera brothers and Riggs is the one you don't want to piss off. They all have tempers, but not like Riggs.

Walking out, I run my fingers through my hair and walk straight to Conrad.

"I took the liberty of getting the check all sorted, come, let's get out of here," he smiles, shuffling out of the booth and clasping my hand in his. I expect to feel something, a spark, tingles, warmth... but I feel nothing. Disappointment surges deep within me.

"I would have paid, you didn't have to do that," my brows furrow and I feel bad for ordering all the shots, especially as Conrad switched to water a while ago, but my once tipsy disposition has been replaced with stone cold soberness.

"Never, I'm a gentleman. A lady never pays," he winks, pulling me gently towards him as he leads me out of the bar. My heart begins to race and by the time I'm at Riggs' table it is full on jack hammering in my chest. Conrad's fingers clasp a little tighter as we approach, and I can't stop my head turning to look at Riggs. He keeps his eyes pinned to me, his lips pressed into a thin line and his jaw clenched tight. I slowly turn to look forward and shake my head softly. Defeat slams in my chest, but I have no idea why.

Conrad pushes the bar door open, the blistering cold weather smothering me, and I feel myself begin to tremble. Conrad lets go of my hand, relief swarms me and I hate it. I hate that I would rather him not have his hand locked with mine than our fingers entwined as one. He shrugs off his soft leather jacket then blankets it over my shoulders.

"Thank you," my voice is quiet, my breath evident in the air in front of me.

"Of course," his fingers lace back through mine, and we walk towards his truck. Unlocking it, he opens my door and I climb in, clasping my hands together and huddling forward to try and keep myself warm until Conrad gets in and turns the engine on so the heating can kick in.

Conrad puts the truck into reverse, pulling back and driving out of the dusty parking lot and onto the country roads.

"Want to stargaze?" he asks, the soft music playing in the background as I stare out the windscreen.

Stargaze.

The way my heart falls from my chest, slowly splintering in a torturous way which makes me rub my aching chest.

Stargazing was always mine and Riggs' thing.

I have never stargazed with anyone other than him. Not that you could really ever see the stars in LA. Even when I could I felt as if I was suffocating, looking up at them and hoping, wishing, that Riggs was looking up at them too.

"Can we take a rain check? I suddenly feel floored," I give him an apologetic smile.

"Not a problem," his hand slips between my thighs and he gives my leg a gentle squeeze before both hands land on the steering wheel again.

The drive home is quiet, but not an awkward silence.

It's nice, chilled, calming even, but it leaves me alone with my thoughts and that isn't good.

Conrad walks me to the door like a true gentleman, scooping my cold hand into his and lifting it to his mouth as he places the softest butterfly like kiss on the back of it.

My cheeks pinch crimson as he stands tall, his eyes glistening under the warm porch light. I begin to shrug his jacket off, but he stops me, pulling it back onto my shoulders.

"Keep it, I'll get it next time."

"Okay," I nod, rolling my lips into a thin line. "Thank you for a fun evening."

"Thank you for agreeing to join me."

I smile, stepping towards the front door and I hear the sound of his boots hitting the decked porch as he walks down the steps and towards his truck. I wait for him to disappear, the only noise reaching me is the sound of his tires crunching on the dusty, graveled driveway.

I let out a shaky breath and slump into one of the rockers that overlooks the darkness, the warm light as my comfort night light while I sit out here. My thoughts flash back to Riggs; how I saw a glimpse of the eighteen-year-old boy that was always so happy and care free.

The Riggs that I crushed on so damn hard. I may have even loved him. I scoff, letting my head fall as I rest it in my hands.

My mind flickers back to the night when everything changed, the night when I decided I was no longer wanted here. I scarpered home, packed my bags and ran. I ran out of this town like a bat out of hell.

• • •

It was a typical Friday night. Me, Austin, Harlow, Riggs, Tripp and Pacey were all in the Old Dusty Boot for good food and even better company.

Tonight though, tension was brewing between the group. I was still upset and angry at Riggs for blowing me off at prom. Riggs was pissed at Pacey for jumping in and taking me. Tripp and Austin were blissfully unaware of anything that was going on between the three of us. Harlow knew what was going on, but like the good best friend she was, she kept her lips tightly shut.

"How was prom a month ago already!?" Harlow sighs as she twirls the straw round in her soda.

"I know, it's gone so quick," I sigh, my heart skipping beats when I see Pacey's gaze flicker between me and Riggs.

"Best night of my life," Pacey gushes and Riggs stiffens beside me.

Shit.

"Why's that?" Austin laughs, turning to face Pacey who is sat two seats down.

"You know... I'm sure you had the same kind of evening," and I fucking swallow down the bile that is burning my throat, acid coating my lungs and I choke out, eyes bugging from my head as they land on Pacey.

"Sorry?" Riggs and Austin say in unison. Riggs turns to glare at me and I can see the fire dancing in his eyes, Austin's gaze is pinned to Pacey and Tripp tuts, groaning and sliding from the booth.

"Pacey," I whisper-shout but I have no idea why I am trying to be discreet.

"What?! I'm not keeping the best night of my life with the girl I love a secret. I don't care, I'll shout it from the damn rooftops about how much I love you."

My skin prickles in goosebumps, my heart slamming against my chest and I am frozen in my spot.

"You love her?" Riggs spits and I can see how the rage is slowly taking over his calm and collected persona.

Regret drenches me an in instant.

"We were drunk," I half laugh, half sob. "It meant nothing," panic laces my quiet voice.

"I wasn't that drunk." I see disappointment slap across Pacey's face.

"It obviously didn't mean nothing..." Riggs scowls and I feel myself wilt like a dying rose.

"Outside," Austin flames next to Pacey, "get the fuck outside, now. You broke the fucking code," he growls, pushing his seat out with force as he storms through the boot and outside.

"Shit," I whisper, my eyes on Harlow who gives me a silent nod.

I scoot from the booth and Pacey is up and ready for a ruck.

"Pacey, no!" I call out as his heavy boots slam against the hardwood floor. I try and grab him but it's no use.

Riggs is behind me and my tears are falling.

"What the fuck Aspen?" Riggs' fingers wrap around my wrist as he tugs me back, my red, glassy eyes fixate on his sage green ones.

"Why him?"

"Don't Riggs, this isn't about you," I tug my wrist from his grasp, which was clearly the wrong move when he reaches for me again and pulls my body flush with his.

"Fuck, did you sleep with him to get back at me 'cos I cancelled on you? That's fucking low Aspen, I didn't realize you were such an easy lay." The words whipped at my skin, lashing at me over and over. Fresh tears built behind my eyes, pricking, stinging until I gave in and let them fall. Lifting my hand, I swipe him across the cheek.

"Fuck you Riggs!" I shout as I turn and run for outside,

wanting to put a stop to the chaos that was currently unfolding in front of me.

Regret poisons me as I watch Austin and Pacey swinging for each other.

"You're a cunt," Austin shouts, swinging for Pacey. Tripp is on Austin's back trying to break it up, but Austin shrugs him off and I watch as Tripp falls to the floor, a dust cloud forming around him from how hard he hit the ground.

Riggs stands next to me, puffing out his cheeks, his fists balled by his side.

"Look what you done," he seethes, a look of disgust coating me as his eyes swipe over me.

"Excuse me," I choke out, "you caused this. You're a coward, don't come for me."

Rage spills out of me and all I see is red.

I look for Harlow but she just stands back, her fingers in her mouth as she watches the brawl unfold in front of us.

"What's wrong?" I ask, walking towards her and she whimpers, hot tears streaming down her face and suddenly, fear consumes me.

Pacey shoves Austin off him and Tripp grabs Austin's arms, holding him back. Riggs storms through the middle of them, his head twisting from side to side as he looks at both of them.

Anxiety swims in my chest, nerves prick my skin and I hope this is over.

"Pacey, you fucked up." Riggs warns, his tone is low and Pacey just smirks, spitting out blood to the side of him.

"Did I?" Pacey challenges and I watch as Riggs' once furrowed brows pinch a little deeper, his eyes darkening before widening at Pacey's words. "What did you do a few weeks ago? Or should I say 'who'."

"Pacey, watch your fucking mouth," Riggs warns him once

more, but this time his tone has venom coating it, his tongue darts out as he runs it along his bottom lip.

Pacey looks past Riggs for a moment and towards my brother.

"What about you? Who did you fuck on prom night because I can't be the only one that broke some sort of code that night," he laughs.

My eyes move between all of them.

Nothing but silence.

"And you!" Pacey takes a few steps towards us, his finger pointing at Harlow, "Crier over there, are they tears of shame? Regret? Guilt?" he continues and Austin looks as confused as me.

"Can someone please explain what is going on?" I plead, my throat tight.

Tripp lets go of Austin and lurches forward, shaking his arms out.

"No one going to speak up?"

Silence falls over the dusty parking lot.

"Fine—"

"Shut up Pacey," Riggs grits, his tone low and full of gravel.

"Nah, people want to come for me, but I'm not the only one who is going to be spilling their secrets tonight," he shakes his head from side to side and he looks manic.

"Please, Pacey... you'll hurt everyone."

"And what?! I'm hurt. I have fallen in love with Aspen and yet it's still not enough. You've pined over her for years, and the same for her with you. I finally done something about it, swooped in like the knight on the horse and saved the day so she could go to prom and for what? To find out she is ashamed of my feelings? Regrets sleeping with me? I didn't force her into it, it was the perfect night. Or so I thought," he twists his lips, his head dropping for a moment. He is hurt. His emotions mask his face. I *edge forward but am soon stopped in my tracks. "Harlow fucked Austin, then Riggs fucked her."*

The words plough through me like a wrecking ball, all the noise that once was clear was now muffled and blended into one, loud noise.

"What the fuck," I whisper, my heart in my throat, my pulse quickening under my skin and suddenly I feel lightheaded.

My best friend.

The one who knew just how much I love Riggs.

How much it's always been him.

And yet...

My eyes are brimming with tears, my stomach churns and nausea replaces the anxiety. Slowly turning to Harlow, she is crying and apologizing.

She isn't apologizing about Austin.

She is apologizing about Riggs.

"I can't," I whisper before I let my head slowly twist to face Riggs who looks broken. Completely and utterly broken. Shoulders sagged forward, eyes fixated on mine and I swear I see the hint of tears forming in his pretty green eyes.

He takes one step forward which causes me to take one step back.

"Fuck you Riggs," my voice trembles. "I fucking hate you. I HATE you." Viciousness laces my tone.

"Hurts doesn't it!" Riggs shouts back, storming towards me but I hold my hand up, stopping him, his eyes fall to my open hand.

"Don't," I threaten, my voice trembling, shaking.

"Aspen."

"Don't," sobs break through and I am humiliated.

The commotion that was unfolding just minutes ago settles just like the kick up of dust. I hear Harlow step towards me and rage burns through my veins.

"I don't even want to look at you," I cover my mouth with my hand before I turn away, the hot tears burning my cheeks. "I was waiting until later tonight to tell you all, but seeing as our group has just been ripped apart, I guess it doesn't matter much anymore. I may as well do it now."

All sets of eyes are on me. Austin is disheveled and crumpled. Tripp can't even look at anyone but me. Riggs just stands, hands on hips and I can see the pain that is etched into his expression. Pacey is pacing, but his eyes don't defer from mine and Harlow is frozen next to me.

"I got into Cornell. I'm done. I'm out and what perfect fucking timing," I throw my hands up, shaking my head from side to side as I step forward, pushing past Riggs ignoring the urge to turn and face him. I push past Pacey and Austin next.

"Aspen!" Austin calls out and I hold my hand up, flipping them all off.

Within seconds, Tripp is next to me, wrapping his arms around my shoulders and that's when I crumble, sobbing uncontrollably into the darkness.

I'M NOT OUT HERE with my memories long when I hear the sound of trucks, but not just any trucks. The Rivera Ranch trucks. Sand colored Dodge Rams, with black rims, grills and matte stripes across the hood but they're a lot more beastly than Conrad's. You know these trucks as soon as you hear them. Everyone knows their trucks.

I stiffen in my seat, silently praying that only Austin gets out the truck. But, both the engines cut and the lights turn off.

Of course they do.

I hear Austin laughing, the truck doors slamming shut

as Riggs rolls out the driver's side and Harlow out the passenger side.

Anger burns like wildfire in my belly. Harlow prances towards Riggs, letting her fingers drag across the shoulder of his beaten, black jacket; his dark brown cowboy hat firmly on his head.

He doesn't look at her.

He looks at me and only me.

My heart flutters in my chest before it crashes and burns in the depths of my empty chest.

Austin comes bowling over, messing up my hair as he rubs his hand back and forth over the top. He has that drunk sparkle in his eyes, his cheeks red and rosy from being in the warmth of the car and now in the icy evening.

Tripp and Pacey climb out the second truck, Pacey a little unsteady on his feet as he walks past Riggs and Harlow and heads straight for me.

I stand, my legs trembling beneath me and I think they're going to buckle on me at any minute. Austin leans over the porch railings, smirking as he eyes Riggs and Harlow.

"Hello you," Pacey says with a little smirk and I swallow down the nerves.

"Hello you, back," I laugh a nervous giggle as he steps closer and swoops me in for a cuddle and once my feet are back firmly on the ground he tilts his head to the side as he studies me.

"I'm sorry I was a bit of a douche, was just a little…"

"It's fine. It must have been a surprise, I wasn't meant to be here," I let out a soft snort, "So, how long have those two been a thing?" I whisper, bracing myself for another round of heartache.

"Ughhhhh," Pacey over exaggerates his groan, "they're not a thing," he shakes his head from side to side. "Personally…" Pacey steps closer to me, his lips hovering by my ear, "I think she is just doing it to spike a reaction from you."

"Course she is," I roll my eyes and step back, wrapping my arms around myself to try and keep the chill out.

"Anyway, night Penny," his rosy cheeks glow, flushed from the cold air, his eyes twinkle and I'm glad he came over to say hello.

"Night Pacey," I exhale, as he turns on his heel and jumps down the steps and back into Tripp's waiting truck. Tripp doesn't move. He stands next to Riggs as if forming some sort of alliance against me.

Tripp whispers something to Riggs which gets a solid nod in return. Seconds slip past when Tripp climbs into his truck and starts the engine.

"I'm going in. Good night, Austin," I say quietly, closing the gap between us and giving him a kiss on his cheek before I turn and walk back into the house.

And finally, I feel as if I can breathe.

CHAPTER SIX
RIGGS

I have been reeling the whole way home. I offered to give Harlow a lift home because she was wasted and as much as she gets under my skin—and one of the many regrets in my life—I'm not an asshole who would leave her stranded and drunk.

Aspen was out on a date.

On a date with Conrad the jerk.

Why was she dating? She was engaged to whatever that douchebag's name was back home in LA.

I tighten my grip on the steering wheel, and as we approach closer to Maple Farm the rage that fills me consumes me whole.

Pulling down the drive, I cut the engine and Austin jumps out before the truck has even stopped, barreling down towards his sister who is sitting in the rocker on the porch, nightlights glowing around her.

Cutting the engine, I jump down and slam my door shut. I move forward but stop myself when Tripp and Pacey stand beside me, I keep my feet grounded. Harlow bounds up beside me, skimming her fingers over my shoulder, back and forth and I know she is trying to spark a reaction from Aspen. I glare when I see Pacey leap over to her like an excited fucking puppy. At least he has the balls to actually not be a dick to her. They embrace, he swings her around and I feel the stab of jealousy erupt deep inside of me. Old feelings rupture on the surface, taking me straight back to when we were younger.

Aspen gives an icy glare over to the two of us before Pacey whispers something in her ear which causes a giggle to come out of her and that shit stirs me crazy. Pacey says his goodbyes and then runs towards Tripp's truck.

"You need to cool it," Tripp mutters quietly so only I can hear, both of our eyes pinned to Aspen. Tripp squeezes my shoulder, "I'm going to get Pacey back, see you soon."

I nod as he gets in the car and starts the engine while I watch Aspen say goodnight to Austin and head inside the house. Sighing heavily, I shrug Harlow's fingers from me and call out to Tripp.

"Yeah?" he asks.

"Can you take Harlow back with you please?"

"But," she says, shock evident in her voice.

"But nothing, you're going home with Tripp," I tsk, marching forward towards Austin who is still standing there all giddy.

My feet stomp up onto the decked porch and I stand next to Austin, leaning over the banister too.

"Why the fuck did you let her go out on a date?" I growl, and I know I have no right even asking that, but I hate the thought that she was sitting with him all night.

"Fuck you man, I'm not her keeper," he scoffs shaking his head from side to side as his eyes stay fixed on where Harlow once stood.

I nudge into him. "Still pining after her are ya?" Humor

laces my voice and I watch as Austin's head snaps around fast.

"At least I'll do something about it unlike you, you grumpy moping asshole," Austin chuckles, slapping me on the back hard, which makes me cough. "I'll see you tomorrow, go get some sleep cowboy."

I snort a laugh as he walks away and shuts the front door behind him.

"Fuck's sake man," I groan into the emptiness and give myself a moment of quiet before I trudge back towards my truck and let my heavy boots drag along the floor.

CHAPTER SEVEN
ASPEN

SEVENTEEN YEARS OLD

*P*rom night.

It was one of the most important nights in a teen girl's life. I know some girls didn't care for prom, but I was not that girl. I was psyched for prom.

I was excited, Riggs agreed to take me to prom and Austin was taking Harlow. I knew she had a crush on him so she thought all of her dreams had come true, but Austin didn't like her like that. He found her annoying and whiny, and I mean, he wasn't wrong but she was my best friend, I knew her inside out and her annoyance was all towards him. She wasn't like that with anyone else but Austin.

When I thought about asking Riggs, I was sure he was going to say no. I mean, he was twenty-one, he was a lot older than me but I didn't care about the age. I just wanted to be on Riggs' arm for one night and for him to see me other than his best friend's kid sister, or the annoying girl from the farm next door. I scoff a little laugh. Ironic that Austin finds Harlow annoying and yet here I am being the same annoying kid in Riggs' eyes.

I still remember it like it was yesterday. I had spent days building up the courage, pacing back and forth and replaying the scripted conversation over in my head, only to go completely off track and buckle on the spot. Riggs was in the bunkhouse, working alongside Bridger, being shown the ropes. I hid in the stables, flustered and worked up, and the words came out in a rush when he'd found me in there. Dirty jodhpurs, knee high riding boots and an old tee of Austin's. I had been riding Blossom, getting ready for our show in the summer.

Prom fell in spring. My favorite time of the year.

I paced up and down outside, nibbling on my bottom lip, picking at the dry skin around my nail bed. I could hear a commotion coming from inside and I froze. Sulking away, I hid in the stables and begun to untack Blossom.

"You were such a good girl today," I say softly as I lift her saddle and blanket off her back and place it on the saddle horse. Unbuckling her bridle, I lift it over her ears then drop her bit into my hands, hanging it over the door ready for me to clean. Turning back to scratch Blossom's neck, my body stiffens when I hear Riggs mumbling and moaning under his breath. The sound of his boot kicking the concrete floor. I gave her a pat then hung over the half door.

"All okay there Riggs?"

"Great," he rumbles, stalking towards me, his green eyes soften when they land on me.

My hair is in a low bun, no doubt the top now flat from my riding hat. Fresh faced, but I wasn't a big make up wearer; it's not that I didn't like wearing it, I just never had time. I suppose when you're raised on a small-town farm with horses and mucking stalls out every day, glamour kind of goes out the window and falls on the back burner. It isn't a priority.

"Wanna talk about it?" I unbolt the stall door and close it behind me. I step towards him, hands pressed onto my hips.

"Not really," he rolls his eyes, stepping past me and leaning over Blossom's door.

I spin, head cocked as I watch him. Dirty denim jeans, heavy black boots and a dirty white tee. Riggs is slender but muscular. The cowboys down at the bunkhouse don't give him an easy ride. Jorge makes them work him, and they treat him like their little pet. He is normally asleep by seven most nights, awake again at four. I miss the sneaking out, now it's just me, Austin, Tripp and Pacey but it won't be long before Tripp is roped into the same fate as Riggs. Live by the ranch, die by the ranch; that was Jorge's motto. Branded across their hearts, those words tattooed into their skin.

"She's looking good," he whitters, lifting his cowboy hat off his head and tossing it to the floor. I tut, picking it up and dusting it off. My fingers trace the rim of the hat and I can't stop the way my heartrate spikes even if I wanted to.

I hover it over my head and give him a grin before he knocks it out of my hand. A soft gasp passes my lips and my eyes fall to where the hat now sits.

"Don't. Don't do that," he sounds pained and my heart sinks, his eyes darken for just a moment as he looks at the floor.

"Why not?"

"You'll belong to me, whether you want it or not and I'm not going to burden you with that. We're friends Aspen, I care a lot about you... too much to tie you to me forever," he lets out a soft chuckle, the green back in his eyes. His shoulders relax as he pops his hat back on the top of his head and rests his back against Blossom's stall door.

I have no idea why but hearing them words sting like a thousand needles pricking my skin.

"Lucky me," I mock in a sarcastic tone.

Silence blankets us for a moment and I swallow, needing to just ask him what has been sitting on the tip of my tongue since this morning.

"Hey, Riggs," I pull his eyes to mine as my voice echoes down the empty stables like a soft spring breeze.

"Yeah?"

"Will you take me to prom?" I rush the words out as if they're venomous.

Riggs blinks at me, and I can see it's taking him a moment to register what has just come from my mouth.

"You sure about that, Dinks?"

"Yeah..." I breathe as he steps closer to me, snatching my breath in an instant. "Unless..." I stammer, stepping back before my back hits the wall behind me. What if he doesn't want to take me. I don't want to force him into it, I didn't want him to think he had to take me.

"Unless what?"

"You don't want to come with me? I don't want you to feel forced... plus, what would the nosey townspeople say about you coming to prom with me? You're older than me..." I whisper because suddenly speaking out loud is too much for me. Nerves swim deep inside of me and maybe this was a bad idea.

"Fuck them assholes, so what?" he spits, and I know I struck a nerve. I watch as he slowly exhales before his eyes land on my lips, my nose, my eyes. The air shifts between us and I no longer feel anchored to the ground. "Dinks, why wouldn't I want to take you to prom? Who else would take you? One of those little weasels from school?" his eyes bounce back and forth between mine.

I shake my head from side to side.

"Only you," my voice cracks, my cheeks flame scarlet.

"Then let me take you to prom, I look good in a tux." He winks, finally stepping back away from me and tipping the rim

of his hat down, "Let's hang out tonight, just me and you. It's been too long."

I smile.

"Are you going to be able to commit to those plans grandpa? You'll be tucked into your bed and asleep by seven," I laugh and he shakes his head slowly, his boots now toe to toe with mine once more.

"I'll be there Dinks, for you... I'll always be there."

My eyes don't leave his and I see a slither of vulnerability slice through his beautiful light green eyes as he presses his lips to my forehead. I knew Riggs didn't feel anything other than a 'sister love' for me. He didn't see me as the young woman I was becoming. I was just Aspen 'Penny' Warren.

I LOITERED by the fence line, checking my watch every few seconds. It had just gone seven and as the minutes pass, I begin to worry that he has fallen asleep or something has come up that he hasn't been able to get out of.

I blow out my cheeks, but don't exhale my breath when I see Riggs walking from the bunkhouse and my heart flutters in my chest. He came.

Riggs is in front of me in seconds and I see the crooked smile that lifts his lips and my own smile grows.

"You made it!"

"Of course, I would always make it."

My cheeks blush. It's mad how easily he puts me under his spell. We stand for a moment, in the stillness of the night, nothing but the rustle of the leaves that dance in the wind surrounding us. No one else to watch us apart from the stars that twinkle above us.

Footing my boot on the bottom of the fence, I climb up and swing my jean covered leg over and jump down the other side.

"New jeans?" he asks, a twinkle in his eye as they roam over me. I'm wearing a cream tee under a cream and brown check flannel shirt and dark wash Levi skinny jeans with brown cowboy boots.

"They are new Mr. Rivera, good eye," I wink as I flick my braid over my shoulder.

"Always," he winks back and we head towards his house.

"Where we going?" I ask as I fall a couple of steps behind him, my brows pinching as we walk towards his house.

"To get the best view of the stars, Dink."

"The best?" I smile, picking up my pace to catch him up, my skin prickling with anticipation, excitement thrumming through me.

"Only the best for you," and my heart jumps in my chest, my inner self already picturing me in a wedding dress, Riggs in a tux as he waits at the end of the aisle for me.

We walk into the Rivera home, and it's not unusual for me to be here, or to go into Riggs' room. Or any of the boys rooms to be honest. We are all friends. We've grown up together. I go to take my boots off like I normally do but Riggs shakes his head.

"Oh." I utter.

He leads me upstairs, and I automatically turn to walk down the large hallway towards his bedroom but he lets out a soft chuckle and gently shakes his head again. Pausing for a moment, he looks up and points to the attic.

Reaching up, I don't miss the opportunity to steal a look as his tee rides up his torso slightly, showing me his tanned skin, his toned stomach peeking at me, teasing me and I can't stop my mind taking me to places I know it shouldn't.

The attic door drops as he tugs the ladder down.

"You coming?" he waits for me to answer and the pause stretches a little longer than I anticipated as my thoughts whirl.

"Yeah," I mutter, my mind finally kicking into gear.

Following him up to the attic, fear prickles deep inside of me at the darkness that awaits me, but as I step onto the hard wood floor, there is no darkness. Fairy lights are hung on every wall, a beautiful glow fills the room and my heart swarms in my chest.

"No need to be scared of the dark up here Dinks."

He was so thoughtful. Kind. Caring. He was just Riggs. He was perfection.

I blink back the tears.

I'm not ashamed to admit I am scared of the dark. Everyone has fears and no one should feel belittled or embarrassed by what scares them. Anyone who says they don't have a fear or they aren't scared of something is lying.

He reaches for my hand and I let him take it willingly, the tingle that pulses through my fingertips shoots straight to my heart. He walks me towards the large windows that sit in the gables at the back of the house. Pushing it open with a bit of force, he opens it as far as it can go. He drops my hand for a moment and I instantly miss his touch. I miss the buzz that consumed me. I watch as he picks up a box step and places it under the gable. He steps up first and crouches as he climbs over the threshold onto the roof of the house. Turning slowly, he leans back through and holds his hand out for me once more. Steadying myself, I climb out onto the roof with him and I lose my breath for a moment as I take in the views in front of me. I am never not in awe of where we live and where I have been lucky enough to grow up but up here, it feels like I am seeing it for the first time.

The way the mountain tops kiss the stars, the dark violet night sky twinkling with the brightest stars, the moon sitting low against the stunning backdrop that is painted in front of me.

"Wow," I whisper, no other words could even describe the way I am feeling at this moment.

"It's something right?" he smiles as we sit and fall into an easy silence.

"Right," I nod, my hands pressed against the old roof tiles and I feel Riggs' fingers tease mine.

I turn to look at him, our eyes lock.

"You know it's always been you Dinks, the thought of never having you in my life... being here without you." His voice is low, his lips edging towards mine.

Suddenly I can't breathe. Is this really happening? Does he like me that way too?

His hand cups my face, his thumb brushing across my cheek as my eyes fall to his parted lips and before I can even respond, his lips are on mine, tongue sweeping past my cushioned lips, taking full control. Every sense in my body is screaming, the fire burning deep inside of me and a thousand bolts of electric zap up and down my skin, singeing and burning me as they do.

"Fuck," he whispers as he pulls away and I giggle.

Slipping my hand into my jean pocket, I pluck out two black, thick material friendship bracelets that I had made, and I hand one to him. I watch as his brows squeeze, causing a crease to form between his eyes. He holds the bracelet between his finger and thumb, studying it.

"Thought we could have matching," I lift my shoulders up and he smiles, widening the string and slipping it onto his wrist then fastens it with his teeth.

"It's perfect," he holds it up for me to see as I slip my own on.

"Best friend bracelets," I dip, lifting his arm. Scooting closer, I snuggle into him and rest my head on his chest as he lays back slightly, our hearts beating at the same, steady pace. His heart singing in my ear whilst we watch the stars dancing.

And that's how we spend the rest of the evening, snuggled into each other and stargazing.

I will never forget this moment.

Ever.

RIGGS

I finally did it. I finally plucked up the courage to kiss her. I knew people would disapprove, but fuck the people. I didn't care. All I cared about was her.

Walking her to the fence line, I scoop her face in my hands and slant my lips across hers to seal our evening with a kiss.

"Night Aspen," I caress her cheek, whispering. My eyes remain closed as I savor this moment.

"Night Riggs," she whispers back, edging her lips closer to mine to let me steal another kiss.

I reluctantly let her go, watching as she swings her leg over the fence and jumps down the other side.

"I'll see you soon then," she smiles, her eyes dancing under the moonlight as she walks back away from me, but not turning her body away from me.

"I'll see you soon then," I tip my cowboy hat towards her and fight the urge to take it off my head and give it to her.

She turns and begins to run back towards the farm, my heart swelling in my chest at the lights that run alongside and down the fields to light her path home.

Her own little nightlights.

I am so focused on her, I don't hear my father's footsteps behind me. It's only when I feel his harsh grasp on my shoulder that I flinch.

"You don't want to go there son," he says quietly as we both watch the farmhouse lights come on and I know she's home.

"Go where?" I mutter, my tone flat as I fixate on the empty

fields where she once was, my lips still burning from our kiss and I am left wanting so much more.

"With Aspen. She's a wild spirit, she won't stay here. She is always going to want more than this," he lets go of my shoulder but not without another punishing squeeze.

"I think you're wrong, she's happy here," I shrug away from him. He's instantly spoiled my good mood.

"You think you can give her what she wants, Riggs? You'll make her a ranch wife and make her throw out a few kids? She wants to see the world, be a professional show jumper. You know as well as I do that her father runs in all the right circles. One call and she is in that world. You really going to keep her locked and chained here? In Lovelock Bay? Her heart might be yours Riggs, but her spirit and soul want so much more than you. She's like a mustang, she needs to be wild and free and she won't get that here with you." He doesn't lie. I know it's the truth but it's not a truth I am willing to accept. I know I can make Aspen happy here, with me.

He gives me a hard pat on the back causing me to fall forward slightly and cough. Anger bubbles deep inside of me, my lips rolled tight and my molars grinding.

"I'm saying this for your own sake. Do what you want with your life kid, I just have an off feeling when it comes to little Aspen Warren," he tsks before turning and walking back towards the house.

I take a moment to mull over his words and sigh deeply.

I can give her more than this if that's what she wants.

The truth was, I didn't want to stay here and be a cowboy. I wanted to see the world too. And if she leaves for the city, so will I.

. . .

*D*RESSED *IN MY TUX*, *my mom slips a carnation into my suit pocket, then gives it a gentle pat.*

"You look very handsome," she cups my cheek with her soft hand and smiles, her thumb brushing across my cheek bone.

I have always been a momma's boy. My dad was hard faced and cruel. He could never show any affection towards us for some reason. As if he was too much of a man to show an ounce of emotion towards us.

I step around my mom and begin walking towards the door when I hear my dad call my name. I turn, his glare thunderous as he curls his finger for me to go to him. I let out a heavy sigh as I drag my feet across the wood floor. One thing I learned from a young age was that you never ignored Jorge Rivera. I did it once and I have never done it again.

"Yup," I say quietly. My dad turns and walks up the stairs and I know it's going to be a shit conversation because he has taken me away from my mom. I follow like a lost puppy dog and wait for my command.

Walking onto the landing area, I tug at my white shirt cuffs and pull them out of my suit jacket sleeve. The excitement that once filled me was now fizzling out by the second.

"What the fuck are you doing?" his voice is low but I can hear the angry tone. His eyes narrow on me, his hand pushes through his thick, dark hair and I don't miss the way his tongue darts out and runs along his bottom lip.

"Taking Aspen to prom, you know that." Confusion crosses my face, my eyes bouncing back and forth and I mirror his moves, a habit I seemed to have picked up from him as I run my hand through my curly brown hair.

"No, you're not," he shakes his head from side to side, his tone clipped and harsh and I internally wince. "You will not be the reason for a broken-hearted Aspen. You could ruin everything. I finally have an amazing business relationship with

Buck and you will not fuck this up for me or this family, do you understand me? So get the fuck out of your tux, Pacey can take her."

I ball my fist. My temper simmering but I know that I'm not going to win this argument.

"Riggs, please. I'm asking you nicely, please don't do this. This summer romance won't last. Don't be the reason for her unhappiness, don't be the reason that she stays back here instead of letting her follow her dream..." he pauses and I ignore the burning lump in my throat as my lungs scream for air but I refuse to even let out a slither of breath. My jaw is locked tight, the unbearable pressure throbs behind my eyes. "Don't be the reason for our downfall," his voice falls even quieter, and I don't even have the words to respond. My brain is ticking over at a hundred miles a minute, my heart crushing in my chest and all I can see is her disappointed face. Standing in her pretty fucking dress, her heart shattering fully, splintering into a thousand shards. She will think I changed my mind, she'll think I lied.

My dad walks past me and as soon as his boots are off the bottom step I can hear my mom.

"What did you do, Jorge?"

I bite the inside of my cheek until my mouth fills with a copper taste. Tears brim in my eyes, my throat aches and burns as I pull my bottom lip between my teeth. I scoff in disbelief, but instead of doing what my heart is screaming at me to do, I listen to my dad like I always do. Giving my head a gentle shake, disappointment strangles me. Turning my face to the left, my eyes fixate on the attic and my heart thumps in my chest, angry hot tears roll down my cheeks and I am so fucking mad. Sucking in a breath, I storm towards my room, unfix my bowtie and let it unravel as I tug it out of my collar and as soon as I step into my room, I slam the door behind me.

ASPEN

"You look beautiful," my mom says as she steps into my bedroom, Harlow smiling as she waits for her compliment, "and Harlow," my mom's eyes sweep over her light blue princess style ball gown, "our very own Lovelock Bay Cinderella." She kisses Harlow on the cheek before embracing me whole.

"Sweetheart," she beams, tears glistening in her pretty blue eyes, "you truly are breath-taking. Riggs is a lucky man to have you on his arm."

My cheeks pinch with heat.

I'm wearing a silver, strapless fitted gown that hugs my hips and thighs. My hair is in a low bun, tidy and neat. I look down at my right wrist and my heart flutters in my chest at the thought of having a corsage on there soon.

"Come on, girls, the guys are waiting," my mom ushers us out of the room and I feel my heart somersaulting, excitement coursing through me.

Walking down the stairs, I see Austin standing there in a black and white tux, a box in his hands with pretty white and blue flowers arranged beautifully. I slice my eyes across to see an empty spot next to Austin and I begin to panic when I see Pacey step from the kitchen dressed in a black and white tuxedo looking every bit handsome.

"Pacey," I press my hand to my heavy rising chest, an unbearable ache coursing through me.

"I'll be taking you this evening now, I hope you don't mind?"

Truth was, I felt devastated.

"Of course not," I smile, but my eyes are brimming with tears. I shrug them off as happy ones and not ones of complete disappointment and heartache.

His fingers tap on the plastic of the corsage box, a trio of stunning white flowers arranged and sitting on silk.

I step off the bottom step and close the gap between me and Pacey. Pacey has pretty, huge brown eyes, dirty blonde hair similar to mine and not like his brothers Riggs and Tripp. His skin has a glow to it and he has a picture perfect smile. Pacey is my age, older by a few months. He has never had a girlfriend, which is crazy because he is a catch. Hard working, loyal, caring and trusting. But I crushed on the moody brother. The grumpy one who seemed to walk around with a permanent thunder cloud over his head.

"You look stunning Pen," his long fingers curl around my wrist, pulling me closer to him as he places a kiss on my cheek.

"Let's get some photos!" My mom chokes, calling my dad in to stand and watch. I can see the unamused look on his face but his lips do twitch with a smile when he sees me and Harlow.

"Well girls, you look beautiful. Perfection," he claps his hands together as my mom begins snapping away, then ushers the boys to join us. Pacey's arm snakes around my waist and I lean into him, a warmness fizzling deep down inside of me, but it's not the fire that burns through to my soul like it does when I am with Riggs.

Stupid Riggs.

"Perfect. You ready to go? Your dad fixed one of the trucks up, put some pretty twinkle fairy lights on it too."

There was that prominent ache in my chest again and I swear my heart was ripping into two. It definitely was not my dad. The fairy lights were a perfect match to the ones that Riggs wrapped around the attic all those weeks ago.

"He will drive you and pick you all up at eleven," my mom beams.

"You do realize I can drive?" Austin snipes in.

"Fully aware darling," she strolls towards him and gives him a little, playful slap on his cheek.

I snigger a little laugh, softly shaking my head as Pacey leads me outside, his hand resting on the small of my back and I wish it was Riggs' hand there and not his brother's.

We step into the warm spring air, the soft breeze dusting over my skin and causing it to pebble. There's a sweet smell in the air from the meadow flowers that are dancing in the beautiful dusk evening whirl around us, the trees swaying and singing as the wind rustles through them, causing them to shiver against a rhythm only they can hear.

Austin opens the truck door for Harlow, she climbs in and Austin gives my mom a kiss goodbye.

"After you Pen," Pacey whispers, pulling me out of my moment with nature and ushers me towards the truck. Just before I step in, I feel his gaze locked on me. Placing one of my sandaled feet onto the step bar of the truck, I turn to look towards the paddocks and see Riggs standing in the shadows. He looks sad and disheveled. Broken even.

Why is he looking so upset when he is the one that stood me up? Perhaps I should feel angry, but all I really feel is hurt and confused. Somehow all I want is to go to him, to make sure he is okay but I don't. I climb into the truck, ignoring my heart as it whimpers away into the depths and crevices of my chest. Wistfulness smothers me when I think of him standing in the dark.

Pacey slides in beside me, giving me a look as if to ask 'are you okay?', and I give him a shallow nod before the car pulls away.

I can't stop myself from looking out the back to see Riggs walking into the dullness of the red dust that is whipping up from the tires, his eyes pinned to the back of the car and I have to look away. I pretend I have a lash or something in my eye as a tear escapes and I swipe it away quickly before I draw attention to myself.

"Prom night!" Harlow calls out, excitement lacing her voice.

"Woo," I force it out, because inside I feel gutted. This is not the prom experience I thought I was going to be having.

I wanted this special night with Riggs.

But instead, I have it with Pacey.

What a bitch I am for feeling disappointed when Pacey has stepped in to be my date at the last minute instead of being with anyone else.

Determination floods me to make this a good night for me and for Pacey. I push thoughts of Riggs away once we're pulled up at Lovelock High and I focus on enjoying my night with Pacey, Harlow and Austin.

CHAPTER EIGHT
RIGGS

I am wrecked. I slept like shit last night and my eyes were still pinned to the ceiling when my alarm went off. Slamming my hand down on the alarm clock I groan, swinging my legs around and I sit on the edge of the bed, reaching up then clicking my neck from side to side. Scrubbing my face with my hand, the roughness of my beard scratches my palm as I run my hand back and forth across my chin. It didn't matter what I did, I couldn't get Aspen off my mind.

Sighing, I push up and drag my heavy body to the bathroom. I spent far too long in the shower and by the time I look at the clock it's already past five a.m. *Shit.*

Grabbing my hat from the back of the door, I place it on my head and trudge downstairs. Everyone else is still asleep, and I am grateful. I'm in no mood to put up with anyone's shit today because all it'll take is one wrong word and I'll bite their heads off like a damn grizzly bear.

Turning the coffee pot on, the buzzing from the refrigerator is humming low, the sound of the coffee machine kicking up, the gurgling of the water filling through the tubes. Every little noise was pushing me that little closer to erupting like a dormant volcano, lava bubbling at the tip of the surface.

Grabbing a mug off the mug tree on the countertop, I shove it under the teat of the machine and watch as it begins to trickle out with the dark, glorious liquid.

Why is everything taking so long?

A headache teases, throbbing at my temples and radiating across the front of my head. Rubbing my fingers over my forehead back and forth, I will for some of the tension to leave. I feel bunched up, everything is wound tight and I don't even know how to unwind myself.

Grabbing my now full mug, I add some creamer and thump out to the bunkhouse. Time to get my day started.

Barging in, the guys are all up and ready for their day. I give them their jobs then turn and get lost in my never ending list. I like the winter months though, everything is more relaxed and I find myself having time to actually get the shit done that I have been putting off for the last however many weeks. My mind wanders to Aspen and her shitty plastic car, I wonder if she has had it fixed yet or whether it's still sitting in the garage.

Why do you care?

Who even has a car like that. My head shakes softly, trying to clear my thoughts of Aspen.

The hours rush by as I steadily make my way through tasks. Once lunch is over, I walk towards the stalls as the other guys move the cows from the front pasture to the back and near the creek.

Leading the last horse out into the paddock, I turn them out and let them roam whilst the others are working.

Mucking out stalls is not usually my job, but we're two cowboys down so I decided to throw the two yard-hands,

Billy and James out with the cowboys. I had a couple of guys apply for the job, and one woman, but I wasn't sure if I wanted the aggravation that came with having a lady in the bunkhouse with filthy mouthed and rowdy cowboys.

I am deep in thought when I hear the sound of footsteps closing in on me. Poking my head over the top of the stall door, I see Aspen walking towards me. She looks a million miles away and it's not till she stops, she realizes where she is.

"Shit," I groan, slipping back and out of her view.

"Riggs?" she calls out and I close my eyes for a moment, my heart thrashing in my chest like a wild horse and I suck in a breath before I respond.

"Yeah," my voice is gruff and low and I finally—after what feels like hours—step out of the stall with the fork in my hand. She seems a little hesitant, playing with the small bit of hair that is loose from her braid. The air knocks out of my lungs with a heavy blow, my bad mood teetering on turning good. I would be lying if I said I didn't find her beautiful.

She was *beautiful*, stunning, exquisite even. She looked so much better in her old gear than she did the tight dress and high heels that she showed up in.

"Hey," she grins at me and her kindness fills me with dread. She hasn't sought me out once, and now here she is trying to make conversation.

"Hey," I pinch my brows and they dig into the center of my forehead, creasing. A low growl vibrates in my throat at the thought of her on her little date yesterday.

"Sorry for just walking in..." she pauses for a moment and looks over her shoulder back to where she just wandered in from. "I was just walking, lost in my own thoughts and well, for some reason I ended up here."

That's because you know this route like the back of your hand. Your body went into autopilot and took you to the one place you feel most safe.

"It's fine, I'm just mucking out so..." I give her a curt nod then turn to go back into the stall not wanting to waste any more time talking to her.

"I could help?" her soft voice slips through the empty stables and my heart jack hammers in my chest. Watching as she cautiously looks round the empty stables and I know it's because of her accident. The fear she feels being around horses is unmissable. I let my eyes do a quick sweep over her body. Her thighs are covered in those tight boot legged Levi's and all I can think about is how fucking good they would look wrapped round my waist. She has a cream roll neck sweater that has loose holes weaved through. Her dirty blonde hair is in a tight braid and all I want to do is wrap it around my fist, tugging her head back and letting my lips dust up the column of her throat. My eyes continue roaming over her, she has her old brown cowboy boots on and fuck, she looks so damn perfect it hurts me, my chest aches.

Never did I think I would see little miss spoiled princess back in her cowboy boots. Her hazel eyes glisten and are wide with anticipation, her cheeks are rosy red from the chill that is whirling through the winter air and her lips are full and parted as she waits for me to answer.

"I've got it, thanks. Plus, I'm pretty sure our spoiled little princess wouldn't want any horse shit under her perfectly manicured nails now, would she?" My tone is rude and curt but the thought of being in here with her alone is too much. Too overbearing. I don't trust myself.

Her eyes widen at the words that fall too easily off my tongue and I can see how they slice through her, hurting her in an instant. But she stands tall, shaking it off and smiling as her voice has a playful tone to it.

"Come on, I'm sure you're busy so just let me help," she shrugs her shoulders up and walks towards me, standing toe-to-toe for just a moment as her warm hazel eyes dance with mine. I don't even realize when her small hand moves forward, her fingers wrapping round the fork handle and slipping it from my grasp.

"Fine." I grunt and I loathe myself for speaking to her this way, but it's the only way I know how to treat her. I pushed her away, listened to my dad and let her live the life she so desperately wanted. But she didn't get the dream. She ended up injured with a broken spirit, and I wasn't the one to do it. Her dreams broke her. Not me.

Not like how my dad said I would.

But it's too late now. She is a perfect little city girl with the perfect fiancé living in LA.

We muck out in silence, but I don't stop myself from peeking at her in secret every now and then. She's too beautiful to ignore.

CHAPTER NINE
ASPEN

The last week has whizzed by in a blur. I hadn't seen Riggs anymore after I helped him muck out the stalls in complete silence. He hasn't been nearby so I think it's safe to assume he is avoiding me. Conrad has been a little more present and asked if I would like to spend New Year's Eve with him but I told him I needed a little space over the holidays. It wasn't a lie, I did need the space. My head is fuzzy, my heart aches and I feel isolated. Trying to find my new normal is proving difficult.

To make things even more uncomfortable, I'm currently helping mom get the table ready as we have Jorge, Orla and the Rivera brothers over for Christmas dinner.

"Remind me again why we are having them over?"

"Because your dad and Jorge have had such an amazing year with work, we thought it was only right for us to host as a thank you for their custom."

I sigh, irritation nipping away at me.

"Did you hear back from Luke?" Her question pierces my heart like a needle to a balloon and I feel the life drain out of me slowly. Licking my lips, I shake my head as I polish the plates and place them at the correct settings.

"He is just too busy with work," the lie is getting easier to spin, not wanting to make eye contact. I know she knows I'm lying. I'm just too much of a coward to admit it out loud to her.

Dad and Austin appear, and my dad looks a little anxious. I know things have moved slightly on the missing cattle from a few ranches down and for some reason, he seems to be taking on the stress of it all. We were told a week back, I say we but I eavesdropped, but Tripp came to tell my dad that a herd of cattle had literally just disappeared. My dad has enough stress, he doesn't need the stress of the Rivera brothers' stuff too.

Placing the last plate, the doorbell chimes through the hallway and my mom nods for me to open the door. I groan inwardly, pulling a loose bit of hair from my face. I'm wearing a black velvet mini dress that flows from the waist and sits mid-thigh. My dirty blonde hair is down with a loose wave to it and half of it is up and clipped back with a matching black bow. Nerves drum through me. Everyone seems okay when I've seen them, apart from Riggs and I can't stand it. I hate the animosity between us, the awkwardness every time one of us enters a room. He was the one that pushed me away. He was the one who didn't show on prom night. Even when I was standing outside his house in the pouring rain, begging for him to tell me why he never came, he just left me standing outside. Alone.

He broke my heart that night and it has never fully recovered. Not even with Luke.

He may have patched it up the best he could, but pieces were still missing from my aching heart and my broken soul.

Swallowing hard, I swing the door open and plaster a wide smile on my face.

"Our girl is home," Orla cries, pushing through the door and holding me tightly. "Oh, we have missed you sweet girl," she chimes, stepping back and cupping my face so she can really look at me.

"Missed you too," I just about manage with my cheeks squished between her palms.

Jorge walks in behind her and gives me a kiss on the cheek. "Merry Christmas Aspen," handing a pie to Orla as she disappears, he then walks through the house to find my dad who hands him a glass of bourbon whilst Orla goes and helps mom in the kitchen.

Tripp walks through the door and embraces me which throws me out a little bit.

"Hey Pen," he squeezes a little tighter.

"Hey Tripp," I step back as he lets go, my hand still curled around the brass doorknob.

He gives me a curt nod as he steps past me to go and find Austin. Pacey bounds towards me, wrapping me in his arms, lifting me off the floor and I squeal. I can hear the heavy sigh from Riggs, and I roll my eyes.

"Wanna hang out later? It's been forever and I really want to just sit and chat," he asks as my feet land on the floor gently.

"Yeah, cool, sounds good," I nod, smiling from ear to ear. Pacey was my best friend growing up. Yes, I had Harlow. But there was something about me and Pacey that was just different. But that friendship grew into something more for one of us and after prom night, all it took was one mistake to blow everything up.

"Perfect," he leans in and kisses me on the cheek, but he lingers a little longer and my cheeks blush crimson under his lips. He walks towards the kitchen and Riggs steps into the house. His eyes are glazed with annoyance, his lips pressed to a thin line and his jaw tight and wound.

"Merry Christmas," I just about manage through the thickness of my throat, but he doesn't respond. He walks straight past me, not even acknowledging me.

What an asshole. I slam the front door with a little more force than intended but he makes me so mad. He makes my blood boil.

Maybe we've just grown too far apart, grown too far from the seventeen-and twenty-one-year-olds we were all those years ago.

Some relationships are just too strained to repair. I was so stupid to think that we could ever work. He lived for this life.

And I wanted so much more. Though look where wanting more had gotten me.

I didn't want to be grounded here, but, who was I kidding? If being grounded here meant I got to love him every day, I would have stayed wherever he wanted me to.

What a sad truth.

Slowly walking into the large kitchen area where everyone seemed to be huddled, I walk through them all, reaching for the bottle of red and grabbing a large wine glass. The satisfying glug of wine leaving the bottle and filling my glass soothes my rage.

"Aspen," my mom blinks at me and I give her a wink.

"It's Christmas," I shrug my shoulders and walk towards the living area. I flop down on the sofa as a large sigh leaves me, puffing air from my lips and causing a light bit of hair to lift from my forehead.

"What's eating you?" Pacey climbs over the back of the sofa and slumps down next to me and I smile.

"Life," I half laugh as I turn my face to look at him.

Why couldn't I have fallen for him. He was perfect, in every single way.

"Talk to me, we're friends, well... we were," he nudges into me, "no but seriously, talk to me... what's going on in that pretty little head of yours?"

I keep quiet for a moment, lifting my legs and resting my feet on the large, rectangular coffee table that sits on a low pile ornate rug.

Letting my head fall back against the leather brown sofa, I turn my face in the opposite direction and let my eyes roam over Riggs.

Cream cable knit jumper, fitted straight leg jeans and heavy black boots. His curly brown hair was neatly styled and not unruly and flat like it normally is. His beard trimmed, his skin glowing and dewy and his eyes are glistening under the kitchen spotlights as he talks to my dad.

Ignoring the stutter of my heart in my chest, I turn back to face Pacey.

"It feels weird being back here, I left home in such a rush that I am still trying to come to terms with everything that had happened before coming back to Lovelock Bay." I lift the glass back to my lips and take a mouthful, my eyes scanning the room to see Butch curled up by the open fire and a small smile tugs at the corner of my lips.

"What happened?" Pacey asks and I know he is genuinely concerned and my face drops, my eyes welling as I look at the engagement ring that is still sitting on my finger. I part my lips, ready to speak to him but I am reminded of what Luke said and for some reason, I *still* decide to protect him.

"Maybe another day, yeah? I don't want to put a

dampener on Christmas," I rest my head on his shoulder and emotions consume me.

The sound of the fire crackling fills the room, the voices from the kitchen floating through occasionally and I am only honing in on Riggs.

"I'm sorry for running and being a shitty friend," I whisper, because I can't muster the courage to say the words out loud.

"Hey," Pacey whispers back, leaning away from me so I have no choice but to lift my head from his shoulder. My eyes widen as I look at him through the windows of his soul. "You have nothing to be sorry for... I was as much to blame for that shit storm that hit us all, none of it should have happened but it did. I'm not sorry for prom night though, Penny, I'm not sorry at all for that. That one moment was hands down the best night of my life." He stalls for a moment, his eyes batting back and forth between mine before they drop to my lips. "I know I wasn't the one you wanted, but I am glad it was me. I know that makes me selfish, but I don't care."

His lips grow into a wider smile, and I drop my head, a soft laugh leaving me.

"Honestly Aspen, don't you apologize. Tripp was just... well, being protective I suppose. He didn't mean anything he said... and Riggs... well..." he sighs, looking over my shoulder at his older brother and I avoid doing the same.

Tripp was nothing but kind and attentive that night, but Pacey just confirmed that he lashed out behind closed doors, and honestly, I was just grateful I wasn't there to witness it.

"He thinks we both betrayed him," I whisper and my heart plummets in my chest at admitting that out loud.

"I think it was a lot more than feeling like we betrayed him," Pacey's eyes find mine.

"Me and Riggs were never anything more than just…"

"Friends?" Pacey's brows lift and I swallow down the nausea. "Aspen, you and Riggs were never just *friends*. You both knew that, and that's why he is struggling so much. You left Aspen, you broke all of our hearts in the process. And we got it, well, most of us did. You wanted a new dream to chase, you wanted to heal and who were we to stop you? You're ours kid, we all adore you, but it seems Riggs adores you a little more than us."

I blink back the tears.

"I wish we could go back to being kids, when none of this had happened, it was just running out and playing until the stars shone above us… and now, here we are, a dysfunctional pack of friends who can hardly bear to be in the same room as one another…" I pause, "And then there is Harlow." I facepalm myself and I feel Pacey's arms wrap around me, pulling me into him.

"Harlow changed when you left… and well… I don't need to bring up old news." I stiffen in his arms. "But just know, and please, you didn't hear this from me…" he pauses, "but Riggs regrets that one night, it never should have happened. Anger, resentment and a flirtatious girl all mixed with too much alcohol was a recipe for disaster, it just so happened that disaster was Harlow."

I have no right to be cross with either of them, but I am. I hate the fact that she slept with Riggs. She knew what we had… she knew how I felt but as soon as I was out of sight, she jumped into bed with him. I push away from Pacey and stand, taking a large swig of my wine.

"Yeah, I hurt Riggs too so I guess we are equal but still. Harlow has avoided me and now, every chance she gets since I've been back she has dangled Riggs in my face like a carrot. She knows what she is doing. It was bad enough she fucked my brother," I whisper-shout now and Pacey just sits there with a stupid grin on his face. "Stop smiling, this isn't funny. Do you hear how fucked up all of this is?" and then I laugh at how ridiculous it all is, a light giggle bubbles out of me and I can't stop. Hysteria finally winning.

<hr>

WE SIT at the dinner table, Austin to my left, Pacey to my right and I am grateful. Riggs sits opposite me between Orla and Tripp. Dinner was delicious and now we all sit amongst light chatter and I focus on my glass of wine. I really should stop, but I need something to get me through this evening and my good old bottle of red will be the one to do that. I reach for the bottle at the same time as Riggs does, our fingertips just brushing and I pull my hand away quickly, my fingers tingling.

"Please, you first," Riggs says lowly and I shake my head from side to side which causes a roll of his eyes as he lifts the bottle and fills my glass up before his anyway.

I finally allow myself to look at him and ignore the way my heart is galloping in my chest like wild horses, but he doesn't look back at me. I lift the glass to my lips and let the smooth, velvety wine slip past my lips, travelling down my throat like silk.

"So, Aspen," Orla says across the table, "tell me all about this famous fiancé of yours and your life in the wonderful LA." My eyes widen, and I choke, placing the glass on the table and grabbing a napkin to cover my mouth.

"You okay?" Austin whispers, rubbing my back and I

nod continuously, giving myself a moment to catch my breath.

"Sorry," I mutter, and I hear an irritated groan from Riggs. Annoyance flickers inside of me causing me to swing my leg forward and kick him under the table which in turn causes him to suck in a breath through his gritted teeth. A satisfied smile creeps onto my lips and I plaster on the nicest façade I can muster.

"No, no, don't apologize." Orla says softly but still her elbows are perched on the table waiting for me to confess all. I feel a squeeze on my bare thigh, and I know it's Pacey.

"Things are amazing, Luke is just so busy on set with his new movie, so instead of being home by myself at Christmas, I thought I would spend it with my family. It's been a hot minute since I have been home," I smile through gritted teeth and my heart is skipping beats in my chest. Pacey's grip tightens and suddenly I feel like I am suffocating. I can't breathe. My chest is tight, my heartbeat is picking up its pace and I feel out of control of my body. I drum my fingers against the tablecloth, hoping that tapping them in a rhythmic pattern would help. It should help, it's a coping mechanism from when I had my accident, but it's not calming me. My chest squeezes tighter, an elastic band wound tight around me and I feel myself struggling to fill my lungs.

"Beautiful engagement ring, you really are glowing Aspen. Good for you for getting out of this time loop and making something of yourself," Orla continues, and I can't take any more.

"Please," I say quietly as I push my chair back and stand up, "excuse me for one moment," and only then do I feel Riggs' beautiful green eyes on mine. The want to turn and look at him overwhelms me but I refuse myself that privilege.

Turning quickly, I walk out of the dining room and into the downstairs restroom, slamming the door behind me. Resting my back against the door, my palms splayed flat on the surface, I slowly slide down until I am sitting on the cool floor.

Knees bent against my chest, head in my hands and only then, do I allow myself to cry.

CHAPTER TEN
RIGGS

Coming here was a bad idea. She was a temptation. One that I couldn't give into. I sit between my mom and Tripp, and directly in front of me is Aspen. She looks so fucking beautiful it hurts. Her hazel eyes are full of joy and I notice the flecks of gold that glisten in certain lights and I never want to stop losing myself in them.

Supper was amazing, Blue was always the better cook out of our moms. I used to prefer coming up here for supper as a kid. Any chance I could, I would be here but it wasn't just because of Blue's home cooked meals, it was also because of Aspen.

But supper was a good cover up.

I need to just get drunk, it'll make this evening a lot easier to get through if I am drunk. Being in such close proximity to the one girl that has my heart, hurts. She takes the air from my lungs, my heart in her hands as she squeezes it until it is nothing more than ash in her hands, pouring out of the gaps and to her feet. But to love her is pointless. Like roping in the wind.

Reaching in the middle for the wine, Aspen moves at

the same time and our fingertips graze, the burn coursing down my arm and I pull away at the same time she does. I fight with everything in me not to look at her as I move closer to the bottle again.

"Please, you first," my voice is low and when I can't feel her beautiful eyes on me, I lift mine and see her shaking her head softly. I inwardly groan, lifting the bottle and filling her wine glass up before doing my own.

Lifting the glass to my lips, I turn my body slightly so I don't have to look at her and take a large mouthful of my wine, willing for it to numb out my feelings.

"So, Aspen," my mom says, her voice loud as she perches herself in the perfect position to pounce like a waiting lioness. "Tell me all about this famous fiancé of yours and your life in the wonderful LA."

My own eyes widen when I hear Aspen begin to cough, her glass being placed roughly on the table as she reaches for a napkin. My eyes narrow as I watch Pacey's hand slip under the table and I have to chill my inner self from losing my shit and exploding on Christmas day.

"You okay?" Austin, her brother, leans into her, his face laced with concern as he rubs her back and she just nods, keeping quiet.

"Sorry," she mutters and I scoff. I'm not buying her shit. She is hiding something, but little miss perfect won't admit it. I feel a swift kick to my shin from under the table which makes me groan and I know it has come from her, a fucking smile plastered along her face as a warning to me.

Fuck, that hurt.

"No, no, don't apologize," my mom says softly but she is still sitting in her position waiting for Aspen to spill all.

"Things are amazing, Luke is just so busy on set with his new movie, so instead of being home by myself at

Christmas, I thought I would spend it with my family. It's been a hot minute since I have been home," she smiles through gritted teeth and that's how I know she is lying.

I watch as her chest rises and falls a little quicker now, her lips parting as if she is trying to inhale as much air as she can to fill her crushing chest, her suffocating lungs. Letting my eyes move, her fingers are tapping on the table in a rhythm and I know she is trying to focus on that rather than my mom's onslaught of nosy questions. The finger tapping became more apparent when she had her accident, whenever she had to open up about it, she tapped.

"Beautiful engagement ring, you really are glowing Aspen. Good for you for getting out of this time loop and making something of yourself," my mom continues, and I see Aspen snap.

"Please," she just about manages as she pushes her chair across the hardwood floor and stands up. "Excuse me for one moment," and only then, do our eyes connect and I feel the air shift between us, the ground moving beneath my feet as I only focus on her. She rushes from the room and it takes everything in me not to follow her. *She's not yours to follow.*

Pacey's eyes move from Austin to Tripp and finally onto me. I have no idea what to do.

"Is she okay Blue?" my mom asks Aspen's mom. Blue's face is turned into the direction her daughter disappeared but slowly moves to look at my mom.

"Yeah, yeah," Blue rushes out, reaching for her water as her eyes move to Buck and I can see the concern that masks Blue's smile.

Yeah, fuck this.

I push away from the table and ignore my mom when she asks me where I am going. I move down to the hallway following Aspen's steps and stop outside the bathroom door. My hand hovers over the doorknob, internally battling with myself whether I should go in or not. Do I knock or just enter?

I should knock, it's the right thing to do.

"Aspen," I knock on the door gently, but she doesn't answer. I inhale, rubbing my hand over my face and feeling my frustration bubbling deep inside of me. I don't like the idea of her being in there and clearly upset.

Lifting my closed fist, I knock again a little harder this time.

Nothing.

My fingers wrap around the doorknob and I twist it, pushing the door open when I feel the resistance of her leaning against it.

"Get out, I'm in here!" she shouts out, her petite frame pushing against the door, but she doesn't stand a chance. I push the door with force and she steps aside just as I do.

I fall through the door and steady myself by placing my hands on the paneled wall in front of me.

Silence surrounds us, I feel the air crackle between us. The tension is thick. My eyes scan over her pretty face and my heart stammers in my chest. Her beautiful golden honey eyes are red rimmed and puffy, tears rolling down her cheeks and she swipes them away with force. Her lips are parted as she sucks in air but chokes on a sob on her intake of breath.

No words are needed.

She throws herself at me and I hold her tightly and that's when I feel her petite body sag into mine. Tightening my grip around her waist, my neck cranes and I press my lips to the top of her head, inhaling her addictive scent, she smells like wildflowers in the spring meadows.

"You okay there *Dinks?*" and I feel her stiffen when her nickname rolls off my tongue like a bad habit.

"I will be," she says quietly, her hands on my chest as she presses away from me, her honey eyes lifting and connecting with mine and I feel my heart swell in my chest.

My eyes fall from hers for just a moment and graze to her parted lips, gliding them back to her wide eyes, I edge closer to her, letting my eyes fall once more as her lips are inches from mine.

"Is everything okay?" Blue's voice echoes around the room and Aspen pushes out of my grasp just as Blue's head pops round the door.

"Fine," she coughs, turning and fixing her already perfect hair.

"Okay," Blue's eyes move between me and her daughter before she walks out of the room and I don't stick around for a moment more before I follow her out.

That was too close.

Far too close.

After tonight, I needed to distance myself from Aspen Warren for my own sake, and hers.

CHAPTER ELEVEN
ASPEN

MARCH

A short trip turned into months, Christmas came and went, and we brought in the new year with a quiet drink down the Old Dusty Boot. January and February flew by in a blink of an eye and now we're in March, spring threatening but it's still a little too cold. Honestly, I can't ever see myself leaving Lovelock Bay again. Everything felt so relaxed and miniscule here.

Looking down at my ringless finger, I felt as if a weight had been lifted by just removing it. After my close call with Riggs, he has kept his distance. It meant nothing anyway, I was in a bad place and he was the one who came to find me. I had no idea what was happening with Luke and I loved that he couldn't just reach out to me when his world inevitably gets ripped to shreds when Tammy takes him for everything he has. One of the small joys of not having a phone.

Pulling my hair into a messy, high ponytail, I am dressed in a light sweatshirt and jeans. Dad wanted to show me the mares that were being put into foal. I felt accustomed to this life and now I didn't want to *not* be part of it. Like I'd truly come home.

Rushing down the stairs and into the kitchen, I smile when I see the fresh pot of brewed coffee. Placing a mug underneath it, I wait as it trickles through. Reaching for some cereal, I fill my bowl and cover the crispy flakes with cold milk. Placing the bowl on the breakfast bar, I grab my coffee and perch myself on the stool, but I'm not alone long when my mom comes in with fresh eggs from the hens.

"Morning sunshine," she smiles as she pulls her woolly hat off. There is still a chill in the air but it's warmer than Christmas was. We got hit with a bad snowstorm just after so all hands were on deck to try and get the animals safe and well whilst we rode it out.

"Morning," I smile, spooning a mouthful of cereal into my mouth, her cheeks rosy as she stacks the eggs into the little egg house that sat just inside the pantry.

I still hadn't admitted what was going on with me and Luke but after three months of no visits, and the removal of my ring, I am sure they had all connected the dots. They knew something was up, but I just hadn't confirmed or denied it. And truthfully, I didn't think I needed to.

"You ready to help your dad? He is super excited to have you out on the ranch with him."

"Mmhmm," my lips part and rest on the lip of the bowl, sipping my milk from the bottom, and I hear my mom's soft giggle bubble from her.

"You have always done that," she bares her teeth with a grin as she puts her basket under the kitchen sink.

"Best part of the cereal," I wink. Pushing from the breakfast bar, I hop down and walk over to the sink to wash my bowl and spoon up.

Walking back and grabbing my mug I take a sip and groan in appreciation. The cold mornings have me needing this coffee like my life depended on it.

I hear the sound of my dad's heavy boots hit the floor.

"Hey pops," I smile as he closes the gap between us and gives me a kiss on the forehead.

"Morning darling," his voice is soft as he strolls across to my mom and gives her a morning kiss then takes a cup of coffee. "Hens okay?" he asks as he perches himself on the edge of the stool.

"Yeah, Peggy has lost some feathers and I'm not sure if the foxes are back."

"If I find them I'll shoot them," my dad groans and I roll my lips.

"You can't shoot them," I turn to face him as I lean against the countertop, my eyes bouncing back and forth. Surely, he is joking.

"I can if they're going after my girls," his face is thunderous, a scowl etched deeply into his face.

"Can we do anything to stop them?" I ask with inquisitiveness.

"We've done everything we can, I'll just have to put some more chicken wire up," he grunts and rubs his face. His hands are dry and rough, his tired eyes surrounded with wrinkles and suddenly I feel guilty for ever leaving. I was so selfish, young and innocent. But I was mainly selfish for wanting to get away from everything after my accident, wanting to get away from Riggs and Pacey and in doing so, I left everything on my dad and Austin's shoulders. The ones I have always loved, the ones that have always loved me no matter the circumstances.

"Well, I'm happy to help," I smile softly as I finish up my coffee.

"Thank you, sweetheart," his stern voice filling the room before he finishes his own cup of coffee. "Right, we ready?" he asks as he stands, pushing out his back as he does and I hear the click. His red, rosy face looks even more flushed than normal. Concern laces my mind for a moment that he may be getting unwell. He shrugs his shoulders back and he pulls his boots on and I hear a grunt. He isn't as agile as he once was, he looks tired. He is still built the same. Solid, broad and stands around five foot seven. Regret floods me at not coming home for three years, that I pushed them aside for Luke and that I used to get aggravated with their Sunday night phone calls.

I regret it all.

"Where is Austin?" I ask as I begin to walk towards the boot store and grab my old riding boots. Memories flash in front of my eyes and my chest tightens at the memory.

"He will join us in a bit," he rolls his lips as he waits for me. Grabbing his flat cap, he pulls it over his head and does his fleece jacket up and under his chin to keep warm in the cold spring air.

"Do you think at some point you could walk with me down to where Blossom is?" I ask, ignoring the sting behind my eyes, the bob in my throat and the way my stomach twists.

"Of course," my dad smiles and I ignore the tears that are threatening to fall as I follow him out onto the porch.

My steps falter when I see Conrad's truck pull down the driveway, my heart dropping from my chest.

"Why didn't you tell me Conrad was coming?" I whisper to my dad and he just laughs.

"I didn't think I had to," he shrugs his shoulders, a ghost of a smirk pulling at the corner of his lips.

Nudging him with my shoulder as we walk down to

where Conrad is pulling in, I murmur so only he can hear, "Idiot."

I inhale deeply and plaster a broad smile on my face stopping behind my dad who has just shaken Conrad's hand. He dips back, and that's when Conrad seeks me out.

"Aspen," he smiles, his beautiful eyes glistening in the high spring evening.

"Hey," I breathe and any awkwardness I was feeling slowly melts away. Conrad is a gentleman, I know that. But I also know that I am not interested in him as anything more than just a friend. Shame swims through my veins at the thought, in no way do I want to lead him on.

"You still owe me another date," he says quietly as we drop back behind my dad as he leads the way to the stables.

"I do, don't I?" I turn to look up at him and my smile widens.

"How about Friday?"

"Friday is good, I'll have a think what we can do," I skip forward, moving closer towards my dad and away from Conrad.

"I'll be here at seven!" he calls out and I look over my shoulder at him, giving him a wink before I focus on the job in hand.

MUCKING OUT THE EMPTY STALL, I opted for this job instead of having to deal with the horses. I hate myself for it, but I need to build myself back up. I should have just climbed on the back of Blossom after my accident, but I didn't. I let fear cripple me more and more as the weeks turned into months, months into years.

I'm not alone long when I hear the sound of galloping

hooves coming down the paddocks and I see Riggs, Tripp and Pacey. Walking towards the large opening, I lean on the fork handle as I see them slow in front of my dad.

Nosiness gets the better of me as I slowly walk towards where the commotion is. I can see Tripp's hands flying around and my dad holding his up trying to calm him. Conrad is standing next to my dad, straightening his back as if gearing up for a fight.

"What is going on?" I say as I walk out onto the dirt track, my eyes narrowed on the three brothers.

"Nothing for you to worry about," my dad gives me a grave look and it panics me.

I look at Conrad then move to the three brothers.

"Is this to do with Clay?" I ask, my brows pinching when Austin barrels in behind us all.

"Is it true?" Austin grits, already grabbing one of the mares and getting ready to tack her up.

"Over a quarter of my cows were maimed along with one of the horses that we left turned out last night," Pacey finally says and my heart stills in my chest.

My eyes are glued to Riggs.

"We had to put them down," he says blasé, no emotion in his voice at all and my gut twists. "Get Marty down there," he orders Pacey, his eyes narrowing.

"I don't understand why you're being targeted," I mutter but I'm not sure if I am directing it to anyone or if it is just my thoughts speaking aloud. Another lot of Riggs' cows got taken down a few weeks back and we put it down to a wolf attack but now, I'm not too sure.

"It's got to have something to do with Clay," Tripp puffs his cheeks out, his grip tightening on the reins of his horse and I don't miss the sparkle of his sheriff badge clipped to the waist of his jeans. "I've pissed him off and he decided to let it get personal. Well, I'll fucking get personal with him." Venom seeps from Tripp's lips, his tongue vicious as the rage saturates him and Riggs turns to look at his brother, a wave of concern lapping over him.

"Well, thanks for letting me know. I'll keep an eye out to see if anything happens over this side," my dad lets out a heavy sigh. "Keep safe boys, we have no idea whom Clay is partnering up with. His dad would be turning in his grave over his behavior."

Riggs grunts before his eyes move to Conrad.

"We could use a hand moving the animals," Riggs says and Conrad gives him a nod.

"Can I borrow a horse?" Conrad asks as he begins walking towards the stalls with my dad.

Austin has already gone with his mare and I am just standing in front of the three brothers.

One can't take his eyes off me.

One has a boyish smirk on his face.

And the other has a thundercloud over his pretty fucking head as his eyes burn into my soul.

"I'll help," I say softly.

"No, princess, you stay here. Wouldn't want you to chip a nail now would we? Plus, how would you help? You won't sit on the back of a horse," Riggs drops his head after hitting me where it truly hurts...

"Fuck you, Riggs," I yell back at him and ignore the way I choke on my inhale. A knife penetrates my skin, straight into my back and lodges itself between my shoulder blades making it impossible to breathe.

It was a cheap shot and a venomous insult, but it didn't stop it from being true.

What help could I be?

My feet stay anchored to the ground as they all stand in

front of me, sitting tall and proud like the knights of the round table. Disgust rolls through my gut. I twist and walk towards the house. Slamming the door in retaliation behind me, the outside world and Riggs fucking Rivera shut away from me before I let the anger consume me whole.

CHAPTER TWELVE
RIGGS

"I'll help," her soft beautiful voice masks her vulnerability, but I see it fucking written in her pretty honey eyes. I know damn well she couldn't stomach it. I know damn well this will just bring everything back, hitting her with a wave of grief that she isn't ready for.

So what did I do? I fucking hit her with a truth she thinks I believe in. All I want to do is protect her, but I know she isn't going to see it like that.

"No princess, you stay here." My stomach knots and twists and I feel the sickly ache in my chest, "Wouldn't want you to chip a nail now would we?" This is when I knew she was going to hate me, but I'm doing this for her, *always*. "Plus, how would you help? You won't sit on the back of a horse," I drop my head, hiding behind my cowboy hat because I am so disappointed in myself that I had even stooped that low. I don't want her to see the sadness in my eyes, but I know she is going to think that I'm mocking her offer of help.

"Fuck you Riggs," her voice cracks, and I see the tears welling in her beautiful eyes as I look back up at her and I hate that I was the one to put them there. She turns quickly, walking towards her house and slamming the front door.

"That was a bit much wasn't it?" Pacey tuts at me, opening his horse's rein and kicking her on as he begins to gallop down the pasture.

"I get it," Tripp mumbles quietly as I follow suit and turn my horse so I am looking up the fields whilst we wait for Austin and Conrad.

"Do you?" I turn to face my brother, his eyes narrowing on me as I ask him the question.

"Yeah, Riggs, I do. Stop acting like an ass. I'm trying to be supportive, so you can stop chewing me out." He shakes his head, a loud tut echoing before he kicks his horse on and leaves me sitting in the dust his mare kicked up.

Exhaling, I rub my temples as I try to alleviate some of the tension.

"We good?" I hear Austin and I nod, clicking my tongue at the top of my mouth, urging my horse on with my boots. Conrad is trotting up beside me as I kick my stallion on and head towards the massacre we have created.

But all I can think about is her.

How it's always been her.

How it will always be her.

I fell in love with Aspen Warren and I have never fallen out of love with her.

"HOLY SHIT," Austin mutters as we all sit on the back of our horses and look at the annihilation in front of us. Conrad covers his mouth with his jersey and I'm not sure if it's because he feels sick from the sight or because he is about to ball his eyes out.

"Dad is bringing a truck down with the horse trailer, we just need to work and get these moved off our land as soon as possible." Tripp grunts. "We need to get the field sorted and the herd back out, then Conrad," Tripp turns to face him, "I want the carcasses decomposed so we can use them as fertilizer when we do the fields in the autumn. Can you speak to Harlow for me?"

Conrad gives him a solid nod and Tripp moves forward into the field when we see our dad pull through the bottom gate that sits alongside the small and narrow country road, Austin following behind.

Pacey doesn't hang back and instead gallops towards our dad.

It's just me and Conrad and I take this moment to turn and look at him, and I mean, really look at him. I get what she sees in him. He is a pretty boy who doesn't mind getting his hands dirty and I am pretty sure he would treat her right, but I can't help but wonder if they've seen each other since their first date.

"We might go down the Boot Friday if all of this is cleaned up by then, did you fancy joining us?" I ask the question with an ulterior motive. Chewing on the inside of my bottom lip, my hands resting on the horn of my horses saddle whilst I wait for his answer.

"Ah," he chuckles, "I would love to but I will be out on a date," he turns to face me and gives me a wide shit-eating grin and I know that his date is with Aspen.

"Oh really," I laugh, tightening up the reins as I lift my horse's head up, tension and anger simmers deep inside me and I am trying real fucking hard to keep my temper at bay.

"Yeah..." he smirks, his eyes scoping over me, "really." His voice is slow as he assesses me one last time, trying to work out my tone.

"Well," I say, nudging my horse on, "we will have to see about that." Looking over my shoulder I give him a wink; I laugh to myself and kick forward, catching up with the rest of them.

Jealousy swarms me and honestly, I am getting a little sick of these men that think they can take what belongs to me.

She might not be mine yet, but she will be.

I'll make sure of it.

I AM EXHAUSTED, my legs are heavy like lead and all I want to do is climb into my bed, but I can't. I need to go and apologize to Aspen. Whether she will forgive me or not is another story entirely, but I need to at least try.

Walking down the fence line, I stop just before the meadow that sits to the side of our ranch and see that some of the wildflowers are battling through the harshness of the cold spring mornings. Swiping up a small bunch I trudge towards my house. Kicking my shoes off, I place the wildflowers on the countertop and climb the stairs for a warm shower. Coldness has gotten into my bones and I can't warm myself up.

Every time I blink, all I see is the bloodshed that was in front of me today. A quarter of our cattle gone in a heartbeat and my dad's beloved retired mare, Honey was destroyed too. Seeing him so cut up over her was enough to make me think my dad's frozen heart was beginning to thaw out, finally.

Stepping under the hot shower water, I let it wash the shit show of a day from me. My muscles ache, my feet burn and my ankles feel swollen.

Letting my eyes close I push the scenes from today out of my mind and it drifts to prom night, my heart splintering inside my hollow chest at the vivid memory.

I PACED UP and down my bedroom, stopping occasionally to look out the window to see if Pacey had brought her back, but the drive was still empty. I hated that I didn't show; hated that I didn't even tell her, but seeing her face when she saw the fairy lights on the truck was enough for me. I told her mom I didn't want her knowing it was me, but as soon as she was told that Buck put the lights on I knew she knew who really did it. I wanted her night to be perfect; I wanted to be perfect for her, but my dad made sure that I couldn't be there for her. He made it clear that I wasn't to get involved with Aspen and like an idiot I listened because I never wanted to disappoint him.

I stilled when I heard the noise of tires crunching on the graveled drive and like some sort of obsessed stalker I perched myself at the window. I watched Pacey stumble out the truck, holding his hand out for Aspen and I felt the air knock from my lungs. Her long blonde hair was loose and not as neat as it was earlier in the evening, the silver-grey silk dress that clung to her little curves sat perfectly on her body and she reminded me of the stars in the night sky, shining bright and glistening. She looked so happy and so carefree and my heart plunged.

I should've looked away but I didn't, I kept my eyes pinned to both of them and that's when I saw Pacey grasp her pretty face between his hands and slide his lips over hers. My insides boiled and I felt rage splinter through me. She pulled away and Pacey whispered something in her ear, and I begged for her to look up at me, silently pleading that she would see me and come to find me. Within a second of that wish, her beautiful face turned towards the house, her honey golden eyes lifted to my window and I forgot how to breathe for just a moment but she didn't leave Pacey. She didn't come and find me. She let Pacey lead her away to the back of the house and I knew she was doing it to punish me. To get back at me for standing her up.

The hours ticked past, the summer rain was hammering down on the double window pane and I couldn't move. I couldn't rest until I knew she was being taken home. I heard a commotion, she was shoving and pushing Pacey off her. He was trying to reason with her but she wasn't having any of it. Sitting up straight, I cracked the window slightly when I saw Pacey admit defeat, staggering off into the darkness.

"Come down Riggs, please" she cries out, her pretty dress getting soaked which only thinned the material, the bright light coming on as she stepped closer to the back of the house, her head tilting back.

"You owe me this at least, please Riggs,"

But I ignored her. My heart thrumming against my chest.

"You promised me Riggs, you said you were going to be there," she screams and my heart cracks, but like the coward I am, I say nothing. Just sit and listen. "This was meant to be our night Riggs, I thought you felt the same but clearly everything I thought I knew was just a lie. You never liked me. You were just too polite to say no when I asked you to take me to prom," she chokes on a sob.

No, baby. My heart only beats for you, I wish I could explain everything.

"I fucking hate you Riggs Rivera."

I rush out of my bedroom, nearly falling down the stairs as I take them two at a time and I tug on the back door, but by the time I am outside, she is nowhere to be seen. I stand in the pouring down rain as I watch the only girl I have ever felt indescribable feelings for run down the muddy fields, guided home by night lights.

I broke her heart.
And she didn't stick around for me to fix it.
Because just after prom, she had her accident.
And I have never forgiven myself for that night.

DRESSED in a crew neck jumper and dark wash jeans, I let my hair dry naturally and I'll kick myself later when it is wild. Placing my cowboy hat back on my head, I slip my feet into my boots and trudge downstairs. My brows pinch when I see the countertop where the flowers were sitting is now empty.

"Mom?" I call out and see her standing at the sink, washing up and the pretty wildflowers from the meadow are sitting in a vase.

"Did you get these for me, Riggs?" she asks, a warm smile on her face and fuck, I'm about to break her damn heart.

"Ah, mom, as much as I would love to say yes..." I pause and I see as her smile slips.

"Aspen?" her brows lift and my cheeks blush.

"Yeah... I owe her an apology. I said some not very nice things." I run my hand round the back of my neck and rub on the skin.

"Riggs Rivera," my mom spins from the sink and puts her soap covered hand on her hip and I can feel her judgmental gaze on me and I hate it.

"I know, I know," I hold my hands up, "I'm going to fix it, well, try and fix it," I give her a small shrug of my shoulders.

"I baked some brownies. Take her a cup of hot cocoa and a brownie and she will be putty in your hands," she winks as she opens the refrigerator and takes a brownie slice out and wraps it up all nicely.

I wait patiently as she whips up a hot cocoa and hands it to me in a thermal flask.

"Thanks mom," I step towards her, bending slightly as I kiss her on the cheek. I tower over my mom. She is short, probably a bit shorter than Aspen. I stand at six foot seven, tallest out of all three of my brothers, but the same height as my dad.

I slowly stand and turn, feeling a slap round the back of my head which causes my cowboy hat to fall on the floor.

"What the hell was that for?" I groan, lifting my eyes from the floor and to my mom as I rub the back of my throbbing head.

"Watch your tone," she points her finger at me and I back away, giving her a submissive nod. "And that, Riggs Rivera, was for making Aspen sad. Now, go make it right with her. We don't want her to run away again now do we?" She gives me a knowing look which makes my heart twist.

I puff out my cheeks as I bend my knees so my mom can put my cowboy hat back on and then she continues picking lint and dusting imaginary dust from my clothes.

"Mom, seriously," I shake my head. "Flowers, please," I give her a toothy grin, "and I'll get you some flowers tomorrow, I promise." Her warm hand finds my cheek, cupping it.

"Everyone reads you so wrong my sweet boy," I lean into her, "you deserve someone to hang the moon and stars for you."

"I don't know about that ma," I snort a laugh as she walks to the vase and picks the flowers out, shaking the excess water off the stalks and handing them to me.

"Now, go make up with *our* girl," she winks and with that, I turn and walk out of the house all the while my heart is in my throat.

Our.

THE CLOSER I get to the stalls, the quicker my heart is racing under my skin. I see the horses still tied outside which makes me think she is still in there.

Placing the hot cocoa on the fence post, I climb over, swinging my leg so I am sitting on the fence as I pick the flask up and jump down, ignoring the way my bones crack and my muscles ache, I continue walking towards the stall.

Ignoring the sickly nervous feeling that is currently coursing through me I approach the steel grate and hear her muttering to herself, but I have no idea what the hell she is going on about. Leaning against the frame of the double sliding stable door, I just stand and watch her for a moment. Her honey blonde hair is still in a ponytail, but a few strands are now hanging down and framing her pretty face. The way the curve of her ass looks in her tight light denim jeans, her long, toned legs that I fantasize about having locked around my waist. Her full chest that is hidden behind her flannel shirt finish off her perfect hourglass figure.

I could stand and watch her all day.

She stands, huffing and dropping the fork to the floor. She tugs her gloves off and throws them on top of the fork. She looks tired.

"How the fuck am I going to get these damn horses in?" she mutters and I can hear the crack in her voice. "*You can't even get on a horse,*" she says in a childish mimic and I let out a low chuckle, but I don't miss the way my heart throbs in my chest, the way it aches.

I step aside, placing her cocoa on the floor and then I place the wrapped brownie on top of the flask and lay the flowers down next to it.

"I didn't say that actually," my voice booms through the stalls and I watch as her eyes widen as they scope me out.

"Fuck you," she flips me off and my lips twist as I feel a chuckle vibrate low in my throat.

"Let me apologize," I step towards her, her lips parting and her eyes falling to my lips, "Let me do something to show you just how *sorry* I am."

"I don't want you to apologize," she stammers, stepping away from me.

"I didn't ask if you wanted me to, I want to. There is a difference." I wink at her as I close the gap between us completely. Looking down at her, it takes everything in me not to run my thumb over her full bottom lip, tracing it down her jaw before I clasp her pretty face in my hands and slant my lips over hers. To kiss her, to remember what it feels like to have her lips on mine. "Now, stop acting like a brat and let me help you."

I watch as she twists her lips and then she crosses her arms across her chest.

"Fine," I hold my arms up in defeat, turning and walking towards the exit of the stables, "get the horses in by yourself," I call out and pray that she takes me up on my offer.

"Fine!" she calls out and my lips twitch.

I spin on my heel and place my hands on my hips. "There's a good girl," I wink at her, "now come on, let's get the mares in."

She walks cautiously towards me and I can see the fear etched into her eyes.

"It's okay, I'm right here, let's just take it slow, okay?" I say softly as she stands beside me and gives a shallow nod.

Stepping onto the yard, the six horses are all stood eating hay bags.

"Any preference?" I ask, squinting as the low afternoon sun comes round and warms us.

"Nope," she just about manages, her voice tight and her breaths ragged.

"Right, let's do the bay mare. We will do it together okay?" my voice is soft as I begin to move towards the horse. I stop once I am next to it, and give the bay a pat on the neck. "Your turn," I step aside as Aspen freezes beside me.

"I can't do it," she shakes her head from side to side.

"You can, I promise Aspen."

"Oh look, another false promise," she snipes at me but I ignore it because truthfully I do deserve it.

Letting my fingers brush against the back of her hand, her breath stutters at the back of her throat as I wrap my fingers around her wrist gently and slowly lift her small hand so it's hovering over the horse's neck. That's when I notice that her engagement ring has gone. My brows pinch, but I ignore the urge to ask her.

The bay mare's ears fold back and she swishes her tail which causes a whimper from Aspen.

"Aspen," I whisper, which causes her to turn and face me, "she can sense your fear, just small steps. You're doing so well," I reassure her as her eyes leave mine and focus on the horse in front of us.

Slowly, she edges her hand forward and places it flat on

the horse's neck and I don't miss the choked gasp that leaves her, silent tears rolling down her cheeks.

"There we go Dinks; you're doing amazing," I praise her and my heart swells in my chest. This might not seem a lot, but this is fucking huge for Aspen.

The mare stamps her back hoof on the ground which makes Aspen jump and she pulls her hand away quickly. Untying the rope, I lead the mare back to her stall and Aspen walks by my side.

We continue this, Aspen stroking the horses' necks, then me leading them back to the stalls.

"Last one," I smile as I turn the horse and slowly walk into the stall when Aspen pauses and points at the flask and flowers. "Ah," I scoff, "they're for you," I shrug as I walk the dun mare into her stable and bolt the door.

Hanging up the last head collar, I turn and see Aspen holding the brownie and the flask and I smile. Walking past her, I pick up the flowers and hold them in front of Aspen.

"I'm sorry for earlier..." the words feel lodged in the back of my throat, "I shouldn't have said any of that to you. I was just..." I pause and Aspen sniffles, licking her top lip.

"Being an asshole," she smirks as she takes a mouthful of her cocoa and I watch as she sags slightly.

"Good?"

"So good, your mom always made the best cocoa," she chimes.

"She really does," I twist and place the wildflowers on the hay bales. Silence surrounds us for a moment as she takes another mouthful and unwraps her brownie. "I heard you're going out on a date this Friday," the words taste bitter on my tongue.

"What's it to you Mr. Rivera?"

"It's a lot to me actually." My tone is flat, my voice gruff.

"And why is that?" her brows lift, her lips pushing into a pout.

"Because I wanna take you out. I don't want you dating captain douchebag."

She giggles, covering her mouth with the unwrapped brownie.

"Hey, he isn't a douchebag; he is actually really nice," she smirks, "and also, who said it was a date? I'm engaged... I'm not really on the market for dating," she shrugs, and I feel the fire burning deep inside of me.

"Is that so?" I step forward which causes her to step back until she has nowhere else to go, so she is cornered.

"Yes," she just about manages to breathe out.

"Then where is your pretty fucking ring?" my eyes scope to her empty finger.

"I'm keeping it safe," she stammers, her fingers tightening around the thermos.

"Bullshit," I growl.

"Don't believe me then," she looks away from me, turning her face to stare at the wall. Placing my hands either side of her, I box her in.

"I don't believe you," my voice is low and slow, but my heart is jackhammering in my chest. "Because Aspen, if you were fucking mine there is no way in hell I would let you take that ring off. I would want everyone to know that you belonged to me. The fact that your poor excuse of a *fiancé* hasn't been by to see you once tells me that something isn't ringing true. So just tell me the truth, because either way, I'm not letting you out of my grasp again."

"I don't have to tell you anything. I have no idea what you have going on in your fucked up head but I don't want to be yours. You hate me, I hate you. We had a moment many years ago but you ruined that. You didn't even bother to check in on me when I left. You shut me out Riggs. You've been horrid to me ever since I came back. You've ignored me for the best part of three months and now because you find out that I am going out with Conrad you think that you can put some burly claim on me?" her eyes volley back and forth between mine and it's taking everything in me right now not to fucking kiss her just to shut her up.

I press my body up close to her so she can feel *everything*.

"Tell me, Wildflower..." I rasp, lowering my face to hers, my eyes falling to her lips, "does this feel like I hate you?" My evident bulge is pushing against her and I hear a light gasp leave her. "I have *never* hated you Aspen, not once in my entire fucking life. Do you want to know who I hated?" I pause for a moment, but she says nothing. "I hated myself. I hated myself for not stopping you from leaving, I hated myself for not going to prom with you, I hated myself for pushing you into Pacey's arms when all I wanted was to hold you in mine. I hate myself, Aspen, I wholly loathe myself over what I've done to you. But now that you're back, you're not going anywhere."

My breaths are ragged, my heart is jumping around in my chest and all she can do in response to my outburst is to slap me. Hard.

The sting of her hand on my cold skin is enough to make my eyes water. She ducks out from under me, dropping the cocoa and brownie on the floor as she tries to get away from me. I reach forward, wrapping my fingers around her wrist and pull her into me, our bodies slamming together.

"Don't run from me," I plead with her, her honey eyes glassing over and my heart squeezes in my chest.

"I'm not the same Aspen that up and left all those years ago Riggs."

"You're right, you're not... because that Aspen wasn't mine, but you..." I pause,

"you are."

Silence fills the stalls for a moment and her eyes bat back and forth between my eyes and lips. The tears evident and I have to fight the urge to not swipe the ones that have escaped with my thumb pad.

"I can't do this Riggs, I'm sorry." Her voice cracks and it destroys me. "I'm not some toy you can pick up and play with when you feel like it Riggs. I have feelings, and my feelings for you were left behind with my broken heart on prom night. I'm sorry, but I'll never be yours," she drops her head and I just stand there as I watch her walk away. Her words wind me, causing me to gasp for air, my lungs burning as they beg for oxygen. My fingers dig into my chest, applying pressure for me to feel something other than heartache.

CHAPTER THIRTEEN
ASPEN

What the fuck.

What the fuck.

What. The. Fuck!

My hands are pressed against my cheeks, my mind racing as I replay the events that just unfolded on repeat in my head.

"This is such a mind fuck," I whisper, letting my fingers drag down my cheeks and slip off my jaw.

I pace up and down my room, my hands now on my hips.

The way he cornered me, the way he pressed himself up against me to *show* me how much he didn't hate me.

He ignores me for months. Literal months. Every time I walked into a room, he walked out. Anywhere I was, he wasn't.

But now, because he has found out I am going out with Conrad on Friday, he wants to put some claim on me.

Well fuck you Riggs Rivera.

Fuck you.

FINALLY ROLLING OUT OF BED, my eyes sting. I hardly slept. My evening was spent with my eyes pinned to the ceiling just playing everything on a constant loop. I didn't have to get up now, but I also didn't want to wallow in self-pity even though I didn't really understand why I felt a slither of the emotion that was weighing heavy on my chest. I walked away from Riggs. He laid everything out and because I got scared, I ran. Again.

Slipping my feet into my slippers, my room is cold and I shudder, wrapping my arms around myself. Why had I thought wearing a cotton vest and matching short set was a good idea? Checking the clock, it's just past eight. I hear the tiny tip tap of feet and smile when I see Butch round the bedroom door.

"Hey there bud," I crouch down and stroke him before I pick him up and hold onto him like a little hot water bottle. His tongue darts out, licking my chin softly. "Let's go get a coffee," I kiss the top of his fluffy head.

Walking downstairs, still holding onto Butch I put him down when I hit the bottom step and he scampers off towards the back of the house.

"Mom, dad?" I call out, but I am greeted with silence and shrug my shoulders up. Pacing down the hall and into the kitchen, I fill the coffee machine with water and replace the filter. Switching it on, it takes a moment or two to kick in before it begins to warm.

Leaning over the countertop, I drum my fingers against the worktop while I wait.

Ten years ago, I would have done anything to have Riggs Rivera tell me I was his. That's all I wanted. Even after he broke me into a million pieces, I would have still glued myself back together again. Because if he'd have said 'jump', I was that kind of girl to say 'how high'.

But now?

I'm not such a rollover.

Being away from Luke has made me realize how much I hated who I'd become. I hated everything about who I was. I was like a Stepford wife, so busy doing everything to make *him* happy that I forgot what made me happy. After my accident, small pieces of my soul and make up chipped away because I was broken in ways I never thought was possible.

I adored that Aspen.

The Aspen I am now? Not so much.

But I was on the way to getting the old me back.

I look over my shoulder to where my dad's office sits, my laptop becoming part of the furniture as it sits with a dead battery and thousands of words that will never see the light of day.

I sigh, the coffee machine beeping to let me know it was hot enough. Pressing onto my tip toes I reach for a mug, closing the cupboard when I hear a cough from behind me and I freeze.

Turning slowly, fingers wrapped round the handle of my mug I press my eyes shut silently praying that it isn't fucking Riggs standing there.

Opening one eye only, my heart races.

"Well, good morning Aspen," my name rolls off Riggs' tongue like silk and the low, gruff growling tone makes my insides quiver.

"It was a good morning until I saw you," I quip, turning round and ignoring the way my blood is thumping in my ears, the way my heart is thrashing in my chest so erratically that I am stammering on my intake of breath.

"That isn't very nice is it," I can hear the playful tone in his voice.

"Truth hurts, big man."

Placing my cup under the coffee machine, I press the button.

"I would *love* one. Thanks," I hear the sound of his boots crossing across the tiled floor, slow and torturous. "I am parched."

"I didn't offer."

"Oh, come on, be a doll and sort me out a cup. I am so *thirsty*," he chuckles to himself, and I twist my lips.

Turning to face him, my brows are pinched, but I can't stop my hungry eyes from roaming over him even if I wanted to.

Dark brown cowboy hat hiding his beautiful, curly, chocolate brown hair. His beard trimmed and short. His light sage eyes filled with so much want and hunger as he stares down at me as if I am his favorite snack.

Dressed in a gray jacket and a black wash shirt with both top buttons undone so I can just see a glimpse of his dark brown dusting of chest hair peeping out. A black belt with a large silver buckle wrapped around the waist of his dark denim jeans and I can't deny that he looks good. He has always looked good.

Handsome. Rugged.

Rough around the edges but so beautifully pieced together.

And hot. I can't forget hot.

Undeniably hot.

The golden tones of his skin flecked with rosy cheeks.

"Pick your jaw up sweetheart."

"In your dreams," I roll my eyes, scoffing as I pull the mug of coffee out of the machine and hand it to him.

"Cream and a sugar please," he winks, lifting his hat and placing it down on the countertop.

I puff out, exasperation clear.

Opening the fridge, I grab the creamer and pour it in then scoop one sugar into his now creamy coffee.

Placing it a little harder on the countertop than I intended he snorts a laugh, shaking his head as he walks round the other side, putting the counter between us and I have never been more grateful.

Silence cracks through the tension that fills the room as I make my own coffee. I suddenly feel very conscious about wearing so little but I didn't think my brother's best friend would have graced me with his presence this morning, especially after yesterday's event.

Slowly, I turn my face to look over my shoulder to see Riggs burning his eyes into mine. Turning my head quickly I ignore the blush that is creeping onto my cheeks and turning them a pretty shade of pink.

I inhale deeply then puff out my cheeks as I turn to face my nemesis again.

My back against the countertop, my legs crossed over at my ankles as I put my weight onto the surface behind me.

"Brr," Riggs shudders in his seat as he wraps his fingers tighter round his mug of steaming coffee. I raise one of my brows, lifting my mug to my lips. "Bit chilly in here isn't it?" he smirks slowly as he drags his mug towards him then lifts it to his lips as his pretty eyes fall from mine to my heaving chest.

Licking my lips then rolling them I can't stop myself from nibbling on my bottom lip as I roll them out. Slowly lowering my chin to my chest I look down to see my nipples hardened and strained underneath my thin vest top.

He chuckles softly to himself.

"You're an asshole." I press my arms into my chest, trying to hide my evident nipple on but all that does is cause a cleavage.

"Hey, darlin' don't be hiding those pretty tits for my sake," his voice rumbles, "I am perfectly fine seeing them," he winks and I feel my whole body warm under his words, under his intense gaze.

"You don't get to look at them, you lost that right many years ago," I plaster a sarky smile across my lips.

"Darlin' I didn't lose anything," he grunts, pushing back on his stool and my heartbeat stills for just a second.

"Why are you even here Riggs? No one is here, you have no need to be here," I swallow thickly ignoring the way my heart has kickstarted and is now galloping like wild horses in my chest.

"I have a meeting with Austin and your dad, and my two brothers," he clicks his tongue to the roof of his mouth as he stands now, my eyes pinned to him.

"Well, they're not here so maybe go back to whatever hole you crawled out of and leave me alone." I nod, stepping forward and towards the doorway leading out to the hallway but he moves quickly, stopping me from leaving the kitchen.

"I have about half an hour before they're due back, and I thought to myself as I walked over, why not spend some time with my favorite girl," he licks his lips and steps towards me which makes me stumble back into the centre island.

"You must be confused, Harlow doesn't live here."

He sucks in a sharp inhale through his teeth.

"I'm not looking for Harlow," he says gravely.

"Shame," is all I manage for a comeback. My mind fuzzy

as Riggs presses close to me, my lower back hitting the edge of the hard, cold worksurface.

"It's not though is it," he glares down at me, his lips parting as my chest rises and falls, heaving breaths consuming me that I fight hard with myself to not let him see.

"I'm not into you," I barely manage a whisper.

"Why are you lying to yourself? Dinks, what we had..." he pauses, pushing his tongue inside his bottom lip.

"Had, Riggs. *Had*." I emphasise the word.

I hear a low rumble of a growl in his throat and I feel my stomach knot, heat swarming between my legs and I hate how my body is betraying me.

His large hand sweeps in, taking my mug from my grasp and places it beside me.

"I hate you," my voice cracks, humiliation mixed with anger causing a storm to brew in my eyes, revealing myself to Riggs.

"Do you sweetheart? Because I bet if I was to slip my hand into your shorts, gliding my finger through your pretty pussy you would be soaked for me," his eyes fall to my parted lips and my cheeks burn crimson.

"I'm as dry as anything," I nod, swallowing the large lump that has formed in my throat. But we both know it's a lie. I can feel wetness pooling on the seams of my light pink pyjamas, and if he looked, he would see I was lying too.

He smirks before a low chuckle vibrates through him.

"Stop fighting what is inevitable."

"I'm not fighting Riggs," I breathe and it's the truth. I'm not fighting. "And we're not inevitable," my voice trembles slightly but I manage to cover it before he even notices.

Licking his top lip slowly, he knocks my legs open with his knee and I curl my fingers around the work surface.

"Nothing has changed from yesterday, any feelings I had for you were left on your front porch in the pouring rain many years ago." I swallow down the burn.

Anger swirls deep inside of me which only seems to heighten my desire.

"I didn't do it out of choice," he whispers and I can see the vulnerability etched over his pretty face.

"I don't care about the reasons Riggs, so much has happened since then. Prom night was years ago and really, it's not even a big deal."

He scoffs, rolling his eyes.

"If it wasn't a big deal, why are you throwing it in my face at every given chance?"

His words whip against my skin, marking me in an instant and my eyes widen at the truths he has just coated me in.

"Because you hurt me! The whispered promises and the future that I had painted for us was destroyed within minutes. You did that Riggs. You ruined any chance of a me and you." I choke on held in sobs. My chest tightens as my heart weeps inside my chest.

"And you hurt me!" His voice is tight, his eyes volleying back and forth between mine and I feel my heart sink into the crevices of my aching chest, my lungs burning as the air is snatched from them so cruelly.

"Well then, we both hurt each other," I spit, wiping a stray, angry tear from my cheek and that gets him stepping back, his large hand rubbing over his beard, and I can see the hurt masking his handsome face as our words replay in his head on a constant loop.

The room that was once filled with heated pants and sexual tension is slowly fizzling into nothingness. And I don't know why. But it hurts deep down in my core.

His green eyes seek mine out, no words are said as we both stare at each other.

The tension slowly builds once more and I know with the one little sentence about to roll off my tongue, I am going to destroy Riggs Rivera once and for all.

"I'm still going out with Conrad on Friday; I'm uptight and I could really do with releasing some... tension..." I trail off and that's all it took for Riggs to fucking lose it.

CHAPTER FOURTEEN
RIGGS

"And you hurt me!" I hurl across at her, my chest heaving, my heart breaking and my whole-body aches at my admission. I hadn't told anybody before about just how broken I was. I'm not talking about prom, or anything before or between.

I'm talking about the night after prom.

What her and Pacey did.

Memories floor me, bitterness coating my tongue at his admission. The pain that has become so natural to me sears through me causing me to suck in a deep, sharp intake of breath.

I watched as her and Tripp walked away, his arm looped around her shoulder and fury bubbled inside of me. I was angry, my eyes pinned to Pacey as I charged for him. He didn't stand a chance. He fell to the floor and I took my frustration out on him. If Austin hadn't stopped me... I don't know how far I would have gone.

The morning after, we walked downstairs and I couldn't

even bring myself to look at him. His face was swollen, his eyes bruised and his nose bloody. I was disgusted with myself but it still didn't simmer down the rage that was burning through my veins.

A week after, my dad came home from his business trip. My mom filled him in, leaving out the gritty details but my dad's expression was thunderous.

"Hit him," my dad orders Pacey and I look at him dumbfounded. "I'm not having you getting one up on your brother Riggs," he shakes his head. "Hit him Pacey, fight it out and once you're finished, get your fucking shit together. I will not tolerate my two sons fighting over a goddamn girl!" he roars and me and my brother both cower. He storms towards the front door, swinging it open and urging us to go outside.

"I told you she was trouble Riggs but you never listen, do you?" I drop my head, shame burning me. "Now fuck off outside and fight it out."

We both turn our faces to look at each other, and on a silent nod, we step outside.

Pacey did hit me, twice.

He told me he didn't want to hit me again. We walked down to the creek and we sat there for most of the day and hashed it out.

I was still mad, and I'm sure as shit he was mad too.

But we got over it. Eventually. Even though my constant pain and heartache stay with me every day, I still get a new kind of pain that splinters through me every now and then when the memories become a little too raw.

It's normal right? They both broke my heart.

THEY DESTROYED me in a way that I never thought was possible. The only girl I have ever loved and my brother.

"Well then," she swipes at her cheek angrily, "we both hurt each other." I step back, my hand moving to my face as I rub my chin, my beard scratching against the palm of my hand and I inhale heavily, my heart heavier.

Silence blankets us, but I don't take my eyes off of her.

She shuffles and her lips part and I wait for her to speak but she says nothing. Seconds tick past as I take a step forward.

"I'm still going out with Conrad on Friday, I'm uptight and I could really do with releasing some... tension..." she trails off and anger consumes me whole. I turn into a green-eyed monster filled with jealousy and I couldn't stop myself even if I wanted to.

"I swear to God, Aspen," I groan, stepping towards her.

"What?" she smiles at me, and I can see the menacing look on her pretty fucking face.

"Like fuck are you going out with Conrad."

"I can do what I want, and I am going Riggs," her voice floats over me and I feel my skin prickle.

Pressing myself against her tight, curvaceous little body, I tuck my hands under her arms and lift her onto the work surface which causes a gasp to leave her, her eyes and wild.

"No one else will be relieving your tension," my lips dust up the column of her throat, my large hands clinging and wrapping around her waist as I keep her pinned to the countertop. "I will be the only one satisfying your pussy, do you understand me?" Rage boils deep inside of me and I know this is wrong, but I can't stop myself. I was the bullet, she was the gun. One swift slip of the finger and I am barrelling towards her, burying and lodging myself deep inside of her.

I nip at her jaw, her gasps echoing round the room.

"Tell me, Aspen, tell me that it's only me," my large, callous hands lift her vest, my fingers skimming over her warm skin as I trace them up over her rib cage, trailing small circles against the silkiness, my heart thrumming in my chest at actually touching her, at feeling her under my fingertips, *finally*.

A possessiveness comes over me when she doesn't answer, lifting my hand from under her vest and wrapping my fingers round the base of her neck, her pulse racing underneath my fingertips, my lip lifting on one corner.

"Tell me," I groan as I tease my other hand on her thigh, skimming it up and dusting the tips just where the hem of her shorts sits.

"Yes," she whispers, "only you," her eyes are pinned on me and my heart gallops at her admission. My hand glides down and presses against her chest and I let it stay there for just a moment to feel the way her heart beats under her skin, my own heart constricts in my chest at the pulsing under my fingers. Pushing her back after a second or two, and laying her down on the countertop, my eyes darken at the pretty sight laid below me.

I lean over her, my lips grazing against her collar bone, trailing down her sternum as I release her tits from her vest top, full and bouncy and my cock hardens against the zip of my pants. Brushing my lips over her hardened nipples, I pull them into my mouth, my tongue rounding her pebbled nipple, teasing her with my hot mouth and rolling my lips across to her other one.

"Oh," she breathes, her fingers still wrapped around the edge of the counter, her head rolling back.

"No one gets to touch you Aspen, no one gets to taste you..." I pause, my hands pushing away the thin material of her vest up, my lips brushing down to the waistband of her shorts and just when she thinks I am going to go further, I stop. Slowly rolling myself up so I am looking down at her. Hooking my fingers into the waistband of her shorts, I slip them down her beautiful, toned legs and they fall off her feet to the floor. My large hand wraps round the inside of her thighs as I push her legs up, her feet on the edge of the countertop and I smile. She looks so fucking pretty, waiting, wanting, dripping fucking wet.

"You want to go against me, you want to tell me that you don't have feelings for me *Dinks*," my voice is low as her eyes burn into mine, my fingers finding their way to the apex of her thighs, her legs widening on their own accord. I tease my finger over her panty covered pussy. The thin cotton beneath my fingers becoming wetter as I rub over her clit in slow, small, circles. Her breaths shuddering on her intake. My eyes fall down as I watch, her legs wide in front of me, moving my fingers over slightly, I tease at the sensitive skin next to her pussy. Grabbing and rubbing as I graze a fingertip over her pussy and go back to focusing on her clit.

"Seems you like to lie Wildflower," I groan as I rub harder, her head rolling round, her eyes falling between her legs.

"Riggs," she moans.

Finally lifting my fingers from her, she whimpers and my cock aches between my legs.

"I'm going to eat this pretty little pussy, claim her as my own." I growl as I slide the thin cotton material over, her pretty pussy glistening. "So wet," I moan, sucking my bottom lip in and letting my teeth graze over it. Rubbing two fingers over her clit, my eyes are pinned as I watch, her breaths ragged. Sliding a finger through her lips, I slip into her hot, soaked, pussy with ease and I clamp down on my bottom lip, stifling my own moan that this is actually happening. All those years of pining over her, all the years of wishing it was me that got to love her and now, I've got my chance.

I hiss as she clenches around my fingers, her knuckles turning white as she tightens her grasp around the edge of the countertop. My thick digits pumping in and out of her.

"I am so fucking desperate to taste you," I growl, slipping them from her then wrapping my hands around her waist and dragging her to the edge of the work surface so her pert ass is right on the edge, my hand cupping her soaked pussy as I rub and tease at her opening.

Slowly falling to my knees, I press one of her legs back up onto the surface, the other hangs beside me so she is wide and open. I curl my hand under her ass where she is overhanging slightly and slip my thumb into her pussy as I hover my lips over her, my hot breaths blanketing her clit before I run my tongue up from where my thumb is pumping inside of her and onto her clit, swirling and sucking.

"Fuck," she moans out, her fingers entwining in my curls as I turn my head, rubbing my tongue over her clit before plunging my tongue into her pussy. Lapping and sucking, my thumb still buried deep inside of her as I run my tongue up and down her parted pussy lips, teasing over her clit before I do it again.

"Riggs," she pants, pressing up onto her elbows, her hand back in my hair as she pushes my face into her, her hips grinding over my face. "Yes, shit, like that, fuck," she pleads as I slip another digit into her, my tongue slowing as I graze my tongue on her clit with force, softly moving my head from side to side as I keep the pace that she has asked for.

Lifting my mouth from her, I stand between her parted legs, letting my thumb slip out as I replace it with a finger and begin to fuck her. Her eyes roll in the back of her head as my thumb pad brushes over her clit before rubbing in circles, her legs widening as she enjoys every second. Craning my neck down, I wrap my fingers around the base of her neck, her chin tipping up as her lips part, soft moans escaping as I fuck her slow, bringing my fingers to the tip as I tease her, stretching her then sliding them back in. My mouth dusts over hers, my tongue dipping just past her full lips as I tease her, letting my fingers tip toe up to her cheeks as I grab them, holding her where I want her. Bringing her to the brink of an orgasm and just when she is close, I stop, my lips hovering millimetres away from hers. Her shaky breath on my face, her eyes fluttering and I can feel her pussy clamping down on my fingers, clenching and squeezing.

"Does that feel good? Do you like having my fingers buried deep inside of you, fucking you?" I whisper into her mouth and she nods, moaning. "How about my tongue?"

"Yes," she gasps as I put pressure on her clit with my thumb, teasing another finger in her soaked cunt.

"I want you to come all over my fingers," I smile against her mouth as I let my hand gently rest at the base of her throat. "I want you to moan my name, Aspen. I want you to tell me you're mine," my tongue dips back into her mouth and just as my lips close over hers, I slide another digit in slowly as I stretch her pretty pussy before fucking her with them.

"Oh fuck, Riggs," she moans into my mouth.

"Say it again," I beg, my eyes closing, my heart swelling in my chest.

"Riggs," she pants, our teeth clashing as our kiss deepens.

"There's my good girl," I groan into her open mouth, her head tipping back as pleasure consumes her and I let my eyes fall between us as I watch my fingers fuck her, coated in her arousal.

"Riggs," she moans once more, "please," she begs.

"Baby, you don't need to say please to come all over my fingers." I smirk, letting my lips find her pulse point in her neck and kiss her gently, feeling her pulse quicken by the second.

"I'm going to..." her whispers make my skin pebble, and I suck on her sensitive skin as she comes undone in front of me, her cunt tightening as her body trembles against mine. Sliding my fingers out, I bring them to her parted lips and push them between as I fall in front of her and let my tongue rub over her pussy, taking all I can from her.

Standing on shaky legs, I cover her over and my eyes skim behind her to see Austin and her dad through the window.

"Hey, darlin'," I grab her face in my hands, her beautiful hazel eyes hazy from her orgasm.

"Mm," she nods.

"Your dad is coming up the drive."

She stiffens and her eyes widen as she pushes me out the way, jumping from the counter and grabbing her shorts.

"This didn't happen," she snaps, looking me up and down with something that looks a lot like disgust on her pretty face and I feel a pain sear through my heart.

"Oh," I chuckle deeply, "baby, it happened."

CHAPTER FIFTEEN
ASPEN

Letting the soap lather up over my still sensitive skin, I replay the last few moments in my head. How the hell did I get from telling Riggs I didn't like him to having him between my legs and giving me the best oral of my life. The way his tongue rolled and rubbed over my clit, his fingers working me up until I was ready to explode.

I clench, my stomach knotting and I feel heat blossoming between my thighs. I always knew me and Riggs would be amazing... but that was out of this world. It was mind blowing.

Rinsing off, I turn the shower off and wrap a towel around my body. My cheeks are still flamed red, the prominent but good ache in my core still throbbing as a constant reminder. I want more.

But I can't.

What happened moments ago was just a slip up. A mistake.

I've moved on from Riggs. I can't go back to the broken-hearted girl I once was.

Slipping my jeans on, I tuck my long-sleeved top into them and brush my still wet hair through.

Part of me wants to stay up here, hide away, but I can't. I have stuff to do and I wasn't going to let my small moment of intimacy with Riggs keep me as a prisoner in my own home. Opening the door, I pace out onto the landing area and I can hear my dad, Austin, Riggs, Tripp and Pacey all talking. I swallow down the nerves and glide down the stairs towards the kitchen.

I hover in the archway when I see Riggs look in my direction. He is standing where I was just sitting whilst he ate me out, his fingers wrapped round the same bit of countertop mine were.

"Morning, Pen. You okay sweetheart?" My dad smiles at me and I force one onto my lips.

"Hey Pops," I keep my feet firmly on the ground, not moving as flashbacks flicker behind my eyes. Heat rising up my chest, my heart racing under my skin.

"You only just woke up?" he asks and lets his eyes move from mine to the clock then back to me.

"Mmhm," I nod, humming in agreement with him because I am terrified to even try and string a sentence together when my mind is otherwise occupied.

"You have a lovely glow to you," Riggs smirks and I feel my body tense under his words.

"I just had a really hot shower, the pressure was amazing on my skin. Really relieved some of that tension that I hadn't managed to get rid of," Riggs' glare is stone cold, fixated on me, but my reply had knocked the shit-eating grin off his face. "Sorry, I didn't mean to interrupt. I was just going to get myself a drink," my eyes move around the room and Pacey, Tripp and Austin give me a nod.

"You're not interrupting darling," my dad says, his cheeks rosy.

"Good," stepping into the kitchen, I brush past Riggs which gets me a low, burly growl in return.

"So, as I was saying..." Tripp continues, "I had a report come in last night about another ten horses disappearing into the night. I'm telling you, this has Clay's name written all over it. I just need to find something to pin it to him" He sips his coffee and I hear my dad sigh.

"I was on his ranch yesterday, he called me over saying some of next door's cattle got into his yard and that they must have purposely moved them because of his cattle grates."

Pacey rolls his eyes, "Honestly, I think he is up to something. All of this smells rotten and I think he is trying to throw us off the scent; trying to cover these missing horses up by calling me out on the shit I haven't got time to deal with," I hear Pacey sigh and I pinch my brows.

"But why would Clay make up stuff?" I ask before I can even stop my mouth running off.

"He was seen with a couple of suits, we think he is trying to sell the land, but no one will sell."

Tripp butts in, "But by getting everyone's cattle and horses out, what have they got left? Really? Most of us here are cattle farmers, you guys break in and sell the horses on. Well, he is trying to drive business out. I might be clutching at straws here, but I do think Clay has an agenda. I just need to know what."

"Why don't you invite him out for a drink?" and the whole kitchen erupts into laughter.

"Oh, baby," Pacey says, and my eyes fly to Riggs who stiffens completely at Pacey's endearment, his jaw wound tight. "Ain't no way we would get Clay out drinking with us," he laughs again and shakes his head, a firm smile plastered across his lips as he looks into his coffee mug.

"Okay, well, what about if I ask Clay out for a drink?"

Riggs chokes on his coffee.

"No fucking way," he growls, his eyes bugging from his head, pushing his large fingers through his curly hair in frustration.

"Pretty sure it's not up to you big boy," I roll my eyes and I look between my dad, brother and the other two Rivera boys. Tripp's eyebrow lifts, his hands on his hips.

"Don't," I hear Riggs warn his brothers as if he can hear their thoughts.

"I mean," Austin half groans, rubbing his hand around the back of his neck and kneads out the skin, "it could work. You and Clay haven't properly met, have you? He goes down to Sunny's every morning between nine and nine thirty to get his coffee and breakfast roll. You could be working there or something? Catch his eye..."

"Yeah, I can do that." I smile but my dad doesn't look pleased and neither does Riggs. I have felt like such a spare part since I have been here, I don't miss the opportunity to throw myself into something to help them.

"Maybe see if you can get him out on Friday?" Tripp murmurs as he lifts his mug to his lips, the whole time his eyes pinned to Riggs. He knows exactly what he is doing. *Touché Tripp.*

"Ah," I rub my lips into a thin line, "I can't do Friday I'm afraid..." I pause as I head for the exit of the kitchen, my eyes raising over to where Riggs is standing all stiff and rigid. "I've got a date with Conrad" and with that, I turn and walk out the room, smiling from ear to ear when Riggs lets out a low, thunderous growl.

"Just give me one minute," I hear his grumpy ass say as he storms after me.

I make it to the bottom of the stairs before I am tugged back, stumbling until I land against Riggs' chest. His hand splaying across my stomach, his rough beard scratching against my cheek as his lips hover by the shell of my ear.

"I'm not sure what you heard whilst my tongue was buried deep inside of your pussy..." he pauses for a moment, his voice low and full of rasp, "but I said you were mine from the moment we crossed that line, yet you're still going on your little date..." I smile as his hand glides up my side, then delicately wrapping his fingers around the base of my throat.

"I gave into a weakness, doesn't mean I'm yours, Riggs."

My hand pulls on his wrist, tugging it from my throat and annoyingly, I miss the way his fingers felt wrapped around me. Turning, my grin widens as I stare him down.

"Fuck you and your possessiveness. I don't belong to anyone," my voice is hushed, mindful of our little audience just across the threshold.

"That's where you're wrong Wildflower, you belong to me. I'll make sure to ruin you for any other man. Once I am finished with you, no one will even be able to look or breathe in your direction."

I roll my eyes and scoff a laugh.

"You don't scare me with your empty threats. What happened this morning was a mistake, and I can assure you baby that it won't happen again."

Riggs is back toe-to-toe with me, towering over me and his large frame shadows me in an instant. A slow and sexy smirk pulling at his lips as his eyes dance with mine.

"I don't make threats darlin'." His hand curls round my hip as he pulls me into him again, his erection evident as it pushes against me. "Go on your little date on Friday and see what happens," his voice is raspy, a guttural groan vibrating in his throat. His eyes darting across my face and I focus on the way his throat bobs.

"Oh, I am going, you don't need to tell me." I yank his hand from my body, storming away and before he can even think about following me, Tripp calls him back into the kitchen.

A victorious smile graces my lips as I walk to my bedroom and slam the door behind me.

SITTING at my dad's desk, my eyes are fixated on the views in front of me, my mind wandering back to this morning. I am ashamed that I let Riggs devour me. I mean, it was hot and it definitely took me away from everything that has been happening, but it shouldn't have happened. We crossed a line that we shouldn't have crossed. It was risky and stupid and now he feels like he has some sort of claim on me. Years ago, I would have been a puddle on the floor for Riggs, and now, well I'm smarter. So much went on between us all that I don't think we can really be anything more than acquaintances and things being just *fine* between us.

Opening my laptop, I inhale deeply as I push the button on and give it a minute to come to life.

I click into the blank word document, my fingers hovering over the keyboard and all my mind fills with is me and Riggs. Everything before, everything between and everything after Riggs. A rush of emotions swarm me; I can't pinpoint a single one and it takes me a moment to realise that words are spilling from me, my eyes fixated to the screen. I feel like everything I have been carrying around with me for the past twenty years is slowly lifting from me, and it all begins from when I first met Riggs.

While the words are flowing I lose track of time until I suddenly feel stiff. Lifting my arms above my head and rolling my neck round. Lifting my head above my laptop screen, I see it's already evening and I have been sitting at my laptop most of the day.

"How's it going?"

I turn to see my mom walking towards me with a steaming hot coffee.

"Okay I think," I half shrug as I take the mug from her and wrap my fingers round it, embracing the warmth that radiates through me. "Well, okay for something that is going to sit on my desktop for months on end and never to see the light of day."

My mom slumps down next to me on the armchair and puffs out her cheeks.

"I don't know... I have a good feeling about this one."

I snort a laugh. "Mom, you say that about every book I try to write."

"It's because I believe that this is your calling. You've just not written *the* one about *the* one. You need your own love story to be able to pour your feelings into the words."

I twist around to look at her, tucking my knees under myself as I drink the frothy coffee she made me, then let out a little moan in appreciation at how good it tastes. I lick the froth from my lips and let my eyes fall to my mug.

"Maybe this isn't what I am destined to do. I went to college to study, ended up engaged to a Hollywood actor and now I am back here and in limbo. I don't quite know where I belong in this world anymore."

She leans forward and places her hand on my knee, giving it a gentle squeeze as she smiles.

"This is where you're meant to be. Write the books, help on the farm, live... just don't go back to Los Angeles." And I hear the plea in the tone of her voice, it wraps around me like a blanket of guilt.

"I don't think I'll be going back to LA mom, or back to Luke for that matter," I whisper, my throat swells as I turn to look at my now black laptop screen because looking at her is too much.

"I figured that one out sweetheart," her hand still on my knee.

"I don't know where it all went so wrong," my voice cracks and I ignore the tear that rolls down my cheek, the back of her fingers brushing against my warm cheek as she wipes it away.

"You never will my love, these things just happen sometimes. Luke was lovely, I would be lying if I said he wasn't, but he wasn't your forever. Call it mom instinct," she lets out a low chuckle and I sniffle, nodding and willing for the blurriness of unshed tears to leave.

A cough pulls my mom's attention for a moment, her head turning towards the door and I don't even have to look in that direction to know it's Riggs.

"Sorry to interrupt Blue, but Buck needs you," and my mom lets out an exasperated sigh.

"You okay?" her hand cups my cheek and I give her a weak smile, bobbing my head up and down.

"Okay," she leans across and places a kiss on the top of my head, lingering for just a moment before she turns and walks out the room, patting Riggs softly on the chest as she does.

Silence crackles, the low, yellow light of the fire burning

away filling the void and I fight with myself not to look in his direction.

The sound of his boots echoes round the room and I shudder on my intake of breath. I watch with bloodshot eyes as he sits in the chair opposite me.

Sucking in a breath, I ignore the way my lungs burn and my eyes sting. His dark and hooded eyes are pinned to mine and suddenly, the weight that was crushing down on me was slowly being lifted.

"Are you okay?" His voice is quiet and soft, concern lacing it tightly. His whole demeanour changing in a moment, he goes from hard and cold to soft and slouched within a matter of seconds.

"Depends on what your definition of okay is." My tone is clipped and my eyes fall to the cup of coffee that sits in my lap.

"Who upset you?" he runs his index finger along his bottom lip, his leg crossing over his lap as he keeps his heavy gaze on me.

I sigh. "I upset myself," I lick my lips free of a salty tear that escaped and ran down my tear-stained cheek. I hear the heavy inhale of breath that Riggs takes and I suddenly feel small.

"I'm always here for you," he whispers into the room and my heart stammers in my chest.

I nod, because I am scared at what might come out of my mouth. I don't want to *want* Riggs. Everything that happened all those years ago is already bubbling on the surface, the cracks are beginning to show and I don't want to fall down the slippery slope of what was my past.

He stands, walking slowly and cautiously over to where I am sitting, knees up around my chest, nose red and eyes bloodshot. He stops, his neck craned down as he looks at me, his large hand slipping from his jean pocket before fisting it back inside as if he changed his mind. I look up at him, eyes glassy, bottom lip trembling as my chin wobbles and suddenly I feel needy of him. Bending over, his lips hover over my forehead before slowly edging them towards my skin and placing a soft kiss there, lingering for a moment or two as I hear him inhale heavily through his nose.

I reach up and wrap my arms around his neck and hold on tightly like a child not wanting to let go of their favorite teddy bear. I cling onto Riggs like he is my lifeline.

CHAPTER SIXTEEN
ASPEN

Riggs kept his distance for the rest of the week, and I was unsure if that was a good or bad thing. We crossed a line. We both knew that. It was a heavenly, explosive line but it was still something that I should have stopped myself doing. But when it comes to Riggs, everything blurs around me and all I can focus on is him.

Unlocking my McLaren, I suddenly feel embarrassed to even get into it, but if I want to catch Clay's attention then this is the way to do it. I wince when I see the damage to the back of the car, I know I need to get it fixed but it hasn't been at the top of my priority list.

But getting finger fucked by your brother's best friend has? My subconscious curls her lip in disgust.

I haven't driven it since the first day I pulled up here with just my dog, my laptop and the clothes on my back. Even though it was a few months ago, it feels like a lifetime since all of it happened. I have no idea whether Luke and Tammy are still together, I haven't been on socials, I have no phone and I'm okay with that. I don't miss it. I don't miss the constant need to check what was happening every five minutes. But being back home, having the views and my family supporting me is everything I did need, I just didn't realise how much.

Unlocking the car, I swing the butterfly wing doors open and lean into the seat, placing my laptop on the passenger seat. I hear a low growl from behind me and roll my eyes in an exaggerated manner. Pushing back, I stand and it takes me a moment to steady myself on my heeled boots. I have lived in sneakers, cowboy boots and work boots for the last few months so heels feel unfamiliar to me suddenly.

"What?" I spin and I am met with a smirking Riggs, his eyes alight with something that dances with the greens of his eyes.

"Nothing," he snorts but he gives me the once over, studying my outfit.

Lowering my chin to my chest, my brows pinch as I look down at myself. I am wearing an off-white jersey dress in a boucle fabric. A soft collar sits open and three out of the four gold buttons are open, revealing maybe a little too much cleavage. Two fake pockets sit on each of my breasts and have matching gold buttons. The sleeves are short and capped and I personally think I look every bit business woman.

"Do you not like the dress?" my head lifts and my eyes burn into his. I have gold hoops sitting in each ear lobe and my dirty blonde hair sits in a styled blowout, layered bangs framing my face.

"That's the problem kid, I *really* like the dress. It's just a shame it's on your body and not on my bedroom floor," he grins a boyish smile, his eyes lower and I feel the crimson hit my cheeks as a nervous giggle rolls out of me.

"Riggs, honey," I flick my hair over my shoulder, "I've

told you there is nothing between you and I, and there will never be." I shrug my shoulders up before giving him a wink as I lower my black square glasses to cover my eyes.

"I see the city princess is back," he tuts, shaking his head from side to side and for some reason his words hurt me, twisting something like disappointment deep in my stomach but I don't let him see how they affected me.

"So it seems," I scrunch my nose and turn my back on him, before slipping into the car. I start the engine, and when I turn to look up at him, he has gone.

He gives me whiplash, I don't want him to be any particular way with me. I just either want nice Riggs or asshole Riggs. At least that way I know which one I am getting all the time.

He is so hot and cold.

Sighing and puffing my cheeks out, I pull the door down and close it before pushing the car into reverse and driving down the driveway towards Sunny's.

The drive was only short, and once I passed the neighboring ranches and farms I was slowing down on the approach of the small town I grew up in. The small school just before the town was where my parents sent me and the whole school had about fifty students. We all knew each other and so did our families. This wasn't just a town. It was a family. A Lovelock Bay family. I scan the street for a parking spot and get one just outside of Sunny's. The town is thriving, the flower shop blooming, the green grocers busy with town folk doing their weekend shopping and the butchers also queuing out the door. I used to love sneaking into the back of the library and inhaling the scent of the old dusty books whilst eating a freshly made buttercream cupcake that I used to spend my cents on every Saturday morning. My mouth waters at the memory and I make a mental note to pop into the bakery at some point.

Cutting the noisy engine, I feel eyes on me. Some will recognise me, some won't, and I am just hoping that no one mentions my name whilst I am sitting with Clay. Grabbing my laptop, I swing the door open and climb out delicately whilst trying not to flash the town my dignity.

Locking the doors, I keep my head down as I walk quickly across the maple tree lined sidewalks and slip into Sunny's. The small bell above my head chimes and I look around finding a small table that faces the sidewalk and I make camp there. Popping my laptop down on the hard surface, I look round the cosy coffee house and smile. The smell of the coffee aromas mixed with the sweetness of muffins, cakes and pies that sit all pretty on the countertop. I am famished.

Looking back at my spot, I feel confident that my table will still be there when I come back from ordering. It isn't overly busy, and Clay isn't here as of yet. I twist my wrist towards me and check the time, it has just gone nine a.m. Tripp's words echo in my head *'he goes down to Sunny's every morning between nine and nine thirty to get his coffee and breakfast roll.'*

Walking to the counter, I brush my hands down my dress to try and alleviate the clamminess of my palms. A woman who I would say was a little younger than me, with beautiful porcelain skin, deep brown eyes and rosy cheeks smiles at me as I approach.

"Welcome to Sunny's, what can I get you?" she chimes, and my eyes fall to her name badge. *Sunny.*

I smile.

"Hey," I play with the ends of my hair as I scan the large selection on the boards behind her, "I'll have a white coffee with oat milk and a poppyseed muffin," my eyes land on hers as she taps the touchscreen filling my order. A young girl behind her starts to prep the coffee beans.

"Take out or in?"

"In please," I reach for my purse and slip out some dollars and place them down on the counter. I watch as she rings it up then gives me three dollars back. I give her a soft smile and pop the dollar notes into her tip jar.

"Thank you, honey; may your coffee be strong and your day beautiful," she beams at me and I feel my insides warm at the small act of kindness just shown.

"You too Sunny," she looks a little confused but then glances down at her name badge and shrugs one of her shoulders up. I throw her a wink before walking to the end of the counter and collecting my coffee and muffin. It smelt and looked delicious. I walk back towards my seat, next to the large windows and I feel some sort of comfort here mixed with a knowing feeling. It's weird but in the best possible way.

Placing my cup and plate down, I take one last look around the room. Rusty orange panelled walls, a large black and gold clock hanging on the wall. Cream bookshelves fill one side of the cosy coffee shop while the other has tables leading down to the back of the shop. Tilting my head back, I look up at the ivory and cream artificial flowers that cover the entire ceiling and have fairy lights entwined between.

It isn't much, but there is definitely something pretty about it. Dragging the wooden chair out, I take my seat and open my laptop as the morning sun beats down on me. I read over the words I had written the night Riggs kissed me on the forehead and I feel my heart flutter. Seeing my feelings and deep desires spilled onto the pages makes me giddy. I have never delved into much, but this story seems to be the one that I want to push for more.

Curling my finger round the handle of my coffee cup, I bring it to my lips, taking a mouthful and moan in appreciation before licking the white froth off the top of my lip. Placing it back down, I pick at the paper muffin case and unfold it before I break a bit off and pop it into my mouth.

My fingers hover over my keyboard and just like that, I fall straight back into it. I'm not working long when I hear the doorbell ring, I lift my eyes from my screen and they land on an impeccably dressed man. Black hair slicked back, tall, high cheekbones and sculpted jaw. He looks every bit a businessman. Not like Riggs and his family who scream *ride me cowboy.*

"Morning Clay," I hear Sunny say and now my interest is piqued even more. I turn in my chair and study him for just a moment longer. I have no idea how I will gain his attention and the longer I am sitting here knowing that I am waiting for him to approach me makes my nerves rise.

Turning my head back round, I pick another piece of my muffin and pop it into my mouth and wash it down with a huge mouthful of coffee. My fingers find their rhythm once more, but as time moves on, my anxiety grows and fills the empty void deep inside of me.

I'm not alone with my words long when I hear a throat clear beside me. My eyes widen and my heart jackhammers in my chest. I slowly turn my face to look up at him and give him a small smile whilst my fingers continue to dance over my keyboard.

"Can I help you?" I say sweetly and I see his eyes sweep over me as if giving me the once over.

A low chuckle vibrates through him, his large hand

wrapped around his takeout coffee whilst one of his fingers was hooked round a paper bag which I am assuming had his breakfast roll in. His spare hand slips from his suit pants as he runs his long finger across his bottom lip.

"You have a little something something here..." he reaches up and touches the bow on his top lip and I retract back, my cheeks burning as I dart my tongue out and lick it away then reach for my napkin and wipe my lips until they hurt.

"Oops," I wince as I feel the crimson blush slip over my skin.

"Out-of-towner?" he asks, his eyes giving me the once over before straightening up and looking out the window, his eyes landing on my McLaren.

"Yeah, just a few towns out. Heard about this place and I am on a deadline so needed some quiet time from people that know me," I half laugh as I turn my attention from him and to my laptop screen. I spun that web of lies pretty damn quick.

"You staying a while?" he asks as he reaches for his phone.

"A couple of days maybe, I'm staying at the little bed and breakfast on the edge of Maple Street."

"Ah, Sylvia's," he nods, looking over his shoulder down the tree lined street.

"Yeah, that's it," I say.

"How about we get dinner some-time while you're still in town. I know a great little steak restaurant just outside the town in Silver End if you fancy it one night?"

Nerves suffocate me. *Shoot.*

"Yeah, that sounds good," I swallow them down, "it would be nice to have one familiar face here," I blush under his intense gaze and I feel perspiration pricking at the back of my neck.

"Monday, eight p.m? I'll collect you from Sylvia's?"

"How about I meet you outside here?" I counter his offer.

"Sounds good to me, here, take my card. You can reach me there if you have any issues," he smiles as he hands me his business card which I take then flip between my fingers, my eyes casting down for just a moment as I read.

"Perfect," I smile widely at him.

"Perfect," he repeats after me, "I'll see you Monday at eight."

"You sure will."

He turns but stops in his tracks after a step or two forward, spinning on his heel to face me once more.

"I didn't catch your name?" one of his thick brows raise as his gaze narrows on me and I feel my heart stutter in my chest.

Smiling, my cheeks pinch, and my throat thickens for just a moment before I swallow the feeling down.

"Aspen" my voice is quiet, but loud enough to float across to where he stands a little in front of me.

"Aspen," he repeats, as if testing my name on his tongue, feeling how it rolls off the tongue.

"Pretty name," a slow wink from him causes my heart to fall from my chest and I give a small but curt nod. And with that, he walks out of the coffee shop with a little bounce in his step. Once he is outside, he passes where I am sitting and lifts his fingers to the side of his head and salutes me on a smirk before he disappears.

As soon as he is out of sight, I suck in air and the realisation smacks me in the face at what I have just agreed to.

Hard.

I spent most of the morning at Sunny's and after three or four coffees I feel like I am buzzing. I normally have one coffee in the morning and I'll have another later on in the afternoon, but I am fully caffeinated out and awaiting the almighty crash.

Pulling into the farm, I see three heads pop up from behind the fence as Tripp, Pacey and Austin barrel over to where I park the car.

Pacey is opening the door before I have even cut the engine.

"Eager, are we?" I groan as Austin holds his hand out for me to take which I am grateful for.

"How did it go?" Tripp asks as he runs his hand round the back of his neck, squeezing slightly as his eyes are glued to mine. They're nervous.

"Fine, he approached me, and I agreed to dinner on Monday," my smile is lopsided and nerves drum away in my chest when I hear a commotion behind me. Turning to face the driveway I see Riggs storming towards me after dropping a couple of barrels to the floor.

"You did what?" his brows raise, his hands on his hips.

"I don't need to repeat myself," I turn my face away from him, "you quite clearly heard what I said." I slam the car door down and head out of the garage and towards the porch.

"You don't understand," Riggs rushes out as he follows me, hot on my heels and the panic is evident in his voice. "Clay ain't someone you can mess around with. My stupid ass brothers don't apply logic to their dumb ass plans," his voice is low, his hot and heavy breaths snort from his nose.

I look past him towards Tripp who is muttering something to Pacey before saying a little louder that he is heading to the office. My eyes flick back towards Riggs.

"I'm not messing with him. He can buy me dinner, I can *innocently* pick his brains... or maybe if I'm not innocent, I can pick a lot more," I snigger knowing full well that'll get under his skin.

Before I can even make it to my front door, I am being pulled and pushed up against the hard cladding of my home, his hips pinning me still as he puts his full weight on me so I am unable to move at all.

"I'm getting a little tired of your bratty behavior."

"Really?" my brows raise, sarcasm dripping from my tone, "Maybe you need to fuck the brat right out of me then."

I watch as his beautiful green eyes widen at my crude words. I feel how his body relaxes against me and I take that as my cue to shove him off me.

"What's the matter Riggs? Cat got your tongue?" I snipe at him, my heart racing in my chest as I knock into him with my shoulder and storm through the front door.

This man is getting on my last nerve.

CHAPTER SEVENTEEN
RIGGS

I stand dumbfounded.

Maybe you need to fuck the brat right out of me then.

Her words replay in my head.

What the fuck.

I mean, honestly, that's all I have thought about. Claiming her and loving her as my own, tracing her skin with my fingertips so I know every mark, every bump and lump, every scratch or scar and down to all of her imperfections. I want to know everything about her. I want to know what her skin feels like beneath my palm, the way her moans fill the room as pleasure takes over, the way her body moves and writhes beneath me. I want to see the glassiness in her eyes, the hollows of her cheeks, the way her pretty fucking lips look when they're locked around me. I want to see and feel everything about her when it comes to Aspen Warren.

I hate the fact that she is going out with Conrad tonight and I am even more pissed that she has agreed to go out with that cunt Clay.

He is no good, we know he is no good, yet dumb and

dumber thought it would be a brilliant idea to use Aspen as bait. He isn't stupid. He will know who she is. She can't lie for shit and it'll take one slip up for him to realise that.

Scrubbing my hand over my face, I groan. I'm so goddamn tired. My days are long and my nights are lonely, except for tonight. Tonight we're going down to the Old Dusty Boot and Aspen is on her date with Conrad. I feel my blood boil beneath my skin.

Fucking Conrad.

I'm not a possessive guy, well, with any other girl I'm not, but when it comes to Aspen I am as possessive as they get. In my head she has always been mine, even after the shit storm that was prom and Pacey taking what I vowed to take and cherish, Aspen was always meant to be mine. I think that's what gutted me the most about that night. I wanted to be her first and her last. I hated that we didn't get to be like that, so instead we ran her out of town because if I couldn't have her, no one could.

Pacey still pines over her now, but we both know she doesn't feel the same. Heck, I don't even know. Aspen is a complex woman, but fuck, she was so goddamn perfect that it hurt to not be able to have her. I hated that she met that idiot back in LA, hated that she was transformed into this sixties stepford wife who stayed home and tended to the house and cooked his fucking meals. When Blue explained her life with him, I thought she was lying, I thought she was telling me this shit to soften the blow that Aspen left and never came back for me. My dad told me to let her go, spread her fucking wings and follow her dreams. But all she ended up getting was the life that my dad feared for her if she stayed with me. She never became a professional show jumper, she didn't make anything of herself except being the fucking arm candy to that prick.

She was a shadow of herself when she showed up back in December. She wasn't the fiery, loving, shoot-for-the-fucking-stars Aspen that we all knew and loved. Everything that she once was disappeared from the moment she left Lovelock Bay, but watching as she transforms back into the girl that left all those years ago is like a fucking dream come true. *My dream come true.*

Showered and dressed, I lift my hat from the back of my door and place it on my head. I trudge down to the bunkhouse and smile when I hear the music playing and the boys singing along.

Opening the door, I smile when I see they're all sitting round the table, Rex is cooking whilst Tyler sings and plays the guitar. The rest of the guys are either drinking beer and listening or drinking beer and playing cards.

"Hey, just checking in," I lift my hat off my head as I take a step further into the bunkhouse.

"Night boss," one of the young lads calls out and I chuckle.

"It's Riggs," I remind him, like I always do. "Don't drink too much, early start tomorrow," I throw them a knowing look then close the door on them when I hear the commotion of them moaning and groaning but they're in good spirits.

Walking back down towards my truck, I unlock it and climb in as I wait for Tripp and Pacey. It's always me that drives. I don't like to drink much, the odd beer here and there or a couple of glasses of whiskey to keep me warm on the cold, winter nights, but I prefer to be in control of myself than be led by poison pumping through my veins, no control over my actions.

Moments pass and I am still waiting for Tripp and

Pacey. I push down on the horn just long enough for my dad to come barrelling down the driveway.

"Riggs!" he shouts and I chuckle, "pack it in!"

"Alright, alright," I shout out the window and lift my hands from the horn. My dad throws his hand up in the air and shakes his head from side to side.

"Damn, I swear my life would be easier if I had three girls," and I laugh louder now.

"And a damn sight more expensive." I honk on the horn again and he flips me off.

Pacey and Tripp finally grace me with their presence, and I roll my eyes in annoyance.

"What took you so long?"

"We wanted to make you wait," Tripp beams and gives me a slap on the back as he sits beside me, Pacey clambering in the back of the truck.

"Come on, we're going to be late," I groan as I push into drive and pull away, the sound of the tires crunching over the drive as I head towards the Boot.

As always, our local is thriving. It sits just on the outskirts of the town and we have been coming here for as long as I can remember. Our parents used to come here every Friday, we would have dinner and then my mom and dad would have a few drinks before walking us back home. But they were always a little more fun once they had a drink or two inside of them.

We didn't have a picture-perfect childhood, but we did have a childhood. Not like kids nowadays being fed an iPad and consoles, kids needed the freedom and fresh air. They needed to get dirty and let their imagination run wild. They needed to be just that, *wild*.

Putting the truck into park, I have zoned out most of the

way and made a few noises here and there to pretend I was listening when in fact all I was focused on was the past. Snapping back into the here and now, my eyes search the car park and I tighten my grip on the steering wheel when I see Conrad's truck parked all snug and I feel my temper rise.

"Calm it," Tripp reaches across the centre of the truck and places his hand on my shoulder, giving it a tight squeeze through the black long-sleeved top I am wearing.

"I am calm," I bite but then soften my tone with a wide smile.

"Oh boy," Pacey whistles as I climb down from the truck and slam the door shut.

I ignore him and lift my cowboy hat from my head as I push my fingers through my tight, long, curly hair. It's unruly but I won't wear my cowboy hat inside the Boot.

Stepping up towards the door, the country music croons through the speakers as I push it open and receive a few hat tilts as me and my brothers walk through the door. This is a small town, everybody knows everybody. A few whispers here and there, some have become a little more cautious since Tripp was assigned sheriff.

Pacey and Tripp head straight to our booth and see Harlow and Austin already sitting there but I stand for a moment as I scan the room for *her*.

My heart spikes when I see her cuddled in the corner with Conrad. I ball my fists by my side and swallow down the bile that is creeping up my throat.

Lowering my eyes and narrowing them in her direction, it's not long before she catches me staring. I clench my jaw, my molars grinding as I try and refrain myself from bolting over there like a mad man. Inhaling, I exhale on a steady breath and walk towards the booth where my brothers, Austin and Harlow sit.

"Oh wow, someone is grumpy tonight," Harlow's voice sounds like nails on a chalkboard, and I shudder. I feel mean because I like Harlow. She is a nice girl and we all grew up together. Her and Aspen used to be best friends until Aspen found out that not only had I slept with her, but she had slept with Austin too. I get it, girl code and all that, but Aspen wasn't a saint. She made Harlow's life hell in the last few months before she left until she completely iced her out. Harlow gave up trying and Aspen moved on with her life, but now they were back living in the same town, something's got to give.

"Don't start," I groan, scrubbing my face and instantly my irritation levels rise.

When my eyes meet with Harlow, she gives me a pout and a wink and I smile back at her.

Daisy, one of the young waitresses, comes over and places down our drinks, scotch on the rocks for me, beer for Pacey, whiskey and coke for Tripp, vodka and orange for Austin and a glass of the cheap white for Harlow.

I lay some notes down on her tray and she gives a curt nod before scampering away.

"We made it through another week," Tripp almost cheers as he moves his drink into the centre, us all following and tapping our glasses together. We have had one hell of a week. I try not to get involved too much with what Tripp and Pacey get up to, but when they need me, I'm ready to go to war. Tripp is a little tighter lipped, he can't tell us everything but he tells us enough. I never want him to jeopardise his job, but some things can't be kept secret when it comes to Lovelock Bay.

"And what a week that was," Pacey chimes in, voicing my thoughts out loud.

"Amen," Austin nods, not that he moves in the same

circle as my brothers, but seeing as Pacey helps sell the horses which Austin breeds and breaks in, he gets it. I take a mouthful of my scotch, wincing slightly when the burn coats my throat.

"Any idea on what the disease was down at Oak Ranch?" I ask, placing my glass on the table and shuffling in my seat. We got told there was a disease that ripped through one of the ranches, killing most of the livestock in a few days.

I hear Pacey sigh, "Nothing as of yet, Harlow is still running tests." Pacey goes silent for a moment as he takes a sip of his beer. "I'm starting to think these are targeted attacks. Firstly, our cows and one of our horses were maimed, plus Clay trying to sell livestock without papers to some out-of-towners and now the cows down at The Oaks? It's all a little bit coincidental."

I hear Austin suck a breath between his teeth.

"What?" my elbows rest on the table.

"It's got to be Clay. We had them suits from out of town a few months ago sniffing around the land, none of us were willing to sell. He made himself pretty damn friendly to them. The only way they could get us to settle is by taking our jobs, all of us are being hit by different things, and it's our animals that are suffering. What's a cowboy with no cows? A horse trainer with no horses? A livestock commissioner with no livestock? A sheriff without his badge?" he pauses for a moment as his eyes float between me and my two brothers who sit beside me.

"Nothing," Tripp grunts.

"Exactly. Our jobs are gone in an instant, no use for the land and with no livestock we have no money. Sure, our parents *have* money, but it'll only go so far." He sits back in his seat opposite us and takes another swig from his beer. "They're trying to push us out."

"Then we need to make sure we don't let them." Pacey pipes up and I can't help but roll my eyes.

"Aspen is going out with Clay on Monday. Who knows what he will say. We've just got to be careful, because once he knows who she is, it's game over. The only saving grace for us here is that Clay moved in as she moved out. There is no way he knows that she is with us," Austin shrugs but it still doesn't sit right with me.

"You're playing with fire."

"Sometimes we need to get burned," Austin glares at me and I think I am just about done with tonight.

CHAPTER EIGHTEEN
ASPEN

My nerves are shot as I sit and anxiously watch the door for Riggs. Conrad is being as sweet as ever, his hands dipping between my thighs and giving me a gentle but reassuring squeeze, his lips brushing against my ear as he whispers sweet nothings, but all I think about is how he isn't Riggs.

His lips are too soft, his hands too smooth. I liked the burn from Riggs' beard between my thighs, the way his full lips grazed against my skin and his callous hands palmed a map that only he knew.

My heart stills for a moment when I see the door open and Riggs steps forward, his eyes scanning the room and I know he is looking for me. Ducking my head down and into Conrad's neck to hide my shameful blush at seeing the guy I have crushed on since I was a kid.

"You okay?" Conrad asks and I nod against his side, inhaling his fresh scent. I inhale deeply as I sit back and keep my eyes pinned to Conrad.

"Thinking..." he trails off for a moment, his picture-perfect smile slipping across his lips as he gazes into my eyes, "how about after here, we go lay on the bed of my truck and just watch the stars?"

My eyes widen and my heart constricts in my chest at the memory of when me and Riggs used to do just that. We used to drive across their fields and down to Crooked Valley where there was nothing around us except rolling hills, mountains and a blanket of stars above us.

"Yeah, sounds good," I manage to squeeze out as I swallow. But I didn't want to stargaze with Conrad. It was always mine and Riggs' thing, connecting us like the constellations we lay under, our hearts threaded. I wasn't ready to let go of that part of us. We never got our happily ever after, but our souls are entwined with the stars, our hearts wrapped in the galaxies.

"Let's get another drink, same again?" he asks turning to face my wine and I nod. "Okay," he murmurs as his lips brush against the top of my head and I wish my heart fluttered in my chest like it did when Riggs kissed me.

Riggs gives me an erratic, galloping heart rate, but with Conrad, it's a flatline. I lift my eyes, finally looking in his direction and that's when his beautiful sage eyes burn into mine.

We hold each other's gaze for only moments, but I feel as if the floor beneath me slips away and sends us free falling into nothingness. Weightless, free, an invisible string linked between him and I slowly gravitating us towards each other, pulling us closer and closer; but the string snaps as soon as Riggs pulls his eyes from mine and suddenly, I am face down on the floor with an unbearable weight crushing in my chest.

I should be sitting over there with my friends. I should have Riggs' hand resting on my thigh, his other arm wrapped around the back of my chair but instead I am sitting as an outsider, watching everything but not being involved and I only have myself to blame.

"Excuse me," I manage as my heart gallops like wild horses and I feel my anxiety begin to slowly suffocate me. I needed out.

"I'll get the drinks," Conrad says softly, and I hate that it's not him my heart yearns for.

I nod, slipping past him and ignore as his finger dusts across the skin of my lower back. I'm wearing a cropped oatmeal jumper and high waisted black jeans with knee-high heeled boots. My hair is down and sits in loose curls that tumble down my back.

Keeping my head down and holding my breath as I walk past their table, their eyes are on me as I push into the restrooms and once I am tucked away I exhale. Running my hands under the cold tap, I pat my hand behind my neck to try to bring my body temperature down. I feel clammy and hot and I know it's because I have got myself in a state. I keep replaying Riggs between my legs, and for some reason it all feels too intimate and makes me feel like I have cheated on Conrad.

I shake it off, grabbing a paper towel and drying my hands when I hear the restroom door go and I know it's Harlow.

I stiffen slightly, standing a little straighter and roll my shoulders back ready for her onslaught but she says nothing. Just stands next to me, her eyes on mine in the reflection of the mirror as the breath catches at the back of my throat.

"Look..." she starts and I break the contact, dropping my head and curling my fingers round the edge of the sink, keeping my lips pressed into a tight line. "I don't want it to be like this between us. Fuck," she pauses for a moment and

I slowly lift my eyes to look at her. Her dark curly brown hair is pulled into a messy ponytail, she wears a knitted mid length dress and her old cowboy boots. "We both done things to hurt each other," and I go to speak but she holds her hand up, "more so me than you…" she gives a small apologetic smile and my lip lifts slightly at one corner. "We were best friends, yes I shouldn't have slept with Riggs or thrown it in your face and I am sorry for sleeping with Austin… it just…"

And now it's my turn to hold my hand up and I slowly turn to face her.

"You have nothing to be sorry for. I was young and naive. Riggs didn't belong to me, he never did and never has. I just was a little cut up because my prom night didn't go the way I wanted it to, that mixed with my accident, I just felt so alone as the visits dwindled into nothing. And when I was well enough to actually leave my room, I found out that you slept with Riggs as well as my brother." I pause and watch as she hides behind her hands, shaking her head from side to side.

"I sound like such a slut," she scoffs and I let out a small laugh as I reach forward and pull her hands from her pretty face.

"No," I snort, "you don't."

She sighs, her head tilting to the side.

"I'm sorry too. I'm sorry for exploding on you, I just…" I trail off and she nods.

"I know."

"I never wanted to fall out with you, God I missed you so much. And when I met Luke, you were the first person I wanted to call but I was too stubborn to make the first move so I am sorry for that too."

I watch as her shoulders visibly relax before she throws

herself at me, her hands pressed against my back as I wrap mine round her slender body.

"Friends?" she whispers, her chin on my shoulder.

"Always."

We walk back to the table hand in hand and I slowly release my grip as we approach her table, I give her one last smile and continue forward to my own table where Conrad sits with a wide grin waiting for me.

"Sorry I was a while, had some bits to sort out," I snort a giggle and he just stands, places a kiss on my cheek and ushers me in beside him.

I knew I could have said so much more to Harlow and I am sure she could have said so much more to me, but what was the point? So many wasted years have passed and for what? We were both always stubborn as mules but I am glad she made the first move.

Settling back in the booth, Conrad talks about his day and what his plans are for the weekend and I just listen, but my eyes are pinned to Riggs. It doesn't matter how much I try and pay attention; Riggs is just too damn distracting.

<hr>

RIGGS

I would be lying if I said I wasn't relieved when I saw Harlow and Aspen walking back hand-in-hand. The boys had a bet going that they would end up fighting. The girls were inseparable before everything went down, but I am glad that they got whatever was needed sorted.

I drain the rest of the glass and hit it down on the table with a little more force than intended.

"I'll be back in a bit," I grunt as I stand up and slide out of the booth and towards the corridor that leads to the restroom. The memories of having Aspen pinned up against this wall flood me and all I can think about is tasting her again. The one time wasn't enough, it will never be enough. Pushing through the door, I go about my business then wash my hands when I see Conrad walk in. My eyes pin to him and I give a low scoff as he walks behind me and stands at the urinals. Drying my hands with the paper towel, I throw it in the bin at the other side of the restroom and then run my fingers through my hair. Fuck, it was such a mess.

I try to keep myself distracted for a moment so my jealousy simmers below boiling point at being in close proximity to him. I can't fuck up the relationship between my family and Austin's because I want what he has.

It would be foolish and reckless.

I hear the sound of Conrad's heavy boots drag across the tiled floor of the restroom as he stands next to me and begins lathering his hands up.

"Am I stepping on your toes at all Riggs?" his tone is not at all malicious, but it does instantly get my back up.

"Sorry?" my brows raise as I turn to face him, my eyes narrowing in on him and my lips pressing into a thin line.

"Being with Aspen? Am I stepping on your toes?" he meets my gaze as his brows sit high in his head.

"Didn't realise you were a *thing* to be honest buddy," I glance away and turn to begin walking towards the exit.

"Damn, you do look pretty when you act dumb," he chuckles, and I hear the sound of his boots thumping behind me.

I stay silent. I will not get into a scuffle with Conrad fucking Stone. He follows me into the corridor.

"Okay so I'm taking your silence as a no, that I am not

stepping on your toes." He continues and I curl my fingers into my palm, my bitten to shit nails digging into my skin. "And if that is the case, I am going to need you to back off and stop with the death glares every time we're together, and I am really going to need you to stop breathing down our necks like an overbearing brother."

"That's fine by me." I swallow the thickness down. "It won't be an issue and you're not stepping on my toes. Aspen doesn't belong to me."

Why have I got to lie.

I'm a fucking idiot.

"That's great. I'm going to slip outta here now anyway; going to take her down to the look-out point at Crooked Valley, lay her on the bed of my truck and watch the stars if you know what I mean," and he fucking belly chuckles.

He may as well be waving a damn red flag before my eyes because I see red like a raging bull. I turn quickly, wrapping my fingers around his throat as I smash his back against the wall and tighten my grip, my eyes volleying back and forth between his and do you know what this cunt does? He fucking smirks at me.

"I fucking knew it man," he laughs, and I loosen my grip in an instant, my eyes widening. "Damn, you're so easy to wind up, but even easier to prove you wrong." I drop my hand from his throat as if his skin has just scalded my palm as Conrad continues laughing, shaking his head, his eyes cast down. I watch as he pushes through the door and back out to where Aspen is sitting.

Shit.

CHAPTER NINETEEN
ASPEN

My fingers drum on the table as I eye the door to where Riggs and Conrad disappeared into approximately—I cast my eyes down at my watch—eleven minutes and fifteen seconds ago.

What if Riggs is telling him about what happened? What if Conrad is antagonising Riggs?

I nibble on my bottom lip when I see the door go and Conrad walks out smiling from ear to ear looking like the damn cat that got the cream. It unnerves me and makes my tummy do an anxious flip.

He slows when he approaches our table, cups his hand round my cheek and turns my face up towards him as his lips hover over mine.

"See ya kiddo," he winks slowly as he steps away from me, my heart stuttering in my chest as my brows pinch and dig into my forehead. Confusion laces my face, my lips part to speak but I can't even string a sentence together.

What the fuck just happened.

I watch as Conrad walks out the door, my eyes not

leaving his back until it shuts behind him. As soon as he is out the door, my eyes glide across to see Riggs standing there, eyes pinned to mine as if I am the only person in his world. My heart thumps. Breaking away, I look towards Harlow who is looking over her shoulder at me and grinning.

Have I missed something?

What the fuck happened in that restroom?

Riggs begins walking over towards me, with each step that brings him closer, my heart thumps that little bit harder.

"Come with me?" he asks, and he seems nervous as he places a hand inside his jean pocket, the other resting on his hip before it lands at his side.

"But..." I mutter but he shakes his head from side to side.

"No buts, leave with me? Take my hand and let me show you the goddamn stars Aspen Warren," his lips slowly break into a smile, his perfect white teeth bearing and his dimples prominent on his beautiful face.

"Show me the stars," I whisper as he holds his hand out for me to take, and I do. Gladly.

RIGGS OPENS my door and I climb into the cab of his truck, nerves swarming me. But the good kind of nerves. The good kind that let you know that this moment is going to change your life forever. He slips in beside me and turns to look at me, the glee in his eyes is evident, his beautiful green eyes sparkle.

"You ready to go Dinks?" My heart aches.

"I am," I roll my lips and drop my face as I smile, my eyes in my lap.

He starts the engine, the rumble of his truck the only noise I can hear and I am grateful that it has silenced my thumping heartbeat. Pulling out onto the quiet roads, the radio kicks in and *Forever After All* by Luke Combes begins playing. My skin tingles as anticipation suffocates me. I know this route like the back of my hand, even after years of being gone, I could find Crooked Valley blindfolded.

I turn to look at Riggs as he pulls off the road and onto the dirt track that takes us across to the look-out point. He seems nervous. One hand is gripped with his fingers wrapped round the steering wheel, the other moves from his thigh, to his mouth before he changes to resting his elbow on the centre armrest and pressing his thumb and index finger to the side of his face.

"What happened between you and Conrad?" I ask, trying to break the tension that is crackling between us.

"Just a little talk," he admits, a small sigh passes his lips and I wonder if he is telling me the truth.

"About?"

He turns to face me and gives me a cheeky smile, his dimples on show once more and I feel my heart skip a beat. I have missed his beautiful smile. I haven't seen his true smile much since I have been back.

"Stepping on toes," he snorts a laugh as he averts his attention back to the road and I smirk, settling into my seat and looking out the window at the clear night sky for the duration of the journey.

Riggs pulls into our old spot and cuts the engine. Silence fills the once music filled car and suddenly I feel awkward. I unbuckle myself, twisting in my seat to face him.

"So," I lick my lips, trying to stop the pull of a smile gracing my lips.

He turns to face me.

"So," he chuckles and unbuckles himself, "shall we go and see the stars?" he asks and I can feel the once innocent Riggs seeping out of him and it makes me giddy. Spending time with Riggs was my favorite thing in the world, apart from riding Blossom of course, but he was my best friend. We did everything together and coming out to Crooked Valley to see the stars was always *our* thing.

Until it wasn't.

I hardly saw the stars back home in LA because of how bright it was, but I missed it. Every time there was a clear night sky and I was lucky enough to see the stars, I wondered if Riggs was looking up at them too. I somehow felt connected to him through the stars; the constellations a map of my heart that only he could see. Riggs Rivera was my very own constellation, the prettiest of them all.

"Let's see the stars," I beam as I excitedly open the truck door and move to the flat bed. Riggs rummages about in the back of the truck before he comes out with two blankets and lays them down on the bed.

"I wasn't prepared for this..." he runs his hand round the back of his head, then lifts his cowboy hat on top.

He passes me a blanket and I climb onto the bed of the truck, laying it down then taking the other from Riggs as I lay them side by side.

"This is perfect," I smile, kneeling on the soft blanket and waiting for him to join me. He groans as he steps up onto the truck, kneeling next to me as he wraps his finger around my wrist, lifting it to his lips and placing a soft kiss on my pulse point. I feel myself relax.

"I only want perfect for you Aspen because you deserve just that."

I can't cope with sweet Riggs. I have been teleported back to when we were helpless teens who knew nothing about this world we lived in, where we were both so silly to think that we would always be together. I never wanted to leave. I wanted to live in this moment forever.

He rolls over, laying on his back as he takes his hat off and lays it on his chest, his knees bent as he gets comfortable. I follow, lying next to him as our fingertips brush, my fingers tapping up as I wait to see if he locks his with mine and within minutes, he does.

The air is crisp, the night is clear, and the stars look beautiful up against the violet night sky. We lay in silence and hours slip past in the blink of an eye. It's not an awkward silence, it's comfortable.

"It's so peaceful out here," I whisper and I roll my head to look at Riggs.

"It is," he mumbles, he sounds tired.

"We can go if you're tired, I know you're up in a few hours," I say softly.

"Baby, I'm not going anywhere. Do you know how long I have waited to be lying next to you like this again? To stargaze with you?"

I nibble on my bottom lip to fight my smile. The once bright moon has been eclipsed by clouds and the stars are becoming harder to spot.

"Maybe the stars have decided for us," I laugh as I sit up slowly, looking out at the view in front of me, the once green fields now blanketed in pitch black.

"Maybe," his fingers find mine again as he locks them together. I scrunch my nose when I feel a drop of rain land on the top of my head and I groan.

I go to move but Riggs tightens his grip.

"Riggs?" I look at him confused.

"I need to make up for when I left you out in the rain," he mutters and I am utterly confused.

"What?" I whisper.

"I fought with myself the whole time you were standing outside my room crying and begging me to come down. All I wanted to do was to run down to you, take your pretty face into my hands and kiss your tears away until you had none left to cry..." he pauses and the breath catches at the back of my throat as the little drop of rain turns into a hundred more.

"Riggs," I breathe.

"Let me kiss you in the rain Aspen," he kneels up and pulls me into him, his hands cupping my face, his eyes falling to my lips as he edges towards me cautiously. My breath stutters, my heart beating along with his deep within my chest, my eyes on his as I fall helplessly into his soul.

"Kiss me in the rain Riggs," I whisper against his lips and before I've even finished his name, his lips are covering mine. His tongue slipping past and caressing mine as he kisses away all the mistakes we both made, the pain that we both put each other through and finally piecing every broken part of us back together to make us whole again. The invisible string that was once slack now pulls tight, knotted and holding us both together. I lean into him, the rain pouring over us through an earth-shattering kiss that leaves both of us panting. He breaks away, his eyes closed and I let out a nervous laugh.

Darting my eyes to the side, I see his cowboy hat and I remember his warning from all those years ago.

"Don't, don't do that," he sounds pained and my heart sinks.

"Why not?"

"You'll belong to me, whether you want it or not and I'm not going to burden you with that. We're friends Aspen, I care a lot about you... too much to tie you to me forever."

The difference now though, is we were already tied together.

My heart gallops and my skin prickles. I reach beside him and lift his hat, hovering it over my now soaked head.

Riggs gives me a knowing look, his lips pressing into a smile.

"You know darlin' as soon as that hat lands on your head, you belong to me, you become mine Wildflower... *forever*"

"Make me yours, Riggs." I just manage to rush out as I let the hat fall onto my head.

His lips crash over mine once more and we're completely unphased that we're kneeling on the back of a truck bed in the pouring rain. We're too lost in each other to notice our clothes are soaked through, tongues dancing, teeth clashing, eyes closed as our hands grope and grab at each other's clothes. I still have Riggs' cowboy hat on and I don't plan on taking it off anytime soon. Something about wearing it and knowing that he has claimed me as his own by the one simple move of wearing his hat fills me with a confidence I have never felt before.

His large hands cling to my waist, his fingers pushing into my skin which makes it pebble under his touch and I feel the heat blossom between my thighs.

Was this finally about to happen? Me and Riggs? My wildest dreams coming true tonight under the stars at our favorite viewpoint.

My hands move to his neck, my fingers wrapping in his wet curls as his fingers skim up my sides, teasing over my side breast before they wrap at the base of my throat and press on the pulse point in my neck. His smile spreads across his lips as he breaks the kiss and I whimper at the loss of his lips on mine.

I gasp in the cool air, my eyes volleying back and forth from his glistening greens.

"Why did you stop?" I ask, my fingers still locked in his hair at the nape of his neck.

"I am just trying to savour every single moment of this night," he smirks, his fingers gripping my chin as he tilts my face up so I have to look at him. "You have no idea how long I have been dreaming of this, how long I have wanted to know how your lips would feel on mine, the way your skin would feel under my fingertips..." he pauses for a moment as he runs his tongue across his bottom lip then pulls it between his teeth. "I know how you taste Wildflower, but I want so much more," he groans and I blush, my cheeks burning and I am grateful that he can't see me blushing under the dark star kissed night.

"I want it all with you too Riggs," I pant, his other hand is resting on my lower back, his fingers drawing circles on my bare skin which causes my skin to prick in goosebumps mixed with the cool spring breeze that seems to have picked up with the rain that coats us.

The smile slips from Riggs' lips for a moment and suddenly I am worried that he is having second thoughts. I sit back, my knees hurting from resting on the truck bed. Riggs moves onto all fours, crawling towards me before he lays me down slowly, so my back is resting on the damp blankets of the truck and I shiver against the coolness on my skin.

"Oh baby," his voice is low and soft, but loud enough to hear over the rain that is belting down onto the truck exterior. "I need to get you warm, I don't want our first time to be the reason for you getting hypothermia."

I giggle as he wraps his arms around me, and I loop my legs around his waist as he stands with ease, his arms tucked under my ass as he walks me to the edge of the truck bed. I lock my arms around his neck and panic courses through me as he jumps from the bed to the ground and I squeeze my eyes shut, fully ready to hit the dirt, but of course he doesn't let me slip out of his arms.

"I've got you," he whispers against my lips as he walks me around to the front of the cab, opening the door and placing me on his driver's seat. I climb over the middle of the truck and wrap myself up in a ball on the passenger seat. Riggs climbs in and I watch as he shudders, lifting his cowboy hat from my soaked head of hair and tossing it into the back.

"Hey, you took my hat," I lick my upper lip and my hazy eyes lock on Riggs'.

"*My* hat princess," he winks as he starts the engine and turns the heating up, the radio playing soft country music.

"I'm yours so the hat is mine okay cowboy?" I shudder as the warm heat from the heater blows onto my skin.

"I feel awful that you're cold, I should have never kept you in the rain," he sighs and breaks his eyes from mine, my heart stammering in my chest.

Pushing to my knees, I climb over the center of the truck once more and straddle myself in his lap, my legs bent on either side of his.

"Baby, don't feel awful. It was the best damn kiss I have ever had," I clasp his face in my hands, lifting his face to look at me as his eyes volley back and forth between mine.

He rolls his lips and I squirm in his lap as I feel his evident bulge in his pants.

Brushing my lips softly against his, I mould into him when his hands grip my hips, holding me in place as I grind my hips over him. I hear the shudder of his breath, my eyes fluttering open to see his eyes wide and pinned to mine.

"I'm never letting you go Dinks; never."

CHAPTER TWENTY
RIGGS

Our lips meet, her fingers fumbling with the hem of my top as her wet, cold hands splay against my hot skin and I suck in a breath as my hand wraps around the back of her head holding her in place. Her gentle fingers skim up the sides of my body before she glides them back down again.

"Let me undress you," she whispers as *cardigan* by Taylor Swift starts playing in the background and I feel her smile against my lips. "Secret Swiftie?" she giggles as she kisses me between words.

"No secret about it," I chuckle as I reluctantly let go of her and she sits up slowly, my hands moving to her damp jeans, squeezing her thighs gently. "You're so beautiful," I rasp and it's the truth. Her sitting here, her skin dewy and glowing with a permanent blush painted onto her cheeks, her freckles that dust over her face, and all I can see when I look at her is the moonlight dancing in her eyes. The stars now hidden behind the clouds and she looks every bit a goddess basking in the darkness that surrounds us.

"So are you," she nibbles on her full cherry red bottom lip and I feel a primal growl vibrate through me.

Her fingers are back and playing with my top, her eyes burning into mine and I could lose myself in her honey golden eyes. Slowly lifting the thick cotton material, I lift my arms as she pulls it over my head and discards it on the passenger seat. I watch her with intent as her soft and playful expression hardens, her eyes trailing down over my chest, her fingers mapping out a trail that only she can see. My heart drums under my skin a little faster now as her feather-like touch brushes through my dark dusting of chest hair and my breath catches at the back of my throat. Her brows pinch and furrow deeply as she traces the scar of my tattoo over my heart, skimming them around in an infinite loop. Her eyes finally lift to meet mine and I can see the pain behind her eyes. She knows my dad's ways. This is no shock to her but it still makes my own heart ache seeing her pained by something that is so natural to me. I instantly miss her gaze when her fingers make their descent and I hear a soft shudder of breath consume her.

"Don't be sad," my voice is low as I grip onto her chin and lift her pretty face to look at me and she meets my eyes with a smile.

Lifting my arm up, my hand is just in front of her face when I watch her eyes center and focus on my wrist and my heart somersaults. Her own hand lifts and her index finger brushes over the black, woven bracelet she gave me the night we sat on the roof to look at the stars. The night we had our first kiss. The night I silently promised her forever.

"You still have it," she whispers, her eyes glassy as they meet mine.

"Always," I breathe and let my fingers graze across her sharp jaw, they brush a strand of her hair over her ear before I let them hook behind her head and pull her lips to mine. She whimpers into my mouth as my spare hand skims up her side, brushing softly against the bare skin between her cropped jumper and waistband of her jeans. She sits back, her beautiful dimples on show as she smiles and now it's my turn. I skim my fingers under the elasticated hem of her jumper and let them trace the back strap of her bra and I feel my cock twitch inside my jeans, rubbing against the zipper.

Drawing small circles on her skin, I lean forward, pressing my lips to the base of her throat and drag them along her collar bone. I curl my fingers back round the hem of her jumper and pull it over her head, my eyes staying on hers as I toss it over on the passenger seat along with mine.

I finally give in to temptation, my chin tucking into my chest as I look at the pure perfection that is straddled on my lap. Her chest heaves up and down, rising and falling as she breathes in shallow breaths. Her tits spill out of the laced white cupped bra that she is wearing and for a moment, anger snipes at me that she may have been wearing this for Conrad. I shut the intrusive thoughts down in an instant and focus on her. It's always been her.

Both hands reach out, kneading and rubbing her full tits that fill my hands nicely. I watch as she tips her head back, a small moan escaping her and filling the car, her scent an intoxicating haze that surrounds us. Pulling the thin lace on the cup of her bra, her nipple pops over the material and I groan as I lower my hot mouth over it; flicking my tongue slowly then letting my warm breath blanket her sensitive skin before taking her breast into my mouth sucking and swirling my tongue once more before popping her pert, hardened nipple from my mouth.

She watches me as I skim my lips across her bursting

chest, licking and nipping at her sweet skin and hooking my finger in the material, pulling it down and covering her other breast with my mouth, giving it the same attention. Her back arches, her hands resting behind her on my thighs as I slowly suck and lick her nipple. Pulling away, I sit back and just admire her for a moment, her chest rising and falling, her bra pushing her full tits up higher and her nipples hard from the warmth of my mouth.

Curling my palm into her hip, my other hand glides up her stomach, past her sternum and up round her neck for just a moment before I glide my fingertips across her collar bone, and up and over her shoulder. I drag them down the back of her shoulder blade, dipping between them and unhooking her bra, smirking as it falls away from her beautiful body.

Edging closer to her, her hands link round the back of my neck as I press my lips on the side of her neck, her pulse quickening under my mouth. Gliding them past her collar bone I focus on her nipples, teasing, licking and biting softly on her sensitive skin and her hips roll over my erection. I am so hard for Aspen that I am afraid I am going to nut in my boxers.

She kneels up, unbuttoning her jeans and my greedy hands are wrapped in her waistband, tugging her jeans down her long, toned legs before her lace covered pussy is back on my lap.

"You're going to be the death of me," I groan, the back of my head resting on the headrest of my seat as she begins to circle her hips, her pussy rubbing over my hard cock.

She gives me a slow wink and I can't wait anymore. My calloused hands grip her waist, lifting her off me as I slide down the seat and internally kicking myself for us being on the driver's side. I hover her lace covered pussy over my face and I hear her gasp.

"Riggs," she wriggles over me, but I just let out a low chuckle and pin her exactly where I want her. Being mindful of the pedals, I move her pussy closer to my mouth, breathing a little heavier as my lips brush over the thin lace and graze her pussy.

Her breath catches and I smile before nipping her panties, teasing her with my tongue as I swipe it through her pussy without moving them to the side. I love teasing her, watching her pant and wriggle because she is desperate for me.

"Patience Wildflower," I growl, uncurling one of my hands from her waist to skim them down her thigh, grazing my fingertips across her thin material as I continue to tease her.

"I'm so wet for you," her face falls forward, her eyes meeting mine as I steady my gaze on her.

"I know baby," I smile as I slip a finger in the side of her panties, rubbing over her swollen clit and a guttural noise vibrates through me, my throat bobbing as I feel my mouth begin to water knowing full well that her pretty pink pussy is going to be over my mouth at any moment. Gliding my finger through her parted pussy lips, I tease a finger at her opening before dragging them back to her clit as I continue rubbing. My cock is aching between my legs and all I can think about is sinking my thick dick into her tight cunt.

I know how good she tastes and how amazing she feels around my fingers, but her tight cunt is going to feel phenomenal when it's wrapped around my cock.

I plunge two fingers into her without warning and her back arches, her head falling back as pleasure explodes deep inside of her. Her hips buck and just as they do, I tug her soaked little panties to the side and swipe my tongue over her clit, massaging her as I fuck her with my fingers, curling them up to rub her g-spot, my tongue gliding back and forth as I bury myself deeper into her. Her skin glistens as the warmth of the heater in my truck makes her sweat, my eyes on her, watching as she begins to crumble above me.

"Don't come," I break away, her arousal coating my lips and my fingers are still buried inside of her as I slip another finger into her and she sucks in a breath as her pussy stretches around me.

"I can't… Riggs," she moans, panting between her words.

"Don't. Fucking. Come," my voice is full of gravel, my tone flat as I command her.

"Then stop," she begs, her voice almost pained and I smile against her wet little pussy, my fingers coated in her arousal as they slip in and out of her with ease.

"Not a fucking chance." Groaning, I press my lips into the crease between her lips and her groin, moving them across the inside of her thighs as I slip my fingers from her and move myself up but I don't let her move. Sitting back in my original position, my hand presses against her chest as I push her onto the steering wheel and move my chair back so we have a little more room.

"Lift your hips for me," I ask, my eyes falling to between our bodies to her glistening cunt. She does as I ask.

My fingers rub against her clit once more, her hands on my chest as she pushes against me, her head forward as she tries to steady her breathing while I slip two of my fingers inside of her hot pussy. The fingers of my other hand fumbling with the button of my own jeans and within minutes, my cock is free and resting against my stomach.

Her mouth gapes, her eyes slightly wide as she takes in my size.

"Riggs, it's not going to…" She moans as I stroke her g-spot again, curling my fingers and drawing her focus on that.

"It'll fit, I'll fucking make it fit. You were made for me Aspen, every part of you was made for me," my thumb pad rubs against her swollen clit and she whines, I feel her pussy tighten and pulse around my fingers. "Don't Aspen, I mean it," I warn, my tone sharp as my eyes pin to hers.

I cover her mouth with mine, my tongue sweeping in as I match my strokes with the same pace as my fingers which causes her to moan into my mouth. Pre-cum seeps from my tip and I groan, slipping myself out of her and rubbing her arousal on the thick head of my cock. Not that I need any lubricant, she is fucking soaked.

My hands are on her hips, my lips moving from her mouth as I tug her bottom lip with my teeth before grazing them across her neck.

"Wildflower…" I rasp against her hot, silky skin.

"Yes," she whispers, her breath raspy, two fingers sinking back inside of her briefly.

"I'm going to fuck you now," and she whines as I slip my fingers from her, rubbing the head of my cock over her clit and dragging it through her wet pussy. I edge my thick head into her tight opening; fuck, she feels so fucking good, I edge a little more into her, teasing her as I slip in and out and suddenly, I panic.

"Wait," I pant and her mouth drops open, her eyes already filled with lust and want.

"Condom," She breathes, disappointment surging through me that we could have been reckless.

"I don't carry them..." I pause and I go back to tease her with my fingers, circling and rubbing in a slow and teasing manner.

"I haven't been with anyone since Luke," she breathes, her head rolling forward as her breath catches, "and I can't even remember the last time we did it." I hate that she is saying his name moments before we seal our fate.

"I'm clean," I rasp, rushing the words out, my fingers still working her up, keeping her ready as wetness pools between her legs, her arousal dripping down my fingers. "I haven't been with anyone in a couple of years, and before those, it was Harlow..." I feel Aspen stiffen at her name. Even saying her name causes my own rage to burn deep inside of me even though I know it was nothing but one night. I didn't feel anything for her, I have never felt anything for anyone but Aspen. "It's always been you," I remind her in a whisper, the truck only filled with the shallow pants of her and the rain beating down on the windshield.

Her eyes are wide when I finally allow myself to look at her, but then I replay what I said; years ago.

Years.

Shit.

"Fuck me Riggs, make me yours... please," she begs, her eyes flutter shut and I take my fingers from her and line my cock back at her opening, and with one, slow but hard roll of my hips, I claim her as my own. Stretching her in the most delicious way and her nails dig into my shoulders as she whimpers.

"You're doing so well baby, just a little more..." I grit my teeth as I roll into her once more, her head falling back as I fill her to the hilt. "Aspen, baby..." I can barely control my emotions in this moment, her face lifts, her honey eyes on mine as I cup her face with one of my hands, my thumb pad sweeping a tear from her cheek, her lips parted as she hangs on my every word.

"You're my wildest love, my wildest dreams and my wildest forever."

CHAPTER TWENTY-ONE
ASPEN

Years.

He said years.

He hasn't been with anyone in years.

I stare, blinking as words fail me. Every time I go to open my mouth, I shut it instantly.

"It's always been you," and I feel my heart lurch in my chest, thrashing around as the words I have always wanted to hear from Riggs' mouth finally fall from his lips.

I shudder on my intake of breath, so wrapped up in this moment that I want him and only him.

"Fuck me Riggs, make me yours... please," I practically beg as heat swarms between my thighs, sweat pricking on my silky skin as I flutter my eyes shut, the tip of his cock nudging into me.

Slowly he rolls his hips up and sinks a little further and my lips form in an 'o'. My fingers wrap over his bare shoulders, my nails hooking into his warm skin as pleasure courses through me and causes a whimper to pass through my lips. He stretches me in the most delicious way. He steadies himself for a moment before edging further into me.

"You're doing so well baby, just a little more..." he grits, his jaw wound tight and in one swift move he fills me to the hilt making me gasp for breath at how amazing he feels deep inside of me.

Neither one of us moves, my heart combusting in my chest as the tension in my lower tummy begins to unravel.

"Aspen, baby..." he croaks, an evident crack in his voice and I let my face lift to look at him as I focus on my own breathing. His large hand cupping my face as his eyes burn into mine and I hadn't even realised tears had left my eyes until I feel his callous thumb swipe away a tear that runs down my cheek, my lips part as his green pools volley back and forth between mine.

"You're my wildest love, my wildest dreams and my wildest forever."

"Always," I pant as I roll my hips over him, his cock buried deep inside of me as I find my own rhythm. His fingers skim down my sides then wrap around my hips as he holds onto me, a slight sting from where he is gripping me tightly. He begins to move beneath me, meeting every roll of my hips and after a moment he lifts me up and down his length. I feel the bubbles begin to pop and rise in my tummy, my skin splintering in shivers, goosebumps blanketing me as I feel the heat consume me, flames licking at my skin. My orgasm teeters on the edge of the cliff overlooking the deep blue sea and I am so close and ready to just free fall into the depths of the pleasure pool that is Riggs.

"Keep going," I pant, lifting one of my hands from Riggs' shoulders, I skim it between my legs and rub my clit, widening my legs and a moan vibrates through me as he sinks even deeper, the head of his thick cock rubbing the ache that pulsated deep within me.

"Riggs," I whisper, my eyes locked on his sage green beauties and one of his large hands wraps around the base of my throat as we lose ourself in this silent rhythm, the soft sounds of the radio filling the car which is mixed with our moans and groans as pleasure swallows us whole. My body begins to tremble under Riggs' grip, my pulse quickening and my heart slamming against my chest as Riggs smiles at me, his breaths shallow as he gasps, fingers digging into my skin. "Fuck, Aspen, I'm gonna... shit," he rasps, his eyes rolling as his thrusts slow to deep, hard pounds into me.

"Me too," I just about manage as I come, my orgasm shattering and obliterating me into a thousand pieces as I wait for Riggs to scoop me back up and carefully put me back together again. My body shakes as I ride out my orgasm. My pussy tightening and pulsing round Riggs' thick cock as he empties himself deep inside of me.

Crimson pinches at my skin, my hands slowly gliding up his bare torso as my fingers loop round his scars, drawing a heart that only he can feel.

His arms circle my waist, pulling me closer to him as we both sit in comfortable silence, our hearts racing against each other and it's back to being just me, Riggs and the stars.

RIGGS SLOWS as he pulls into my driveway, the tires crunching across the gravelled drive. His hand has been resting between my thighs the entire drive, the odd stare at me when we halt at stoplights, his lips pulling at the corner and all I can do is smile back as my cheeks burn with a cherry red blush. The truck rolls to a halt and my heart skips in my chest as I unbuckle myself and twist to face Riggs.

"Thank you for tonight..." I drop my head and smirk, hidden by the shadows. Within seconds, his fingers are gripping my chin and lifting my face up so I'm no longer hidden.

"Baby," he rasps, smiling, his eyes exploring my face, "you don't need to thank me..." my chest rises and falls as my breaths become a little shallower.

He leans across and softly brushes his lips against mine, the fire that was gently crackling away was now a burning ember slowly losing its control in the depths of me. I let my tongue explore his mouth as our kiss deepens, his fingers loosening their grip on my chin but his hand scoops round the back of my head as he holds me in place, our kiss slow as we savour every second that passes in the moment.

It was the perfect kiss for the perfect night.

Reluctantly, I pull away and I hear him suck in a breath as I do, his hand still firmly in place.

"I better get going," I whisper as *Wild Love* by James Bay begins to play through the radio, my skin prickling in goosebumps as Riggs breaks his eye contact and gives a gentle nod. My heart thrums in my chest, the thought of leaving him makes my soul ache but I know I have to.

"See you soon then?" Riggs smiles as he settles back in his seat, and my own smile grows.

"See you soon then," I nod, a nervous girl-like giggle bubbling out of me as I open the door and jump out the truck.

I hover for a moment, turning to get one last look at

him in the cab of his truck, a glowing aura around him and I know it's from the dim streetlamps that my dad put in place for my fear of the dark. But his aura is pure and wholesome and even without the streetlamps I can see how it radiates from him. I feel myself gravitate towards him, and all I want to do is tie myself to him, tie our souls together so we're in an infinite bond that no one can ever break.

"You are beautiful Riggs Rivera," I whisper into the darkness before closing the door behind me and practically skipping through the front door.

Sneaking upstairs, I miss the creaky floorboard as I slip into my room and press it closed softly.

My eyes cast to the time, it's just after midnight and I smile as my mind retraces over the night's events, the way his mouth was on mine, the way his fingers played me as if he was the only man to have ever touched me in that way. I nibble on my bottom lip, suddenly feeling hot and flushed.

Lifting my jumper over my head, I bring it to my nose and inhale deeply as Riggs' scent consumes me. I walk towards my bathroom and drop my clothes into the wash hamper. Turning the faucet, the water grumbles and bangs through the pipes. I wait for a moment or two for the hot water to kick in, so I skim across to the mirror that hangs over the sink and I look back at myself. I look so different than I did when I turned up here four months ago. I feel better, look healthier and my skin has a natural glow to it without the need for thick foundation to give me what I have now and the constant need I felt to be picture perfect no longer plagues me. My skin is a little dryer, my lips a little more chapped, but my eyes are bright and full of life, my heart even feels as if it beats a little harder in my chest each day I've been back here. And I realise it's because I have found myself again, I am back home where I am loved and where I love to be.

I left a sad, broken-hearted young girl but I have returned strong, still a little broken woman.

But I am happy. I am loved.

And for a few years, I forgot what feeling loved truly felt like.

DRESSED in an oversized tee and stone-coloured leggings, my feet are snug in my slippers. The mornings are still a little cool and I am snuggled in my dad's office sitting in front of my laptop. My fingers are curled around a mug of cocoa as I read back over what I had written a few days ago. Sighing, I play *exile* by Taylor Swift featuring Bon Iver as I let the music pulse through me, my heart thumping against my chest as the words echo around my mind. The lyrics feel so raw to me suddenly because of how me and Riggs started and how we just existed in a world without each other for a while. It had always been Riggs. Even when I was with Luke, Riggs was always my first thought of a morning and my last one of an evening, I just didn't let the thoughts linger for too long.

My fingers begin dancing over the keys, my head cocking to the side slightly as I lose myself in this fictional world that comes from a locked safe place, tucked away in the depths of my heart, the story of me and Riggs. The one I'd let myself play out in my mind on lonely nights. The one where we didn't leave each other. The one where he did show for prom. The one where we got our happily ever after.

Engrossed, I didn't even realise that footsteps had

approached behind me until I felt his arms skim around my waist, his head brushing against the top of my head and I smile, my skin prickling and my insides warm and cosy.

"Hey you," Riggs' voice is low and raspy, one of my favorites.

"Hey you," I mimic and spin around in my chair to see him, but not before locking my laptop screen.

"You okay?" he asks as he falls into the seat opposite me, a silly ass grin on his face.

"I am," I reach for my cocoa and turn my attention to him once more. "Are you?"

"Darlin' I am perfect," his smile widens, and I can't help but widen mine, my jaw aching.

"Why are you hiding out in here? Not busy?"

"Wildflower, I am always busy, but I couldn't not come here and pop in to see my favorite girl," he winks and my heart swells to double its size. *Favorite girl.*

"Don't think your daddy will be too happy with your slacking," I smirk, a giggle bubbling from me as Riggs stands and slowly closes the gap between us. My breath catches in the back of my throat, my lips parting.

"I don't care about what my daddy thinks," he rasps, his large hands wrapping around the arms of my chair, his lips hovering before mine. "Do you?" he asks, and I am rendered speechless. Just as his lips are about to cover mine, we hear the front door bang and Riggs jumps back, his hand now round the back of his head as he begins pacing the room.

"Riggs, you in here?" Austin shouts out as Riggs moves towards his voice, but before he disappears, he looks over his shoulder and winks.

"Yeah, I'm here," he groans, his grumpiness back in full force and I giggle to myself as I swing back round to face my laptop and a blissful sigh slips from my lips. Unlocking my laptop, I go over where I stopped and picked up the pace with ease.

CHAPTER TWENTY-TWO
RIGGS

Storming down the hallway of the Warren's house and towards Austin, I slip my mask back on and go back to the grumpy asshole cowboy they all know and loathe. My lips twitch at the thought of her wide eyes, her innocence seeping out of her, her beautiful full lips pursed and ready for me and then Austin fucking ruined it.

"What?" I snap as I meet Austin in the doorway.

"Don't 'what' me." He huffs, turning and walking down the steps with a speed that contradicts his usually laid back manner.

I scoff, following him until we're out front, our boots on the dusty gravel drive. Austin seems uncomfortable, his eyes wild as he struggles to focus on just one thing, one hand pressed to his hip, the other running through his dirty blond hair.

"What's wrong?" I ask, worry bubbles deep inside of me but I don't let him know that.

"Something is brewing," he rushes out, his hand now dragging down the side of his face.

"What do you mean? With Clay?" my eyes bounce back and forth as I watch him. He is agitated.

He shakes his head from side to side.

"Pacey was in a meeting with Tripp and Marty at the town hall discussing the little issues we have been facing," he pauses for a moment.

"Right?"

"The suits are back, they've already acquired Bluebeak Ranch," he mutters, his eyes bloodshot and I can see the panic that looks back at me.

"The fuck!" I roar, pulling my hat from the top of my head and running my own hand through my curly hair.

"They're going for The Oak," he utters and I pale.

"What the fuck happened to solidarity between the ranches?"

"I have no idea man, but they're moving in... it won't be long," he rambles and I feel my own anxiety begin to claw at my throat.

"It's fine. I'll ride down and talk to Tom, he won't sell. He is having his hand forced and isn't it funny that the first ranch that has rolled over to these assholes is Bluebeak?" I grunt, placing my hat back on my head and storming across the fields.

"Where are the guys now?" I turn round and call out as Austin stays back.

"On their way home I presume."

I nod, turning forward and marching back to the ranch.

These suits can fuck off.

They won't get these ranches.

They won't get our land.

They won't get anything from me.

I would lay my body down and sacrifice myself and

even then, even over my dead body, they still wouldn't get them.

SADDLING UP, I call on Hudson to help me. One of the older cowboys, but one of the only ones I can trust too.

"You ready to go?" I ask as I widen the rein on my dark dun and kick her forward. We all have our own horses, but I'm greedy and have two. Raff and Travis.

Raff is a dark dun Quarter Horse, and Travis is a chestnut mustang.

"Ready as I'll ever be boss," he gives me a curt nod and kicks his own horse forward.

"Then let's go," I click my tongue to the roof of my mouth and kick Raff on as we canter out the large open area and onto the fields. As we gallop alongside the fence line, I see Tripp and Pacey stop the truck, glaring at me as they get out. I slow up, bringing Raff to a halt and circling back round.

"You have fire in your eyes," Tripp says with a knowing smirk.

"You know me brother," I throw a wink in his direction and circle round again. Raff is picking up on my brewing anxiety and can't stand still.

"Where is Marty?"

"Heading back to the offices."

I give a steady nod.

"Want us to come?" Pacey asks.

"I mean, a little back up wouldn't go amiss." I chuckle and tighten my grip on the reins.

"See you at The Oaks."

"See you there," I nod and kick on, Hudson close the

whole time as we ride down to Tom's ranch. He and my father are of similar age, his ranch is a lot smaller than ours and they have sheep and goats, not one cow in sight. Rivera Ranch is the biggest cattle ranch on this side of the state and it took decades to get the reputation we did. People know who we are, my great grandfather built this ranch from the ground up and it's grown stronger ever since. I am proud of my heritage and our land and I am not about to roll over so some suit can come in and destroy everything we have all worked so hard to build.

I am lost in my own thoughts, rage boiling through me, passion coursing through my veins and for just a moment, my thoughts move to Aspen and every emotion that had just consumed me suddenly quietens down. All I can feel is her.

Slowing Raff down, I loosen the reins as I approach Tom's land. His gate is shut which is unusual. Hudson hops down and unhooks the gate, pushing it wide as I kick my horse on, Hudson by my side within seconds on his.

My lips twitch when I hear the sound of the tires crunching down the gravel of The Oaks driveway and I am glad that my brothers are here. I slow again when I see Tom approach, his cowboy hat firmly on his head. I cross my hands over the horn, my horse's rein softly looped over one of my gloved fingers, but his neck is stretched and grazing on the grass.

"What do I owe the pleasure of having Riggs Rivera on my property?" Tom side-eyes Pacey and Tripp who are walking towards where we stand. I can't help but notice a little bit of bitterness in Tom's tone and it suddenly gets my back up. "And the Sheriff?" His brows raise.

"We're neighbors are we not? Friends I thought?" I cock my head to the side, reaching up and taking my black sunglasses off, folding them down and placing them between my hands as they go back to resting on my saddle.

"I wouldn't say friends," Tom grumbles as he takes another step forward.

"You're right there," I chuckle softly, Pacey leaning against Raff's shoulder, Tripp standing just a little further left of us. "Friends don't fuck each other over, Tom," my voice is steady as I keep my eyes on him and I watch as he shrinks slightly, his head dropping.

"I don't have a choice Riggs. We're not a huge ranch like you guys up at Rivera. Business is dying, there isn't a need for wool and meat at the moment... and after the disease that broke out... well," he rubs the back of his head.

"We both know it wasn't a disease," Tripp growls.

Tom's head snaps up, his icy gaze narrowing on Tripp, falling to his badge before they settle on his eyes once more.

"What?"

"There is a certain puppet master that is orchestrating all of this... funny how the *diseased* ranch was the first to sell, hm?" Pacey's brows raise as he takes a step closer towards Tom.

"We're being fucked over Tom, and you rolling over and selling off the land is you being submissive." I growl, "You might as well buy the strap on and let them fuck you with it."

Pacey drops his head and lets out a low rumble of a laugh.

"Riggs," Tripp rolls his eyes, his tone coated in a soft warning.

"Just stating facts," I grunt, shuffling in my horse's saddle and he moves forward.

Tom's eyes move between me and my brothers, seconds passing between each fixed gaze.

"Don't sell," I feel my heart quicken when Tom's dark brown eyes settle on me.

"Riggs," the crack in his voice evident as he eyes the ground.

"Let us help, we can get the herd moving. Pacey and Marty will help where they can to get the meat shifted as well as the wool. We're a family, us ranchers need to stay together. We can't let the suits win..." I trail off and I hear the heavy sigh leave Tom, his shoulders sagging. It was the truth. We were all family. Especially Tom. He was never blessed with children, so my dad used to throw us down here a couple of days a week to help him out which he was always grateful for and when his wife died suddenly, we all surrounded him to remind him that he wasn't alone. We were ranchers, and ranchers are for life. *Family.*

"I'm too old for all of this shit." He admits on a grumble.

"Let us buy the ranch, nothing will change, we're just securing it," I feel Tripp's eyes on me and even I am wondering why I have just offered to buy a sinking fucking ranch that is hemorrhaging money.

"What the fuck?" I hear Pacey whisper under his breath, but I ignore it. They can grill me later.

Tom takes a moment to mull it over, his eyes on me the entire time.

"Look, sleep on it, but just promise me one thing... don't fucking sell to the suits."

I watch as Tom steps forward, the sound of his boots on the gravel crunching beneath him. He looks up at me on my horse, lifts his hat from his head as he holds it across his chest and holds his hand out for me to shake.

"You got yourself a deal, son," he nods, and I don't miss the way his eyes glass over.

"I'll get the contracts drawn up and over by end of the

day tomorrow. Sit tight, keep quiet and I mean it, not a word on this."

"My lips are sealed," he gives me a nod and places his hat back on his head.

"We will see you tomorrow," I return his nod then slip my glasses back in place and kick Raff forward, Hudson following.

I know I am going to get it in the neck from Pacey and Tripp but at this moment, I give no fucks.

I did what was right and they both know that deep down.

Live by the ranch, die by the ranch.

PUTTING THE HORSES AWAY, I head off to the bunkhouse to sink a couple of beers with the guys. I feel like I haven't been around them much lately as everything else has consumed all my time. Pushing the door, they all groan and grunt something in the form of a *hello* and I drag a chair out, twisting it round and straddling it as I sit.

"Do your rounds tomorrow and take the day off, it's Sunday after all. God's day of rest," I sigh, taking my hat off and placing it on the floor beside me.

A few of them whisper amongst themselves, a couple stay quiet.

"If you've got something to say just say it," I grit, my eyes moving from each of them.

"Any reason?" Billy pipes up.

"I felt like being nice," I shrug my shoulders up and they chuckle.

"Riggs Rivera being nice... is there a special lady that might be making you nice?" Paul chimes and the bunkhouse explodes and I just shake my head from side to side as I fight to hide my smile.

"Give it a rest will ya," I laugh, taking a bottle of beer off Hudson and sinking it in one.

I reach for another and this time, I savour it.

I've missed the ambience in here, it feels like home somehow. This life is all I have known.

I ROLL out of bed with a groan. I sunk one too many beers last night and after having to stop myself from knocking on Aspen's door. All I wanted was to slip into her bed and hold her in my arms so I could bury my nose in her hair and rest my head against her chest so I could listen to the steady beat of her heart. But I spent the night alone, my dreams filled with her and only her.

Pacing downstairs, I see my dad and my brothers all sitting at the table and I know they've ratted on me.

"Morning," I say, pushing the button on the coffee machine and watching as it fills my cup.

"Why are you interfering and buying Tom's ranch?" my dad's cold tone fills the room.

I sigh, spinning on my heel.

"Because I want to. He is being forced out, he is the first and when all our neighbors hear that he sold, they'll follow. These suits are not stupid, they know what they're doing. They've already bought Bluebeak, and once the ball gets rolling, we won't be able to stop it. So," I walk and get the creamer from the fridge and splash a bit in my cup before adding a sugar, "I bought it, I have my own money and nothing will change. Just helping Tom out like we have always helped him out." My eyes steady on my dad as I bring my mug to my lips, blowing for just a moment as I take a mouthful and groan in appreciation as the coffee wakes my tired, grouchy soul.

"I appreciate and respect what you're doing Riggs, I'm just a little..." he pauses on a heavy exhale.

"I know dad, and I get it... I really do. But let me do this, let me save our neighboring ranch. We're in a position to help, if it's not us buying it, the suits will and then it's game over. It's bad enough Clay has sold, but this just cements the fact that he has his fingers in many pies." Fury rages through me at the thought of Clay and that Aspen is meant to be going on her little *date* tomorrow evening. I growl.

I hear my dad sigh, no words are spoken from his lips but I hear the quiet rumbles from my brothers.

"Speak up, I can't hear you," I bark, annoyance brimming with rage and their heads snap up.

"We back you," Tripp nods before turning to look at Pacey.

"We do," he smiles and now I am hanging on the silence from my dad. I'm a grown ass man, but I still like my dad's blessing. I want him to be proud of everything I do and achieve and without it, it feels wrong.

"Just be careful Tripp, we don't need people making noise surrounding you and your authority over certain things," I give a curt nod in his direction as a warning. We all know what the towns people will think if the sheriff gets too involved. He returns a bob of his head back to me in a silent agreement.

"Let's get the contract drafted. Tom's family." My dad finally says and relief swarms me.

I stroll across to the table and pull out a chair, sitting with my brothers and dad as we start working out our plan.

Once we're done and contracts have been signed, I am going to see *my* girl.

We all go to Tom's, minus Tripp but we're still a united front. If these pieces of shit are watching, we will give them something to watch. The truck rolls to a stop and I push it into park. Hopping out, my dad jumps out the passenger side and my brothers leave the truck from the back. My heart thumps a little louder in my chest and I can hear the blood thrashing in my ears. I am just grateful Tom gave us the go ahead, at least it's two ranches I know I can save.

Two is better than losing them all.

I slow as we approach the front door, climbing the two steps up to the front door. Tom's ranch is worn and weathered. The wooden panels that were once white were now slightly gray and peeling. It'll look brand new with a lick of paint. That's one of the first jobs I'll be starting once the The Oaks is officially mine. I lift my gloved hand and knock on the door, my brows pinching in confusion when the old, crooked door creaks open.

"Tom?" I call out, then turn to look over my shoulder at my dad and brothers. The grimace apparent on my dad's face and his eyes tell me everything I needed confirming, I just didn't want to believe it.

I step inside, walking down the long, dark and narrow hallway until I come to the lounge and my heart drops from my chest, my throat thick when I see Tom sitting in the armchair, his fingers linked together and his hands resting on his stomach.

He looks so peaceful, heartbreakingly peaceful.

"Shit," I grit, my voice cracking and I feel emotion swarm me. I sniff, lifting my hat from my head and placing it over my chest as I send a silent prayer above.

"Call the sheriff," I roll my lips as I turn and walk out of the house because suddenly, I feel like I am suffocating.

As soon as I am outside, the fresh spring air hits me before I collapse on the steps, my hat still in my hands as grief hits me like a freight train.

"FUCK!" Anger consumes me, my throat hoarse from my screaming.

I'm not alone long when Pacey sits beside me, patting me on the back before rolling and squeezing my shoulder in a comforting way.

"You okay?"

I nod, unable to speak.

"Shocked?"

Another nod.

I go to speak but change my mind, rolling and pressing my lips tight.

My dad walks out, shaking his head softly and I watch as he leans over the battered wooden railing that boxes round the small house.

"Tripp is on his way," my dad mutters.

"I've got to go," I finally manage, rushing towards my truck. Turning the ignition on, I boot out of the lot and ignore the screeching of my tires. I don't even care that I have left my brother and dad eating my dust. I needed out.

Abandoning the truck outside my house, I climb the fence and walk the fence line down to the only place I feel any comfort, to the only person I can bear to be near at the moment. I don't even know if she is in, but that still doesn't stop me from heading there.

I push through the paddock fence and I hear her giggles coming from the stables. My skin pricks as I lean against the frame of the sliding paddock door and I wait for her to come into view.

I am not waiting long before I see the pure beauty that is Aspen. She's throwing hay at her brother, and I am in awe watching how carefree she is. Austin catches me staring at her before she does and I swallow down the thickness in my throat.

"Riggs," his voice echoes through the empty stalls and I wait for her eyes to find mine, my heart skipping a beat.

"Hey man," I clear my throat and step over the threshold.

"You okay? How did it go with Tom?" he asks and I can't even get the words out. I just freeze on the spot.

"Can you give me and your sister a minute..." I try so hard to not let my voice crack and give myself away.

"Yeah sure, no problem," Austin looks over at Aspen and she shrugs her shoulders up but she is still wearing her pretty little smile and my heart soars in my chest.

Austin walks past me, gripping my shoulder as he does and I just give him a gentle nod. I let my eyes follow him over my shoulder and once I know he is gone, I turn to face my girl.

"You okay Riggs?" she asks as she stands up, her hands on her hips as her pretty little face tilts to the side and her beautiful eyes widen slightly.

"No Dinks... I'm not..." I just about manage and the crack in my voice is so clear now that I can't even hide it if I wanted to.

She begins to walk towards me, but I'm also walking towards her and I throw myself into her open arms as she embraces me. And only when I am in her arms, do I feel like I can breathe.

CHAPTER TWENTY-THREE
ASPEN

Resting against the hay bales, Riggs' head is on my lap. He hasn't told me what is wrong, I just knew he needed me. I run my fingers through his curly hair, fixated on the tight curls that wrap around my fingers so perfectly. The evening is drawing in, the coolness filling the stalls but neither of us move.

"Wanna talk about it?" I ask, dipping my head to look at him.

I hear him sigh as he shuffles slightly so he is now looking up at me, his head still on my lower stomach.

"Your stomach is making some weird noises," he smirks and I swat him round the back of the head which causes a low grumble to vibrate through him.

"I was on about why you're clinging to me like I am your lifeline."

"Because Aspen, you are my lifeline."

I smile wholly down at him and I feel a tear roll down my cheek but swipe it away quickly.

"That still doesn't answer my question," a small laugh escapes me.

"I found out that Tom passed away earlier today…" he pauses and I feel his body shudder, his breath shaky.

"I'm so sorry Riggs," I whisper, my fingers back to locking in his hair.

"It's life, it happens… I just wasn't expecting it so suddenly. I saw him yesterday, I was going to buy his ranch and now he's just…" he pauses and my heart aches.

"Gone," I whisper into the cool air and Riggs nods.

"I have no idea what I'm going to do about this shit show now," Riggs sits up, his whole demeanour changing in an instant.

"What are your options?"

"Take down Clay," he grunts as he pushes from the floor and pulls me up with him.

"And how you going to do that big boy?" I ask in a playful manner, my fingers skimming across the waistband of his jeans, trying to relight any other form of emotion from Riggs than anger.

I hear the low growl as he swoops me up in his arms and I let out a loud, shrill giggle as I circle my legs around his waist before he pushes me against the hay bale.

"Don't you worry about that Wildflower," he winks before his lips are on mine.

I STAND LEANING over the paddock fence as I watch Austin readying the girls for the stallions.

"Wanna help?" he asks as he passes one of the mares to Harlow and she smiles at him.

"No thanks," I smile but on the inside fear is consuming me whole.

"I could really do with some help," he pleads but I shake my head from side to side.

"Fine," he rolls his eyes before focusing back on the one he has always had a thing for. My old best friend. Harlow Ballerini.

They have a quiet conversation between the both of them, I squint slightly as the low sun rises a little higher and I push my sunglasses onto my face so I can continue watching them. The stolen glances, the small giggles that erupt between them and the odd finger brushing.

I'm not watching them long when I see Harlow walking towards me. A slither of a smile graces my lips as she leans over the fence on the opposite side.

"Hey," she beams and she is honestly like a ray of sunshine.

"Hey," I half laugh then look behind her to see Austin standing just staring at us both.

"I feel like we need a girls' night, it's been so long and well, after everything I would really like to spend an evening with you if that's okay?" she asks sweetly and I sigh.

"That would be lovely, I've missed you." I admit and I see her smile widen.

"I've missed you more," she lowers her glasses for a moment and I can see the sincerity in her eyes.

"It's a date then?"

"Oh yes, Friday next week? The Boot?"

"Yeah, why break the habit of a lifetime," a laugh bubbles out of me.

"Okay," she nods, pushing her hands into her back pockets, "and we could really do with some help, so if you're feeling brave you'll have to help out 'cause in a few months there will hopefully be some beautiful foals prancing round your meadows," she looks over her shoulder at Austin, her shoulders instantly relaxing as she does.

"Yeah maybe," I mutter, rolling my lips as I do. I don't think I'll ever be ready to help the way they all want me to.

"See ya later," she throws me a wink, pushing her glasses up her nose then heads back towards Austin.

I hold my hand up and turn my back on them, walking into the house and spend the rest of the day typing all the words, whilst Butch is out exploring with my mom. He definitely has a new favorite.

Before I know it, Monday evening is drawing in and I am standing in my bedroom trying to work out what I want to wear. I know this isn't a real date, but it sure as hell feels like one.

I'm not even sure how fancy this restaurant is, it's been a hot minute since I had been taken out for dinner in these small towns. I was used to all the well-known restaurants in LA where there was a certain dress code.

Tightening my grip on my towel when I hear a knock on my bedroom door, I step towards it and swing it open to see Mom standing there.

"All okay?" I ask.

"The Rivera brothers are downstairs, they want to have a quick chat with you," she smiles.

"Okay, make them a pot of tea. I'll be down in ten."

"Okay sweetie," she calls out and she is already on her way down the stairs.

Nerves drum deep inside of me.

I move back towards my closet and pull out a casual but pretty sage green dress and excitement courses through me that the colour matches Riggs' eyes.

Dropping the towel, I pull a lacey nude thong over my

curves and let it sit on my hip bone and pull out a matching bra that supports my full breasts. Placing the dress over my head, I smooth it down my thighs and smile at my reflection. It has a plunge neckline and hugs my body. The skirt cuts off just under my knees, the sleeves capped. Slipping my feet into black heeled pumps, I run my fingers through the ends of my wavy hair and half smile at my reflection. I wish I was going out with Riggs tonight, I wish he was taking me out for the fancy dinner then drinks and even maybe stargazing at our favorite spot. As much as I loved Crooked Valley, my favorite place to watch the stars was from the roof of his house, where we used to sit and watch it, putting the world to rights until one day it stopped. Then our spot was Crooked Valley, but I never knew why we had to move from his house to there.

At the time, all I cared about was being with him.

He consumed my every waking thought, he devoured me in my dreams but then when reality kicked in and I lost him, the dreams stopped and so did my never-ending thoughts.

Sighing, I walk over to my bed and grab my clutch bag then make my way downstairs. Nerves rattle through me when I walk into the living room and all three of the boys stand from the sofa. Each pair of eyes sweep over me but Riggs lingers a little longer and heat flames my cheeks.

"You look beautiful Aspen," Pacey says all bashful and I watch as his cheeks flush red.

"Thank you, Pacey."

He bows his head, as if looking at me for too long would cause a problem. Tripp says nothing and Riggs just stares at me with a smug grin on his face.

"What do I owe the pleasure of the Rivera men standing in my living room on the evening of my date?" I tease as I step towards them and take a seat on the large armchair in the corner of the room.

"We thought it best to just give you a little update on what's been happening and what we want you to try and get out of Clay," Tripp's tone is serious, and I watch as Riggs rolls his eyes. Suddenly, I am anxious about going out with Clay.

"Okay..." my voice trails off as I pick the skin around the nail bed of my fingers, nerves burying themselves deep within.

"Don't panic," Riggs' smooth voice coats my skin and I am drawn to him in an instant, my eyes locking with his and a sense of calm pulses through me.

I nod, swallowing the thickness that has formed in my throat. Pacey's throat bobs as he exchanges looks with his brother.

Uneasiness settles at the pit of my stomach when Tripp begins talking and my eyes drift from Riggs and land on him.

"We believe Clay is working with the suits, he has sold his ranch to them and then they made their way to The Oaks. They want to buy all the land so they have it at their disposal. We could be completely off the mark here, but I am certain Clay is working with them. First it was the illegal selling of livestock, and now he has sold his ranch the first moment he gets. His family haven't been here long, they're newbies, but they also bring nothing to our town. All of our ranches work together, we're a family... Bluebeak Ranch was never part of that. They made it clear from the get-go that they weren't about the ranch life. They knew the rules when it came to selling, and if left, they would have gotten away with it for much longer, but we have loyal friends here in Lovelock Bay so it wasn't going to be long until one of us found out," Tripp sighs and drops his head for a moment.

"Try and see if you can get anything out of him about Tom's ranch, The Oaks. I have a feeling they were sniffing around a little too closely to that one. They preyed on his vulnerability knowing full well he had nothing to lose by selling to them," Riggs takes over the conversation and I slowly swing my head to look at him.

"Riggs," I hear Tripp's warning tone, but Riggs ignores him, keeping his eyes focused on me.

"Tom was one of us. I offered to buy... the next day he dies?" He shakes his head from side to side as if in disbelief and my heart aches.

"He was old," Pacey steps in, looking across to his brother and tries to reason with him, pulling the idea of Tom's death being anything more than natural causes.

"I don't care, I wanna know what he knows," Riggs answers abruptly, and I know he is hurting.

"I better be off, Clay thinks I'm staying down at Sylvia's and I need to meet him outside Sunny's."

I puff out my cheeks, already feeling the pressure and anxiety of the web of lies I will be spinning off to him.

I give the boys a curt nod and turn to walk out the room when I feel a grip on my elbow, slowly pulling me back. Spinning, I see Riggs staring at me, his eyes volleying back and forth between mine.

"Be careful, okay?" he is concerned.

I half laugh but he doesn't return it.

"Riggs, I'm just going for dinner," my voice is quiet.

"I know Dinks, but just be careful. Keep your wits about you at all times." He lowers his voice, his eyes hooded.

"Yeah I will," I nod.

"Okay, good. I'll tail ya."

"No," I shake my head from side to side as I pull my elbow from his tightening grip slowly. "He knows your trucks, you'll blow it all in five minutes."

He sighs and fully drops his head so I can't see his pretty eyes anymore.

"Oh," Tripp calls out and stands in front of me which causes Riggs to turn away and walk back over to Pacey. "Nearly forgot to give you this," his smile is crooked as he slips me a mobile phone. "I know you don't have one, and well, it would be silly for you to go into this without any way of contacting us. Mine, Pacey and Riggs' numbers are in here, as well as Austin's and your parents'." I take the phone from him and give it a once over. Feels weird having a phone again. I have been so used to being disconnected to the outside world that suddenly I feel weighted by it.

"If you're in trouble, drop us a two-ring call. We will be there within seconds."

My lips twist, "Well, not seconds... it's at least a ten-minute drive." When I lift my eyes to look at Tripp and his brothers, they all have a stern look on their faces. "Of course, you'll be sitting outside the restaurant." I roll my eyes and I can't hide my laugh.

"You know it, now go... you don't wanna be late for your date," he gives me a quick wink and flashes his cheeky smile and I take that as my cue to leave, ignoring the low rumble of a growl that leaves Riggs.

Climbing into the McLaren, I smile as the engine roars and as I pull out I see the Rivera brothers standing in the dimly lit doorway. I give them a salute through the driver's window as I push on the gas and drive a little faster down the winding driveway than I should. Turning left onto the road, I boot it down the empty country lanes and head for town. Nerves consume me but I need to focus on the task. A little sigh slips out of me as I pull into a spot a little further down from Sunny's. I don't want Clay to see me and blow it within the first few minutes.

Locking the obscenely out of place car, I make my way down the sidewalk, my heeled pumps clicking along the concrete, the soft spring breeze dancing in the leaves and a small smile plays against my lips. I wish I was with Riggs and I was meeting him outside Sunny's. I wanna say that I hate that I have fallen for him again and so quickly, but the truth is, I don't hate it at all.

I have always been smitten with Riggs, but I am scared in case this doesn't work out. We have never done this before, we were only ever friends and now, well... we're... I don't even know what we are. A lot happened between us all, me with Pacey, Riggs with Harlow...

"Hey, Aspen!" I hear Clay's voice float towards me and my thoughts shut down in an instant. I hold my hand up to greet him, my legs carrying me a little quicker now as I close the gap between us. He is dressed in a dark navy suit, his black hair is slicked back like it was on Friday and he still looks every bit businessman. I would be lying if I said he wasn't easy on the eye, but he is no Riggs. I prefer the rough and rugged type it seems, and Clay is a little too clean shaven for me. He doesn't hang about, he swoops in and places a kiss on my cheek and my stomach knots with anxiety, nerves rippling through me.

"Thought you were gonna stand me up," he gives me a wink and steps back slightly and I let out a nervous giggle.

"No, was just taking in the beautiful evening," I drop my head to my chin and take a deep breath to try and calm my erratic heart.

"It is something, isn't it," he chimes as he falls back so he is beside me and we begin walking.

"It really is," my hands rest in front of me, my fingers wrapped around my clutch as we walk slowly down the sidewalk.

"How's Sylvia's?" I turn to look at him as he asks and smile.

"Yeah it's okay, not home though…" I cough and let out a small laugh, "nothing like your own bed."

"You're so right," he pushes his hands into his pockets and pulls out a set of keys to a Mustang and I see the side lights of a red one flash.

"Nice car," I admire it, sleek and beautiful.

"Thanks, you into cars?" he asks as he gets my door, opening it up for me and I silently thank him with a smile before slipping in.

"A little…" I blush under his intense stare before he shuts the door, and when I know I am alone for a second or two, I close my eyes and inhale deeply through my nose and let out a slow but shaky breath.

The driver door opens and I turn my face to look at Clay.

"Ready?" he asks as the car vibrates, the engine purring.

"I am," I plaster a fake smile onto my lips. Why the hell did I agree to this?

CHAPTER TWENTY-FOUR
RIGGS

I pace back and forth in the lounge of our home, my arms crossed against my chest and I can feel eyes on me.

"Damn it Riggs," my dad groans, "at least change course, you're going to make a tread in the carpet," and I hear my brothers laugh and my mom tut.

"I can't relax," I stop suddenly and turn to face my family. "We should never have let her go with him," my chest heaves and I feel sick to my stomach.

"She's a grown woman Riggs," my mom pipes up and I narrow my gaze on her.

"Oh okay," I throw my hands up, "so that makes a difference then?" my brows furrow, my lips turn up in confusion at what just came out of her mouth.

"Give it twenty and we will hop in the truck and head over to where they're eating dinner. I put a tracker on her phone anyway so we can keep an eye on her."

"You done what?" Tripp turns to look at our younger brother Pacey and my lips twitch.

"Yeah, contacted some dudes in New York and asked them to put a tracker in her phone."

"Some dudes?" Tripp's brows raise.

"Yeah, a firm called…" he pauses as he slips his phone out of his dirty jeans and scrolls, his cap turned backwards making him look more like an adolescent teen than he normally does. "Mills, Spencer, King."

"Is that some made up company? You sure you haven't been scammed?" Tripp asks and I scrub my face.

"Nah, I checked it all out and popped their address on the world wide web and it all checked out."

"Did it now?" I ask.

"Yeah, it's all legit. Don't you old fuckers worry about this tech stuff, I have us covered," he winks before sitting back in his chair proud as punch.

"Goddamn it, what did I do to get three hellions like you lot," my dad groans as he stands up and strolls towards his crystal decanter, popping the topper before pouring himself a rather large glass.

"Orla," he calls out, holding the decanter up and she gives him a nod, he turns back round and pours her a large glass too.

I clear my throat a little louder than usual and I hear Tripp snigger and Pacey looks up and round the room.

"My throat is ever so dry…" I cough again.

"Parched. I am parched," Tripp joins in and it takes Pacey a moment or two to catch up.

"I feel like I have swallowed a desert."

"Oh, give it up you three, you're going out in a minute," my dad waves us off as he begins to walk away, my mom rolling her eyes and smirking as she follows him.

"They're so over our shit," a laugh rumbles through me.

"Yup," Tripp laughs and Pacey just sits back shaking his head.

A few minutes tick by and silence fills the room.

"Time to go yet?"

Pacey rolls his eyes.

"Let's go," Tripp slaps his hands on his thighs before he stands up, "because you're doing my head in," he slaps me on the back and lets a laugh slip past his lips.

Pacey eyes me as he stops in front of me and I keep my cool.

He knows I've always had feelings for Aspen.

He just didn't like that it was me she wanted and not him.

And I hate that when he finds out, it'll crush him inside.

But she's my girl.

She will always be my girl.

CHAPTER TWENTY-FIVE
ASPEN

My fingers drum on the table as I wait for Clay to finish his phone call. He didn't leave the table, just sat opposite me whilst talking.

"Yeah, all is going perfect." He smiles at me and gives me a slow wink and I return his smile. He starts nodding and then runs his finger along his bottom lip, but all the time his eyes are on me. It unnerves me.

"Few last bits of the puzzle to slot in, but I have my eye on the prize," he sucks in a breath then says goodbye, cutting his phone off. "Sorry about that," he locks his phone and places it face down to stop any more distractions.

"Not a problem," I say sweetly as I wrap my fingers around the stem of the wine glass and lift it to my lips. The chilled white wine slipping down my throat a little too easily.

The restaurant is cosy but busy. The lights are dimmed, there is a nice ambience filling the room and the music that plays in the background is soft classical.

"So how was your day?" Clay asks as he takes a mouthful of his own wine and makes the most over the top noise as he appreciates the good taste. I mean, it is delicious, but he was so eccentric with it.

"Not too bad, had a few errands to run then spent the rest of it working." There was no lie there, I did have to run errands for my mom and then I lost myself in my words. The way I feel as my words wrap around me before transporting me into the pages of my work. I have never been so in love with a story until this one, which makes me think that this might be *the one.*

Excitement ripples through me momentarily before I am brought back down to earth with a thud.

"What do you do if you don't mind me asking?" he asks, the waiter walking over to take our order and I have never been more grateful to be interrupted. "Can I order for you?" Clay asks and it's an instant ick.

"Yeah," I mumble, I know I am only here to get information, but it still bothers me.

"Can we have two of the sirloins, medium, a side of mash and green vegetables," he flashes her a toothy grin and the waitress gives him a curt nod before she disappears into the back of the restaurant.

"Where were we?" Clay asks and I take it as my turn to turn the tables.

"You were telling me what you do for work," my cheeks pinch and I softly walk my fingers across the table and tease them over the back of his hand. I watch as one of his brows hitch up. My spare hand teases at the back of my neck then skims down the side and across my collarbone. I am internally cringing, I have never flirted like this... well, if you can call it flirting. I am an embarrassment.

"Well," Clay hooks one of his long, skinny fingers round mine and I feel a shudder rise up and down my spine. And not in a good way. "I work within the family business. We own Bluebeak Ranch, well I say *we*, but it's mainly a one man run operation."

I nod as if I am showing interest.

"Oh really, what do you do on your ranch? Livery sales? Cattle?" I reach across and take a large mouthful of wine to dampen my now dry throat.

"It's just a ranch," he shrugs his shoulders, and I draw back my hand slightly but his fingertips reach for mine.

A laugh bubbles up from deep inside of me. "It's never *just* a ranch."

"Well, what can I tell ya sweetness, it is just a ranch to us. We bought it a few years back and honestly," he chuckles as he sits back in his chair, "it's just haemorrhaging money."

"Spoken like a true rancher," I wink.

"Yeah? You know much about ranching?"

"Nope, told ya, I'm not from around here. I am on a deadline and I needed some downtime, but that doesn't stop me from eavesdropping on some of the locals." A high chime coats my voice.

Clay laughs, "I have no idea what the appeal is to be honest, but after living here for a few years I have realised I am set for city life. I've had enough of the country... well, I did... until I met you," his hand skims across the table and scoops mine in his and I will for my stomach to stop churning in nauseating whirls.

My skin crawls and I desperately want to scrub my skin clean until I bleed.

"Well, isn't that romantic. Was that plucked straight from a romance book," I laugh and he laughs with me.

"No, but it's true. There is something about you."

"You're sweet," I put on my sweetest voice and bat my eye lashes a few times.

Our moment is interrupted when our dinner is placed down in front of us. Clay asks the waiter for another top up of wine.

"No more for me," I decline softly, shaking my head. "So, what is your plan going forward, will you move out of Lovelock Bay?" I ask as I stick my fork into my vegetables and pop a carrot into my mouth.

"Yeah, we actually sold the ranch a couple of days back."

My brows lift as I try and act surprised, cutting into the medium rare steak, the meat like butter.

"Really? Did you sell it to a local rancher? I bet any of the ranchers in this picturesque little town would love to expand."

Clay's lips twist as he cuts into his steak, his eyes cast down for just a moment.

"Nah, we sold to an out-of-towner. All these ranch boys don't need to feed their egos, it's all a dick measuring contest in their eyes. The bigger the ranch... well..." he pauses and pushes his tongue into his cheek before popping a mouthful of steak past his lips and making that irritating moan again.

I cock my head to the side, straining my neck slightly and nibble on the inside of my lip to try and distract me from the noise he is making.

"Bet you've upset the big, dicked ranch boys now then..." I purse my lips to fight my smile. I only have one big, dicked ranch boy on my mind and that boy is Riggs Rivera.

"I'm sure I have, but there is one family that I know has taken the news a little sourer than the others."

"Oh?" I act dumb and pop a piece of steak into my

mouth, it melts on my tongue. Reaching for my glass, I lift the rim to my lips and take a mouthful.

"Have you heard of the Rivera brothers?" Clay asks as the waitress pops a fresh glass of wine on the table.

I choke on my wine, swallowing it before I gasp. Pulling my napkin from the table, I cover my mouth as I cough, eyes wide.

"Are you okay?" he looks panicked and I hold my hand up.

"Fine, just went down the wrong hole," my voice is hoarse.

He stands from his chair and leans across the table to pour me a glass of water.

I thank him and reach for the glass to try and stop the burn in the back of my throat from inhaling my wine.

After a moment or two I place my napkin back on the table when my phone pings inside my bag.

"Excuse me for just one minute."

Slowly bending down, I reach for my bag and place it on my lap as I open it up and slip the phone out that I was given.

RIGGS

You're taking too long

I fight my smirk.

RIGGS

And I don't like the way that he keeps
touching you.

Possessive big, dicked rancher. I twist my lips and slip the phone away when it beeps again.

RIGGS

You have ten more minutes, then I am coming to get you. Either you come willingly or I'll drag you out of there myself and show you just who you belong to.

I ignore him, but before I go back to my dinner, I change his name in my phone to BDR and the eggplant emoji.

"So sorry about that, it was my parents," I place my bag back by my feet and pick up my knife and fork.

"Are you close to your parents?" he asks and it sounds as if he is genuinely concerned. The issue is, he probably is. I'm the one on a fake date. Not him.

"Very, how about you?" I scoop up a forkful of mash and hover it over my plate as I wait for him to answer.

"My mom, yes, but not my dad. He passed a while back and I don't remember much of that time to be honest, I blurred a lot of it out."

And I feel my heart bottom out.

"I am so sorry," I say a little quieter, my eyes soft as I watch him with intent.

"It's okay, don't be sorry."

I nod, pushing the tip of the fork past my lips and chewing for a moment.

"I heard about one of the locals passing away on one of the neighboring ranches," I try going straight in for the kill. "Did you know him?"

"Tom Ranking? Yeah. I know he put his ranch up for sale when he got wind of what we were up to. Seems a lot of the older folk are getting ready to up and leave." His brows raise.

"Why would they do that? Ranching is their life, surely."

"It was, but when someone comes in with an offer they can't refuse well…"

"Well?" his answer piques my interest.

"They sell their land to the big suits and this becomes a hot spot, it's so beautiful here and not many people know about it, but once the ranches sell and the land is at their disposal well… they will make it even better than it is now. Ranching is a dying trade, why do we need ranchers and farmers when we can just go to local supermarkets and get our meat for half the price?" he laughs a little louder now. "Plus, there is so much more to these ranches, much more than livestock etcetera," and I sit dumbfounded at the sheer idiocy that has just fallen from his mouth.

"Oh yeah, I completely get it," I nod a little too enthusiastically. I roll my lips, rage bubbling deep inside of me. "What about the trade of world class horses? The wool to the local clothing shops for example? Aside from the meat, there is a lot more that these ranchers do. You know the circle of life and all that? Well the ranchers have the same morals. Live by the ranch, die by the ranch. This is their lives, their heritage… and you think they're just going to roll over and sell it?"

I am mad at myself for getting myself riled up this easy, but I can't stand the stupidity that comes with certain people.

He says nothing. Just sits with one elbow on the table, his index finger pushed to his lips and a knowing smirk on his face.

"Seems little miss out-of-towner knows a little more than she let on, hm?"

"I've done some research. My work is about ranching and livestock," I swallow and suddenly I have lost my appetite.

"Sounds interesting," he places his fork down on his plate then wipes his lips with his napkin.

"It really is," I nod, mirroring him and placing my own knife and fork down.

Silence echoes around us and the tension slowly begins to build.

"Will you excuse me for just a moment, I need the restroom," my tone is soft as I collect my clutch from by my feet and push my chair out, walking across the cosy restaurant to the restroom and only when I am in there and alone, I let out a heavy sigh.

Shit.

Pressing my back to the restroom door, I inhale heavily. I was a fool to agree to this.

I pull my phone out and hover my thumb over Riggs' number, but just as I am about to press the button someone pushes against the door and knocks me forward.

"Hey!" I call out but my eyes widen when I see Riggs standing in front of me.

"Hey," he rasps, his large hand pushing through his curls.

"You're gonna blow my cover."

"Wank Stain didn't even see me. Too busy on his phone, probably looking at pictures of peoples toes."

I scrunch my nose up.

"What is wrong with you?" I smirk but his eyes are dark and hooded and there isn't a hint of a smile on his lips.

"You've ignored me," he stalks towards me as I walk back, hitting the wall in the small restroom. He drops his jacket to the floor, my eyes fall for a moment before they're back on him as I watch him unbutton the top two buttons of his shirt.

"I'm on a date," I chime and he shakes his head from

side to side.

"It's been longer than ten minutes," and I press my thighs together to try and dull the ache that presents itself between them.

"Has it?" I just about manage, trying to ignore the delicious pulse that's beating with my want.

"Yes," he growls and with one large step, he has closed the gap that was between us. His hands skim down my body, gripping the hem of my skirt and bunching it round my waist, I hear him suck in a breath as his beautiful eyes cast down to where he so desperately wants to be.

My chest rises and falls fast, I'm practically panting. Silently begging.

Swiping his finger through my panties and through my soaked core, I shiver at the pleasure that courses through me.

"Riggs," I whisper, panicking that anyone could walk in, my hands pressed against the wall.

"I don't like you out with someone else," he nips at my jaw, his beard scratching against my sensitive skin. I burn for him. "The way he was touching you," he growls as he grips my thigh and lifts it over his hip, his fingers skimming my panties to the side as he sinks a finger inside of me.

"Only you," I breathe, my eyes fluttering as pleasure pools deep within.

"Are you sure?" he asks, his eyes steadying on mine and I hear the sound of his belt unbuckling.

"Yes," I nod, trying not to moan as he continues to fuck me with his finger.

"Good girl," he growls, slipping his finger from me and pushing it between my lips, I suck and lick him clean whilst he lines his thick cock at my opening, and fills me in one thrust.

"Fuck," I gasp, still clinging onto the wall as my other leg is wrapped around his waist.

"I'm going to fuck you hard and fast darlin'. I'm going to ruin your pussy for any other man, even your hand or toys won't please you like I do," he grits as he pounds in and out of me, my orgasm building and burning in my stomach, my skin scattering in goosebumps as he pushes me further to exploding around him.

"Ruin me Riggs, I don't care." I moan, one of my hands grips onto his shoulder, holding myself up as his cock slips in and out of me with ease.

"Fuck, you feel so good Wildflower," he rasps, his head tipping back and I watch as his throat bobs.

"So do you," I whisper, my pussy tightening around him.

"You were made for me and only me." He groans, his eyes levelling with mine.

"Keep going, I'm going to come," I cry out and I don't care if anyone walks in now. I am too far gone, my orgasm teetering.

"Then fucking come for me, show me darlin'," he pulls out to the tip, holding himself still but the thickness of his head is stretching me.

"Show me how good I make you feel, I want to feel your tight little cunt tighten and pulse around me as you come all over my cock," and as soon as the last word slips from his tongue, he slams back into me and that's all it takes.

My eyes roll, my mouth dropping open as my orgasm shatters through me.

"Fuck, you look so damn pretty when you come Dinks," and with one last stroke, he stills, his body shuddering as he comes and empties inside of me.

We stand for a moment and my legs begin trembling.

Gently and slowly placing me down, I try and tug my dress back down but Riggs shakes his head from side to side. He kneels in front of me, swiping his tongue through my pussy and sucks on my clit which causes a spark to ignite inside of me.

"Just a little taste to keep me going," he murmurs before swiping his tongue through me again.

I still when he hooks his fingers in the side of my panties and slides them down my legs as I step out of them.

"What you doing?" I breathe as I look down at him all starry eyed.

"I'm taking your panties," he stands, bringing them to his nose and inhaling before he grips my cheeks and kisses me, hard.

He snatches my breath away and I am left starving of oxygen.

"Let's hope my cum doesn't run down your leg whilst you walk out there... Enjoy your food," he winks then fucking turns and walks away from me with my panties bunched in his hand.

"Silly big dicked rancher," I huff, but I can't fight the smile that creeps onto my lips.

After giving myself a moment, I make my way out the restroom and walk back towards the table and see in fact, that Clay is sitting with his head buried in his phone. I roll my eyes. Dragging my chair out, I take a seat and press my thighs together now very conscious that I don't have any panties on.

"You okay? Your cheeks are a little flushed," Clay looks up from his phone as his eyes search my face.

"I'm just peachy, thanks," I twist my lips and pick up my fork and stab into my steak.

"Oh okay," he nods, his plate is empty but his wine glass is still full.

"Would you happen to have the number of the buyers?" I catch him off guard and his brows pinch.

"Sorry?"

"When I was in the restroom, I overheard someone from town saying they were thinking of selling and well. As much as I don't agree with your logic or the ranchers selling to land grabbers, I thought I might as well be a good neighbor and pop the number across?" I smile at him, blinking a little more than usual.

"How about you tell me their name and I'll pass the details on."

"Are you the buyer then?" I sit back, cutlery still in hand.

"No," a deep laugh rumbles through him.

"Then can I have the number?"

Clay sits back and laces his fingers together before settling them in his lap.

"I'll take care of it," and all I do is nod.

"Fine," my tongue darts out as I lick my lips, dropping my cutlery onto my plate and reaching for my wine glass to drain it.

I take a breath, trying to calm my racing heart.

My phone beeps.

BDR 'EGGPLANT EMOJI'

You okay?

I softly shake my head, my heart stammering in my chest.

"Everything okay?" Clay asks and I can hear the sincerity in his voice.

"Yeah," I smile sweetly and after a moment or two of

awkward silence, we fall into an easy conversation. The talk of ranch, land and suits a distant memory.

Clay walks me to his car, the spring air is a little cooler than it was before we walked in and I shiver into the darkness.

"Here," Clay hangs his suit jacket on my shoulders and warmth blankets me. Within seconds my phone pings.

A knowing smile crosses my lips.

"Thank you," I mutter as we walk in silence to his car.

He opens my door and I slip in, shrugging his jacket off and laying it across my lap. Clay slides in beside me and starts the engine as he pulls out onto the road, my eyes shift to the side and I see the Rivera truck pull out about ten seconds after us, but Clay is oblivious.

"I had a real nice time tonight," and even though it's not the whole truth, it isn't a lie either.

"So did I, thank you for accepting to come out with me," he smiles, his large hand slipping across the center of the car as his fingers brush over the back of my hands and I stiffen in my seat.

He pulls into a parking spot a few cars down from my McLaren and I see his eyes focus on that.

"Such a stunning car, I saw that last week," he whistles through his teeth as he unbuckles himself.

"Yeah, stands out like a sore thumb here doesn't it," a nervous giggle bubbles from me.

"A little yeah, but what a beauty," he turns his face towards me.

"It is," I smile, lifting his jacket from my legs and placing it in the middle of his car. He takes that as his moment to skim his hand between my thighs and give it a gentle squeeze.

"Can I see you again?" he leans his head against the headrest of his seat.

"Maybe," I smirk and shuffle in my seat and he takes that as his cue to take his hand from my thigh.

"Okay then, I'll have to keep an eye out for you," he winks and I swallow the lump that's lodged in my throat back down.

"Maybe you'll see me at Sunny's" I say with hope in my voice as I open the passenger door.

"Oh, I hope so. It was a pleasant surprise to see such a pretty face sitting in the window, the sun shining on you and making your skin glow."

My cheeks burn.

"Maybe you'll get lucky again," I shrug and climb out the car before I fall deeper into this back and forth we have going on.

The cool air catches at the back of my throat as I bend down, lowering myself so my eyes are at his level.

"Thanks again," I smile. "And thanks for dinner, I would have paid for myself."

"I know you would have, and thank you," he gives me a curt nod and I stand, closing the door shut and walk onto the sidewalk, not looking back as I head towards Sylvia's but I take my time. I hear the sound of his engine rumble and within moments, he is pulling out onto the road and driving in the direction of his ranch.

Once his taillights are gone, I let out my held breath and rush for my car. Unlocking it, I start the engine and whizz onto the road as I boot it home.

I see lights flash me, and when I look in my rear-view I see it's the Riveras and my racing heart begins to slow. Lifting my foot from the gas, I fall into a steady speed and make my way home.

CHAPTER TWENTY-SIX
RIGGS

We stay on her tail as we follow her home. I hated having to watch her be with someone else. Sure, no one else knows what has been going on between us, but still. I claimed her and now she is mine. I won't let her out of my grasp again. She is my home and I never want to feel what it would be like to lose her again.

"Wonder what shit she managed to get out of him," Pacey asks, his fingers wrapping round the metal bar of the head rest.

"Probably not a lot," Tripp puffs his cheeks out as he drives. My eyes focus on the back of her stupid car, the back end of it still battered. I wonder why she hasn't had it fixed and I make a mental note to ask her. But not tonight. Tonight, I want to spend the night with her. I hate being without her.

We pull into Maple Farm driveway and slow as we follow her, the little lights coming on in a sequence as she passes them and it makes my heart ache that everywhere she goes, there are lights so she won't be scared of the dark.

She parks her car in the garage and before the truck

even rolls to a stop, I hop out and rush down towards her. She smiles when she sees me but her eyes soon leave mine when they land behind me on Tripp and Pacey.

"You okay?" Pacey asks and I watch his eyes dip and sweep over her body and I feel a jealous streak course through me.

He knows he is playing with fire, though in his eyes everything is banter. But it's not when it's the girl I have always loved and wanted. It's always been her. He averts his gaze to me and rolls his lips into a thin line.

He may have been her first, but I will be her last.

***

ASPEN

I don't miss the way Pacey's eyes dance over my body, and for some reason it suddenly makes me feel self-conscious.

"Let's get inside, yeah?" I shudder as the cool breeze dances over my skin. I feel Riggs behind me as we walk in silence up towards my home. Opening the door, the warmth blankets me in an instant. I kick my shoes off and move towards the lounge to collapse on the sofa. The balls of my feet burn. My mom and dad are sitting in the back living room, the television playing quietly, and I have no idea where Austin is.

The three men walk into the lounge and hover.

"You can sit down," I laugh, my eyes moving between the three of them. Pacey doesn't even wait for me to finish my sentence; he claims the large armchair next to where I am laying. I see him side eye Riggs then gives him a quick nonchalant shrug of the shoulders.

I scoff, rolling my eyes as Riggs perches himself on the arm of the sofa I am sitting on, Tripp sits next to Pacey.

My eyes roam quickly over Riggs and my cheeks burn, little flashbacks of how he devoured me in the bathroom, my skin prickling and heat swarms between my legs and suddenly, I need him again.

"Hello loves," my mom says as she steps into the room, "are you all okay?" her eyes bounce around the room and we all groan and grunt something that merges together as a bunch of yes's.

"Drinks? Cocoa?"

"I'll have a cocoa please."

"And me," Pacey pipes up, holding his hand up.

"Oh go on then," Tripp beams and then I hear the sound of Riggs' hand rubbing over his beard.

"I suppose it would be rude for me to say no now, so yes please Blue," Riggs turns up the sweetness for my mom and it melts my heart.

"I'll go get it started," her eyes glisten and she has always liked to take care of people.

"Mom," I call out just as she turns to walk out the room.

"Sweetie?"

"Where is Austin?" I ask, I feel like I have hardly seen him.

"He was meeting someone down at the Boot," she gives a knowing smile and I know it's Harlow.

She disappears and I sit in silence waiting for one of the brothers to ask the burning question that lays on their tongues.

"Nothing to say?" I play with the ends of my hair as my eyes move between them. The Rivera brothers are all pretty similar.

Riggs is the broadest and tallest. He is rugged and rough

round the edges. His curly brown hair, his piercing sage green eyes that sometimes look hazel depending on the weather. His tanned skin is mostly hidden by a thick but trimmed beard. His lips are full and delicious and he has a sharp jaw that would make any woman weak at the knees.

Tripp is a little less rugged. Short dark brown hair which is cropped short round the sides and sits in tufty waves and always styled, even under his cowboy hat. Where Riggs is more of a roll out of bed, run his fingers through his hair and hide it under his hat. My lips twitch at the thought. Tripp has dark brown eyes, almost black in colour. He has neat stubble, his nose a little crooked and a scar above his eye from when Riggs hit him in the eye with a horseshoe. Tripp is a little shorter than Riggs and a lot slimmer. They're all lean, but Tripp is very defined.

Then you have pretty boy Pacey. Light brown hair that sits to his jaw. Messy but glossy and soft with the same curls as his brother but a lot looser. His eyes are hazel and a little brighter than Riggs. He is slim, petite. He is real pretty, a clean face and well looked after skin. They're all handsome, but together, they're beautiful. Real fucking beautiful.

"Aspen," Riggs pulls me from my thoughts and my eyes widen.

"You back with us?" Tripp laughs and I blush.

"I think so," I roll my lips, shuffling, my knees touching and my thighs clenched. I really should have put some panties on before I sat down.

My mom walks in and hands us all our cocoa, handing me mine last. I take it from her and give her a smile. Her hand cups my face as her soft eyes land on mine.

"You okay?" I whisper and she nods, leaning down and placing a kiss on my forehead.

"I'll leave you to it," she stands tall and walks out of the living area, sliding the lounge doors across, but not closing them completely so there is still a small gap.

I take a mouthful of my cocoa and then lick my lip of the chocolate moustash I was sporting.

"So, how did it go?" Tripp asks, I can hear the desperation in his voice.

I sigh, placing the bottom of the mug on my bare thigh and welcoming the burn that radiates through me.

"Well, for starters he said that you ranchers were basically just doing a dick measuring contest when it came to your ranches, so I named you the big dicked ranchers." I hear Riggs splutter, coughing and Pacey's jaw drops, Tripp just stares at me wide eyed and I giggle.

"I mean, I really like the nickname, B-D-R," I sound the letters out on my tongue, "Could also be Big Dicked Rivera's…"

"That's enough," Riggs pushes his hand through his hair and I giggle a little more at his flushed cheeks.

"Did you say who had the biggest dick or…?" Pacey asks dead pan, his face serious all of a sudden and I lean over and swat him on the arm with the back of my hand.

"Idiot," my laugh is a little louder now, but it's only me and Pacey who are laughing, the other two grumpy fuckers keep their poker faces on. "Anyway," I manage to calm myself down after a moment or two, "he didn't really say much more than you already know. I asked for the buyers number but he wouldn't give it. I said I overheard someone saying they wanted to sell," I hold my hand out, "he said that there was more to the ranches than *just* the ranches." I watch as Riggs sits a little taller, him and Tripp exchanging looks.

"What was he on about?" my eyes bounce around the room and I feel clammy suddenly.

Tripp cocks his head slightly, as if trying to give a warning look at Riggs to not open his mouth.

"There is an old gold mine that sits beneath us all, bang in the middle. If you were to look at a birds-eye view of Lovelock Bay, you would see the point where it's situated. No one has been down there in decades, there was nothing down there, but it seems whoever Clay is working with is aware of this little abandoned mine and they think they can destroy our heritage just to explore a redundant mine." A heavy sigh leaves him.

"Is it redundant?" I ask twisting round to look at Riggs.

He shuffles on the arm of the sofa, his palms rubbing up and down his jean covered thighs, silent words move between the three brothers. My eyes jolt to each one of them and none of them can look at me.

"What are you not telling me?" My palms start getting twitchy, my heart thumps in my chest and I can hear the blood thumping in my ears.

"Dinks," Riggs pauses and clears his throat as his brothers look between us. "Aspen," he sighs. "Our understanding was that it was, yes. But the suits began moving in and Clay became more known in our little town so we started digging." I pin my eyes to him. "No one has been down there since the early 1900's, they bled it dry." He breaks his gaze.

"So why do you think he is interested in the mine if it's empty?"

Riggs shrugs his shoulders up.

"He might not even be hinting at the mine, I just think it's weird how they're so focused on our town. Why, all of a sudden, the interest in buying all the ranches when we all sit on a common denominator."

I sit back, my fingers clasped round my mug as I just listen for a moment.

"Could it be drug related?" I shoot my question towards Riggs and he returns another shrug of his shoulders.

"Could be, I mean they could be using the livestock carcases that are..." he pauses and uses bunny ears, "'dying' to carry the drugs out without anyone even realising."

And it's like a lightbulb has just gone off over all of their heads at the same time.

"No fucking way," Pacey's tone is slow and low as the realisation kicks in.

"Easily done, we had ours cremated... didn't we?" Riggs asks and Tripp steadies his gaze.

"Yeah, our usual guys couldn't do it so I had to call on someone else, Harlow said they were fully booked."

Realisation smashes them all in their pretty faces for the second time in as many minutes.

"I've got to go," Tripp stands, placing his mug down as he darts from the room, and with a curt nod, Pacey follows behind him.

"Well, that escalated quickly," anxiousness courses through me and I hear a deep rumble that leaves Riggs.

I stand slowly, stepping towards Riggs and after three steps I'm in front of him.

"Maybe I shouldn't have gone out with Clay," I whisper, and for some reason I feel guilty. Riggs didn't want me to go, but I wanted to help.

"No, baby, no," Riggs lifts his face to look at me, his eyes volleying as his large hands rest on my waist. His eyes look dull, a smile forcing across his lips but it doesn't meet his eyes. "You helped. Fuck," he drops his head for a moment, shaking his head from side to side. I clasp his face, lifting his face to look at me. "I didn't want you to go, but you managed to possibly find out what these assholes want with our land."

"I just hope we're not too late."

"There is a long way to go Wildflower, we're not selling anytime soon. There is one more ranch that is a few miles down which we may be able to convince not to sell."

"Really?"

"Yeah. It's pretty run down, but the potential is amazing. They used to raise bulls and also had horses. Their son was killed in a road traffic accident. He wanted to be a bull rider and damn, he would have been the best there was. Wrapped up in grief, they slowly sold the bulls off and now they're living out the last of their days on their empty ranch."

"That's sad."

"It is, their son was their world. No one should have to bury their children."

I rub out the ache in my chest that presents itself, Riggs' grip tightening on my waist.

"What's the ranch called?" I ask.

"Crooked Creek."

"As in Crooked Valley?" my eyes widen and Riggs nods. "I would love to buy it. Could you imagine... one of our favorite spots and I get to live there and wake up every day to that view..." I pause for a moment, my heart galloping in my chest, "with you."

"Wouldn't it be amazing," his voice is low and I begin to see the glisten in his eyes seeping its way back in.

"It really would be." I blissfully exhale.

"Anyway..." he pauses, his hands trailing down, his fingers playing with the hem of my sage green dress.

"Anyway," I smirk, craning my neck to look down at him, my arms wrapping loosely around his neck. His finger dips under my dress, grazing under the curve of my ass and teasing at the crease.

"God I love you bare underneath your dress."

My insides quiver, his fingertips teasing in featherlight strokes against my sensitive skin.

"Not here," I rub my lips together, my eyes not leaving his for a moment as I place my hands on top of his and lift them from my body and I miss the feel of him instantly. I reluctantly slip away from him, my fingers linking between his before it's just our tips brushing.

"I want so much more than the secret hook ups," I feel my cheeks flame under his intense gaze and suddenly I feel embarrassed.

"Fuck Aspen," he rasps pushing to his feet and closing the gap between us in two steps. His large hand moves from his side where I have watched him pick a bit of thread in the seam of his jeans and lifts it to my face, his knuckles brushing across my cheek bone and my eyes flutter shut, my heart stammering in my chest.

"Open your pretty honey eyes, baby," and I do as he asks, our souls entwining as I feel the burning desire that penetrates through me. Our gazes lock and I could lose myself in his beautiful eyes forever.

"I don't want the hook ups and the secrets. I want you Aspen and I want all of you."

I blink to try and clear the blurriness that is misting my view.

"I want all of you Riggs, I've been without you for too long and now being back here with you..." I whisper, his hand clasping my cheek now, his thumb brushing across my full bottom lip.

"It's always been you Aspen, from the first time I saw you when we were kids. Beautiful golden hair that was always braided, sun kissed skin and freckles that I used to trace with my eyes because I loved every single one. No one has compared to you, my heart has always beat along to yours, Wildflower."

I pull in my bottom lip with my teeth as he pours out the words I have longed to hear from the moment I met him on his ranch all those years ago.

"I'm waiting for something to mess this all up," I admit, fear crippling me and anxiety wrecks my stomach.

"Darlin' nothing is going to mess this up," he presses a soft kiss in the center of my forehead and I let my eyes close as I place my hands over his chest to feel the steady rhythm of his heartbeat under my fingers. I wish I could stay here and in this moment forever.

The sound of a door slamming has me jumping back, Riggs rubs his hand over his bearded chin and I go back to sitting on the edge of the sofa. We wait and listen and I hear Austin thumping down the hallway.

My gaze shoots up at Riggs and I twist my lips to try and fight my smile. He smirks at me, his hands on his hips and all I can think about is how much I want his hands on me. Touching me, teasing me, pleasuring me in a way he never has before.

I snap from my thoughts when Austin barrels through the double doors, a wide grin on his face as he looks between me and Riggs.

"Ah, two of my favorite people." His voice echoes round the room and I watch as he stumbles into the living room. "I had the best date."

"Yeah?" I ask, my eyes darting to Riggs when I notice my lace panties hanging out his back pocket.

Fuck. Fuck. Fuck.

Austin swings his arms round Riggs' shoulders, using him as a support and fear prickles inside of me. I rush up, running over and wrapping one of my arms around Austin's body and with my other hand I tuck my panties deeper into Riggs' pocket. I watch as his brows raise, his eyes widening when he feels a hand on his ass.

"Austin, why are you touching me up?" His voice is gruff and I give him a gentle kick in the shin, with a *what the fuck* look on my face and realisation settles inside of him. The shocked expression soon turns to a smirk and playfulness.

"I'm not touching you up bro, I mean, you're handsome and everything but it's not me." He sighs, swaying and I push him back into Riggs' arms. "There is someone I wish I was touching though," he wiggles his brows at Riggs then winks as if Riggs knows what he is on about.

"Shall we get you up to bed?" I rush out, not wanting to hear any more of Austin's drunken admissions. "I think you need to sleep the alcohol off."

He mutters something then moans in a protest.

I go to pull him off Riggs but he shakes his head. He re loops Austin's floppy arm round his neck and holds him close to his side with his arm and walks him upstairs to his bedroom.

I take that as my moment to check him out before my eyes land on his firm, peachy ass. Boots, jeans, shirt and his a jacket. A signature look, but so Riggs. He is every bit a ranch boy, but he is my ranch boy.

CHAPTER TWENTY-SEVEN
RIGGS

"There we go buddy," I groan as I lay Austin down on his bed. He mutters something incoherent and I smirk.

"Riggs? Is everything okay?" I look over my shoulder at Blue's voice as she appears in his room, her head twisting between me and Austin. Concern laces her voice, but I soon smooth any feelings of uneasiness away. I don't want her worrying.

"Yes ma'am, Austin had a bit too much to drink so I helped him into bed."

I hear her tut and watch her eyes roll.

"He will have a sore head tomorrow," she says softly, her eyes pinned to a softly snoring Austin.

"He sure will," I chuckle as I step a little closer to the door and I catch her gaze.

"You're a good friend and a good man Riggs Rivera." Her thin lips spread in front of her teeth as she smiles at me, her head tilting slightly and her eyes are filled with adoration.

"My children are lucky to have you," she says as she walks towards me and places her hand on my heart.

"And I'm lucky to have them too," I snort a gentle laugh as she pats me a few times on the chest.

"Always look after each other, never turn your backs or hurt one another." She gives her motherly advice and I listen intently, and I somehow get the feeling she doesn't know what happened before Aspen up and left all those years ago. "And look after our girl."

I swallow. My throat bobbing as my eyes widen and I clear my throat to try to move whatever has suddenly lodged there.

"She deserves the world Riggs. She won't cope with any more hurt in her life, so if your feelings for her are not genuine then let her go, because she deserves her happily ever after; you both do." And on that last warning note, she walks out the room and leaves me standing in the room with a snoring Austin behind me.

"Come on Buck, let's get to bed," my head follows the noise and I watch as she waits at the top of the stairs, and within moments, Buck is there. His arm wrapping around her waist as they both talk quietly amongst themselves and slip into their bedroom.

My heart drums in my chest.

Was that a blessing or a threat?

I turn back to face Austin and suddenly, mixed emotions consume me.

When I finally manage to walk back downstairs, the house is pretty much in darkness except for Aspen's nightlights. My heart sinks, but I continue to search for her and it doesn't take me long to find her.

She is leaning across the kitchen countertop tucking into a freshly baked blueberry pie.

"I always thought your favorite was strawberry," I smirk, leaning against the door frame as I study her. Her pretty green dress hugs her figure, her ankles crossed at the bottom of her long legs, the skirt of her dress sitting a little higher so I can just peek the top of her golden thighs. Her dirty blonde hair is styled in pretty curls but they look a little messy and messy curled Aspen is my favorite.

"Strawberry is my favorite, but I'm having to settle for blueberry." She rolls her eyes as if the pie choice is not acceptable.

"The audacity," I tsk then let out a gentle laugh.

"Want some?" she holds a forkful of blueberry pie out for me but I politely decline.

"Shame, more for me," her voice is sultry as she stares at me, her eyes lustful as she slowly parts her lips and teasingly feeds the tip of the fork past her lips and into her mouth, her eyes closing in a sensual way as she moans around her mouthful and suddenly I am hot, bothered and fucking hard.

"You're teasing me."

"What if I am? What are you going to do about it from all the way over there *Riggs*? I remember when you laid me down on this countertop and feasted on me like I was your favorite meal in the whole... wide... world," her words come out slow as she teasingly presses up and twists, leaning against the worktop, her fingers curling round the edge as she pulls herself up and sits there looking all fucking pretty.

"Aspen," I rasp, but my tone has warning. I can't do this, not here. Not whilst they're all upstairs.

"Riggs," she challenges, her delicate fingers tracing over her bare thighs and hitching up the skirt of her dress a little higher, her legs parting for me.

"Aspen," I can just about manage as my eyes fall between her pretty little thighs.

Running my hand down the side of my hair, my legs begin to move as I slowly walk towards her, and within two steps I am in front of her. Her beautiful hair framing her face, her full lips parted as her hazel eyes dart back and forth between my eyes and lips. My fingertips brush over her exposed skin and I hear her breath hitch, catching at the back of her throat.

She parts her legs a little more and I bury my body between them, both my hands clasping on her thighs, digging my fingers in. I am obsessed with everything about Aspen. Her chin lifts, her head tipping back slightly as I edge my lips closer to hers, and just as they brush, my phone screeches from my pocket.

"Ignore it," she pants and as much I want to, I can't.

I drop my head and shake it softly, stepping back away from her on an inhale as I fish for my phone. Tripp.

"Yeah?"

"We've got a plan," he says into the earpiece.

"Okay, I'm on my way."

I cut him off and let my eyes land on her.

She is still sitting on the work surface, her eyes a little glassy and her legs pressed closed.

"I'm sorry," I whisper and with that, I turn and walk out of the kitchen, down the hallway and out the front door, and I don't once look back.

AFTER RETURNING HOME and listening to what my brothers had to say, I kept pretty quiet. They hashed out all the details and I trusted their plan entirely.

Heaviness weighs me down as the guilt creeps further

and further through me. The way I just left her there, I didn't have to leave at all, but I felt I needed to. Blue's words echo in my head any moment I am alone.

"She deserves the world Riggs."

Fuck, don't I know it.

I wanted to give her it all.

All my love, all my time. The moon, the stars and the galaxies in-between.

But people forget that she hurt me too. The difference was I kept silent. I kept silent for her and for Pacey. I did what was asked of me.

I didn't take her to prom.

I hurt her.

Then I let her follow her new dream. She was so broken when she left. Her soul shattered into a million pieces because the dream she had was no more. I will never forget the day it happened.

It was early summer, the warm days were in full swing and she was getting ready for her show jumping show in Austin the following week. She was on form and so was Blossom. They were the perfect duo. The equestrian world knew they were a force to be reckoned with.

The pretty Palomino and the beautiful blonde.

I was first out, stepped on the bottom of the fence as I leaned my upper body over and watched in awe as they became one in the training ring, cantering a steady pace before soaring over the jumps. Aspen always lifted herself from the saddle two footfalls before the jump, I loved how it seemed that she was standing in the stirrups, her hands up Blossom's neck as the reins were loose for just a moment, putting all of her trust in her trusty steed.

Then came the colossal fall, the blood curdling scream.

I shudder at the memory that haunts me and when I lift my head, I see my dad standing in the doorway of my room.

"Riggs?"

"Yeah?" I shuffle in the chair that sits in the corner of my room and closest to the large sash window.

"What do you make off this Clay situation?" he asks me as he steps over the threshold of my room and sits on the edge of my bed facing me.

"Honestly, dad?" I sigh, drumming my fingers on the arm of my chair, "I have no idea. I feel like we're being played somehow but I just can't work it out. Does that make sense?"

I watch as he nods.

"I never thought it would come to this, where our own would sell so easily."

"Is it worth it though? That's what they're probably thinking. I mean, most of them know no different, take Tom for example. He lived and breathed for this town. It's all he knew, they were never blessed with kids and then when Ivy passed... well," I sigh and swallow the lump that has formed in my throat. "Why would he agree to sell?" my voice cracks and I am annoyed at myself that I am letting emotion fill me.

"Because of what you said. He had nothing left, his ranch was sinking and losing money and he probably sat there and thought *is it worth it*."

I sniff, ignoring the burn that is coursing deep inside of me.

"It doesn't matter now though does it. Those greedy cunts have got their hands on that land now. Won't be long before they take Crooked Creek down."

My dad exhales heavily as he stands and walks across the hardwood floor of my room towards me, his hand resting on my shoulder as he gives my tense muscle a squeeze and I think that was the most fatherly and loving contact he has given me since I was just a child.

I lift my face to look at him, his eyes searching my face. He lifts his hand from me and slips it inside his flannelled shirt, pulling out a white envelope and holding it out for me to take.

"What's this?" I blink at him.

"Have a look."

I take the envelope from him, flipping it over and my brows crinkle when I see it's not sealed. Running my finger under the flap, I pinch the piece of paper from the envelope and slowly slide it out. Resting the envelope on my knee, I turn the paper over and open the letter.

Last Testament and Will.
Tom Ranking.

My eyes trace the words out as I read down the letter and that's when I see it.

Property deeds: The Oaks Ranch, Lovelock Bay, MT.
Riggs Jorge Rivera.

"What," I whisper and read the letter again. And again. And again so that by the time it finally registers, the words are scorned into my corneas.

"The Oaks is yours son," I lift my face to my father who is smiling down at me, "Now let's stop these fuckers in their tracks before they take any more of our town."

I push from the seat, and wrap my arms around my father's shoulders as I embrace him. Endearment swarms me, and I just hold onto him until I feel his hands on my back, patting me in a soft rhythm. This has never happened before and for the first time I really do feel my father's love.

"Thanks dad."

"No need to thank me son, you owe your thanks to Tom." He mutters as I step back from him and look back at the letter that is still clutched between my fingers.

"Yeah, you're right," I sniff.

"Now, get some sleep." He orders, stepping away from me "And tomorrow, I would like you to go down and check on the mares, see what studs have been used so we can get some new horses on the ranch this summer."

I chuckle. Straight back into work mode.

"Okay dad," I nod, and his lips waver into a smile before he turns and walks towards the door, pulling it too as he leaves.

I cast my eyes back down at the letter and smile. I fall back into my seat and look at the clear, starry night sky. "Thanks Tom."

Folding the letter back up, I slip it into its envelope. I stand and walk across the room to open my bedside unit and I place the letter in there for safe keeping tonight. Finally kicking my heavy boots off, I let them fall against the floor. I hang my jacket up in my closet and reach down the back of my shirt, grabbing it and tugging it over my head as I toss it into the wash bin. Tugging my jeans down, I fold them up and place them on the ottoman at the end of the bed. Finally, I fall onto my bed and groan as my muscles feel tense and achy.

Placing my arm behind my head, I stare at my ceiling and my thoughts drift back to Aspen sitting on the edge of the worktop, legs parted and her pretty little pussy on show.

I smirk, my cock instantly hard.

My phone pings and I groan, rolling over and grabbing it from the nightstand. My lips twitch when I see Aspen's name on the screen.

Tapping it, I wait for the message to open.

ASPEN

I'm making a mess.

You left me to sort myself out...

1 attachment.

My lips roll as I lay back down and tap the attachment. It's her laying on her bed, thighs spread and her fingers teasing down towards her pussy.

"Fuck," I groan.

I read her message again, my heart drumming, the blood beating in my ears.

RIGGS

Well, that's no good is it princess...

I send it and wait for a moment.

RIGGS

Do you know how fucking pretty you looked sitting on the worktop, legs parted... I wanted to devour you Aspen.

I watch as the ticks change colour, showing me she has read it, and within seconds, she is typing.

ASPEN

I do know how pretty I looked... what I don't know is why you walked out on me.

I lick my lips.

RIGGS

I had to take care of something, but I am kicking myself right about now.

She replies instantly.

ASPEN

So you should.

1 attachment.

I have never opened an attachment so quick in my life.

The angle of the camera has changed, her fingers are pressed against her clit, her bare pussy on show and I swear I'm about to nut.

RIGGS

Aspen...

It's all I can manage because I am fucking jealous and ravenous for her all at the same time.

ASPEN

Yes Riggs.

My cock aches between my legs and I am restraining from touching myself because I am so desperate too.

RIGGS

I want you. I want to sink myself between them pretty fucking thighs and replace your fingers with my tongue.

I fire back quickly and wait.

ASPEN

You could have had me but you ran home.
So now I am touching myself imagining it's
your tongue on me, your mouth hot and wet
as you pleasure me. I'm right here Riggs…

I sit up, frustration coursing through me. I stand from the bed and look out across the dark fields. I am so fucking tempted. I storm back over to the bed, grabbing my phone but I don't sit down.

RIGGS

Don't tempt me.

I'm already tugging my jeans back on and pulling out a new pair of socks.

ASPEN

That was nothing, I am so wet for you
Riggs.

1 video attachment.

Her soaked pussy is glistening as she slowly pumps one of her fingers in and out of her opening, her arousal covering her skin.

"Fuck this."

Walking across the room, I grab an oatmeal v-neck tee from my closet and pull it over my head, the arms sitting quarter length on my thick arms. Then I reach for my baseball cap that sits on the bedpost of my bed and place it on my head. Slipping my feet into my boots, I grab my truck keys and my phone and head downstairs.

The house is quiet but I can hear the television still playing. I have no idea where Tripp and Pacey are but, in this moment, I don't care.

I'm hot, my blood boiling and my cock throbs for release.

Passing through the front door, I jog across to where my truck is and climb in, starting it up, I open the messages.

RIGGS

You better be ready because I'm about to fucking ruin you and your pussy.

I toss my phone over on the passenger side and reverse out of my space before pulling out the driveway and within minutes, I am slowly pulling into Maple Farm.

I hear my phone ping but I ignore it, I am too focused on getting up to her fucking room. I park the truck around the back of the stables, tucked away so no one sees it. I should have walked, but it would have taken too long. I am *that* desperate for her.

Cutting the engine, I grab my phone and jump out the truck. Her room is situated at the back and I know there is a drainpipe and trellis that I could use to climb up. She has a small ledge just underneath her window that slips down onto a flat roof. There is no way I can knock, Blue and Buck would kill me.

Sneaking round the back, I see her bedroom lit dimly. My eyes scan for the trellis and I weigh up my options. Her pussy is worth dying for. It's a solid ten, I can't risk passing it up. I did it once already tonight, I'm not about to do it again. Footing the bottom of the trellis, I wrap my fingers in the wooden slats and I pull myself up. My heart is thrashing in my chest with each step I take, and I know once I am at a decent height, I can use the drainpipe too.

Lugging myself higher, the bottom of my stomach drops as my boot slips and I curse internally.

Giving myself a moment, I pull myself further and reach for the drainpipe, pulling my body weight up and swinging my legs onto the ledge. Finally standing I give myself a moment for my heart to calm down and look at the ground below me.

Jesus fucking Christ.

Walking towards her window, my phone pings again. Opening her two messages, I smirk.

ASPEN

Empty threat Rivera? You could have ruined me earlier but you walked away.

ASPEN

What's the matter, cat got your tongue?

Fucking cat got your tongue, I know one pussy that's about to get tongued. I tap on her window a couple of times and stand back, bearing a toothy grin as she walks to the window in a pretty silk night dress and I watch as the colour of her cheeks change to a pretty shade of pink.

She lifts the window then steps back with a coy look on her face.

"What's the matter, cat got your tongue?" I wink at her as I climb through her window like a fucking naughty teenager.

As soon as my boots hit her floor, my eyes roam over her body and what a beautiful treat she is. White silk nightie, lace sitting on her thighs, just covering the apex between her legs. Her full breasts rounded and filling the lace cups.

"Did you wear this just for me?" I ask, a certain rasp to my voice as lust consumes me. She stays mute.

"Oh come on Aspen, you seemed *very* vocal on your text messages." I tease her as I take another step closer. I am desperate to have my lips on hers.

The corner of her mouth lifts as I am now inches from her, her neck craning back as she looks up at me, her small hands reaching up and lifting my cap off my head and placing it back on so the peak is on my neck.

"You look so fucking hot Rivera," her voice is quiet and I am done waiting. I loop my arms around her waist and pick her up, her bare legs circling around me as I carry her over to her bed and lay her down gently.

Her dirty blonde hair fans out on her white bedspread, her chest rises and falls and her toned, tanned legs are pressed together at the knees and bent.

"Did you enjoy teasing me?" I whisper as I press my hands either side of her head, as they dip into the soft mattress.

Her lips part and roll over her perfectly straight teeth before she sinks them into her bottom one and nods eagerly.

"I'm glad, because now I want you to be a little pillow princess whilst I enjoy teasing you," I rasp, lowering my upper half down as I slide down her body and kneel on the floor beneath me. "You're not to come until I say so," I order, my hands skimming over her chest, tits, stomach, pelvis before they land on the bare skin of her thighs. "Do you understand me?" my eyes lift and burn into hers as she props herself up on her elbows, looking down at me and she nods.

"Words, Aspen." I growl, my lips pressing against her shins.

"Yes" she whispers.

"Good girl," I praise, then push her legs wide and grin like a damn Cheshire cat when I see her pretty pink pussy.

Gliding my large, calloused hands on the inside of her thighs then rubbing them out to her outer leg, kneading as I do. I edge forward, my fingers brushing against her pussy lips then tracing over her pubic bone and grip the lace of her nightdress, pushing it up, exposing more of her glowing tanned skin. I have to compose myself and refrain from pushing a little higher so her perfect tits are out. Dragging my short nails over her skin, I watch as her stomach erupts in goosebumps, before continuing to glide them down her thighs.

I resume my teasing strokes, brushing against her pussy lips and skimming over where I know she so desperately wants me.

Lowering my mouth over her pussy, I breathe a little heavier so my hot breath blows over her clit and I watch as her hips circle beneath me. My hand pushes down on her lower stomach pinning her to the bed.

"Patience Wildflower," my lips graze against her pubic bone softly, my other hand pushing against her inner thigh widening her legs.

My own patience is wearing thin, but I want to tease her to the point where she can't take any more.

Darting my tongue out, I stroke up and down her pussy lips, just edging across slightly, my hand skimming down and cupping her cunt. She quivers under my touch and I smirk against her skin, nibbling and sucking as I do.

"Please," she whispers, still propped on her elbows as she watches with her mouth popped open.

I shake my head purposefully side to side slowly and let my lips brush against her clit.

"Oh," she whimpers, her hips lifting silently begging for more.

"Not a chance," I groan as I place kisses on the inside of her thighs, my thumb hovering over her clit but I lower it, just skimming and gliding it through her center, and spreading her lips wider as I reach the bottom of her pussy. The want to stretch her out, to see just how good her tight little cunt looks stretched, is far too strong. My cock hardens and rubs against the seam of my jeans.

Her sweet little pants get heavier, my eyes locking on hers as I graze my lips over her clit, my thumb teasing at her soaked opening.

She circles her hips once more, trying to get what she wants but that only makes me slip my thumb further away.

I smirk and she huffs, her eyes rolling in frustration.

Lifting my face, I hover my hand over her clit and spank her, which causes a strangled moan.

"Don't roll your eyes at me," my voice is full of gravel as my hand curls around her hip and I drag her pussy closer to me, her ass just hanging off the bed.

"Fuck," she whimpers as I brush my thumb back and forth over her swollen clit. I let go, and I see the confusion all over her pretty little face.

Standing, I crane my neck in front of her and unbuckle my jeans, pushing them down just enough for her to get to where I want her.

Leaning down, I cup her face in mine and brush my lips over hers, our kiss soft and my eyes flicker with a burning desire.

"Now be a good girl and get on your fucking knees," I slowly stand and watch as she does as she is asked, scooting off the bed and sitting on her knees. "You're such a good girl Aspen," I groan, my hand moving to her hair as I tangle my fingers through her curls. "Do you know how jealous I was that he was touching you tonight?" I rasp, my spare hand slipping down the front of my boxers as I pull myself out, letting my hand stroke up and down my hard cock.

"Very," she rasps, her eyes on me.

"Fuck, you look so pretty on your knees Wildflower."

"I want you and only you Riggs," she breathes.

I watch as her lips part and she kneels a little higher, pursing her full lips around the thick head of my cock before taking me deep into her mouth.

"Shit," I groan, looking down at her with her lips locked around me, moving back and forth and fuck, does it feel good. "Suck me harder, Aspen, show me how much you want me," I pant, my fingers locking in her hair tighter, moving her head a little faster and she moans around me, her mouth full of me and it's such a beautiful sight. Her eyes glisten with tears as she keeps up the steady pace.

I watch as her cheeks hollow out and she's staring straight into my soul. My cock pulses in her mouth and I know I'm not going to last long.

"How deep can you take me Wildflower; can you take me all the way?" I challenge her in a teasing manner and watch her cheeks flood with colour.

I grip under her chin and tilt her head back slightly, slowing my thrusts into her pretty mouth as I slide down the back of her throat, my eyes rolling in the back of my head as pleasure erupts deep inside of me.

"Fuck," I seethe, sinking my teeth into my bottom lip to stop myself from being loud. I pull back, the tip of my cock on her cushioned lips. "You're so damn good," I praise her and I watch as she clenches her thighs together. "Are you wet Aspen? Are you dripping at having my cock in your mouth and down your throat," I continue and she moans, her breath shivering.

"Yes," she whispers and I watch as her hand slips between her thighs and fuck, she looks so hot. I shake my head and her hands press back against her thighs.

"You have a job to finish," one of my brows lift and I smirk down at her, rolling my hips forward as I slip back into her wet mouth.

Her fingers wrap around my thickness, gliding them up and down in time with her wet little mouth and it feels like ecstasy.

"You give head so good," I moan, my fingers still locked in her hair and I refrain from pushing her down deeper.

She smiles around my cock and it does something to me. My hips move faster as I fuck the back of her throat, my spare hand back under her chin as I tilt her back and slip further down, a guttural moan escaping me. Lowering my chin to my chest, I let out hot and heavy breaths as I watch her push me to my impending orgasm.

"Open your mouth baby," I can feel the veins in my neck protrude, my veiny arms more prominent as I tighten my grip on her hair and let my other hand fall from her chin. Slipping my cock from her mouth, it feels as if ice has been dropped down the back of my tee, a shiver dancing up and down my spine.

She does as I say, sitting there on her knees like a good girl with her mouth wide open. I wrap my own hand around my thick cock and slowly begin to pump up and down all whilst looking at her with her wide doe eyes on me.

"Fuck," I moan, clamping my teeth down and grinding my back molars as my cock pulses in my hand, and my orgasm floors me, ripping me in two as I press the tip of my cock on her bottom lip and cum into her mouth, a pleasant shudder floating over me. "Don't swallow," I rasp, my eyes closing for just a moment and letting my heart rate slow.

When I open my eyes, she's sitting there like I ask with her mouth popped open. I lean down, my fingers pressing into her cheek as I look at the mess I have made and my lips twitch, my pulse elevating and my cock throbbing against my stomach, the waistband of my boxers rubbing the underside of my thick girth.

"Such a good girl," I lower my lips over hers and whisper, "swallow," before kissing her.

CHAPTER TWENTY-EIGHT
RIGGS

Steadying her on her feet, I nudge her back onto the bed once more, but this time my hand slips between her thighs as I push her to the top of the bed and not on the edge like she was before. She is flustered and her eyes full of lust and want. She doesn't lift them from mine and I love how relaxed and calm she looks, in her own haze as she waits for my next move. I crawl over her, my fingers gripping her cheeks and I cover her lips, my tongue slowly slipping in and entwining with hers. She moans into my mouth as my spare hand glides down her sides, my fingers skimming under her nightie and across her bare thighs.

"I need you," she speaks against my lips, her voice vibrating through me.

"I know baby," I smile, our teeth clashing momentarily, "and I promise I am going to fulfil all your *needs.*"

She squirms beneath me and I push up, rolling my body down hers as I position myself between her legs. Swiping my fingers through her pussy, I grin when I feel how wet she is.

"You really did like sucking my cock didn't you?" I rasp,

my lips brushing the inside of her thighs as my finger slips into her tight pussy and I hear the gasp that passes her lips. I slip another into her, stretching her as I cast my eyes down and graze my lips across her clit before darting my tongue out, licking gently then sucking on her swollen clit. Her hips roll and a soft moan leaves on her exhale of breath. My fingers pump in and out of her slowly, my tongue rubbing on her clit gently.

Pulling my fingers from her, I let them sit at the tip. My tongue flattens and glides up and down her pussy before I tease the tip of my tongue at her opening, my fingers still sitting just inside her warm pussy.

"Riggs," she whispers, propping herself on her elbows and watching as I eat her pretty little cunt. My tongue teasingly glides back towards her clit, swirling the tip. I push my fingers deep inside of her, curling them up as I rub her g-spot. Aspen's legs part wider and her pelvis tilts up as her moans begin to fill the room. Her hips grind, her pussy riding my face as my tongue laps at her core.

"You taste so good," I groan and run my tongue across my bottom lip, my fingers buried deep inside of her. Her head falls back, her pretty thighs parted and I dive back in, eating her cunt until she is crying out, her body trembling and just as I feel her pussy pulse and throb, I still my fingers and lift my tongue from where it was buried.

She whimpers as I slip my fingers out to the tip, stretching her as I smirk down at her.

"Please," she begs.

"I told you, I'll tell you when you can come."

Another whimper leaves her and my smirk turns into a grin as I slip back inside of her, lowering my mouth over her pussy and gently blowing on her sensitive clit. Flattening my tongue, rubbing it harder over her clit and pubic bone, I feel her hips buck as I slip a third digit in with ease. My eyes lift for a moment as I watch her mouth drop open, her eyes rolling in the back of her head and I gently graze my teeth against her clit, nibbling and sucking as my fingers stretch her and fuck her until she is ready to come but I stop her, slipping my fingers to the tips again and leaving them there, teasing her as she grinds her pussy trying to get herself off.

"You look so pretty when you're desperate." I whisper, kissing the insides of her thighs as I slowly push my three fingers inside of her, my thumb replacing my tongue as I roll her clit under my touch, my teeth sinking into my bottom lip as I watch her writhe in the bedsheets, her hips rolling over my fingers, her pussy being fucked as the palm of my hand rubs against her.

"It's too much..." her voice cracks, "please Riggs," and I hear the desperation that leaves her lips, her chest rising and falling, her silk nightdress up and round her waist. Her hair messy and still curled, her cheeks pinched red. I kneel up slowly, my fingers still buried inside of her as I reach one of my hands down to the base of my neck and grab my shirt, dragging it over my head. I slow my fingers when I realise I can't get my tee off until my fingers aren't buried in her wet little cunt.

"Oops," I rasp, my thumb rubbing, my fingers pumping.

"Let me come," she begs, her body beginning to tremble. I smirk, my cock hard against my jeans.

"You forgot the magic word," I whisper as I lean across her body and bite the thin lace of her nightdress to drag it down, my teeth grazing her nipple as I do. Her tits are perfect. They're full and round, the perfect handful. Locking my tongue around her hard and pert nipple, I flick my tongue quickly as I fuck her with my fingers; my hot mouth back on her sternum as I kiss her, trailing my lips down and dipping my tongue into her navel for just a second. before my lips are back on her skin, grazing across her pelvis and she squirms under me.

Slipping my fingers from her, I kneel back and look down at her, pushing my fingers between my lips and sucking them clean.

"Fuck, you taste so good."

"Please Riggs, pl-ea-se," her breaths are laboured as she stutters out her plea.

With my hand now free, I pull my tee off the rest of the way, throwing it aside. I grin, slowly gliding my hands back up the side of her thighs, my fingers wrapping around her hips as they dig in. Her brows pinch for just a moment as I flip her onto her front, her peachy ass on show, her legs laid straight and open and my cock throbs. I glide my fingertips up and down her spine and bunch her silk night dress higher to expose more of her beautiful skin.

"What a sight," I whisper, pulling my bottom lip between my teeth as I take a second to just appreciate her. Her eyes find mine over her shoulder and I feel my heart skip a beat in my chest. "Lift your ass in the air baby, let me get to your pretty little pussy." I rasp.

She lifts her hips just off the bed and gives me the perfect view. I lean forward, lowering myself down as I place soft kisses along the crease of her ass, nipping on her sensitive skin as I do.

Skimming across to her soaked cunt, I glide my tongue through her slick folds and tease at her opening, groaning when I hear her whimpers. Lifting my mouth from her and pressing my palm to the base of her spine, I then glide my fingers down between her cheeks and slip one finger into her, pumping in and out slowly before filling her with another.

Watching her tight pussy stretch around my fingers as she pulses and clenches.

"You're such a good girl," I praise, her eyes finding mine again, her teeth sinking into the skin on her upper arm. My spare hand runs up the back of her thigh, massaging my palm into her skin, gliding until I land on the round of ass, giving a gentle squeeze before my fingers curl round her hip and pull her up onto her knees. Slipping my fingers out slowly, I turn and lay on my back as both of my hands land on her waist, pulling her down over my face.

She hovers over me, and my eyes steady on her. I watch as her chest heaves up and down, my hands wrapped around the curve of her hips and the shimmer of perspiration coats her lower skin. She reaches for her bunched night dress, dragging it over her head and discarding it to her floor and I smirk.

Fuck, she is so goddamn beautiful. She's completely naked and I am dressed from my waist down and I don't know why but there is something so hot about it. She looks down at me, the bottom of my face hidden underneath her and having her pussy this close to me is torture.

Squeezing her hips, I dart my tongue out and lick through her lips, sucking on her clit as she moans, I feel the blood rush to my throbbing cock.

"Ride my face Wildflower," I rasp, pulling her pussy onto my face, burying my tongue deep inside of her as her hips begin to move over me. She's soaked and I feel her body tense.

"Riggs," she pants, "I'm close."

Loosening my grip on her hips, I roll them over her hip bones and down to her ass giving her a gentle squeeze then pushing her forward so her hands fall above my head so now she is on all fours.

I grin when I hear the gasp that leaves her, my fingers trailing the inside of her thighs, my tongue rubbing across her clit as I graze my fingertips over her pussy and her body shudders over me.

"I can't take much more, please," she whispers and I don't miss the whine in her tone. My tongue flicking across her clit once more.

"Beg," I rasp just as I sink two fingers deep inside of her.

"Wh-what?" she stammers and I can imagine her cheeks have turned a pretty shade of pink.

"Beg." I order and smirk against her clit before I stroke my tongue against her, "you want to come, you need to beg me."

I tease at a third and she clenches.

"Oh," she moans, her hips rocking back and forth as I edge my third finger into her.

"I'm assuming you don't want to come," I tease as I fill her to my knuckles, her arousal coating my fingers.

"Please," her voice quivers and I flatten my tongue against her swollen clit, shaking my head from side to side softly. Breaking my lips away I look up through my lashes at her.

"Not enough," I growl, my tongue back on her clit.

"Please Riggs, I..." she moans as I slip my fingers to the tip and tease her. I swirl my tongue at her opening, running it along my coated fingers and plunge the tip into her wet, hot cunt. "Shit," she whispers, her nails curling in her comforter as her hips buck, moving back and forth as she silently pleads to be filled once more.

"That's not a beg darlin'" I grin as I watch my fingers slowly slip into her and she shudders.

"Riggs, please, let me come," she cries, whimpering on her inhale of breath and I can't lift my eyes from watching my fingers fuck her perfect pussy.

"Beg one more time Dinks, I want to watch you beg," I rasp, my lips grazing against the inside of her thighs. I pull my fingers from her and she whines at the loss. I fist myself from my pants, my cock aching and so ready to be inside of her.

Lifting her, I move her down so she is hovering over my hard cock.

"Beg me baby," I rasp, my cock bobbing at the thought of sinking deep into her pussy.

"Make me come Riggs, let me come all over your cock," and I feel a guttural growl from deep inside of me erupt and vibrate in my throat. Wrapping my fingers around my cock, I line myself up and rub the head of my cock over her swollen clit before I edge myself into her. I watch as her eyes roll in the back of her head. Her soaked cunt feels amazing as I slowly fill her in one roll of my hips, her hands pressed against my chest, my mouth falling open as pleasure pulses through me but I ignore it, trying to push it back down as I'm not ready to have this all over with a few strokes of being inside of her.

"Ride my cock and touch yourself Wildflower," I smirk, my fingers trailing up her side as I grope her tits, squeezing and kneading before rolling her nipples between my finger and thumb. Her hand shakily skims down her sternum, across her stomach and dips between her legs as her fingers rub in small, soft circles over her clit. Letting my hands fall to her hips, she lifts herself up and down on my cock, her knees bent, her feet resting on the mattress. One of her hands skims across my thigh as she steadies herself and leans back as I get a better view of her cunt riding me, her arousal coating me.

"Riggs," she cries, her movements getting sloppy and her fingers rubbing a little harder now.

"Fuck, you look so pretty filled with my cock. I want you to come now baby and I want to watch you fall apart whilst coating my cock in your cum," I pant, my fingers digging harder into her skin as I pin her still, my hips lifting as I impale her down on me. Her pussy tightens and clamps as her sweet as fuck moans fill the room, the sound of my skin and hers clashing and fuck, it sounds fucking heavenly mixed with her erotic moans.

I slow for a moment, lifting her to the head of my thick cock and I slowly slip in and out of her.

"Yes, oh fuck, please Riggs. I need you, please, *please*," her fucking pleas are desperate and with that, I squeeze her hips and slam her down onto my cock, filling her like she asked. I fuck her hard and fast, her whole body quivers as she comes hard, her head falling back and I feel her pussy pulse around my cock.

"There's a good girl, coming all over my cock," I grit, my teeth clenched as I try and hold off my own orgasm.

I don't give her a minute to breathe, lifting her off me I push her forward so her cum filled cunt is over my face and I bury my tongue deep inside of her, moaning as I eat her like she was my last meal.

"Fuck," she rasps and I am desperate to fuck her how I want. Sliding out from underneath her, I keep her on all fours. Kneeling behind her, I disregard my jeans fully. Rubbing my hand over her ass, I give her a moment to come down from her almighty high and I focus on her dripping cunt. My spare hand runs underneath her as I rub her sensitive clit then slip my fingers through her soaked pussy, sinking two inside of her. Her arms give out, her chest flat to the bed and her ass is in the air. Her legs spread wider, tilting her pelvis back giving me a fucking spectacular view of her pussy and I spit on her drenched opening then rub my fingers roughly, mixing my spit and her arousal together.

"I am going to ruin you Aspen, no other man will ever be able to make you feel the way I do," I groan, edging closer and lining my cock at her opening. "I'm not going to go easy on you, I am going to fuck you so hard."

She whimpers as I edge into her, I feel her walls clench around me. Stilling for a moment and inhaling on a shaky breath because I am so close to exploding.

After a second or two, my fingers dig into her hips and I lift her ass up a little higher, her fingers crunch the bedding beneath her, her eyes finding mine over her shoulder. Her hazel eyes are full of lust and want and I growl, my whole body a blaze with heat, my skin on fire as I slam my hips forward, my cock sliding deep inside of her as she mewls. I don't slow or warm her up, I plough into her, my hips pushing in and out of her at a fast but steady pace. My head tips back for a moment as I relish in the pleasure that is coursing through me, the familiar tingle that has me in a chokehold, my orgasm brimming.

My head falls forward when Aspen lets out a loud moan.

"Quiet darlin' we don't want to get caught now do we..." I lean across her back, whispering in her ear, my hand wrapping in her hair as I tug her head back, her back arching.

She whimpers, my cock pumping deep, slow strokes into her.

"I'm going to fill you up with all of me," I rasp, pushing

up from her back and I curl my hand around her hip. I pick up my pace, my cock slipping in and out of her with ease when I feel her legs tremble. "You going to come again for me Wildflower?" my voice strained, my jaw tight as I feel my orgasm building.

"Yes," she whispers and I slow completely, my cock buried deep inside of her.

"Then use me, move those hips and fuck me," I grin down at her, watching as her hips begin to move over me, pulling me to the tip, holding for a moment and I roll my eyes as she pushes down onto me, burying my aching cock deep inside of her. "You're such a good girl." I praise her as she does it again, "and now I am going to fill you up pretty girl," I groan, wanting to take full control.

I pull myself out, holding her hips and flipping her onto her back. My hands skim up the inside of her thighs and push her legs wide and into the bed, I fist my cock, lining the head of my cock up. Rolling my hips forward I fill her in one move, fucking her. Hard. Riding her into the mattress until my orgasm possesses me completely, driving forward as my cock spears in and out of her perfect pussy and I feel her tighten round me. Her fingers rub over her clit, her chest rising and falling fast and I watch her lips part, her eyes hazy as they flutter shut, I continue riding my orgasm, my cock pulsing inside of her.

"You promised me one more," I grit, my fingers digging into the skin on her thighs and I lift her slightly, smirking when I watch her come undone beneath me, her back arching, her body trembling. She is covered in a sheen of sweat and it's not until my hips slow that I see she is crying.

"Shit," I pant, slowly removing my fingers from her skin as I lay across her, my lips brushing against her lips, my thumbs wiping away her tears. "Are you okay? Did I hurt you?" Panic claws from deep inside of me.

She smiles, her eyes glassy as she shakes her head from side to side. "I am perfect Riggs, my orgasm was just so *intense,*" she whispers, her hands clasping my face as she pulls my lips down to hers. "I love you Riggs," she whispers into my mouth, her lips brushing against mine.

"Not as much as I love you, Aspen." I say before consuming her once more.

CHAPTER TWENTY-NINE
ASPEN

APRIL

Shutting the lid of my laptop down, I take my mug and place it in the dishwasher. The house is quiet. Mom is out with friends, while dad and Austin are with the mares. My confidence is growing each day around the horses and I am proud of myself. I still don't know whether I will ever get on the back of one again, but to be able to stand next to one now and run my hands over their neck is a huge step for me. From being crippled with fear and paralyzed to now feeling a sense of calm. I slip on my cowboy boots and grab the hat that Riggs got me a few weeks ago to stop me from taking his.

I smirk as I lower the brown cowboy hat onto my head. Quickly spinning round, I give myself a once over in the mirror. Last week I decided to cut my hair short and tone down the lighter blonde strands that were once there. It sits in choppy waves on my shoulders and I honestly love it. My eyes skim down to the yellow summer dress I am wearing with small daisies on. The skirt sits just on my thighs, four buttons trail down from just above my sternum revealing a little bit of cleavage. Twisting my lips at the thought of Riggs seeing me in this dress then sneaking me off somewhere and fucking me senseless thrills me. Ignoring my thoughts, I push through the front door, Butch follows me out and I am surprised as he is normally with my mom. Traitor.

Skipping down the steps, I walk across to the stables where I am guessing my dad and Austin are. Pacing forward, I smile when I hear their voices.

"Hey, all okay?" I call out as I step over the threshold of the stables and I can't stop the anxiety that prickles deep within me, a shiver dancing up and down my spine as I take another step closer.

"All good, we're just waiting to find out if Peach is pregnant. This will be her first foal, she didn't fall last year." My dad pauses for a moment as Harlow begins her checks.

I step a little closer and look around into the stable to see the dapple mare, ears back as Harlow gets ready to do her examination.

"Have you used the same stallion?" I ask, swallowing down my nerves.

"No, Kray is a new stallion." Austin pipes up, his hands fisted in his pocket.

"Don't forget you owe me a night out," I say softly to Harlow. We had to cancel our catch up because Harlow caught a stomach bug and between the mares and her work, the days have just slipped past.

"I know, I promise I'll make it up to you." She looks over at me and gives me a wink as she gloves up.

"Cool," I nod, stepping back for a moment and removing myself out of view whilst she does her examinations.

"You okay?" Harlow calls out, her voice strained.

"Yup," I shout back.

I hear my dad chuckle and Austin pops his head round the stable door.

"Sure you're alright?" he asks, his brows furrowed as his eyes search my face.

"Yeah fine," I wave him off and smile.

"Go and check Bonnie, I was in the middle of doing their hay when Harlow turned up."

I nod, kicking the toe of my boot onto the concrete floor and sigh as I force myself down there. Walking to the back of the stall, I grab an empty net and start filling it with haylage. As the sweet smell fills my nose something deep inside of me sparks, a warmth coursing through me. It sparks a familiarity, an old love for something that nearly destroyed me. Tightening the now full hay net, I throw it over my shoulder and walk towards Bonnie's stall. Bonnie is in foal, she was confirmed last week and Harlow thinks she should birth early March next year and I can't wait to see the little colts and fillies prance round the fields.

Sliding the bolt of Bonnie's stall, I pause for a moment before slowly opening her door. She grunts, her eyes on me and I watch as her ears turn and flatten. *Don't panic.* Bonnie is a leopard Appaloosa. She really is beautiful. But she is stubborn and a bit of a bitch.

"Hey girl," I try and say as confident as I can but I know she can sense my fear.

Shuffling my feet across the concrete, I try and move a little quicker but my heart is jackhammering in my chest, nausea rolling in my stomach.

Bonnie stamps her hoof to the floor and I try to stop the tremor that is threatening to seep out of me.

"I just want to put your hay in," I say quietly, moving a little closer as I see the silver ring on the stable wall.

"You've got this Wildflower," I hear Riggs' voice float across me. I look over my shoulder at him and my heart slows, his beautiful green eyes land on mine and I feel the ground slip from beneath my feet for just a moment. "I'm so proud of how far you've come," he praises me and I feel the tears prick behind my eyes, my throat bobbing as I try and swallow down the lump that begins to form. I ignore the burning in my throat, like someone has shoved a hot stake down and suddenly I can't breathe.

He closes the gap in one long stride, his body pressed against mine but his hands stay off my body. I close my eyes for a moment, his breath on the back of my neck.

"You look so fucking beautiful in that dress, what I would do to hitch it up and have my wicked way with you," he lowers his lips between my neck and shoulder, smiling against my hot skin.

"Stop that," I giggle and I am grateful for the small distraction.

"Only trying to make you feel better Dinks."

"And you have," I breathe, taking half a step forward as I loop the string through the silver ring and freeze when Bonnie nudges at my shoulder with her nuzzle.

"Don't panic," Riggs' eyes pin to mine and I suddenly forget how to breathe.

"Riggs," I whisper, my eyes widening. Riggs steps a little closer, his lips lifting slowly before he breaks into a smile.

"She just wants to say hello," he reassures me, now inside the stable as he steps towards Bonnie, standing next to her and rubbing behind her now pointed ears. I manage to tie the string and I rush out the stable so I finally feel as if I can breathe.

Riggs scratches Bonnie's neck then gives her a pat before walking out of the stable and bolting it across.

His back is to me and I sweep my eyes over him, feeling the heat blossom between my thighs. When he turns to face me, he catches me staring.

"Like what you see darlin'?" he winks as he slowly walks towards me and I nod. "I'll let you have a proper look later, but right now, we're getting you on the back of a horse."

My eyes widen and panic courses through me.

"Aspen, baby, I promise it'll be okay. Do you trust me?" he cocks his head to the side, his eyes volleying between mine waiting for me to answer.

After what feels like hours, I finally nod.

He smiles, his fingertips brushing against mine and I don't miss the spark of electricity that courses through me, my heart racing.

"I've got you."

As I follow Riggs out of the stables, we walk along the fence line down to his ranch and my mind wanders back to the day of my accident.

RIGGS WAS WATCHING in complete awe of me and Blossom. We were a team and a strong one. I knew we had what it took to be one of the best. I was clearing the jumps, we moved in sync, Blossom's strides immaculate. We were more than ready, but I needed to practice until I knew we were as perfect as could be. I was rounding the outside arena just before the final jump which was a Swedish Oxer. I could do this jump with my eyes closed.

My heart beat slowed, matching Blossom's canter strides and in the moment I was approaching the jump, all I could hear was the way my heart beat in my chest, the way the blood pumped in my ears. Lifting myself out of the saddle, I dropped my heels and nudged her on and my hands moved up Blossom's neck as I gave her a little more slack on her mouthpiece.

Four.

Three.

Two.

I kicked her on a little harder to push her over the jump, I was stood in the stirrups, my legs straight and instead of Blossom soaring over the poles, she spooked just at the last moment, her front legs coming down on the bars before she bucked and as much as I tried to stay on, I couldn't. One of my feet slipped from my stirrup, the other boot slipping forward so most of my foot was through it, she reared up then kicked her back legs out once more, my fingers were tight around her reins and just when I thought I had a hold of her, a loud bang from behind the bunkhouse spooked her again. She jolted to the side giving one last buck for good measure and I was thrown off her back, my arm stuck through her rein and as much as I tried, I couldn't get my boot free. Everything moved in slow motion as I was thrown over Blossom's neck, but all I could hear was Riggs shouting out my name.

My back landed on the poles of the jump and I fell through them, my arm was still entangled in the reins and it felt as if my shoulder was ripped from my socket and I knew my leg was broken. It was a matter of seconds before the pain radiated through me and I let out a blood curdling scream.

"You okay darlin'?" Riggs asks as he pulls me out of my flashback and I mutter back. We duck and climb through the fence and towards the stables. "I'm going to put you on the lazy cob," he gives me a wink as I fall a little behind him, anxiety making itself known as my stomach knots. Tay, the piebald cob was more of a companion mare, she was well loved but she definitely wasn't a cowboy's horse.

"I'm not sure about this Riggs," I say as I slow my steps, my eyes looking round the ranch at a few of the cowboys, all their eyes on me.

"Ignore everyone else around you. We should have got you back on a horse years ago, you need to do this for you Aspen." He turns to face me and gives me a small smile. "Trust me?"

And I have no idea why, but I am nodding.

"Paul, go tack up Tay," he orders the young ranch hand.

"Sure thing Riggs," Paul says quickly as he disappears into the stables. Riggs makes his way back over to me and stands close to me.

"One step at a time baby, okay?"

I stay mute when I see Paul return with Tay all saddled up and my heart drops into my stomach, suddenly feeling sick.

"Can we just leave this as the first step?" my words are rushed, my tongue feeling as if it's swelling in my mouth and suddenly my chest hurts as I try and suck in as much air as I can to fill my lungs.

"You can do this," he says quietly before stepping forward and taking the reins from Paul and walking the pretty cob over to me.

He stops her just in front of me and my eyes roam over her body.

"Take your time, stroke her and let her know you're not afraid," he says softly as he scratches behind her ear and throws the reins over her head so they're resting on the nape of her mane.

"But I am afraid," I swallow down the bitter taste that is coating my tongue and I realise it's bile.

"She'll sense it, I need you to be brave baby," his voice is low so the other cowboys don't hear. "Horses are great healers, give her a hug, I promise you'll feel so much better," he cocks his head to the side and I contemplate it for a moment as my eyes move between him and the cob.

Sighing, I ignore the way my heart is thumping so hard in my chest and the way my blood is thrashing in my ears. I stand just to the side of Tay's head so she can see me. I hold my hand up then slowly move my trembling fingers to her nose, trying to still my fingers as I feel the hot air coming from her nostrils.

Slowing my breathing, I run the tips of my fingers on the end of her nuzzle, stroking the soft pink area of her nose and my stomach flips.

"She's a gentle giant. Mom of the mares without actually being a mom," Riggs smiles as he looks at Tay. I step a little closer, my heart feels like it's in my throat and I am struggling to breathe. Holding my other trembling hand up, I hold it over her neck for a second then slowly and gently place it on the warm skin of Tay's neck.

"You're doing so well Aspen," Riggs goes back to his praise and pride swarms me. This might not seem like a big deal, but to me, this was huge.

Leaning in slightly, I place my cheek against the soft fur and inhale deeply, my arm looping over her mane and I still for a moment and ignore the way my heart is galloping in my chest, but I don't feel as nervous now that I am close to her. Letting my emotions and anxiety seep into the ground below me ready to bury themselves deep and root underground.

Moments pass when I feel Riggs softly grabbing my elbow and pulling me closer to him.

"Let's get you on the back of her," he whispers, burying his lips into my hair and then planting a feather like kiss on my cheek. I pull on my fingers to try and keep myself from getting anxious again. I look at the stirrup and then at the seat of the saddle.

I could do this.

I knew I could do this.

I just *had* to do it.

Fumbling about for a moment as I reach for the reins I then drop my hand again, my eyes focusing on the stirrups. Inhaling deeply, I look over my shoulder at my growing audience.

"Hey, Dinks, eyes on me," Riggs' husky voice pulls my attention and my hazel eyes settle on him. "Focus on me, ignore everyone else. It's just you and me," he gives a slow but soft nod.

I nod back at him, then look back up at the reins. My eyes close and I ignore everything else around me.

Look how far you have come.

Look how much you have grown since being back home.

You've got this Aspen.

You can do this.

Letting my eyes flutter open, I reach up with my left hand and grab hold of the reins. Riggs is standing at my side and I ignore the way my heart is racing in my chest like a wild mustang who is stabled up and kept from running free. I turn to give Riggs one last look and he winks, lifting his hat off his head.

I pause for a moment, anxiety and panic swarming me.

"I can't." I shake my head, my voice barely audible.

Riggs' eyes darken for a moment and he closes the gap with two steps, his eyes penetrating mine.

"You can, and you will," his tone is curt and low and it makes my skin pebble. "Remember when you said you couldn't come four times in one night?" he rasps and my cheeks turn crimson, my insides heat and the apex between my thighs burns. "Well, you surpassed that didn't you my little pillow princess," he slowly licks his bottom lip as if reliving the moment. "Get on the horse," he nods towards Tay and my eyes follow his.

"I can do it."

"Yes, you can."

"I can," I say a little louder and before I can even let fear get the best of me, I tighten my grip on the reins and slip the toe of my cowboy boot into the stirrup. Just as I go to pull myself up, Riggs moves close behind me and confusion masks my face until I realise. I have a dress on and we have an audience. Riggs moves his hat to where the back of my dress sits, midway down my thighs, so as I swing my leg over the back of Tay, he covers me from prying eyes with his hat until my ass is on the saddle.

I freeze, my face turned to look at Riggs and he beams with pride, his arm lifting as he places his hat back on his head.

"That's my girl," he gives Tay a pat on the neck and then lowers his lips, brushing them against my bare thigh. "You did it baby, I'm so damn proud of you."

And without realising, tears are rolling down my cheeks.

CHAPTER THIRTY
ASPEN

Sitting in the front of Riggs' truck, my feet are pressed against the dash as Harlow and Austin sit in the back, soft country songs surrounding us and we're all sitting in comfortable silence. We had been away for the weekend at one of the horse shows and my god it felt so good to be back in the environment. My heart leaped as I watched the riders and their horses combat the show jumping course, each and every single one of them excelled and I watched in awe, but I also had a sickening jealousy that the dream I once had was no more. What made me even more sick to my stomach was that it was my fault. I could have climbed back on the horse once I was healed and worked my confidence back, but instead I sunk into the shadows and focused on literature and moving out of Lovelock Bay and into New York. I sigh, that part of my life feels like a lifetime ago when in reality, it was only a few years. I have done a full circle and I am back home where I have never felt more myself.

I watch as Riggs looks in the rearview mirror at Austin

and Harlow who are turned and facing each other, their voices quiet as it seems they share a private moment between themselves. I face Riggs and let out a little sigh just as Riggs' hand skims across the center of his truck and rests on my thigh for just a moment. I missed him this weekend and I know that sounds silly because I have been with him, but having to share a room with Harlow wasn't what I wanted. I give him a flirtatious smirk as his fingers drag off my jeans and land back on the steering wheel. My thoughts wander back to Saturday night when I snuck out of the hotel room whilst Harlow was sleeping.

IT HAD JUST PASSED one a.m. and me and Riggs had been texting each other. I was desperate to see him, to have his hands on me, his lips on mine and I knew I needed to go to him. I snuck out of our room and tiptoed across to his and Austin's. We agreed I would give one gentle knock on the solid red hotel room door. Lifting my hand, I do just that and the waiting is the worse part. What if Austin opens the door and sees me, what the hell would I say? I am dressed in a cream trench coat and nothing underneath but a pair of black lacy panties.

I hear the lock slide across the hotel door and relief swarms me when I see Riggs standing there, his curly hair messy and a wide grin on his face.

He says nothing, but looks over his shoulder to make sure we're clear before he wraps his fingers around my wrist and pulls me into the hotel room. Closing the door quietly, he pushes me against it and I grin up at him, my heart racing. My hands are in his hair, locking through his soft curls as his large, hard, calloused hands cup my face.

"You're so fucking beautiful. Damn I've missed you," he

rasps, his lips brushing against mine before he drags them down to my jaw and trailing them to my neck.

"It's been a few hours big boy."

"A few hours is too long." He smirks against the sensitive skin on my neck, his lips pursing over my pulse point.

"We're so wrong for doing this," I whisper and a spike of fear impales me.

"It's only wrong if we get caught," his beautiful green eyes are on mine and my heart stammers in my chest.

"We need to tell them, I don't want to sneak around anymore," I say as Riggs' hands skim down my side, his arms wrapping around my waist as my legs circle his.

"We will, I'm being selfish because I like you being mine and only mine." His lips press against mine. "But for you, I'm ready to shout it from the rooftops," he smiles and walks me towards the bathroom and sits me on the edge of the sink unit. He turns, sliding the lock across and testing it just to be safe.

When he is facing me again, I let my eyes sweep over the beautiful man in front of me. Broad, muscular shoulders, his chest dusted with brown hair, his chest and torso toned but not overly defined. Skimming my hazel eyes down, I pull my bottom lip between my teeth slowly at the light trail of hair that disappears into the waist of his boxers. His hard cock evident as it bulges in the pouch of his boxers.

"You turned on Riggs?" I wink as I let my fingers fumble with the tie that sits round my waist. Untying it, I pull it open and I watch as Riggs' eyes darken and they roam over me and the want is evident. I have never been made to feel as desirable as Riggs makes me feel.

"Fuck," he groans, stepping towards me his hands pushing my legs wide as he settles between them. "Can you be quiet Aspen?" his hands knead my breast, rolling my nipples between his fingers. "And remember I love you okay?"

I nod in response to both his questions.

"Good, because I am about to fuck you like I hate you."

MY CHEEKS REDDEN and I feel flustered at the memory.

"You okay?" Riggs asks as he grabs my attention and I nod, blushing even harder now.

"Just reliving a memory over the weekend," I say just low enough for him to hear me over the music and I roll my lips to hide my smirk.

"Oh," is all he says, his sunglasses on as his lips widen into a beautiful smile.

"Hey," Harlow sits forward, her head popping through the middle of mine and Riggs' seats.

"Hey," I tuck a strand of my hair behind my ear and turn in my seat to face her.

"Shall we go for drinks tonight? The mares are all in foal now and my schedule is not as busy over the next couple of weeks. We can go somewhere different if you don't fancy the Boot?"

"Nah the Boot is fine, it's familiar isn't it." I smile and I see Riggs side eye me.

"It's a date then," she falls back into her seat and beams.

"I've got Conrad coming later on this afternoon to take care of a few things," Austin breaks his silence and I hear Riggs grunt.

"Shall we get some drinks in Riggs? Get Pacey and Tripp together and maybe roll down to the bunkhouse?" Austin asks and I see Riggs tighten his grip on his steering wheel before smiling into the rearview mirror.

"Yeah, sounds good."

"You're welcome to join us?" I say softly, already

dreading heading out without Riggs. I am so needy and I have never been this girl. I have never been clingy but with Riggs, I feel like I am a whole new person.

"It's okay ba..." Riggs' eyes widen and as he snaps his head to me then focuses back on the road ahead. "Aspen," he coughs, clearing his throat and I let out a little giggle.

"Yeah, you have girls night, we can have boys night," Austin chimes and I settle myself back into my seat as we finish the last leg of our journey.

Pulling into Rivera Ranch, Riggs parks in the car port and Austin and Harlow jump out. Dusk is just setting in and I feel exhausted. She stops by my window as she gives it a gentle tap, "I'll see you at eight? That work with you?"

"Yeah, I need to wash the road off me. I feel wrecked," a laugh bubbles out of me and she nods.

"I feel that," she chimes, "I'll knock at eight." Turning, she runs to catch up with Austin who lugs both their bags over his shoulders and I watch as they walk down the fence line towards our house.

I let out a deep exhale, my head resting on the headrest as I turn my face to Riggs. He mirrors me, resting his own head but facing me. He scoops my hand in his and brings the back of it to his lips, soft butterfly kisses trailing back and forth and my skin pebbles.

"I don't want to know what life feels like without you," my voice cracks and I have no idea why I am suddenly feeling so emotional and overwhelmed.

"Baby," I don't miss the concern that is wrapped in his gravelly tone, "you never have to imagine what a life without me feels like. We're endgame Wildflower, it's me and you against the world. I let you slip from my grasp once, there is no way I am letting you go again."

He drops my hand from his and brushes his thumb against my cheek, my eyes cast down as I steady my breathing for a moment.

"Why didn't you stop me from leaving?" my eyes lift, and I feel my soul shatter at the emotions that hide behind his eyes.

"I..." he rasps then pauses for a moment, rubbing his hand under his beard.

"I wanted you to beg me to stay Riggs," my voice cracks.

I hear him sigh.

"Would you have stayed?" he asks deadpan, and I open my mouth before shutting it again. Because honestly, I probably wouldn't have. I wanted out. I felt suffocated here when I was younger and I felt after my accident I was destined for so much more than what this small town had to offer.

I shake my head from side to side and I hear the deep sigh that fills his lungs.

"I suppose everything changed after prom night..." I trail off and I feel my heart thump a little louder in my chest.

"I'll regret that night for the rest of my life," his voice is low as his fingers link through mine and gives my hand a tight squeeze and I smile as my head casts down, my eyes fluttering shut. "I should have never listened to my dad."

I blink. Snapping my head up, I turn to look at him.

"What do you mean?" I pinch my brows and my heart skips a nervous beat.

"My dad told me not to take you to prom, told me not to go there with you because work with your dad was too important. He thought I was going to fuck their deal up or some shit..." he pauses and I can see the remorse in his eyes.

"Riggs," I whisper, because if I say his name aloud, he will hear the sadness in my voice. And everything I once thought about Riggs was about to change in this moment.

CHAPTER THIRTY-ONE
RIGGS

"I suppose everything changed after prom night…" and I hear the sadness in her voice as she trails off and falls silent. The blood thumps in my ears almost deafening me. Now is my time to come clean. After all of these years of her thinking I didn't want to take her to prom, all the years thinking I rejected her which pushed her into Pacey's arms all comes down to this moment right here.

"I'll regret that night for the rest of my life," my voice is low, almost a whisper as my fingers link through hers and I give her small, warm hand a tight squeeze. I watch her with intent, memorising every feature of her in case she gets out of this truck and never looks back. I watch as her lips tug at the sides, a sweet smile playing on her lips as she lets her head dip and her eyelids flutter to hide her beautiful hazel eyes. "I should have never listened to my dad."

"What do you mean?" Her head snaps up, her face turning to face me as her brows crease along her beautiful face.

I swallow.

It's now or never.

"My dad told me not to take you to prom, told me not to go there with you because work with your dad was too important. He thought I was going to fuck their deal up or some shit..." I pause and remorse flicks through my eyes, guilt squeezing my heart.

"Riggs," she whispers, and I can see the sadness behind her eyes and my heart drops. Suddenly my chest aches and I ignore the want to rub the ache away. The pain that radiates from her is crystal clear and I feel like I've ripped the band-aid off a bullet hole, knowing full well I'll never be able to stop the bleeding.

My throat is thick and my heart is galloping like a wild horse in my chest.

"He told me that I would ruin you by keeping you in Lovelock Bay. He knew you liked me and that I liked you, but he didn't want me to keep you caged and living in a life that you never really wanted. You were so passionate about your dreams and getting out of this town that I didn't want to be the one to hold you back." I give her hand another squeeze but her small hand feels loose around my grip and suddenly she pulls it from mine.

"You should have followed me instead of listening to your dad! You should have shown me that you wanted me Riggs because honestly, I always *just* felt like Austin's kid sister to you!" she raises her voice now and she has every right to.

I feel my own rage bubbling away inside of me, I hate that I have made her upset and angry.

"I did follow!" I finally snap and her wide honey eyes steady on mine.

She says nothing.

"I went against my dad's wishes and followed you into the city, and do you know what I saw Aspen?" I pause for a beat or two and wait for her to respond, but she just shakes her head from side to side. "You. I saw you Aspen; flourishing. You were your own person; you were finding a new dream without me or anyone here in Lovelock Bay." I choke, my voice cracking, my heart hurts and I swear it is cracking in my chest, slowly disintegrating as I finally speak my truth.

I catch her glassy eyes volleying back and forth between mine, a tear rolling down her cheek and I am desperate to wipe it away, but I don't. I watch as she angrily swipes it away.

"I wanted you to live the life you wanted Aspen, a life you deserved and that meant a life without me," I sniffle, my throat tight and my voice thick. "But the truth was Aspen, I *still* wanted you after everything happened between you and Pacey. You moved on, your world spun and you thrived whilst we all stayed here, frozen in time it seemed." I scrub my face, "I even ran out into the rain on prom night, but you were already gone."

Curling my fingers round the steering wheel, I tighten my grip and look straight ahead of me and out of the windscreen.

"I wanted you Riggs. I wanted it all with you. I left because I didn't think you wanted me... I couldn't bear to live so close to you knowing that you didn't feel the same. The shame and embarrassment I felt after prom night was too much, I love all of you, but you, Riggs. You were the one for me. It's always been you," and my heart thumps a little harder, a little stronger as slowly, the pieces seem to fix back into place. "But I just need a minute to absorb all of this," she unbuckles herself and reaches for her bag by her feet and opens the truck door.

"I'm not mad at you Riggs, not even a little bit. I just feel like my life would have been so different if I had known the truth," she gives me a sad smile and I will for her to look at me, but she doesn't. She slips out the door and slams it shut and instead of following, I listen to her demands.

Like I always do.

Just like I did with my dad when I let the only girl I have ever truly loved, walk away.

CHAPTER THIRTY-TWO
ASPEN

Riggs words replay in my head on a loop. He never stood me up, he never regretted asking me to prom and he never changed his mind. He put on his tux and was ready to walk out the door, yet he never made it to me because of his father.

I get it.

I do.

Work is important, but so were my feelings for Riggs Rivera.

Confusion consumes me with a hint of sadness, and I feel like our weekend has been somehow tainted.

Tarnished like overworn silver.

Pushing through the door of my house, I sigh when I realise I've left my luggage in the back of Riggs' truck.

"Sweetie?" my mom calls as she rounds the corner of the kitchen and smiles when she sees me, her arms wide as she waits to embrace me and I run into her open arms, tightening my grip around her body and I cling onto her like a needy toddler.

"Are you okay?"

I nod as I choke out sobs that seep into her t-shirt.

"Oh Aspen," she coos, wrapping her arms a little tighter round me as she lets me cry it out. I feel ashamed for crying, but it's true what I said to Riggs, if I knew his truth, if I knew how he really felt my whole life would have been different. I forced myself to love a man because my true love didn't want me back. But that all changed minutes ago when Riggs poured his heart and soul out to me in his truck.

"You don't have to say anything, but are you hurt? Did someone hurt you?" I shake my head from side to side as I sniffle, my intake of breath stuttering at the back of my throat.

"Okay," she places her mouth on the top of my head and places a soft kiss.

After a moment or two, I unwrap myself from her and run my ring fingers under my now puffy, bloodshot eyes.

"Go upstairs, I'll bring you a nice cup of tea up," my mom smiles sweetly at me and all I can do is nod.

Tightening my fingers round the strap of my bag, I begin to walk up the stairs and I somehow feel a little heavier since Riggs' admission.

Flopping onto my bed, my whole room reminds me of him. I feel like his scent is on everything and it feels like a comfort blanket swaddled around me. I curl on my bed and instantly my head is filled with *exile* by Taylor Swift.

I'm not alone long when my mom perches herself on the edge of my bed as she reaches and places my tea on the nightstand. Her hand resting on my forehead as her fingers delicately brush the few strands away from my eyes.

"It'll be okay, it always works out in the end," she says softly, and I tremble.

Because I know it's the truth.

Everything works out in the end.

And this is far from the end of mine and Riggs' story.

***

IT'S JUST past six and I am sitting at my laptop, my eyes feel dry and bloodshot from the tears that I have shed, but my fingers are dancing across the keyboard as I use this emotion that is simmering inside of me and pour it into my words. I know Riggs didn't mean to hurt me, I am more upset that he listened to his dad but then again, he was a kid himself. His dad isn't someone you say no to, and Riggs' life was always the ranch. *Live by the ranch, die by the ranch,* Jorge's motto echoes around my head.

The minutes slip by and eight p.m. soon rolls right around and I internally groan. I debated cancelling on Harlow, but honestly, I think the night is more needed now than it was when we agreed to it back in the truck.

Saving my work, I close the lid of my laptop and I let out a heavy sigh. This story is flowing and I am so proud of myself for nearly finishing it and I know this is the one I want to publish and throw into the world because it's raw, it's real and it's my ending. The ending I want, the ending I am wishing comes true for me and Riggs but now, I have no idea if my happily ever after will stay a work of fiction or whether I will get to live it out in real life.

Pushing away from my desk, I stand and stroll towards the door. Grabbing my purse, I toss in the phone that Tripp gave me, my lipstick and keys. I have no idea how late we will stay out but I don't want to risk waking my mom and dad. A toot of a horn lets me know she is here and I give myself a once over in the mirror in the hallway of my home. I'm wearing high-waisted light denim jeans and a white frilled cropped shirt, the buttons a little low and exposing some of my chest. My hair sits in loose curls and rests on my shoulders and my make-up is minimal, but my dark eye circles are covered. That was my main concern when I was doing my make-up. I looked as if I had been dug up and that was certainly not the look I was going for.

Tearing my eyes away from my reflection, I plaster a fake smile on my face and walk out into one of the warmer evenings we've had in the past week. My pace picks up as I climb down the steps and head towards Austin's truck and Harlow is sitting up front. Opening the passenger door to the cab, I climb in and Harlow looks behind the seat and into the back to where I am sitting and she smiles wide at me.

"You look pretty."

"Thanks," I swallow, rubbing my palms down my jeans, "so do you," I return the compliment.

Austin catches my sigh in the rear-view.

"You okay Pen?" he asks using my kid nickname and my heart swells.

"Yeah, fine. Tired. Been a long weekend but thank you for convincing me to go... I really enjoyed it. Was nice watching something I once loved."

"You're welcome, I'm glad you came too. I spent most of my time watching your face light up as soon as the riders and their horses entered the ring," he smiles and I see the glisten in his eyes as he swings the truck round and drives slowly down our driveway.

"Ha," I half laugh, "I was just in awe of them." I lick my lips and check my phone to see if Riggs had messaged, but he hadn't and I'm not sure why but disappointment surges through me. We haven't even had a fight, yet it feels like we have. We're not even official and yet it feels as if we have broken up.

I ignore the anxiety that swarms deep inside of me, nerves pricking at the back of my neck and making me sweat a little.

My phone beeps and I jump as Austin and Harlow speak quietly.

Fumbling, I pull it out and see a message from Riggs and my heart skips a beat.

RIGGS

Be safe. I love you Aspen, it's infinite. It always has been. It's always been you. R x

My eyes gloss over and I swallow down the tears. I re-read his message and send him one back.

ASPEN

'The infinity symbol', forever and always.

Slipping my phone back into my bag, I listen in on Austin and Harlow's conversation.

"So, anything you two want to tell me?" I ask, ignoring the way my heart is banging in my chest.

"Er," Austin nervously laughs as he slices his gaze across to Harlow and then to me in the mirror. "I have no idea what you're talking about Pen," he shakes his head from side to side.

"Give me some credit," I roll my eyes, "Harlow has always had a thing for you, and you Austin have always had a thing for her," I scoff a laugh.

I hear Harlow giggle through her nerves.

"We're just friends," I hear Harlow counter back and I just shake my own head.

"If you say so," I puff out my cheeks as I see the Boot

come into view, the tires crunching across the gravel as Austin slows.

"Have fun with Riggs and the guys tonight," I say, leaning through the middle of the two front seats and give Austin a kiss on the cheek.

"You too," he smiles, lifting his cap off his head, his fingers scraping through his hair before he puts it back on.

"Yeah, have fun," Harlow mutters, lingering for a moment and Austin reaches across and shakes her hand.

What the fuck.

I snort a laugh as I clamber out of the truck and my boots hit the dusty ground beneath me.

"Come on," I call out and Harlow walks round the front of the truck and turns her head away from Austin. "You two are shit at lying," I cackle, slipping my arm through hers as we walk arm in arm into the Boot.

Walking into the busy bar, we walk across to the back and take a seat in one of the smaller booths. Tabitha walks over with a huge smile on her face.

"Well, it's been a while since I have seen you both together," her eyes batting between me and Harlow and I smile back at her.

"We've been so busy but we're here now," Harlow sings, her fingers drumming on the wooden table.

"I'm glad," she nods and waits to take our orders.

"Bottle of white?" Harlow asks. I don't fancy wine but to be honest, anything that has alcohol in seems like a good option at the moment.

"Sure," I reply and Tabitha walks away to fetch it.

We're not waiting long when she comes back with two glasses and the bottle of wine.

"The hot cowboys not joining you tonight?" she asks, hopeful.

"Afraid not, it's girls' night," I give her a soft shrug of my shoulders.

"Damn, I've missed them rough and growly men too," she sighs, waving us off then heads back behind the bar. Harlow reaches for the bottle, unscrewing the lid and filling our glasses to the rim.

Placing it back on the wooden table, I wrap my fingers round the stem of the glass the same time Harlow does and we hold our glasses out in front and smile at each other.

"To old friends," she chimes.

"And shit liars," I say through a laugh, even though I try my hardest to keep a straight face.

Harlow's eyes widen and I watch as her cheeks pinch crimson.

"Look," I say, my voice steady as I take a mouthful of my wine and wince at the taste, "out of all the girls my brother could date, I would rather it be you... but don't lie about it. It is so obvious that there is something going on between the both of you."

"That's the thing," she laughs, but I can see the sadness growing on her pretty face, "there isn't anything going on between us. I mean, we both want it... but," she pauses and takes a large mouthful of her wine.

"But?" I wait for her to answer but she just shakes her head from side to side.

"Don't worry about it. Me and Austin are friends, and we're both okay with that because we would rather be friends than not have each other in our lives."

And her words hit me deep inside.

Maybe that's how Riggs felt.

Maybe that's why he didn't go against his dad because he knew I would always be in his life, whether an acquaintance, friend or lover, I would always be there. The one constant in his life, and in mine. Sure, the years slipped past but there wasn't a day that went by where I didn't think of him.

"Now, speaking of liars," her brows wiggle up and down and I know where she is going with this.

"Just want to point out, I've not once lied," I smile back at her, sitting a little taller.

"Well, you kind of have. You told us you moved home because Luke was so busy... but yet here we are, four months later and he hasn't been by once..."

I swallow. Bile rising in my throat and it burns.

"Let's just say my life in LA wasn't as perfect as it seemed." My voice is quiet and I take a mouthful of my wine, and this time, I didn't wince.

"Were you okay though?" she asks and I can hear the concern that laces her voice.

"Yeah," I roll my lips, "I was, he never hurt me until the day I left, but he was a really good man and for what it's worth, I did love him to some extent. Not as fiercely as I have loved others, but I did love him. If I denied my feelings, *then* I would be a liar and I would wear the title with a huge smile on my face," I cock my head to the side. "But my heart has never really belonged to anyone other than the one that got away, the one I left behind standing on the driveway as my parents drove me away from the farm and out of Lovelock Bay."

"Riggs," she whispers and my eyes glass over.

"Yeah, Riggs."

RIGGS

I'm in a sour mood.

My heart aches, my emotions are all over the place and all I want is to be with Aspen.

I re-read her message, silencing out the noise around me from the rowdy bunkhouse.

WILDFLOWER

'The infinity symbol', forever and always.

Sighing, I lock my phone and place it face down on the table as I reach for my beer, sliding it towards me and taking a large mouthful.

"What's eating you?" Tripp asks as he nudges into me, the smell of bourbon on his breath.

"Just not really in the mood," I look up at him, willing for him to not ask me why and I can tell by his expression he has heard my thoughts loud and fucking clear.

She needed to know.

And now I wait for her to come home.

I wanted to take her to The Oaks, show her the ranch and what my plans are so when the house is fixed up, I can tell her I did it for us. But somehow, The Oaks seemed a little tainted, yet I knew one ranch where we could start our new beginning.

But that now seems like a million miles away.

Inhaling heavily, I try my hardest to fall into the evening and enjoy it and not spend every single second thinking of her.

My Aspen.

My Wildflower.

My Dinks.

CHAPTER THIRTY-THREE
ASPEN

We're on our third bottle of wine. I am feeling hazy and tipsy. We have laughed and cried and relived most of our teenage years. We were never bad kids, but we weren't angels either.

My eyes move to the door and I feel my skin prickle when I see Clay walk in, his eyes searching the room. I fixate on him for a moment before my sole focus is on Harlow.

My whole body stiffens and Harlow doesn't miss it.

I drop my head, turning my body away from where he is standing and trying to hide myself.

"What is it?" she leans across the table, her dark hair framing her face as she whispers.

"Clay," I mouth and her eyes widen before she sits up and looks over her shoulder, then snaps her head back round.

"What the fuck, he knows that I hang out with the Riveras and your brother!"

"Fuck."

"It's fine, just keep your head down."

"I've avoided Sunny's because I didn't want to go back out with him. He has probably been hanging out by Sylvia's," I get the giggles suddenly, and she shakes her head from side to side, her eyes look slightly menacing, her lips twisting and pouting and I know it's the nerves that is causing this outburst of hysteria.

"Aspen, stop," she swats me and then I see him look over and I freeze.

"Oh bollocks," I sink into my chair, covering my face with my hands.

"That isn't going to help," she leans over and swats me again, "oh fuck, he is coming over."

"Hide me," I squeal but I can hear the sound of his shoes on the hardwood floor and I know it's too late.

"Aspen," his tone is warm and I open my fingers that are covering my eyes to look at him then drop my hands and give him a huge smile.

"Clay!" I say a little too enthusiastically and Harlow is just staring at me.

"I haven't seen you around much, I didn't know if you had skipped town after our date," he fists his hand into his pocket and lets out a soft chuckle.

"Oh, no, no," I shake my head then let out a rumble of a laugh, "I have just been really busy with my deadline."

"I see, I even hung out at Sylvia's and when I asked about you she said she didn't know an *Aspen*."

My heart is jumping around my chest so fast, I struggle to catch my breath.

"I used a fake name, I'm quite big in the book world so have to use a different name. I was under Annette Curtain," and I internally curse at myself when Harlow sniggers, covering her mouth and nose instantly, dropping her head.

"Annette?" His brows raise and I nod.

"Mmhmm," I hum.

"Well, how about that second date then? I had a real good time and I think I can make this one even better," he winks and I feel nausea roll through my stomach.

"I would love to, but my deadline is right on my ass and I can't afford to have any distractions…" I bat my lashes at him, "no matter how beautiful they are."

"Well, that's a damn shame, how about when the deadline is finished?"

"Sounds great," I put my thumb up and I want the ground to swallow me up.

"Cool, enjoy your night, *Annette*." His voice is smooth as he turns and I catch him give Harlow a double take. "Hey," he points at her and she slowly turns her face towards him, her eyes wide. "I know you, you're the vet girl that works down at the Rivera's ranch and the little farm across the field."

She nods, keeping mute.

Clay reaches into his pocket and pulls out a business card, sliding it across the table with his index and middle finger.

"Give that to Jorge Rivera or his guard dog, Riggs. I have someone interested in their land."

"Will do," Harlow squeaks, quickly taking the card from him and flipping it between her fingers.

"Enjoy your evening ladies." He says again, but this time he directs his well wishes towards the both of us. Once he is out of sight, I feel like I can breathe again and suddenly I feel sick to the pit of my stomach.

I wait for a few moments before I push up from the table.

"Where you going?" Harlow asks.

"I need some fresh air," I nod, reaching over and giving her hand a squeeze. "I won't be long."

"Okay, if you're not back in five I'll come and find you," she winks.

"I'll be back," I smile, lifting my hand from hers and I walk towards the front of the bar, then push through the door and once I am outside I stop, my head tipping back as I take in as much of the fresh air as I can, filling my lungs until they burn.

I hear the front door click and I smirk thinking that Harlow has come out a little earlier, but it's not until I turn round to look that I see Clay walking towards me with a thunderous look on his face.

"You think you're smart, don't you?" his head tilts to the side and I see an evil smirk play across his lips, a glint of darkness in his eyes.

"Sorry?" I cross my arms against my chest, suddenly very aware that I am out here by myself.

"How long did you think it was going to be until I found out who you really were?" he steps closer to me again, and within seconds he is in front of me, towering over me. "You're Riggs' little whore, Aspen fucking Warren." He sucks in air through his teeth. "I'll be honest, I had no clue who you were when I bumped into you at Sunny's, but when you started getting ill-tempered over the ranches, I knew you had to have some connection to them cunts... and then my little friend confirmed it for me," his hand swipes up and grips my cheeks, pressing them into my teeth and I ignore the pain that radiates through me.

"Who?" I manage to squeeze out my small voice through my pursed lips.

"Me," and the voice that fills my ears makes my skin erupt in goosebumps and the hairs on the back of my neck stand. My heart plummets out of my chest and falls into the stomach.

"Hello darling."

And my blood runs cold.

RIGGS

In my own little daydream, I zone in and out of the conversations that are being had in front of me. Austin's phone begins buzzing on the table and after a few rings, it dies off. Within seconds it's flashing up again. Groaning, I reach forward and see Harlow's name flashing and fear cripples me.

"Austin!" I shout across the loud bunkhouse and I see his head pop up from his card game. "Harlow is calling," I wave his phone around that is still buzzing in my hand.

He walks over quickly, ignoring my warning looks as he takes it from me and answers.

"Hey, yo—" I see Austin turn to look at me, eyes wide and he pales. "Slow down, what? Clay? Fuck!" he shouts, reaching for his jacket off the coat rack and I am up and out of my seat, pushing my fingers between my lips as I whistle for Pacey and Tripp. "Stay put, we're on our way." Austin cuts the phone off and runs for the door, me and my brothers behind him.

"What the fuck is going on?" I growl, my temper rising by the second.

"Clay showed up at the Boot, asked Aspen on another date and she turned him down. He seemed fine and walked away and then a few moments later, Aspen needed some air and Harlow watched as Clay followed her out there. She hasn't come back. I told Harlow to stay put but whether she listens or not—"

I cut Austin off.

"Fuck!" I shout, opening the truck door, climbing inside and slamming it shut as I slip the key into the ignition, booting the pedal to the floor, not even caring if Tripp and Pacey made it in the back of the truck. "This is why I didn't want her involved," I am fucking furious, my whole body convulses, and I punch the steering wheel over and over as I drive out of the ranch and straight onto the road that leads us up to the Boot.

My eyes are on my brothers in the back and I can see the guilt etched all over their faces. Tripp feels for his gun and his eyes flutter shut for a moment.

My heart is racing, I feel sick with worry and Austin is back on the phone with Harlow.

"Tell her we're five minutes away."

I fucking speed all the way there, not giving two fucks about any law.

ASPEN

"Hello darling," Luke's voice echoes through the eerie silent night and my heart bottoms out. Clay drops my cheek and I ignore the want to rub the ache out. I slowly turn round to see Luke step forward out of the shadows and my eyes widen.

"What the fuck?" I just about manage and I cover my mouth with my hand.

"Surprised?" he smirks and takes another step closer to me which has my back straight into Clay's front.

"Worked like a charm," I hear Clay's tone and my eyes lift to the Boot parking lot hoping to see someone who can help, but it's empty and my nerves consume me.

"You're an asshole," I turn quickly, lifting my hand and slapping him hard across the face.

"You little whore, you're going to regret that," his arm jolts out as he wraps his fingers round my throat and squeezes, choking me. "Shame, I had another vision in my head for choking you and it wasn't out of violence," he smirks, so I spit in his face, but he doesn't falter, just smiles as his other hand reaches up and wipes my saliva from his eye.

I hear the sounds of tires screeching to a halt in the parking lot, and I pray that whoever is parking will help me.

"Get your fucking hands off her," Riggs' voice bellows across the parking lot and relief swarms me.

"Not a problem," Clay lets go of me and I gasp for air, coughing and choking as I desperately try and fill my lungs, crumpling on the floor like a piece of used paper. Riggs grabs me, holding me tightly as Tripp, Pacey and Austin surround us.

"I don't know who you think you are, Clay, coming onto our stomping ground then putting hands on *my* girl." Riggs growls, rolling me behind him as he steps forward.

"*Your* girl?" Luke pipes up as he steps towards Riggs and Riggs twists his neck round to look at Luke.

"Who the fuck are you?" Riggs voice booms and I hear Austin laugh.

"Her fiancé."

I watch as Riggs stiffens.

"Don't think so, bud," Riggs laughs and turns to face Clay once more.

"Yeah, check her hand for her ring," Luke stammers, but

puffs his chest out. Riggs spins to face me, I watch as his eyes give me the once over to make sure I am okay as his wrist reaches down and his fingers wrap around my slim wrist, holding it up and looking at it, squinting.

"There ain't no ring on her finger, and even if there was, I wouldn't have given a shit about the ring or about you anyway," Riggs lets my hand fall and my heart thrashes in my chest as I look at Luke.

"You broke up with me, Luke, you left me for that tramp back in LA."

I hear Riggs suck in air through his teeth before he lets out a soft whistle.

"Big mistake there, my man," Riggs taunts and I know where this conversation is going before it has even happened. "She hasn't mentioned you once, but there has been one name that has sounded real fucking pretty coming from her mouth and that's mine. Only mine. It sounds so good when she is moaning it, so no, Luke, is it?" Riggs steps up to Luke and I watch as Luke cowers, "you ain't nothing to her, just like she isn't anything to you. Now run along and fuck off back where you came from."

I watch as it plays out in slow motion. Luke swings for Riggs and catches him just off the jaw then winces and holds his fist as the pain consumes his hand. Riggs doesn't falter, just smirks and pulls his arm back before throwing it forward and lumping Luke and that's when it all kicks off. Luke and Riggs fight as I scream for them to stop. I hadn't even noticed that Harlow was standing next to Austin. Tripp and Pacey are on Luke, restraining him so Riggs gets the upper hand.

"Riggs!" I scream, tears pricking in my eyes, "Stop! Please," I beg and it's not because I still love Luke, I just don't want to see him beaten to a pulp for something I don't think he has any idea he is entangled in. Austin runs for Riggs, grabbing his arms and pulling them behind his back as he tries his hardest to lead Riggs away.

"Leave it man, he ain't worth it," and I know Austin must be cursing me and Riggs out at hearing the revelation that his sister and his best friend have indeed been sleeping together and I can't even bring myself to look in Pacey and Tripp's direction.

A loud clap fills the parking lot and we all turn to face Clay.

"What a show," Clay chuckles and his eyes roam to each and every one of us before they land on Riggs. "They're coming for your land, Riggs. There isn't anything you can do about it. They're already moving forward with their application to revisit the gold mine that sits at the bottom of Crooked Creek."

Riggs stiffens.

I watch as Tripp reaches for his gun, hoovering his hand over the handle.

"We ain't selling the land, tell your fucking suits that," Riggs growls.

"Don't say I didn't warn you," Clay turns and begins walking away.

"Oh no you don't," Austin runs for him, grabbing him by his shoulder as he spins him around and lands a fist right between his eyes, splitting his nose before Clay falls to the ground out cold.

Riggs sweeps me up, his hands cupping my face as his eyes volley back and forth between mine.

"Are you okay? Did he hurt you?" I can hear the sheer panic in his voice, my chest rising and falling as my heart skips beats.

"I'm fine, and no," I shake my head from side to side

before Riggs pulls me into him, my head on his chest and I feel my heart beat slow as I listen to the steady beat of Riggs'.

"Look, Aspen," I hear Luke say amongst the commotion of Tripp and Pacey dragging a limp Clay into the back of their truck.

Riggs stands all protective in front of me, Austin by his side.

"I'm owed money, like *a lot*. I was promised it if I confirmed your identity. It was a shit thing to do but I had no idea what kind of guys they were..." he pauses for a moment and I step to the side of Riggs but his arm stretches out to stop me from going any further. Luke is bloody and bruised but I want to hear what he has to say.

"Why do you need money, Luke?" my tone is flat as I look at the man who once claimed I was the love of his life, but look how quick he sold me out for money.

"Tammy," he mutters, and I can't help the shit-eating grin that spreads across my face.

"The local tramp?" humour laces my voice.

"She took me for all I had, I'm in shit. Clay promised to clear my debt with the money he got from the ranches he sold, I thought it would be a quick trade." He pauses and Tripp and Pacey join us, standing behind Luke now.

"He fucked you over," Riggs laughs, lifting his arm from where it was once blocking me and folding it across his chest.

"Tammy left, then before I knew it, I was somehow roped into this with the big suits and now... well..." he looks at me and I can see the remorse in his eyes.

"I fucked up Aspen and I am so sorry," he steps forward and falls to his knees at my feet and I suddenly feel sorry and embarrassed for him. Tripp, Pacey and Riggs all share a knowing look as I step around Riggs so I am now in front of him.

"I don't want your apology, Luke, you did fuck up… big time," I lower my face to his, "but you cheating on me and kicking me out of my home with nothing but the dress on my back, Butch and my laptop was the best thing you could have ever done for me." I smile at him and I watch as his head drops.

"I suggest you run, Luke, far far away and don't ever come back to Lovelock Bay because I can't promise you'll make it out alive next time," and I know my threat is empty but I want to scare him away. He sags, his head falling back and Riggs steps forward, pressing the sole of his boot into Luke's chest as he kicks him back, his body hitting the dirt beneath him.

"Tell your fucking suits we ain't selling." Riggs spits on the floor beside him then wraps his arm round my shoulders as he walks me away. I look over my shoulder at Luke sitting on the dirt and Austin, Harlow and the Rivera brothers following behind us.

"Let's get you home, Wildflower," Riggs whispers in my ear and I hear Austin groan.

"This is not the way I wanted to find out that you and my sister were a thing!" Austin shouts out and I giggle under Riggs' arms as his head turns and he places a soft kiss on the top of my head.

I stop in my tracks as Riggs opens the back of the truck and his brows furrow.

"Er, Tripp," he calls, his eyes not leaving the cab.

"Yeah?"

"Didn't you put Clay in the back of the truck?"

"Yeah…" and Tripp's words fall short.

"Well, you didn't do a very good job," Tripp and Pacey stand next to Riggs as they all eye the empty cab.

"Fuck," Tripp just about manages, his hand on his mouth.

"Yeah, fuck."

CHAPTER THIRTY-FOUR
ASPEN

It had been a week since Clay and Luke showed up at the Boot.

It had been four days since Clay's body was found on the Rivera's land.

We all knew it was a trap and so did the newly appointed sheriff for this case, but with no proof and the last witnesses claimed they saw Austin and Clay fighting before Clay's body was dragged into the back of the Rivera's truck, it wasn't looking good. We know Tripp believes it had nothing to do with Austin, but he was still part of the law. He couldn't be seen taking sides, especially when it came to his family.

But right now we had to focus on moving forward. Tripp and Pacey were working on finding out what happened to Clay, and Austin has been told to keep a low profile. Harlow has been trying to find out who these suits are and as much as Luke offered to help, no one has been able to reach him since his little visit.

"You ready to do this?" Riggs asks as he sits upon his

horse, smiling down at me as I stand next to Raff, my fingers locked round his reins.

"I am," I nod, footing the stirrup and swinging my leg over Raff's back and slip my other foot into the stirrup.

"Look at you," Riggs winks and I feel my heart somersault. "You take the lead, darlin'," he smirks and I inhale deeply, closing my eyes for a moment before I nudge Raff on, moving him forward through the paddock gates and as soon as the open field is in front of us, I open his rein up and kick him on, holding my breath as I do. He falls into a steady canter and in this moment, the spring breeze blowing in my hair, riding on the back of a horse again it felt like I had never stopped. Riggs rode up beside me, his smile so damn wide and his eyes glistening.

"That's my girl," he praises and I couldn't love that man any more than I do. I lead the way down to Crooked Valley, the starlight sky looming on the horizon. My heart is galloping in my chest as I free the reins of my horse and let him lower his neck as he begins to graze. Holding onto the horn of the saddle, I swing myself off and pull the reins over Raff's head and tie him to the fence post that secures where we're standing. I turn and smile as I see Riggs canter towards us, before he slows his horse to a complete stop and climbs off. He loops Travis' reins round the same fence post and lets them graze together before his arms wrap around me, pulling me close. I can't pull my eyes from him, even if I wanted to and right here, right now, I am wrapped in the perfect moment.

My hand reaches up and I grab his hat to place it on my head, my nose scrunching as it does. My hands find their place on his white shirt, my fingers tapping to the sound of his heart beating and his hands are on the small of my back, playing with the belt loops of my jeans, my cropped white tee giving him access to a small bit of my tingling skin.

"Never did I think I would feel this content," I whisper as we stand at our familiar place. The place where me and Riggs moulded into one, the place where he kissed me under the stars and our souls entwined in an infinite bond, an invisible string tying us together, finally.

"Never did I think I would get this moment," his lips lower over mine for just a second and my eyes flutter shut but within seconds, Riggs pulls away, his gaze steady on mine and I feel the way his heart races a little faster under his skin.

"What moment?" I whisper, not wanting to ruin anything.

He smiles, his teeth on show and I see the glisten in his eyes.

"Marry me, Aspen." He chokes and my throat bobs. "I am so in love with you, our hearts tied together for infinity. Our souls locked as one. You're my wildest love, my wildest dreams and now... my wildest forever... marry me," his voice cracks and I slowly let my hands rise up his chest before they loop round his neck and I can't hide the smile any longer, a tear rolls down my cheek. "It's always been you," he whispers.

"Yes—" is the only word I can manage to get out before Riggs wraps me up in his arms and lifts my feet off the ground. "It's always been you too," I rush out on a breathy whisper before my lips lower over his.

An infinite love.

A full circle.

Our first kiss was under the stars, and now the start of our forever under them too.

I no longer had to be afraid of the dark, because Riggs was the brightest light in my life, and as long as I had him by my side. I would always be home.

EPILOGUE
RIGGS

I finally had the girl.

The woman of my dreams.

And she really is a dream.

Proudness seeps out of me when I think back to how far she has come and grown from the broken woman she was when she returned.

Her debut novel, *Wildest Love* is finished and has been submitted to a couple of publishers. She is doubting herself, but I never doubted her for a second.

OUR ENGAGEMENT WAS a little under two weeks ago, and with everything going on we haven't been able to celebrate the way I would have liked.

But today, I get to show Aspen another surprise.

Stepping into her room, my eyes fixate on her. She is curled up and asleep, her left hand resting on the comforter, and I watch as the sun reflects off her tear drop diamond that sits on a thin, gold band.

Smiling from ear to ear, I sit on the edge of the bed,

leaning across and skimming my fingers across her soft skin as I tuck a strand of her hair behind her ear. She inhales deeply, rolling on her back and her eyes flutter open.

"Morning, Wildflower," my voice is low, a rasp etched into it.

"Morning," she smiles, her dimples on show as she stretches up.

"Happy thirtieth birthday," and I watch as her cheeks pinch crimson.

This date was engraved in my brain. *The first of May*. The love of my life's birthday and every year after she left, it became one of the saddest days of my life.

"Shit, I'm thirty," she groans covering her face with her hands and I chuckle, lifting her hands from her pretty face.

"It's just a number, baby."

She huffs, letting her arms fall by her side.

"Get dressed, I'm taking you for breakfast and then I want to show you your birthday present... or presents?" I smirk, leaning close to her and my lips hover over hers.

"I love you," she whispers just as my lips press against hers.

DRIVING OUT OF TOWN, I pull down a small country road which leads us towards Crooked Valley and I watch as her brows furrow, confusion all over her pretty face.

"Why are we heading to the valley? It isn't night-time?" she asks and I just let out a low, slow laugh.

"You have never been good with patience have you, Wildflower?"

She stays quiet and I shake my head as I turn my blinker on and pull down a private road.

"Riggs," she whispers as we roll to a stop in front of the wooden paddock gate.

"Yes, baby?"

"Why are we at Crooked Creek?" her eyes are wide as she turns her attention from me and out the windshield, the noise of the flowing creek fills the car as I slide down the window, the sound of the late spring breeze dancing with the trees.

"I'll show you," I smile, unbuckling myself and jumping out the truck. She doesn't move, she waits for me to let her out like I always do. "Come," I whisper, taking her hand and leading her down towards the empty ranch.

Her fingers lace through mine, her spare hand wrapped around my forearm. Unhooking the gate, I push it open and we walk down the winding path towards the pretty little ranch house.

Crooked Creek sits on three acres worth of land, the stables are a little run down and our favorite creek trickles through the land. Her eyes narrow when she sees her McLaren sitting in the garage, shiny and brand new.

"Why is my car here?" a nervous giggle escapes her as she rounds the back of the garage, "and it's fixed?" she whispers, her eyes averting to me and I just stand there proud as punch with a huge grin on my face. "You fixed it?" her smile grows and I give her a nod. "Riggs," she shakes her head, her eyes back on her car. "But why is it here?" she asks, hands on her hips.

"Because this is ours baby, this is our *home*."

"What?" she whispers, her beautiful hazel eyes brimming with tears.

"Welcome home Dinks, happy birthday," I just about manage before her legs are circling my waist, her arms locked round my neck and I have never been more grateful for the pretty, cream summer dress she has on. Her tanned cowboy boots press into the ass of my jeans and my cock rubs against the seam.

"Make love to me Riggs," she whispers against my lips, breaking away from our kiss.

"Who am I to deny the birthday girl of her wish?" I smirk at her, pressing her against the car bonnet.

She had the key to my heart, and finally, we were home. Locked and sealed away in our perfect happiness.

I dreamt of this day from the moment I met her, and now, it's finally here and the dream has never looked better than it does right now.

***

TRIPP

I hadn't said anything, but the word on the street was Austin was going to be arrested.

I'm not buying it. Sheriff Kelcie hasn't mentioned a single thing to me, but then again, maybe he wasn't allowed to.

We all know Austin didn't kill Clay.

Deep down Kelcie knew that too, but they have to have a suspect and it's easier to arrest Austin on suspicion than to not find anyone. My blood runs cold, I always thought I could protect my family, but even wearing a badge doesn't promise that.

The suits had gone quiet, and Luke was nowhere to be found and it has me wondering whether he met the same fate as Clay, but fortunately, it wasn't on our ranch.

Kicking off my heavy boots, I settle down in the back

room and pour myself a large whiskey. Pondering over the last few weeks, I feel exhausted with it all.

Pacey has shut down; Riggs and Aspen are caught up in their whirlwind and I feel like I am left here picking up the pieces.

Tapping on the side of my glass, I'm not alone with my thoughts long when I hear the sound of tires screeching.

Bolting up, I run for the large window at the front of the house and see a beaten ass car sitting on the side of the road just outside our ranch, smoke funnelling under the hood. Placing my glass down, I move to the front door and grab my hat, placing it on my head as I run up the driveway to where the car is parked.

"Ma'am!" I call out when I see a woman leaning in the back of the car and fear prickles at the back of my neck, the smoke thick and gray. She ignores me and I hear the sound of a high-pitched cry.

My legs begin to slow as I approach the car, my brows knitting, and my heart is drumming hard against my rib cage.

"Ma'am, is everything okay?" I ask and when the woman stands, wavy brown hair blowing in the wind and eyes as wide as saucers, I feel the air snatch from my lungs.

Standing in front of me, cradling a small bundle in her arms, is the one that got away.

Ten years ago she left town. Ten years ago she left me standing in the dust of her car. Ten years ago she never looked back.

My best kept secret.

The worst heartache of my life.

My wildest dreams.

"Tripp," her voice trembles and all I can do is stare.

Fuck.

. . .

THE END

Wildest Dreams is book two in the Lovelock Bay series and will follow Tripp and Dixie.
Wildest Dreams is a second chance, small town, teen friends to lovers to strangers, single mom and the one that got away romance.
The Rivera boys, Aspen, Austin and the drama that follows will continue through this interconnected standalone.
And maybe, just maybe a certain red head and her crystal blue eyed bodyguard may tumble through Lovelock Bay, but not without their baggage that is Xavier.

ACKNOWLEDGMENTS

Dan. My best friend. My husband. My world. Thank you for pushing me to start this crazy journey. I love you to the moon and back.

Thanks firstly to Robyn, for keeping me in check and always being there when I needed you.

My Rosie Posies, thank you for everything. I would be lost without you.

Leanne, thank you for always being here for me. You're a friend for life. I am grateful for you coming into my world when you did.

Lea Joan, thank you for editing Wildest Love and continuing to work with me.

My BETA's, Carrie, Katie and Jasmine - thank you.

And lastly, my readers... without you, none of this would have been possible.
    My loyal fans, I owe it all to you.

www.ingramcontent.com/pod-product-compliance
Lightning Source LLC
Chambersburg PA
CBHW021238190726
48289CB00005B/1382